Andr... temporary romances filled with seduction and sass. She has been a lover of reading and writing stories since she was young. A dedicated West Coast girl transplanted into the Deep South, she is thrilled to share her special blend of ... lity and dry, sarcastic humor with readers.

...ical Piscean, *USA TODAY* bestselling author **...ne Lindsay** has always preferred her imagination ... real world. Married to her blind-date hero and ... two adult children, she spends her days crafting the ...s of her heart, and in her spare time she can be ...d with her nose in a book reliving the power of love, ...nitting socks and daydreaming. Contact her via her site, www.yvonnelindsay.com.

ONE UNFORGETTABLE WEEKEND

ANDREA LAURENCE

TANGLED VOWS

YVONNE LINDSAY

MILLS & BOON

First Published in Great Britain 2018
by Mills & Boon, an imprint of HarperCollinsPublishers,
1 London Bridge Street, London, SE1 9GF

One Unforgettable Weekend © 2018 Andrea Laurence
Tangled Vows © 2018 Dolce Vita Trust

ISBN: 978-0-263-93607-0

51-0618

MIX
Paper from
responsible sources
FSC™ C007454

This book is produced from independently certified FSC™ paper to ensure responsible forest management.

For more information visit: www.harpercollins.co.uk/green

Printed and bound in Spain
by CPI, Barcelona

ONE UNFORGETTABLE WEEKEND

ANDREA LAURENCE

To Eric—

I was lost when you found me.
Thank you for helping me believe again.

One

"Miss Niarchos will see you now."

Aidan Murphy stood, buttoning his suit coat and smoothing his tie. Wearing a suit again felt a bit surreal after so long without it. At one time, it had been like a second skin to him. Then his world fell apart and the way he lived his life changed forever. A bartender had no need for fancy suits and silk ties. A bartender at Murphy's Irish Pub would be looked at with suspicion by its regular clientele if they walked in wearing this monkey suit.

But today wasn't about Murphy's or the life Aidan lived now or five years ago. Today was about his deceased parents, a deathbed promise and the halfway house he needed to open to honor their memory.

Losing both his parents within a few years of each

other had left him things he'd never anticipated—primarily a struggling Irish pub in Manhattan and a huge house in the East Bronx. As a former advertising executive with a degree in marketing, he had enough business savvy to get the bar back up and running, but he had no interest in a house that far away or frankly, that big. He just wasn't ready to part with his childhood home quite so soon after losing them, too.

His parents had bought the place to house the large Irish Catholic family they'd hoped to someday have together and never did. The house itself was paid for, but even if he wanted to sell it, it wouldn't be so easy. The neighborhood was declining and even the rental market there was soft. His mother had known that and urged him to keep it and use the property as a transitional home for alcoholics leaving in-house rehabilitation programs. After dealing with his father's alcoholism, she'd known that a transitional home was the one thing he had always needed after his trips to rehab, but never had, usually sending him right back to the bottle within a few weeks.

That was where the Niarchos Foundation came in, as much as he hated the idea of asking anyone—especially entitled rich people—for help. Unfortunately Aidan needed money to make his mom's dream a reality. Lots of money. And his personal cash reserves were long gone thanks to his drunken father's poor business practices. So here he was, applying for a grant from the foundation against his better judgment. Somehow that sounded better than begging for money.

He opened the door to the foreboding office and

held his breath. It was now or never. Hopefully Miss Niarchos would be susceptible to his charms. He'd found that a smile and a little light flirting could get him what he needed from most ladies. He tried not to abuse his powers, but today, it would make this whole process easier.

Aidan stepped across the threshold into the brightly decorated space and stopped short when his gaze narrowed in on the dark, exotic eyes of the woman who'd vanished from his life well over a year ago. All thoughts of charming the foundation administrator faded as he realized who she was.

Violet.

Violet *Niarchos*, apparently, although full names had never been a topic of conversation during the short time they were together. If they had, perhaps he would've been able to track down his elusive beauty after she disappeared without a trace.

Before Aidan could say hello, he stopped himself. The blank expression on Violet's face was disconcerting. There wasn't a flicker of recognition as she looked at him, like he was just another person coming to her for the support of her foundation, not a man she'd made love to. Obviously the experience had made a bigger impression on him than he had on her.

"Violet?" he asked, just to prove to himself that he was talking to the right woman. He would've sworn it was her, but time could distort the memory. The woman in front of him was more beautiful than even he recalled, and he wouldn't have thought that possible.

"Yes," she replied, standing up and rounding her

desk to greet him in a stiff, formal way. She was wearing a lavender silk blouse with a gray pencil skirt, stockings and conservative but attractive gray pumps. There were gray pearls on her ears and a matching strand around her throat. This version of Violet was far more proper and dignified than the one that had stumbled into his bar that night.

"You don't recognize me," he said, stating the obvious. "I'm Aidan. We met at Murphy's Pub about a year and a half ago."

The delicate porcelain of her face suddenly cracked. Her dark, almond-shaped eyes widened and her dark pink lips parted with surprise. It seemed she'd finally pieced together who he was. "Oh my God," she said, bringing her hands to cover her nose and mouth.

Aidan tried not to outwardly panic as tears started to glitter in her eyes, but inside, he was twisted into knots. In all the nights he'd lain in bed wondering what had happened to her, why she'd never come by the bar, imagining what it would be like to see her again…he'd never anticipated tears. He hadn't done anything to her that would warrant tears.

Had he?

After all, she was the one who walked out of his life, vanishing in the early hours of the morning like a ghost he'd started to think he'd imagined. If he wasn't a teetotaler he'd worry she had been a drunken delusion. She'd felt like one. No real woman could've affected him, touched him, the way Violet had.

If it hadn't been for the taste of her still lingering

on his lips and the torn lace panties left behind on his bedroom floor, he might have believed she wasn't real.

"Aidan," she said in a hushed whisper, almost as though she was speaking to someone other than him. A moment later, the tears started spilling onto her cheeks.

He fought the urge to rush over and wrap her delicate frame in his protective embrace. He didn't want to see her cry, especially not at the mere sight of him. But something about the way she eyed Aidan gave him pause. It was probably regret. From the looks of her, Violet was a pretty posh lady. It was likely that she'd forgotten about her two-day tryst with the hot bartender and now that he was standing in her office, she was having to cope with the embarrassment she felt for stooping so low. Otherwise she wouldn't be crying or looking as though she wanted to escape from her pleasant and comfortable office through the nearby window.

"Are you all right?" he asked.

His words seemed to snap her out of her emotional state. She quickly wiped the tears from her cheeks and turned away for a moment to compose herself. "Yes, of course," she said, although he didn't believe her. She turned back, all polite smiles. "I'm sorry. I just…"

She thrust out her hand to shake his. He accepted it, feeling the familiar tingle dance across his skin. Touching her that first night had set his nervous system ablaze and that hadn't changed. The tension in her grip was new, though. It didn't lessen as he touched her. In fact, her hand grew stiffer until she finally pulled away and gestured toward the nearby guest chair.

"Please sit down. We have a lot to discuss."

Aidan took a seat across from her with the massive cherrywood desk separating them. The chair was more comfortable than he expected, the whole office being more an extension of the woman he remembered than the one fidgeting with her paperwork at the moment. It wasn't the typical, sterile business office. There was a seating area with plush chairs and colorful fabrics. The walls had bright pieces of art and photographs of beautiful locations with white buildings against turquoise-blue waters. Where was the woman who decorated this office? The one who strolled into Murphy's Pub looking for something and someone to help her forget her troubles?

"Before we discuss your grant application, I feel like I need to apologize," Violet began. "I'm sure you think quite poorly of me for disappearing. At the moment, I feel awful for doing it."

"I just want to know what happened to you," Aidan replied and that was the truth.

She wasn't the first woman in the world to sneak out of a hookup at dawn, but she never texted or came by the pub again. He practically lived at Murphy's. She could've found him there any time she wanted to, but she hadn't. Their time together had made a huge impact on him, so it had surprised him that she could just walk away from it without a glance back. He'd wanted to look for her a dozen times but had had no way to go about it.

"I was in an accident." Violet frowned at the desk as she visibly strained to piece together her story. "I guess it must've been right after I left your apartment.

My stupid taxi slammed into the back of a bus and I hit my head on the partition. I woke up in the hospital."

Aidan's heart started to sink. He'd never imagined that she hadn't contacted him because she couldn't. He'd been home grumbling into a bowl of cereal and she'd been in the hospital. "Are you okay?"

"Yes," she said with a smile. "I had a good knot on my head, but mostly just bruises. No lasting damage aside from some memory loss. I basically lost the week leading up to the accident. The last thing I remembered when I woke up was leaving my office after a big meeting the week before. I've tried everything over the past few months to recover those memories, but nothing worked. I didn't contact you because I didn't remember you, or the time we spent together, until you walked into my office and said your name just now."

"Are you saying you've got *amnesia*?"

Violet wanted to cringe at the way Aidan said the word. It was the same way whenever someone said it. *Amnesia* sounded like something that only existed in a soap opera, not a real-life medical condition. And yet that was what it was. An entire week of her life had been erased from her brain as though it never happened.

The doctors told her that eventually, the memories would return, but they couldn't predict when or how. She might get little flashes over time or a sense of déjà vu, or it might come back suddenly like a tidal wave washing over her.

It had been the latter. When he looked at her with

those big, blue eyes and said his name, it was like the earth had shifted beneath her feet. In an instant, her mind was flooded with images of the two of them together. Naked and sweaty. Laughing. Eating takeout in bed and talking for hours. She fought the urge to blush in embarrassment having such intimate memories about a virtual stranger. But those thoughts were quickly wiped away by the realization of what it all meant for her.

That was what had caused the tears.

She'd spent fifteen months wondering what she'd forgotten when she'd lost that week of her life. Right after the accident, she'd been determined to recover her memories. Eventually she'd put those worries aside when she'd realized she was pregnant. From there on out, her attention turned to her engagement with her longtime boyfriend, Beau Rosso, and planning for the arrival of their first baby together.

Then the baby arrived and the missing week of her life became more important than ever before.

"I know," she said, raising her hand to halt any argument he might have. "It sounds crazy. Until it happened to me, I would've said it was ridiculous, but that's what the doctors told me. I've spent nearly a year and a half trying to get those memories back. But there was nothing, not a flicker of that week of my life, until just now."

Aidan ran his hand through the shaggy ginger curls of his hair and arched his brow. "So, what exactly did you just remember about me?" He awaited her response with a smug curl of his lips.

This time, Violet couldn't prevent the blush the memories brought to her cheeks. She didn't like feeling as though she were at a disadvantage in any situation and knowing he had the ability to ruffle her was unsettling enough. "I, uh," she began, "remember coming into the bar. You worked there?"

At that, he grinned. "Worse. I own it."

Violet nodded, trying not to sigh in relief. She wasn't one to make a habit of having flings with bartenders. She was a shipping heiress to one of the largest family fortunes in Europe and she'd been raised to act accordingly. Her grandfather would roll in his grave if he thought Violet was slumming with a bartender. Then again, she wasn't prone to having flings with bar owners, either, but at least he was a business owner and not a hot guy who paid his rent with a seductive smile and tips.

Violet bit at her lip, trying to sort through all her new memories. She remembered going to the bar, although she didn't know why. It wasn't a place she'd ever visited before. She could recall the exact moment she'd laid eyes on Aidan. Laughing, talking, closing the bar down. "I remember going back to your place."

Her cheeks were burning. There was no way her blush wasn't obvious now. If the red-hot memories weren't enough, the way Aidan looked at her from over the desk would do it. "I think we both know what happened after that," she said.

Aidan nodded slowly. "I've relived that weekend with you in my mind dozens of times, trying to figure out what I did wrong."

Violet pushed aside the stirring images, suppressing the heat that had started circling in her belly. "What do you mean? I may not remember everything yet, but I don't remember you doing anything wrong."

"Well, you left, didn't you? I woke up Sunday morning with a cold stretch of mattress beside me. When did you even leave? I didn't hear a thing."

Violet tried to remember. She had left his apartment early in the morning, but why? Had she had something she'd needed to do? She felt like that was the answer, although she didn't know what it could be. Whatever it was, she'd never made it since she'd ended up in the hospital instead. "I had somewhere I needed to be. I didn't want to wake you up. I was going to call you later."

"But you got amnesia," Aidan interjected with a flat, disbelieving tone.

"Yes. My phone was crushed in the accident, so I lost any new data since my last backup, which probably included your number. Any memories or traces of our time together were erased from my life." Well, most of them. One huge daily reminder remained— she just hadn't realized the significance of it until now.

"That's all very convenient."

Violet didn't like his tone. "Are you suggesting that I'm lying about all of this?"

Aidan just shrugged. "It's just a pretty big pill to swallow, that's all."

"I assure you that if all I wanted was to discontinue our…" What was it, exactly? Relationship? Affair? Hookup? "*Time* together, I would've had no problem just saying so. There's no need to make up a story about amnesia and broken phones just to get out of seeing you again."

"So you did *want* to see me again." It was a statement, not a question. His subdued grin was unnerving, making her muscles tense and her stomach flip. He seemed to like having that effect on her.

Violet wasn't entirely sure she minded it, either. She couldn't remember another man being able to make her stomach flutter with just a glance. Without a touch, with just the memory of a touch, she felt her resolve crumbling beneath her. She wouldn't tell him the truth, but the nights they'd spent together had been the best she'd ever had. He'd mastered her body almost instantly, playing her like a violin until she nearly made herself hoarse screaming out his name. How could she ever have forgotten it?

"I did," she said, swallowing the lump in her throat.

She followed his gaze as it flickered over to her bare left hand. For months, she'd worn Beau's engagement ring. Now the tan line had faded and she'd lost the strange sensation that going without it caused.

"And what about now?"

That was a dangerous question. Spending a weekend with Aidan was one thing, but now…everything had changed. It just wasn't that simple any longer.

"Now isn't relevant," she said, avoiding the answer.

"The hell it isn't!" Aidan stood up from his seat and rounded her desk. He leaned over her, planting his hands on the arms of her chair. He was close without touching her, his warm scent invading her space even as he hovered at the edge of it.

Violet's breath caught in her throat. The large, hulking figure of manhood was so close, tempting her to reach out and close the gap he'd left. The last few months had been scary and lonely. She was tempted to give in to her attraction to him again and let him remind her of everything she'd missed.

"I've spent almost a year and a half wondering what happened to you, Violet. Even when I didn't want to think about you, when I wanted to just move on, the vision of your naked body writhing beneath mine would creep into my head and derail my thoughts." He paused, his gaze flicking over her body then returning to her face. "Now you show back up in my life with this wild story and your big doe eyes and you tell me that your attraction to me isn't relevant?"

How could she explain that things were more complicated than just whether or not she was attracted to him? There were more factors at play, things she needed to tell him, stuff that went beyond her work at the foundation.

Aidan leaned in farther, pausing when their lips were a fraction of an inch apart. Violet's heart was pounding in her chest, her lungs burning with the rapid breaths she was taking. Each one drew his scent into her lungs, reminding her of burying her face in his neck and snuggling into the pillows that smelled like him. He was so close. If she moved, they would be kissing and if she was honest with herself, it took everything she had to stay still.

"Say it," he demanded.

Violet couldn't turn away from his commanding gaze. When he looked at her that way, she'd do anything he wanted. But this wouldn't be just a simple admission of attraction. "Aidan..."

"Say it."

She swallowed hard. "Okay, fine. Yes, I'm still attracted to you. Does that make you happy?"

He narrowed his gaze and eased back from her. "Not really. I've never met a woman who fought her desires so strongly. You don't want to want me at all. Is it because I'm a bartender and not some flashy investment banker like your boyfriend?"

Violet flinched. That wasn't the reason, but it certainly didn't help their situation. She didn't need a man's money—she was a billionaire in her own right—but she had made a habit of dating wealthy men in the past. It made her feel less like a prize to be won, a lottery ticket to change a man's fortune forever. Although they were rarely discussed, there were plenty of male gold-diggers in the world, too.

"No," Violet argued. "It's not about that. And anyway, he's my ex-boyfriend. Listen, there's something we need to talk about." She pressed her hand to his chest, hoping to get some breathing room, but he didn't budge. All she ended up doing was getting a handful of his hard muscles beneath his dress shirt. "Please have a seat so we can talk for a minute."

He didn't respond. He didn't even move. She realized then that his attention had shifted to something over her shoulder.

"Aidan?" Was he even listening to her?

Violet turned and followed Aidan's gaze to the framed photograph on her desk. It was the only picture of Knox she kept in the office, and now she regretted even having this one here. Everyone who saw it asked about the cherubic baby with the bright red curls and big blue eyes. Apparently it had caught his attention as well, but not just because her son was adorable. The similarities were impossible to ignore, a fact that had nearly blown her over when the memories of their time together hit her all at once. At last, the final, crucial puzzle piece had fallen into place.

The panic was evident by his big eyes and slack jaw. He knew what the photo meant. There was no need to do math or conduct a paternity test for him to understand the truth. Finally, he turned back to her and swallowed hard. "Is that your baby?"

She nodded and he stood upright, leaving her personal space and making her suddenly feel cold without him. "Yes. That's Lennox, my son. He's almost six months old."

"Lennox," he repeated, as though he were trying to get used to the sound of the name.

"I call him Knox for short. He's amazing. So smart, so loving. I've truly been blessed as a mother."

Aidan turned back to the photo, the unasked question hanging on his lips.

"And yes," Violet began, with a mix of relief and apprehension climbing up the back of her throat. How long had she worried she would never get to say these words to someone? That she might never know the truth about Knox? Now in the moment, she wasn't even sure she could get the words out. She gripped the arms of her chair to steady herself and looked up into the familiar sky-blue eyes of the near-stranger standing in front of her.

"I'm pretty sure that he's...your son."

Two

"My son?"

Her words were like a swift kick to his gut. Aidan had known—known from the moment he'd laid eyes on the baby in the picture—that it was his, but hearing it aloud carried an impact he didn't expect.

"Yes. I'm sorry this is how you had to find out. Please sit down so we can talk about this."

Aidan reluctantly pulled away and returned to his seat. It was better that he sit, anyway, before his legs failed him and he had no choice. His mind was spinning with thoughts he couldn't grab ahold of. He'd come here to apply for money to start a halfway house and had managed, instead, to get a son. A son named Knox. A son he'd never met before.

The thought made his stomach twist into knots. He'd

always wanted a family of his own when the time came. He'd wanted a chance to be a better father than his own had been, to prove that he was better than his alcoholic, waste-of-space dad. He knew that when he decided to get married and start a family, he would dedicate his world to them, because that was the way it should be.

But instead, he'd just found out his son was six months old and he'd missed everything so far. He would remedy that, and soon. He wasn't sure what Violet had in mind, but he would be a father to Knox. He would take him to Yankees games, be there for every T-ball tryout and parent-teacher conference.

"Why didn't you tell me I had a son?" He was surprised at how cold his own voice sounded, but he was choking back a sea of emotions. It was better to show none at all than to let them rush out of him all at once.

Violet's expression twisted in irritation. "You're really asking me that?"

Apparently she was going to stick fast to her amnesia story. He didn't really buy it, but he'd go along with it for now. "So I guess you're saying since you forgot we slept together, you forgot I was the father?"

She slid her chair closer to the desk and folded her neatly manicured hands over the leather and parchment blotter. Her brow furrowed as she seemed to search for her words. "The way you say it sounds so convenient, as though I haven't spent the last six months of my life agonizing over the fact that I had no idea who my baby's father was."

"Who did you think it belonged to for the months before that?"

Her gaze dropped down to her desk, avoiding him. "I thought it was Beau's child—my ex you mentioned before. Since I had no memory of our time together, I had no reason to think otherwise. We got engaged. We planned a wedding and future together. And then the doctor in the delivery room handed him a baby with a full head of curly red hair and the whole room just went into shock."

Aidan tried not to laugh. He could just picture the scene with everyone wondering where this pasty Irish kid had come from. It would be funny if it hadn't meant that he'd missed the birth of his first child in the process. "How'd he take that? Not well I'd imagine."

Violet sighed and looked up at him. "That doesn't matter. What matters is that we're not together anymore and we know he isn't Knox's father. I've got the lab results to prove it."

"What did your parents say?"

She narrowed her gaze at him. "Did we discuss my parents before?"

It seemed as though Violet didn't remember their conversation. That probably had more to do with the tequila than her head injury. She'd been pretty upset when she'd strolled into his bar and demanded a shot with tears in her eyes. He'd listened to her story and made it his mission to make her smile again, never imagining that decision would lead them to this point. To a child.

"Not at length," he explained. "Only that they were pushing you to be with this guy even though he was a grade-A jerk. I can imagine having another man's baby was a disappointment for them after thinking you two were going to get married and they'd get their way."

"Well, yes, but not as much of a disappointment as having an unknown man's baby. They certainly can't have their fancy friends and family finding out the truth. They'd be much happier if I just took Beau back and pretended like Knox belonged to him. I think they're still telling people that Beau is the father and we're just having a rough patch. My mother tried to convince me that we had a recessive pale, redheaded gene in our Greek and Israeli heritage." She shook her head. "I've never met one. They're just grasping at straws."

"I suppose that means they're not going to be too happy to find out his real father is a broke Irishman who owns a bar."

Violet looked at him with an expression of grave seriousness. He could tell the past year had weighed heavily on her mind. If she was telling the truth about forgetting everything, he imagined it would be difficult. The one week you forget ending up being the most important week of your life.

"I'm not worried about them. In the past few months, I've done a lot of soul-searching and one of the things I've discovered is that I'm no longer concerned with what makes my parents happy. My whole life has been about what makes them happy. Now my focus is on myself and my son, where it should be."

Needing to see it again, Aidan reached out and took the framed portrait from her desk. He ran his finger across the rosy cheeks and bright smile of the child he'd never met. Knox definitely had his coloring, but he had Violet's almond-shaped eyes and full lips. He had her smile, even though his was toothless at the moment. He imagined their son had an infectious giggle the way babies did. He hoped to hear it in person as soon as possible.

"I would've told you," Violet said in a small voice. He looked up from the photo and searched her dark eyes for the truth of her words. "This isn't about other people's opinions or whether or not I wanted you in Knox's life. If I had known, I wouldn't have hesitated to tell you, or to find you again. But I truly didn't remember until now. That's why I cried when it all came back at once. It was an overwhelming sense of relief, finally knowing the truth after all these months."

Aidan sighed and looked back at his son. He wasn't sure if she was telling the truth, but at the moment it didn't really matter. If he wanted to see his child, he'd take her at her word and hope for the best. "So now what?" he asked.

Violet tapped her fingers anxiously at the edge of her desk. "Well, I suppose I should start by calling my attorney. He can get the ball rolling on setting up a paternity test, just to be certain, then we can start working on arrangements for visitation and such."

Only a rich person would start off this process with calling their attorney instead of going for the obvious choice of allowing him to meet his son. Aidan didn't even have an attorney, much less one on retainer who took his calls whenever he needed him.

Of course, Aidan didn't have anywhere near the

amount of the money he suspected Violet had. The Niarchos Foundation gave away millions of dollars every year to worthy causes, and that was just a small fraction of the family's fortune. He'd done a little reading about the family when he was looking for places to help with his project. Her grandfather had made a fortune in Greece shipping steel to the United States. When the family came to America, their wealth only grew by leaps and bounds.

Aidan couldn't imagine how many billions of dollars the Niarchos family empire controlled. They probably just started this foundation so the IRS didn't eat them alive. He didn't really like or trust the rich as a rule, but if they were handing out money, he certainly could use some. All he wanted was a small piece to help him kick off his halfway house since every penny he'd saved went into Murphy's.

He never dreamed the daughter and chair of the foundation would be the woman he remembered from all those nights ago. Or that coming here today would put him on a path to meeting the son he never knew about.

"That's all well and good," he said, "and I'm sure it needs to be done, but I was thinking something a little less legally binding to start off with."

"Like what?" Violet asked.

"Like a playdate with my son."

Violet couldn't shake the anxiety that curled up in her belly. It was one thing to agree to Aidan coming over to her apartment so he could meet Knox; it was another to know he'd arrive any moment.

It had been two days since he'd walked into her office and turned her world upside down. Two days of memories circling in her mind at the most inopportune of times. Memories of the nights she'd spent with Aidan. How he'd held her, how he'd touched her. How he'd made her feel things, both physically and emotionally, that she'd never experienced before.

Losing her memory had at first been an annoyance. When Knox was born, it became an unfortunate complication. Now, knowing how much she'd missed out from her time with Aidan, it had become downright tragic.

How many months had she settled with Beau because she didn't remember how amazing it was with Aidan? All that time, in the back of her mind, she'd had a nagging worry. It wasn't ever something she could put her finger on. Just a feeling that things weren't right. That Beau was the wrong man for her, despite her having no reason to think otherwise.

Now she knew what her subconscious was trying to tell her all this time. Aidan was the man who had been missing from her life. From Knox's life. One look into those sky-blue eyes and she'd nearly been knocked off her feet by the power of that realization. How could she have forgotten that hard, stubble-covered jaw, those skilled lips and those strong hands? Even now, she could easily bring to mind the feel of the coarse, auburn chest hair that spread across his firm pecs. The beat of his heart beneath her palm.

The days and nights they'd spent together had been about more than just sex. It was not at all what she expected, going home with a bartender after last call, but they had really connected. He'd been right about that. Knowing he was back in her life both thrilled and scared her. They'd come together on a level she'd never felt with a man before. It had been as though they'd always known each other after just a few short hours. Like her heart would break if she had to be away from him.

Violet craved that connection again after the tumultuous relationship with Beau ending and the months of emotional upheaval and loneliness that followed. And yet, it frightened her. No matter what happened between them, she hoped that Aidan would be in Knox's life. That was as it should be. But the two of them? Could something that intense maintain itself? Would it eventually consume them?

Even if he was still interested in her—and she wasn't entirely sure that he was—the attraction would eventually die out. They might be drawn to each other just because they'd had their chance taken away. If it ended poorly, she didn't want it to impact his relationship with her son. And if she were honest with herself, she wasn't sure if she could bear the intensity, the passion, and then the crippling grief.

In this situation, it might be better if she kept her distance. Polite. Cordial. Businesslike. After all, they were going to be working together on his grant in addition to raising a child together.

When all the drama had been hashed out, they'd finally sat down to discuss the proposal he'd come for. If the board accepted it, there would be several weeks of working side by side on the project. Her foundation didn't just cut checks, they gave charities the tools they needed to learn how to keep themselves afloat in the future. It was an important key to the success of the Niarchos Foundation, and one that would keep her and Aidan working together no matter what happened between the two of them personally.

Violet heard footsteps coming down the stairs and turned in time to see Tara with Knox in her arms. He was wearing a white onesie with blue and green cartoon dinosaurs on it and little matching blue shorts. It was one of her favorite outfits, a gift from her friend Lucy, whose twins were due any day now. The nanny handed over the baby to his mother and she held him close, breathing in the unexpected scent of his baby soap.

"We had an unscheduled bath just now," Tara said with a chuckle. "We tried a little applesauce with our breakfast and we got it everywhere. I'm not even sure how much got in our tummy." She reached out and tickled at the infant's belly, making him laugh and squirm in Violet's arms. "He's ready to go, though. All dressed and clean. Do you need me to stay and wrangle him while your company is here?"

Violet bit at her lip, but shook her head no. She'd told the live-in nanny that someone was coming over, but she hadn't said who it was. Good news traveled fast and scandalous news traveled even faster. For now, she wanted to keep Aidan and his relationship with her to herself. "We'll be okay. It's your day off. Enjoy yourself."

Tara smiled and grabbed her jacket from the closet. "Okay. You guys have fun. Text me if you need me."

Tara disappeared down the hallway and Violet breathed a sigh of relief. At least they hadn't run into each other as she left. Aidan was taller than most men, with a solid build that demanded the attention of every woman he passed. Tara would notice him for sure. And with that fiery red hair and those icy blue eyes, there was no way anyone would look at Aidan and not know exactly who he was.

That wasn't to say that Violet didn't trust Tara. She loved her. Any doubts or concerns she'd had about hiring a nanny had gone out the window when Tara interviewed for the position. Violet had basically been raised by nannies. Her parents were always on the move, touring the world, securing business deals back in Greece and a dozen other countries. Their private jet had more miles on it than most jumbo airliners. But that meant that Violet had grown up alone with no one but her hired caretakers.

They had all been lovely women. Not horribly strict or harsh, but they hadn't been suitable replacements for her parents, either. When Knox came along, she knew she needed help doing this all on her own. She had a job and since it was a family business, she could take him in with her if she had to, but he really needed someone during the day. Tara had been the perfect someone. A helping hand, but not a substitute like her own had been.

But the situation with Aidan was a precarious one. She wasn't ready to trust anyone with it yet, even Tara. She hadn't even told her best friends from college— Emma, Lucy and Harper—about Aidan's arrival. That would come in time, she was sure, but on her own terms, not because of out-of-control gossip.

Violet looked down at her son. He was chewing intently on his fist with slobber running down his arms. He might be clean, but her little monkey was never perfect for long. She walked over to the Pack 'n Play that was set up in her home office and grabbed a clean burp cloth to wipe away the drool. "We don't want you drooling all over Daddy first thing, now, do we?"

Knox just grinned, shoving his fist back into his mouth the moment she released it. The books said he was teething and any moment now, the first few would start to break through. She anticipated quite a few long nights with a cranky baby in her future.

The phone rang. Violet eyed the number, knowing it should be the bellman calling about her guest. A "Mr. Murphy" was waiting for her in the lobby. She told them to send him up and tried to prepare herself for his arrival.

It seemed to take ten minutes for the elevator to crawl the five stories to her apartment. She wasn't in the penthouse, but she was fairly high up in the building with her apartment taking up the west side of the fifth and sixth floors. It gave her nice treetop views of Park Avenue. She'd had the apartment—a graduation present from her parents—since she'd graduated from Yale and moved back to Manhattan. It almost made up for the fact that they hadn't been able to attend her commencement in New Haven. They'd been stuck in Istanbul. She wasn't surprised. That had been their MO her whole life—lavish gifts in exchange for the emotional and physical distance between them.

Soon, though, Violet wanted to make a change. The apartment was spacious when Violet was alone, but a little too small for her, Knox and Tara. Baby things seemed to fill every corner. She wanted more room and to be closer to a park where Knox could run around. Central Park was a little too chaotic for her to keep up with him there. She got a feeling that this little monkey would be on the move the minute he learned to walk.

The doorbell rang. Violet took a deep breath to prepare herself. It should be easy. Today wasn't about her. It was about Aidan and his son. But that didn't mean it wouldn't be a heart-wrenching moment for everyone involved.

Violet walked to the front door and opened it, stepping back far enough to allow Aidan a full view of her standing there with Knox in her arms. "Hello, Aidan. Come in."

She might as well not have spoken because the instant his eyes connected to his son, the whole world faded away for a moment. He didn't move. He didn't even appear to breathe. Aidan was frozen to the spot as he studied his child for the first time.

Knox, however, was oblivious to their visitor. He'd become fascinated with the scalloped edge of Violet's collar, pinching it between his clumsy, chubby fingers.

She turned a bit so Aidan had a better view, then

tugged Knox's hand from her shirt. "Lennox, we have a visitor. Can you say hi?" He couldn't, of course, but Aidan had finally caught his attention. Knox's big eyes locked in on him and he grinned wide.

"It's amazing how much you two look alike," Violet chattered nervously in the silence. "I bet in your baby pictures you couldn't tell you two apart."

Aidan just shook his head, apparently ignoring everything but Knox. "A part of me didn't really believe all this until now, but it's true. He's my son."

Violet winced and glanced over his shoulder into the hall beyond him. The neighbor she shared a vestibule with was incredibly nosey. "He is. Come in and you two can spend some quality bonding time together."

He finally took a few steps into the apartment, allowing Violet to shut the door. He studied the child in her arms like an exhibit at an art gallery, trying to absorb and process every detail from a distance.

Violet looked down and noticed he had a gift bag in his hand. He'd need to put that down to hold Knox, which she was certain would come next if he could work up the nerve. He seemed both anxious and terrified about the prospect. "Why don't you follow me into the living room where you can set your things down and get more comfortable?"

She turned, and he followed her until the hall opened up to a large contemporary space filled with light from the nearly floor-to-ceiling windows along two sides of her corner unit. In the center of the room, she'd put a grouping of comfortable white couches, the only splash of color being some blue throw pillows in the mostly white and gray space.

"Have you been around many babies before?" she asked. She wasn't sure what his level of skill or comfort was with an infant. He could've raised his siblings or have another child she didn't know about, unlike herself who had almost never even held a baby before Emma's daughter, Georgette, arrived. For some reason, the thought of Aidan having another child made her jealous on Knox's behalf.

"No, not really," he said at last. "I was an only child. I don't have any kids of my own—I mean, I don't have any *other* kids. He's my first. Basically, I'm clueless."

Violet smiled. It seemed like a big admission for a man like him. She could tell that coming to the foundation for a grant had bothered him. His initial posture as he'd come through her office door had been defensive. He read like the kind of man who was used to being able to handle anything thrown his way without assistance from anyone. The fact that he'd come to her anyway because his project was important was something she appreciated. Knox was obviously important to him as well, or he likely wouldn't have admitted his inexperience there, either.

"You'll do fine. I didn't know much when I started either. He's not a small and fragile newborn anymore, so you won't have trouble. He's a sturdy boy, at the top of his percentile of weight and height for his age."

At that, Aidan beamed with paternal pride. "I've always been pretty solid. I would've made a decent football player if I'd wanted to, but baseball was always my sport." He held up the bag to show it to Violet before setting it on the coffee table. "That's actually some Yankees outfits for him to wear and baby's first baseball mitt. Now that I'm involved, I've got to make sure you're raising him right."

Violet chuckled. "We're not Mets fans in my family, so no worries there. The foundation actually has a box suite at the new Yankees stadium if you'd like to take him to a game." She shifted Knox in her arms until he was facing out. "Here," she said. "Why don't you go ahead and hold him? You'll get over your nerves faster that way."

She watched as all the muscles in his body tensed. Memories of touching each and every inch of them flashed through her mind as they flexed beneath his skin. She missed touching a man—the hard muscles, coarse hair and heated skin against her own. So different and yet so comforting. Now wasn't the time to reminisce about what she'd lost. She pushed the thoughts aside and focused on easing their son into his arms for the first time.

Aidan appeared nervous for a moment, but Knox snuggled comfortably against his chest and the tension lessened in him. He cradled him easily, instinctively bouncing a bit on the balls of his feet. "Hey there, little guy," he said.

Violet took a step back to give them some space and shield him from the tears that were forming in her eyes. She watched through blurry vision as Knox put his hand against Aidan's cheek and giggled at the feel of his stubble. He hadn't been around very many men, but he seemed to instantly take to Aidan. Perhaps he knew his father instinctually. Or perhaps Knox was just as drawn to Aidan as his mother was.

Watching the two together was such a touching moment for Violet. After everything she'd experienced over the past year, she'd begun to wonder if she'd ever get to witness a moment like this…if Knox would ever get to know the protective embrace of his real father. She'd been racked with guilt after Knox was born. Guilt for misleading Beau, although unintentionally. Guilt for not being able to remember something as important as who her baby's father was. Guilt of knowing he might grow up never knowing his father, and his father never knowing he had a son, just because a taxi driver got impatient and wiped the memories from her mind.

Then Aidan had walked into her office and the opportunity suddenly appeared to put everything to rights. They'd all been given a chance to start again and do things the way they should've been done to begin with. Now she couldn't understand why she'd been so anxious about Aidan's visit. She couldn't be more grateful to witness this touching moment between father and son. She'd cherish this memory forever.

It was special. *Perfect*.

And then Knox puked applesauce down the front of Aidan's polo shirt.

Three

If you'd told Aidan six months ago that he'd be half-naked in Violet's apartment today, he would've laughed. Then again, back then he hadn't known about his new son or factored in how far the boy could projectile vomit applesauce.

"I just put your shirt in the dryer, so you should be able to wear it home," Violet said as she came back into the room with Knox on her hip.

After the applesauce incident, Aidan and Knox had played while Violet cleaned up and threw their clothes in the washer. She'd quickly changed the baby into a little outfit with a train embroidered on the chest.

"I don't really have anything in the house that would fit you." Violet's gaze ran over his bare chest, then shifted quickly to the art on the wall over his shoulder.

"I'm sorry about the mess. Having an infant has been hard on my drive for perfection."

"It's my fault," Aidan admitted. "I should know better than to bounce a baby if I'm not sure how long it's been since he's eaten last."

"I suppose you'll always remember the first time you held your son, now," she said with a chuckle.

"How could I forget? Even without the spit up it's a pretty momentous event."

Aidan noted that his words brought a shadow across Violet's face, stealing the light humor from her words. Her gaze dropped to the floor in contemplation. Suddenly she seemed sad, although he wasn't sure if it was because he'd missed out on the first few months of his son's life, or because he'd finally caught up with her. His unexpected arrival had to be a complication to her life.

Aidan took the moment to study Violet. He hadn't really had the chance to do that in a long time. When she'd shared his bed, he'd lain beside her and tried to memorize every line and curve of her face. The delicate arch of her dark eyebrows, the thick fringe of her lashes against her cheeks as she slept…

Today she looked different than before. Like that night at Murphy's, she was still dressed flawlessly from head to toe with styled hair and a full face of makeup. This time, she had on impeccably tailored plum slacks and a silk blouse with a collar embroidered with tiny flowers. But something wasn't quite right. She looked less peaceful than she'd been sleeping in his arms all those months ago. More at the mercy of life's stresses, with lines around the edges of her eyes and etched into her forehead. Despite having been pregnant, she seemed thinner than before the baby. Almost hollow. Drained. The last year and a half had clearly been hard on Violet.

Although you wouldn't know it to look at him, it had been hard on Aidan, too. Losing his father three years ago had turned his life upside down, but it hadn't been unexpected. He'd bounced back. Murphy's was doing good business again and although he wasn't a hotshot advertising executive anymore, he'd been happy with where he was in life.

Then his mother got sick.

Owning their own business, they'd never had medical insurance growing up and health care reform had done little to help where she was concerned. She'd had the cheapest catastrophic plan, all she could afford, but it hadn't been enough once she got sick. The best treatments, the latest and greatest advancements in Europe, were well out of their reach. The big pharmaceutical industries were charging thousands of dollars for a single dose of medication that could've worked wonders for his mother. They had to recoup what they spent on research and development, they argued. But that argument couldn't keep his mother from succumbing to her illness.

Aidan had never felt more helpless in his life as he had watching her waste away in a state-run hospital. His father had killed himself with alcohol, but his mother hadn't done anything but be too poor to afford the treatment that could have saved her.

Before she passed, his mother did leave him with one task he could control—the halfway house. It had been her idea, one she couldn't see through to the end. But Aidan could, and he would do it with the help of Violet's foundation. Life had come full circle in a strange way.

Violet turned to look at Knox as he yawned. "I think it's naptime for this little guy. Would you like to help me put him down?"

He looked up at Violet and Knox and smiled. "Sure," he said and accepted the baby into his arms.

The clean, babbling ginger baby went contentedly to Aidan. He hadn't been around many babies but those he had tried to hold had never been too happy about it. He was thankful his son felt differently. He liked holding his son just as much as Knox liked being held. He smelled like baby shampoo and talc, a combination Aidan wasn't used to but found soothing somehow. Knox curled contentedly against Aidan's bare chest and shoved his fist into his mouth.

"Be careful he doesn't get ahold of that chest hair," Violet warned. "Come this way and I'll show you his nursery."

Looking anxiously at the chest hair he wanted to keep, Aidan fell in step behind Violet. He followed her upstairs and down a hallway to a door that opened up to a spacious and beautiful room for a baby. It was decorated in a gray-and-white chevron pattern with pops of bright yellow and dark blue. There were elephants on the curtains and a large stuffed elephant in the corner of the room. He couldn't imagine a more perfect nursery.

Violet stopped in front of the large white crib with elephants on the bedding. Aidan watched as she turned the switch on the mobile overhead, making the matching menagerie of elephants in different colors and sizes dance around in a circle to soft music.

"You can just lay him down there," she said. "He'll be out cold in minutes."

Aidan eased his son into the crib, knowing he needed his nap and yet not ready to let go just yet. He had to remind himself that he would see Knox again.

The baby squirmed for a moment, then reached out to snatch a pacifier from Violet. He sucked contentedly as his eyes fluttered closed.

"Told you," she said. "He loves his naps."

"Like father, like son," Aidan replied with a smile.

Violet grinned. "Let's go."

They crept quietly out of the nursery, and Violet shut the door behind him. Instead of heading into the living room again, however, Violet crossed the hall to the door opposite Knox's. When she opened it, Aidan was taken aback to find it was her bedroom.

Why were they going into her bedroom?

She went inside without hesitation or so much as giving him a second glance. He stayed in the hallway, not quite sure what the right course of action was. When they were at her office, before he'd known about Knox, he'd pressed Violet about her attraction to him. He didn't really need to ask. Aidan could tell by the flush of her cheeks and the way she nervously chewed at her bottom lip that she still wanted him. He just needed her to say it out loud so she would admit it to herself.

Violet had finally broken down and confessed that she still wanted him, but that conversation had gotten sidetracked not long after and they'd never returned to the topic. Was this her way of circling back to where they'd left off?

He didn't know Violet well. At all, really. But he couldn't believe for a second that the beautiful, rich perfectionist he'd come to know was leading him into her room to seduce him while their son napped across the hall. He'd like it if she did, of course, but he doubted it would happen.

"Aidan, you can come in," she said from the far side of her bedroom. She was standing in front of a large oak dresser with a mirror. Between them was a queen-size bed with a plush floral comforter, an upholstered headboard and about a dozen different fancy pillows. Apparently rich people liked to spend their money on pillows.

He gripped the door frame and held his ground. He wasn't entirely sure that he could refrain from touching her once he set foot into her bedroom. It was too personal somehow, like she was opening up to him. He could already smell her familiar and enticing scent as it lingered there. It called to him. Another touch, another taste, another aspect of his missing fantasy woman was all he'd craved these past lonely months.

"I don't know if that's a very good idea."

Violet frowned at him, her gaze traveling to his

bare chest again and staying there a moment too long. When her eyes met his, he could tell she'd been admiring his physique and thinking the kind of thoughts that could get them both into trouble. The blush had returned to her cheeks as she licked her dry lips. He understood how she felt. He'd been having enough of those thoughts about her since he'd arrived and she'd been fully dressed the whole time.

"I'm grabbing something out of my dresser. I'm not trying to seduce you, Aidan."

He crossed his arms over his chest in a thoughtful posture. He wasn't so certain of that. "Are you sure? You were just looking at me like I was a tall, cool glass of water you were dying to drink. And to be honest, I'm pretty thirsty myself."

"I may have been looking, but that's all I was doing." She turned back to the dresser and pulled out something folded. "I can't help but look when you're half-naked like that. Here. It's the largest, manliest shirt I own and I need you to put it on, please."

Violet tossed the shirt to Aidan. He caught the wad of fabric and shook it out to investigate what she'd offered him. If this was the largest, manliest thing she had, he couldn't imagine what the rest was like—lace and bows and glitter? For one thing, the shirt was too small. He had broad shoulders and a wide chest that demanded an XL top even when his waistline was on the narrow side. The top was a medium, and a woman's medium at that. It was also a purply sort of color. Its only redeeming attribute was the black logo on the front for a local rock band that he'd heard play a time or two.

"This is too small."

"Please put it on."

"I'm going to tear it."

"It doesn't matter. I just need you to wear it until your shirt dries. It's that or a pink silk robe. Your choice, but you've got to wear something."

There was a pleading in her eyes that he couldn't ignore. She was desperate not to want him. There were lots of reasons she could feel that way. Perhaps she didn't want to complicate the issue with sharing custody of their son. Maybe she was in a relationship with someone else. Or she could be embarrassed that she had little self-control when it came to her attraction to a lowly barkeep. That was one reason to fight your feelings. Not a good one, but still a reason.

With a shrug, he attempted to pull the T-shirt over his head. It wasn't the easiest thing he'd ever done, but after some tugging and grunting, he was able to pull it down to cover most of his stomach. "Okay, it's on."

She didn't respond right away. He looked up at Violet and found the stunned expression on her face unexpected. Despite the fact that he was wearing a ridiculously small purple shirt that belonged on a woman, she looked at him as though she could eat him with a spoon. She was actually gripping the footboard of her bed with white-knuckled intensity.

"What?" he said, looking down at himself. It was easy to see the issue. The shirt was tight. Painted-on tight. Every twitch of his muscles, every line of his six-pack abs, was magnified by the clingy top she'd forced him to put on. Her plan had backfired spectacularly.

"Oh, dear. We should've gone with the robe." She sighed, shaking her head. "Just take it off. It didn't help."

"The pants, too?" Aidan asked with a sly grin.

Violet swallowed hard before shaking her head. "Uh, no. Just the shirt."

For now at least, he thought with a wry smile as he tugged the purple fabric over his shoulders.

"You've been quiet this week, Violet," Harper noted over her traditional girls' night glass of dry merlot.

"Is Knox teething yet?" Emma asked. "When Georgie started teething, she hardly slept a wink at night, so neither did I. I was a zombie for weeks and that was with a nanny helping during the day."

"Is that what I have to look forward to?" Lucy asked with concern lining her brow.

"Times two," Harper pointed out with a smug grin. She was the only single one in the group without a baby on the way, so she was well-rested, thin and living a fabulous life from all outward appearances. "So expect it to be exponentially worse than Emma and Violet have had it."

"I appreciate you pointing that out, dear sister-in-law," Lucy grumbled into her glass of Perrier and lemon instead of her usual sweet rosé. She was thirty-five weeks pregnant with Harper's niece and nephew. She and Harper's brother, Oliver, had gotten married a few months ago and had been anxiously awaiting the arrival of the twins.

"That's what I'm here for," Harper quipped. "So seriously, what's going on with you, Vi?"

Violet had much preferred her friends continue with the banter so she didn't have to answer Harper's pointed question. Unfortunately, she could tell her friend wasn't going to let it go. She knew that girls' night would be the night she'd have to come clean to them. They could sniff out a secret like a bloodhound.

Knowing it was time to spill the truth to her best friends, she took a deep breath and began. "Knox *is* starting to teethe, but that isn't it. Something else has happened."

"Oh, really?" Emma said, leaning in curiously to hear the latest news. "Do tell."

"Beau hasn't started sniffing around again, has he?" Lucy asked in a worried tone.

It wasn't the first time she'd heard that, and for good reason. Violet's ex-boyfriend had tried to reconcile with her a few times in the six months since Knox was born. He'd actually been all too happy to continue their engagement and marry knowing Knox wasn't his son. He insisted that he loved her and he didn't care about Knox's parentage. It had been Violet who'd demanded the paternity test, and Violet who had returned the ring and ended things when the results came back the way her gut had anticipated them to. Beau hadn't been any happier about the breakup than her parents had been, but she knew she had to do it.

"No, thankfully I haven't heard from Beau in several weeks. This is actually good news. I had a major breakthrough with my amnesia."

"You remembered something?" Lucy asked with wide brown eyes.

Violet nodded. "Not everything," she admitted. "But the most important parts, I think."

"Knox's father?" Emma asked with a breathy voice.

"Yes."

Violet's three best friends in the world whooped with excitement, drawing stares from others around the restaurant. They quickly started a rapid fire of questions, hardly leaving Violet time to answer.

"Just relax for a minute and I'll tell you everything," Violet said, holding up her hand to slow their words. She shook her head and steeled her own nerves with a large sip of her chardonnay. "Last Monday, a man came into the foundation."

"Did he have red hair?" Lucy asked.

"Let her tell it," Harper complained.

"I am letting her tell it," Lucy snapped.

"Yes, he had red hair," Violet interjected into their argument. "And blue eyes just like Knox, but even then I didn't recognize him at first. He knew me, though. Apparently he thought I had run out on him the morning of my accident and he didn't know how to find me."

"When did you get your memories back?" Emma prompted.

"When he said his name. I didn't have the slightest idea who he was and then all of a sudden, it was like a bucket of memories was dumped on my head. I remembered nearly every second of the two amazing days we spent together. And at that point, there was no doubt in my mind that Aidan was Knox's father."

"Ohmigosh," Lucy gasped and clutched her huge belly. "This is so exciting I just might go into labor."

"Please don't!" Harper said with panicked eyes. "The twins need to stay in there as long as they can. If you go into labor on girls' night, my brother will blame me. I don't want to have to hear him complain."

"That has to be a relief for you," Emma said, ignoring the others and reaching out to clasp Violet's hand. "Now you finally know who your baby's father is. I only went a couple months when I first got pregnant before I tracked down Jonah. I can't imagine how you've dealt with the uncertainty for all these months."

"I didn't really have a choice," Violet said with a dismissive shrug. The last six months had been hard, no doubt, but there wasn't much she could do about it when her brain wouldn't unveil its secrets.

"What's his name?" Harper asked. "I have a friend at FlynnSoft that can run a background check on him if you'd like me to ask."

"No, that won't be necessary, I don't think. I know plenty about him already from his grant application. His name is Aidan Murphy." It felt nice to finally know that answer when she was asked. Even when she remembered him she didn't know his last name. They hadn't exchanged much personal information, including last names, when they spent time together before. She didn't know it until she looked over his paperwork.

"So did you tell him about Knox?" Lucy asked.

Violet nodded and reached out to grab some spinach dip from the bowl in the middle of the table. She was suddenly more interested in eating than talking but at this rate, the dip would be cold before she got any if she didn't just dig in. "He figured it out before

I got the chance when he saw the baby picture on my desk. That's when I came clean…"

The girls pestered her for the next hour, asking her to go over every detail of her reunion with Aidan and his first visit with Knox. They gave her a break long enough for everyone to order dinner, but the questions continued as they ate their entrées and ordered another round of drinks.

"Wow," Harper said as Violet wrapped up her tale. "Did you remember anything else about that week? The time with Aidan was just the last two days before your accident, right? You don't remember what happened before that?"

"No, not yet." That had bothered Violet, but she'd been too busy with the situation with Aidan to give it much thought. Something had sent her to Murphy's Pub looking to drown her sorrows in liquor. She wished she knew what it was. At the same time, one major breakthrough at once was more than enough. It would come to her eventually, she hoped.

"You don't seem very happy," Emma noted. "I thought you would be more excited about all this. I mean, you didn't even tell us about it and it's been almost a week since it happened. What are you leaving out?"

Violet was hoping they wouldn't pick up on that, but of course they would. "Maybe I'm just overwhelmed by the whole thing. It's a lot to take in. Now I have to start the process of sharing Knox with his father when he's been all mine since the day he was born."

Harper shook her head. "That's not it. There's something else. Have you told your parents about Aidan yet?"

"Heavens no!" Violet exclaimed. "I want Aidan and I to work things out in terms of raising Knox and get it settled with our attorneys before we bring my parents into the situation. You know how they are. Besides, they're in Dubai right now. Or Qatar. I forget which."

"I get the feeling it wouldn't matter if they were at the next table. What are you leaving out? What's wrong with Aidan? Is he weird? Annoying? A Communist?"

"There's nothing wrong with him," Violet argued. "He's just not what I was expecting. Not the kind of guy I would usually date."

"The kind of guy you usually date is an asshole. So that's a good thing, right?" Harper wasn't holding back tonight.

"Beau wasn't an asshole," Violet argued. "We were good on paper. It just didn't work as well in real life. Aidan is…"

"Poor?" Lucy interjected.

Violet turned to her friend and wished that she could say she was wrong because it sounded so snobby that way. Lucy had grown up with nothing, and until she inherited a fortune from her employer—Harper's great-aunt—she probably had less than Aidan.

"Poor isn't exactly how I'd phrase it," she argued. "He owns his own business, but he's in a different social circle than I usually date in. I know that sounds horrible, but you all know why I do that! My family is famous and any guy with a computer can Google my net worth without much trouble."

"Poor billionaire Violet," Harper said with a smile that undercut her sarcasm. "So what kind of business does he own?"

"A bar. An Irish pub to be exact."

"That's why you haven't told your parents, and took your time telling us," Harper said with an accusing tone. "You had an affair with some sexy bartender!"

Four

It had been a couple days since girls' night, but their words still echoed in Violet's head. That she was keeping secrets about Aidan. That she hadn't told her parents or her friends because she was embarrassed about slumming with a bartender. That maybe, deep down, it was true.

No. It wasn't true, and yet their words haunted her. She knew Aidan was more than just a bartender. Along with her hotter memories had come some of their pillow talk. She knew he was a smart, capable, caring man. One who would be a good father for Knox.

But that still didn't mean she was going to tell her parents about him.

It wasn't about Aidan, not really. It was her parents who were the problem. They jet-setted around the world, ignoring her most of the year. When she did see them, they were filled with criticisms and loaded down with gifts. The gifts soothed their conscience and also doubled as bribes. While she was still lying in the recovery room, her father had offered her a luxury yacht if she'd agree to marry Beau and tell the world he was Knox's father.

She'd turned that offer down.

It was probably one of the first times in her life she'd put her foot down with her parents. They hadn't quite known how to take her answer. So they'd given her a diamond watch as a push present, opened a trust fund for Knox and got back on a plane to somewhere else.

Her parents loved her. Violet knew that on a practical level. But they weren't the hands-on, demonstrative parents she'd always wanted. She wanted that for Knox and she felt like Aidan would provide the warm father figure he needed.

She just knew her parents wouldn't see the good in Aidan. Only his "flaws," the way they focused on hers. She'd already done enough to Aidan, albeit not deliberately. If she'd had her memories she would've told him about Knox the moment she realized she was pregnant. He didn't deserve the kind of casual abuse her parents would heap on him—comparing him to Beau at every chance, criticizing his work, his family, his upbringing… No good would come from that. For now, it was easier to let them think her memories were still lost in some dark corner of her mind.

She had spoken with her attorney, however, and wanted to talk to Aidan about his recommendations going forward. Violet decided to stop into Murphy's before it opened. He texted that he would leave the door unlocked so she could pop in whenever she could.

When she arrived outside the bar, she felt the intense sensation of déjà vu. This was the place where her life had changed forever, even if she hadn't known it until recently. As she pushed open the heavy door to step inside, the familiar scents and sounds of the bar surrounded her. Behind the bar was Aidan, polishing glasses from the dishwasher and putting them away in their respective homes.

"Welcome to Murphy's Pub." He greeted her with a warm smile that made her belly clench.

That smile was probably what had lured her to him the night they met. He had almost a magnetic pull on her. She wanted to be close to him. Even now, although she wrestled with it, she felt the draw. Of course she wanted him as a father for her son. And she still wanted him for herself if her jacked-up pulse and aching breasts were any indication. But did they have long-term potential?

She wasn't sure about that. They were from disparate worlds. Different cultures, different religions, different neighborhoods. He might never be comfortable rubbing elbows with the ultra-wealthy families the Niarchoses associated with. It had been easy to ignore those differences for a weekend when there was no promise of anything more, but for a lifetime? It would eventually be an issue.

"Where is Knox?" Aidan asked when she came through the door with nothing but her designer handbag.

"He's with Tara." Violet couldn't very well bring her six-month-old son to a bar, even if it was to see his father. She set her purse on the newly cleaned bar top and climbed onto one of the worn stools that lined it.

"Who's Tara?"

"She's the nanny."

Aidan got a funny look on his face. It was a mix of surprise, irritation and a complete loss of vocabulary. She wasn't sure why he was confused by something that simple. He should've expected that she had someone to help her with the baby. Violet was a single, working mother. Someone had to keep Knox during the day. Eventually, he would go to a prestigious preschool, but until then, she had to choose between a nanny and day care. The nanny route won in the end.

"What?" she asked at last. "There's something on your mind, say it."

Aidan sighed and slumped onto the bar stool beside her. "What do you really know about this Tara? Did you do a background check on her? Get references from other families?" he asked.

Violet snorted and shook her head. Did he really think she would leave her child with just some random person off the street? "'Yes' to all of that. I actually know more about her than I know about you. She checks out on every level and she's amazing, so you can take the protective dad thing down a notch."

He shrugged off her concerns. "I can't help it. I'm new at this, but it's amazing how quickly the parental panic sets in."

"I know. When they took him from my arms to do

his checkup at the hospital, I started to worry. By the time they gave him back to me, I was on the verge of tears. I had never loved anyone as much as I loved that little boy the moment I laid eyes on him."

Violet noticed a sad look in Aidan's eyes before he shook it off and pasted his bright smile back on. She wished she could give him back the six months he'd lost. Or at least kiss him until the sadness faded away.

"So whatcha drinking?" he asked, changing the subject.

"Do you have anything sweet?"

"I have a Magner's Irish Hard Cider on tap."

"I'll take that." She picked up a cardboard coaster and started spinning it absently between her fingers while he moved down the bar to pour her drink.

Aidan set the glass on a napkin in front of her. "So you mentioned when you called earlier that you spoke with your attorney. What did he have to say about our little situation?" he asked.

"He's going ahead with a draft custody agreement for us to meet and redline. His assistant will also call you with a time and place to go for the paternity testing. The lab already has Knox's profile from his first testing with Beau. Basically, we'll start from there."

"Okay, but I'll need to know how much I'll owe in monthly child support and things like that, too."

The mention of child support brought Violet's fidgeting to a standstill. "I didn't tell my attorney to ask for child support."

Aidan stopped and looked at her with his ginger

brow furrowed in confusion. "Why not? I'm willing to do the right thing and help support my son."

Violet felt her stomach tighten with anxiety. She hated talking about money, especially her own money. It was one thing to talk about the family wealth in abstract or the foundation, but her personal finances always seemed to open up a door to angst. People never looked at her the same way when they knew how much she was worth. She liked the way Aidan looked at her that night after Murphy's closed. His blue eyes had reflected pure desire and nothing more. Even now, she could catch the light of appreciation there as he admired her appearance from across the room. She didn't want that to change. But she couldn't take his money just to end the awkward conversation.

"I don't need it, Aidan," she said at last. "With you trying to start the halfway house and keep the bar running, you can put that money to good use elsewhere. At the very least, save it for things to do when you and Knox are together."

"I have to," he insisted with a stern set of his square, stubbled jaw. "I'm his father. I don't want people to say I didn't step up when the time came."

"And I'm telling you that I can't take a dime from you. I mean it." Violet crossed her arms over her chest in defiance. She doubted it made her appear more adamant, but she'd try it anyway. Male pride could be so frustrating sometimes. That was one thing about Beau that was easier to handle. He was happy to let her pay for things when she wanted to.

Maybe too happy in retrospect.

Aidan looked around the bar and held out his arms. "Listen, you're well-off, Violet. I can tell by the apartment bigger than my bar and the nanny and everything else. But I—"

"I'm not just well-off," she interrupted, feeling the frustration building in her neck and shoulders and pulsating a familiar pain down her arms. She took a sip of cider, hoping it would relax her and dull the pain.

Although she had a really nice apartment and most everything she needed or wanted, she tried to live a more modest lifestyle by Manhattan standards. Her parents' collection of homes was so lavish she was embarrassed to take anyone to visit them. As a teenager in prep school, she'd never hosted a single sleepover. Not that her parents were ever home to oversee one. Her schoolmates didn't need to see the gold-plated furniture and the marble statues of Greek gods in the foyer. It was an over-the-top display of wealth that made her uncomfortable.

"Aidan, I'm one of the wealthiest women in the country," Violet said, finally spitting out the words she'd been holding in. "We're talking billions. With a *B*. I'm sorry to be so blunt about it, but I need you to understand that I'm not just being nice when I say that I don't need any of your money."

"She's a frickin' billionaire?"

Aidan winced as one of his regulars, Stanley, said the *B* word a little louder than he would've liked. "Why don't you yell it again, Stan? I don't think the whole bar heard you the first time."

"Sorry," Stan said, taking a big swig of his dark brown pint of Guinness. "I thought you were bragging. I know I'd be happy to be involved with a sexy billionaire. I'd shout it from the rooftops."

"You'd shout it from the rooftops if you were involved with *any* woman."

Stan chuckled and took another drink. "Probably so. But what's so wrong with a rich girl?"

"Nothing. And everything." Aidan didn't like to admit it aloud, but he didn't really care for rich people. Give him blue collar…give him salt of the earth people who worked with their hands and were willing to give you the shirt off their backs… He'd rubbed elbows with all types and the working class were the kind of people he preferred to associate with in both his personal and private life.

There were never ulterior motives to their friendship. They weren't out to make a buck off you or use your shoulders to climb higher up the social ladder. Most of them knew they were never going to be upper class, much less rich, and they were okay with that. Aidan had aimed high, trying to better his situation for his and his mother's sake, and he'd done well. Working at one of Madison Avenue's biggest and most prestigious advertising agencies had come with lots of cash and plenty of perks.

But he was happier here behind the bar at Murphy's Pub. Aidan had had a taste of upper class and it was far more sour than he'd expected it to be. Here, if something tasted bad, he just changed out the keg and the problem was solved.

"This is about what happened with you and fancy pants Iris, isn't it?"

Aidan winced at the mention of his ex-fiancée's name. "I paid you fifty bucks to never say her name again."

Stan rubbed his stubbly chin thoughtfully. "You said you would. Never did, as I recall. So I'll say it again. That nasty breakup with Iris must've made you bitter."

Bitter? Aidan thought over Stan's choice of words and eventually shrugged it off. "Maybe so. Wouldn't you be bitter if your supposedly loving fiancée left you for your wealthier, more successful boss?"

"He wasn't your boss," Stan pointed out. "You'd quit the agency by then to come work at the pub. I remember her coming in here to break it off."

"Technicality. What's important is that she decided—within weeks of my father's death, I might add—that marrying a bar owner wasn't good enough for her. If I wasn't going to be a hot shot advertising exec with a chance at making partner at the agency, she wasn't interested."

"That was pretty cold. But what makes you think this new woman you're involved with would do the same thing?"

"I don't." Aidan shook his head and wiped down the worn wood countertop of Murphy's Pub. Most of the day-to-day tasks of running Murphy's were the kind he could go through almost robotically without concentrating too hard. Unfortunately today, that meant his mind was free to run through his earlier conversation with Violet again and again. "It's just a general distrust of the wealthy. The rich get richer, the poor get poorer, and the rich are happy to keep it that way. Anyway, I'm not *involved* with Violet. I was. We have a child together thanks to some tequila and a three percent failure rate on condoms. I don't think she's interested in, uh…"

"Banging the bartender on the regular?"

"Nice choice of words there, Stan. But yes. Our fling was one thing. An actual relationship is totally different."

"Just because it's different doesn't mean she's disinterested."

"She didn't exactly run out to find me when she realized she was pregnant. Would you if you were in her shoes? I'm just a bartender barely keeping afloat, Stan. She's probably embarrassed to tell people about me."

"I thought she hit her head or something."

"That's what she says."

"You don't believe her?"

Aidan sighed and leaned his elbows on the countertop. "I don't know. It seems awfully fantastical. The far simpler answer is that she wanted to forget she ever met me and when put on the spot, she came up with that story so she didn't look like the bad guy."

"Or she really did have an accident and forget. She's been very accommodating since you two ran into each other, hasn't she?"

She had. That was part of the problem. The Violet he knew didn't seem like the kind of woman who would make up a story like that. She'd seemed genuinely relieved to know his name and connect the dots of her past. But did that Violet from all those months ago have anything in common with the high-class lady who had his baby? It was hard to associate those two parts of her personality.

"Let me ask you this, then," Stan said when Aidan didn't respond to his question. "You say she wouldn't want to date you. But what about you? Are you interested in a relationship with her?"

Aidan's jaw clenched tightly as he thought over his response. Easily, the answer came that he wanted her. How could he not want her? She was the most beautiful, sensual creature to ever waltz into his life. But the Violet he wanted was the one who had stumbled into his bar all those months ago. Was billionaire socialite Violet going to be as uninhibited and free? Knowing more about her and who she really was by the light of day had changed things for him.

As Stan had mentioned, Aidan didn't exactly have the greatest impression of rich people, and it wasn't just because of Iris and that toad Trevor. No, he'd been burned more than once by people with more money than moral fiber. Violet may not fit into that category, but he didn't know for sure. As she'd pointed out earlier that afternoon, they didn't really know much about each other. It wasn't long ago that he didn't know her last name or where she lived or worked. What he did know—what he had burned into his brain—was every curve of her body, the taste of her skin and the soft sounds she made just seconds before her orgasm broke.

"It's too early to say." Aidan answered the question at last. "It's complicated."

Out of the corner of his eye, he caught the unmistakable gesture of the two men drinking in the far corner. They wanted another round. Aidan moved away from Stan and poured two pints of beer. Then he carried them over to the table and bussed their empty glasses.

"All relationships are complicated," Stan pointed out when he returned. "What makes this more complicated than usual?"

"Aside from her being ridiculously wealthy? How about that if something were to happen between us now it has the potential to complicate our coparenting arrangement?"

"Coparenting?" Stan said with an expression of distaste. "What's that, raising a kid together?"

"Yeah. That's what they call it now."

"When I was young enough to get a woman in trouble, they called it *marriage*."

Marriage? He supposed that some people would think that was the answer. Aidan was actually lucky his devout Irish Catholic parents were both dead and buried or the news of their illegitimate grandson might have killed them.

"Yeah, well, the topic of marriage hasn't even come up and I'm not in the least bit surprised. Why would she want to marry me, Stan? She doesn't need me to raise our son. She has a fortune at her disposal. The biggest Manhattan apartment I've ever set foot in. A live-in nanny. Me showing up in her life is mostly a complication for her, I'm sure. She's letting me be involved in Knox's life to be nice. There's nothing I can offer her or my son."

"That's not true," Stan said in as comforting a tone as he could muster. The older, burly, rough construction worker was hardly the comforting type. "You're his father. At least you're pretty sure you are. Once the tests come back and you're certain, there's nothing that will ever change that and no one else that should take that place in his life. You don't need money or a fancy job to be there for your son. Just be a dad. That's important. More important than bleeding your checking account dry trying to pay for the kid's fancy private schools. She can handle that. You stick to what you're good at."

"And what's that?" Aidan asked. "I used to be good at getting people to buy things they didn't need. In high school, I was a decent baseball pitcher. I can pour a perfect beer. None of those skills will help me where Knox is concerned."

"Just be the best dad you know how to be," Stan grumbled. "Is that so hard?"

"I don't know. Do I know how to be a good dad?" Aidan asked.

Stan looked at him with a narrowed gaze. "You didn't have the best example in your father," he admitted. He'd been a patron of Murphy's Pub long before Aidan took over and had been good friends with Patrick Murphy, his father. "But I've known you since you were a kid and you've grown into a good man, Aidan. You gave up your career to take over this place after your dad died. You took care of your mother while she was sick, God rest her soul. You know how to be a good dad because you're a good person. I'm certain of it."

Aidan thought over his regular customer's words

carefully before he nodded. "You're right," he said at last. "Being there is more than some dads do, rich or poor. I'm just not sure if that's enough for a kid like him."

"A kid like what?"

"A rich kid. I can't buy him a sports car or send him to some Ivy League school like other dads can. But I want to play catch with him and take him to his first Yankees game. I want to teach him what he needs to know to be a strong, honorable man in this world, so when he grows up with a fortune at his disposal, he doesn't abuse his powers. I also want him to have a normal childhood."

"What's normal?"

"Having a trust fund opened the day you're born isn't normal. Neither are boarding schools, live-in nannies and being captain of the polo team." Aidan shook his head. "No matter what I say or do, my son is going to be a rich kid. That's a given. All I can do is try to keep him levelheaded so he isn't a spoiled, obnoxious rich kid."

"Good luck with that," Stan said, taking the last sip out of his pint glass. He shuffled off his stool and tugged his coat back on.

Aidan chuckled at his regular and went to close out his tab. "Thanks."

Five

The sound of the phone ringing—again—was enough to set Violet's teeth on edge.

That morning, she'd stepped out into her kitchen and found herself ankle deep in cold, murky water. Understandably, her day had gone downhill from there. Hours of phone calls, troops of repairmen and insurance company paperwork had left her slightly less damp, temporarily homeless and extremely irritable. So when the doorman rang to let her know she had another guest, she wasn't exactly receptive to the news. But it was Aidan, so she said to send him up anyway.

She waited in the foyer as Aidan stepped out of the elevator and stopped. Her front door was standing wide-open with a huge industrial fan blowing in on the wood floors. His eyes were wide with surprise as he ran his hands through his long strands of auburn hair.

"What the hell happened here?" he asked as he took a giant step over the fan into her apartment.

Violet sighed and pointed to the disaster area she once called a kitchen. "Apparently one of the pipes from the upstairs bathroom corroded and finally burst in the night. It took out my kitchen ceiling and filled most of the apartment with several inches of water. This is one of the joys of living in a pre-war building, I guess. I never expected to wake up to a mess like this."

Aidan looked around with a grim set to his jaw. "This is going to take a while to fix. The wood floors will have to be replaced. They're already warping. Some of the floor and ceiling supports, too. The insulation soaks up the water inside the walls, so that might have to get ripped out and replaced along with all the drywall that got wet. Maybe even the cabinetry. It's a big job, for sure."

"Do you know much about construction?" Violet asked.

He shrugged. "Not really, but I've done some jobs here and there. Dad's bar flooded during Superstorm Sandy and I had to help with some of that. I'm going to be doing most of the renovation of my mother's house when we get the money. It will help me stretch the dollars further. I know it takes time, though. Did the repairmen give you a timeline?"

"No, but I've basically given them a week to get it back to functional. If they do a good job I might pay them later to renovate the kitchen. I was thinking about doing that at some point anyway."

"A week isn't very long for all that work."

"Well, with the amount of money I'm willing to pay to fix this, they can figure out how to get it done. I can't stand to stay in a hotel for longer than a week at a time, and that was before Knox came along. As it is, it's going to be a tight squeeze with Tara, the baby and me. Even a suite at the Plaza is going to feel claustrophobic after too long with all of Knox's things."

"The Plaza?" Aidan said with a strange expression twisting his face. "Are you serious?"

"Yes," Violet said, not entirely sure why he thought it was an odd choice. It was just down the street and convenient. "I already made the reservations. We can't stay in the apartment when it's a construction zone. Tara is packing up her and Knox's things right now."

"You don't have family you can stay with? What about your parents?"

Violet stifled a laugh, covering her mouth with her hand and softly shaking her head. While it did seem like a logical option, there was no way she was packing up and going home unless she had no other choice. Even with her parents out of the country, she'd suddenly be fourteen again and they'd be in her business, having the housekeeper spy on her and report back. And they'd be in Aidan's business if he came around the apartment, as well.

"No, thank you. I'd rather stay in a hotel than do that. I've told you how they are."

His blue eyes searched around the room for an answer, although she doubted he'd find it among the warped wood and soggy insulation tiles. "What about staying with me, then?"

Violet stopped and it was her turn to frown. "With you? Don't be ridiculous."

"It's not ridiculous," Aidan said. "You've been to my place before. It's not the Plaza by any stretch, but I've got two roomy bedrooms and a full kitchen, which you won't have at the Plaza. I'm at work most of the time, so you'd have the place to yourself. It's just for a week and it would give me more time with Knox."

Violet tried not to be offended that he wasn't interested in more time with her, although his offer did leave her with a few important questions. "That's a sweet offer, but two bedrooms," she repeated, "for three adults and one baby." Where did he think everyone would end up sleeping in this scenario of his?

"Tara and Knox can share the guest room. It has a double bed and his Pack 'n Play will fit in there just fine. You can sleep in my room. And I..." Aidan's deep voice drifted off as his bright blue eyes met hers from beneath their heavy ginger brows.

Her belly tightened when he looked at her that way, the possibilities dangling in the air between them. Sharing an apartment, a bedroom, a bed... It didn't matter if it was for a week, a day or an hour, Violet wasn't sure she had the willpower to keep away from Aidan. Images of him standing shirtless in her bedroom still haunted her at night. It had taken everything she had not to run her fingers through the auburn curls on his chest and drag her nails across the hard muscles of his stomach.

"…I will sleep on the couch."

Or maybe she wouldn't have to use willpower.

Even then, she couldn't accept his offer. Staying at the Plaza was hardly an imposition. They would have housekeeping and room service and they would survive. "No, really, Aidan. I'm not going to impose on your life. The hotel is fine. They're sending over a shuttle van to pick us and our things up in an hour."

Aidan grabbed her cell phone from the kitchen counter and handed it to her. "Call and cancel it."

"What? Why?" Violet snatched the phone out of his hand but didn't have any intention of calling anyone. Instead, she shoved it into the back pocket of her jeans.

"Because I'm not letting you and my son live in a hotel when I can do something about it."

"Let me?" Violet couldn't help the edge in her voice. She wasn't the kind of person who asked permission from anyone. At one time, her parents had watched and critiqued her every step, even from halfway around the world. As she grew up, she decided that anyone else could mind their own business. She learned early on that there were plenty of people in the world—men especially—who would be happy to control her and her money. But she was not a prize to be won. Violet had to grow a backbone or she might as well give her fortune away.

"Who are you to *let me* do anything? I am a grown woman—a single mother at that—who makes her own decisions."

Aidan's eyes widened as he realized his mistake and held up his hands to buffer the blowback. "That's not what I meant. I know you make your own decisions, probably better ones than I do. I just want to do something nice for you, okay? You've been great helping me with the foundation grant and working through the custody situation with Knox. There isn't much I can do for you or Knox. I'm sure the Plaza will be great— far superior to anything I can offer you. But I'm asking you to consider staying with me instead. Let me do this for you."

Violet sighed and crossed her arms over her chest. The pleading expression on Aidan's face was hard for her to resist. She knew it was tough to be involved with her in any capacity. The few friends she'd kept around and the men she'd dated over the years had told her as much. Buying her presents seemed impossible. What do you buy the person who can quite literally buy almost anything they want? And helping her? With what? She could pay for all the help she might ever need.

True kindness though... That wasn't something you could put a price on. She could tell Aidan wanted to do this for her. Not to impress her or keep an eye on her, but because he wanted to be nice. From what she remembered of his place, it was a nice apartment in Hell's Kitchen. It wasn't all the way downtown or worse, far off in Jersey or something. She remembered him telling her that the place was the only thing left from his old life, although she couldn't remember what he was referring to now.

"It would be nice to have a full kitchen for Knox,"

she admitted. The Plaza only offered a mini bar and she doubted they had baby food and warmed formula on the room service menu. "Okay. We can try it. But if it's too tight of quarters or it's just not working out for some reason, the three of us will head to the Plaza."

"Absolutely. And I'll gladly help you move there if I'm wrong." The wide grin on Aidan's face was the best thank-you she could've gotten. "But I think it's going to be great."

Violet wasn't so sure, but she knew it would be a better alternative than living in the disaster area of her apartment for the next few days. There was no way Knox could nap or Violet could think with all the work going on. "Thank you, Aidan. This is a very kind offer. I hope we don't make you regret it. Knox is cutting his bottom teeth with a vengeance."

"No worries. I've missed so much that I'll happily endure teething to spend time with him. And you," he added with a pointed look into her eyes before he quickly shifted attention to his watch. "Uh, listen, I'm going to run home and clean up so everything is ready when you get there." He scribbled the address onto a slip of paper in his pocket and handed it to her with a brass key. "I've got to head to Murphy's about two, so if you're not there before I leave, you'll need this."

Violet accepted the address and the key, holding the cool metal tightly in her hand. "Thank you, Aidan."

He nodded and slipped back out the door, stepping wide over the fan drying the floors. Once he was gone, Violet looked down at the key in her hand. The ache in her stomach made her think she'd made the wrong decision staying with him. The ache in her core when he'd looked at her that way made her certain of it. If she didn't want a relationship with Aidan, she needed to tread very carefully. But what was done was done.

It was only a week, right?

With a sigh of resignation, she went up the stairs to the nursery and let Tara know about their sudden change of plans.

Aidan quietly unlocked the front door of his apartment and slipped inside, not sure of what he might find when he got there. He'd had to leave for work in the midst of their settling in. He'd called home to check in a few times throughout the evening and Violet insisted everything was fine, but he wasn't so sure. There was an edge of anxiety in her voice. Then again, she'd had a long and frustrating day that started with wet ankles and ended in another man's apartment.

The apartment was dark and quiet. It looked almost as though nothing had changed today aside from little touches—bottles in the drain tray by the sink, the stroller sitting in the foyer and Violet curled up on his couch with a book.

The only light in the room was shining down on her, highlighting her form like she was an angel sitting there. Her long, dark hair was twisted up into a messy knot on top of her head and she was wearing a pair of navy silk pajamas as she read. He wasn't sure if she'd ever looked as beautiful as she did then, fresh faced and relaxed.

When she finally looked up at him and smiled with

a divinely serene look on her face, Aidan had to brace his hand on the back of a chair to steady himself. "Hi," he said, as ineloquently as he could manage.

"Hi." Violet put a bookmark between the pages and closed her book.

It was then that he noticed it was a historical romance novel—the kind where the man on the cover was wearing nothing more than a kilt and a broadsword while he gripped a woman in his arms. The golden script on the front said something about The Highlander's Bride. Prize? The Highlander's Pride? He wasn't sure. Either way it was not what he would've thought would be in Violet's "to be read" pile. She'd always struck him as the book club type. Interesting.

"I didn't expect you to still be up." He hadn't closed tonight, but when he did, it was after four in the morning when he got home.

"I've got a lot on my mind," she said in a low voice as she stood up from the couch and walked over to him. "How was work?"

"Same as any night," he said. He didn't want to bore Violet with the realities of drunks he dealt with every evening. "Did you guys get settled in here okay? Does everything suit you so far?"

"Everything has been great. It's a single man's apartment for sure, but we're doing fine. We spent the afternoon doing a little childproofing, but nothing too major. Knox isn't on the move yet."

For that, Aidan was thankful. He wasn't that great with childproof locks. Grown-man-proof locks was more like it.

"I also did some work from home," Violet continued. "When I checked my email this morning, I got a message from the foundation chairman. They met this morning and you'll be happy to know that the board approved your grant proposal for the full amount you requested."

Aidan's heart nearly stopped in his chest. The full amount? Approved? He almost didn't believe it. "Are you serious?"

Violet nodded and grinned. Before he could stop himself, he reached out and scooped her into his arms. She squealed with surprise as he lifted her off the ground and spun her around the living room.

"We got the money!" he shouted, growing dizzy with excitement and the circles they were spinning around his blue shag area rug.

"Aidan!" she scolded in a harsh whisper, but he hardly heard her. It wasn't until the words "wake up the baby" made it to his ears that he realized it was three in the morning and not the best time for celebrations.

He slowly lowered her back to the ground, torturing himself by letting each inch of her body rub along his own until she was back on her bare feet. His pulse started pounding furiously in his throat, making it hard for him to draw in a much-needed breath of cool air. He also had a hard time letting go of Violet now that he had her in his arms again.

Aidan hadn't intended to touch her, hadn't let himself do more than shake hands with Violet since they'd reunited, and for good reason. Sweeping her into his arms had been a reflex and now, a part of him regretted it. Now that he'd done it, it would be ten times more painful to let her go. If he could let her go. The part of him that didn't regret touching her wanted to continue. He forced himself to disentangle from around her, but his hands stayed firmly in place at her waist. He willed himself to release her, but he couldn't do it.

What he did notice was that Violet wasn't pulling away, either.

They stood close together, both of them struggling to catch their breaths from the sudden rush of excitement surging through them. He was relieved to know he wasn't the only one affected by this. Violet was physically flustered with a rosy pink highlighting her cheeks.

"I'm sorry," Aidan whispered as he dropped his forehead to rest against hers. "I just was in desperate need of some good news and you gave it to me."

Violet's gaze shifted toward the guest room as she held silent and still for a moment listening. "I don't think we woke him up," she said at last with a heavy sigh of relief. Her eyes met his with a mischievous twinkle lighting their dark brown depths. "Not for your lack of trying." She smacked him playfully on the chest.

Aidan feigned pain, but all he felt was the pleasurable surge that went through his body as she touched him again. What he noticed was that she didn't move her hand away after she hit him. They both stood there in his living room—his hands encircling her narrow waist, her palm caressing his chest. He wished he could whip his shirt over his head so she could run her fingers though his chest hair. He loved it when she did that. Aidan could still remember the feel of her fingernails grazing across his skin. Just the thought of it combined with their bodies so close was enough to build the pulsating arousal in him.

Aidan tried to wish it away. This whole physical interaction between them tonight was a fluke. He hadn't even kissed Violet since that day all those months ago. Them sharing his apartment for the week wouldn't change anything between them.

Or would it?

"Aidan?" Violet's soft voice called to him, both a question and a plea.

He knew how to answer it. Aidan leaned in to her and brought his lips to hers. The moment they touched, it was like a wormhole opened up and sucked them in. Suddenly they were together again, fifteen months ago, with none of the complications or repercussions in their way. It was just Aidan and Violet giving in to the pleasure of one another's embrace.

Violet didn't flinch or pull away. In fact, her mouth was soft and welcoming, opening to him and letting her tongue gently caress his. She melted against him, the soft curves of her body molding to his hard edges.

Aidan groaned softly against her lips, hoping he wasn't too loud. He wasn't about to let this moment be interrupted by babies or nannies or anything else. He'd fantasized about and waited for the opportunity to hold her again. For fifteen months, he'd wondered if she would remain a memory and nothing more.

And now, her hands were roaming across his chest, and his tongue was grazing her teeth.

"Aidan?" she whispered against his lips a second time.

This time he paused, still cupping her flesh by the handful through her blue silk pajamas. "Yes?" he asked as he silently prayed for her not to put the brakes on this encounter. He wasn't ready to give up this moment quite yet, even if it was a bad idea. He would deal with that in the morning.

"Take me to your room," she said instead.

His heart leaped with joy in his chest and he didn't hesitate for a moment. Instead, he took her by the hand and led her through the dark apartment to his bedroom. Thankfully, his room and the guest room were separated by the kitchen, giving them a little privacy.

He tugged her inside and swung the door closed. With that barrier up between them and the outside world, it was as if a dam had broken. Whatever willpower Aidan had was washed away in an instant and all he could do, all he could think about, was getting a naked Violet beneath him.

She seemed to feel the same way. They both tugged at each other's clothes, her silk and his cotton being tossed unceremoniously onto the floor. The moment new skin was exposed, they'd stop to caress and taste the newfound territory before moving on.

The next thing he knew they were both completely naked and falling back onto his bed. The queen-size mattress had a good bit of give, breaking their fall and sending them bouncing several inches back into the air. Between laughter and kisses, they settled into the bed, pushing aside pillows and blankets until they were fully aligned and unfettered.

This first time, Aidan knew, would be about letting the pressure off. Months of denial, days of wanting and not touching, had built up between them. Romance, foreplay…it was all out the window in the quest to satiate the need inside them both.

"Condom," Violet whispered between panting breaths as Aidan knelt between her thighs and sucked hard at her breast. He teased at her opening, pressing into her moist flesh. She was right. He knew if he didn't stop now to get it, he would do something they both regretted.

Not that doing the right thing last time had made a bit of difference. They'd used plenty of condoms without fail, and yet they had a son together anyway. This time, as he reached for the bedside drawer, he was comforted to see he'd purchased a different brand than before. Just to be safe.

Aidan slipped the latex over the length of his desire and returned his lips to hers. His hands caressed her breasts, her rib cage, then slid down her side to her hips, where his fingertips pressed into the ample flesh of her rear. He held her perfectly still as he slowly moved forward. When he was fully buried in her welcoming warmth, he let out a ragged breath of relief.

He'd thought he'd never experience this divine feeling with Violet again and yet against all odds, she was in his bed. He hadn't expected it or planned for it when he'd walked in the front door that night, and yet here he was, reliving his fantasy with her.

Violet drew her legs up and wrapped them around his hips, pulling him deeper. Aidan let out a groan, smothering it against her lips.

"Give me everything you've got," Violet whispered with a twinkle of mischief in her dark eyes.

Aidan didn't hesitate to fill her request. He wrapped his arms around her, holding her tight and still against him as he began thrusting hard into her. Again and again he pounded into her body to the chorus of Violet's muffled cries. She buried her face in his neck to stifle the sounds, alternating between moans and sharp nips against his throat.

It was all too much for him to take—overstimulation to the max. As much as he wanted to hold on, to make this moment last all night, he couldn't maintain this for much longer. She was too beautiful, it felt too good and his senses were on overload. He was counting down to his climax, but before he could give into it, he felt Violet start to squirm and buck her hips hard against him. He responded in kind, thrusting harder and faster until he felt her start to tense and finally come undone beneath him.

At last she broke into a silent scream as she clawed at his back. Her head went back and her body bowed up against his, then began to shudder and writhe with her pleasurable spasms. Her inner muscles clamped down on Aidan and before he could stop himself, he found his own release inside of her.

Then, just as quickly as the moment had come upon

him, it was over. After hovering over her, breathing hard in his recovery, Aidan rolled onto his back and pulled away. Snuggling was nice, but leaking condoms were not. He needed to deal with that. And then…he realized he wasn't quite sure what to do after that point.

Their constant live wire of sexual tension had propelled them forward faster than their burgeoning relationship called for. After taking that leap to intimacy, where did that leave them? Were they dating now? Was it a onetime thing? Would she want him to stay in the bed with her or would the awkwardness fill the space that had once held passion? Aidan wanted to avoid an embarrassing situation between them at all costs. They would be spending the next week together in close quarters no matter what happened tonight.

Finally he got up and went to the bathroom to clean up. That was step one. He'd worry about the rest after that. When he returned to the bedroom, he grabbed a pillow and a pair of jogging shorts to take with him to the sofa. That was easier than asking if she wanted him to go.

"Where are you going?" Violet asked, still naked and strewn temptingly across his mattress.

Aidan shrugged. "To sleep on the couch."

Violet arched a brow at him and chuckled as she pushed up onto her elbows. "Do you really think that's a necessary precaution after everything that just happened between us?"

That was a good question. A part of him was relieved that she didn't expect him to leave. But he had promised her this room and that he would sleep on the couch when they discussed staying here. He didn't intend to break his word, but with her lying naked in his bed, tangled in his sheets with swollen lips and tousled hair, he didn't really want to walk away, either.

To be honest, he wanted her again. Slowly. A second chance to take his time and indulge his every sense in her body. By the light of morning, everything might change and he needed to make the most of this while he could. "I don't know," he answered.

"You get back into this bed right now!" she demanded at his hesitation. Then she smiled with the wicked glint returning to her eyes. "I'm not done with you yet."

This time he was all too happy to comply.

Six

Violet was having a hard time focusing today.

Aidan was in the office going over plans and paperwork for his grant and she couldn't concentrate on the task at hand. Not with him looking at her so seductively and smelling like her favorite tasty treat—him. All she could think about was burying her face in his throat, tasting his skin and drawing his distinctly male scent into her lungs.

Practically, she knew she should regret last night, but she had a hard time making herself feel that way. It didn't feel like a mistake to give into her desires for Aidan. It felt like the most natural thing in the world. Their time together in the past had been so amazing it was difficult to deny herself something she knew they both wanted. They'd wanted it enough to succumb to temptation four times that night before the sun came up. Every movement of her body brought an achy reminder of their time together.

Then again, their situation was more complicated than it had been the first time they came together. She tried not to let herself go down the rabbit hole of wondering what it would mean if they continued to see each other, and how they would handle other people finding out about them. Violet had no concerns about Aidan's background, job or financial situation, but she knew others would feel differently. Like her parents. Their friends. She wanted to protect Aidan from the uglier parts of her social circles—the ones that would judge and whisper about him. They did it about everyone for one reason or another, but he would be fresh meat for the gossipmongers. He didn't deserve to be dragged through the mud just for being with Violet.

But really, there was no "them," so her worries were premature. Yes, they shared a child and for a short period of time, an apartment, but sleeping together one night wasn't a guarantee of a relationship by any means.

And for now, she was okay with that. Relationships were hard work, if the one with Beau was anything to compare to, and they both had enough on their plate right now. Giving in to their attraction and having fun while they were together was almost therapeutic—a stress reliever better than a glass of wine or a run on the treadmill. Could the physical turn into more? There was certainly that possibility, but that didn't make her want him any less.

Right now, she couldn't imagine anything that would be a turnoff where Aidan was concerned. To be honest, if she knew her assistant, Betsy, might leave early today, she'd lock her office door and let him take her across her desk. All he'd have to do was push up her skirt...

Violet glanced up from the paperwork she'd been blankly starting at and found Aidan looking at her with a sly grin plastered across his face. "What?" she asked, as she felt a blush warm her cheeks. Did he know what she'd been imagining just now? It felt like she'd been caught red-handed.

"You're not listening to me at all. You're a thousand miles away."

She bit at her lip sheepishly and shook her head. "No, I wasn't listening to you. I'm sorry. I got lost in my thoughts for a minute. Repeat what you said, please."

"I hope they were dirty thoughts," he teased.

If he only knew...

Aidan shuffled the paperwork and pointed his finger at one of the sections he'd highlighted in yellow. "But seriously, I was asking about this part in the paperwork that talks about helping my new organization build its own donor base. How will we do that?"

Violet took a deep breath and launched back into work mode. She was more comfortable there than in thoughts about her involvement with Aidan. "While we provide funds to you, we also provide connections to a network of other charitably minded people and organizations. Typically, we will do some kind of event to help you draw donor support, raise some additional funds and connect you with people that may want to be involved with your organization in the long-term. Our hope is that the money we give you is seed money to get the charity off the ground and that eventually, you can support yourselves."

"What kind of event are you talking about?"

Violet picked up a couple invitations from past occasions they'd put together. She kept a file of them to use as examples. "Sometimes we do a walk or fun run. Themed parties or galas are always well attended. There's been a few carnivals. A concert. You get the idea. Galas are probably our most successful events. The return on investment is pretty good and you don't have the major outlay for bringing in a celebrity or something. Rich people like to dress up and mingle, and doing it for charity makes them feel good. With any event, you're really just looking for something to get some publicity for your charity."

Aidan flipped through the cards she handed him with a thoughtful look on his face. "I never imagined doing something on this scale."

"You've got to if you're going to get word out about— By the way, what are you going to be calling it? I never quite know what to refer to your halfway house as when I'm speaking about it."

He sat back in his chair and thought for a moment. "For a while I was playing around with Stepping Stones or something like that, but eventually I let that go and decided I kind of liked Molly's House. That was my mother's name and it was her house, after all. It was her dream to help people like my dad recover from their addictions since she couldn't save him."

"Your father was an alcoholic?"

Aidan nodded. "It's what killed him in the end. And I can't help but think that the years of stress on my mother contributed to her illness, too."

Violet tried not to think about how rough it must have been on Aidan to lose both his dad and his mother, and so close together. He was older when it happened, but it still seemed to define him in some ways. He dedicated his life to running that bar and making it successful again. He fought to open this facility in his mother's memory when it would've been so much easier to just sell the house and move on.

She appreciated how much he cared about the people in his life. He would be a great father for Knox, and a wonderful husband to whatever lucky lady snagged him. Somehow, she didn't think that would be her, even if she wanted it to be.

"That's a great name." Violet reached for one of the forms and filled out the line for the organization title. She needed to focus on the event, not on who might be lucky enough to be with Aidan someday. "Having a name can also help with the event planning," she continued. "See what flows well, like the Friday Suppers Fun Run. We did that race for a local soup kitchen."

Aidan looked down at the stack of invitations she'd handed him before dropping them onto the table. "You know, I think a party would be the thing to do. You said they turn a nice profit and that's what we need. Maybe a Midnight Ball for Molly's House?"

That wasn't bad. A shame it wasn't closer to the New Year. "How about a Masquerade for Molly's House? We could do a black-tie party and encourage everyone to wear Mardi Gras or Venetian-style masks. That's a little different from the usual party and yet I think a lot of people will have fun with it."

He nodded. "I like that. A Masquerade for Molly's House. I think Mom would've liked that, too, especially everyone wearing masks. She always made a big deal out of making my costumes for Halloween each year."

"Great. With that kind of setup, Molly's House will earn the profits on every ticket sold after we recoup costs for renting the venue, entertainment, refreshments and such. The most valuable part of the event is collecting the names and contact information of all the attendees for your future fundraisers, but the cash is great, too. We can do some additional things like a raffle to raise more money. Perhaps we can get a local company to donate something valuable, like a diamond necklace or a car to raffle off."

"An actual car?" Aidan asked with wide, surprised eyes.

"I've done it before. We gave away a sporty little BMW one year. The dealer basically sold us the car below his cost for the advertising they would get. We charged twenty-five dollars for each raffle ticket, and it did so well, we paid for the car and made a tidy profit on top of that. It was something different that the attendees enjoyed. It doesn't have to be a car, of course. We could come up with something that's meaningful to you and your organization."

Aidan looked at her for a moment as his brow furrowed with thought, then he ran his fingers through the strands of his copper hair. "What about a trip?"

That wasn't a bad idea. They hadn't done that before. "What kind of trip?"

"My mother always wanted to go to Ireland. It had been her dream to visit the village her family came from and tour all the sites. After my father died, she even made plans to go there with a group of ladies from the church, but she got sick and had to cancel before they went. She was diagnosed with pancreatic cancer, which is so aggressive and difficult to treat. She fought so hard and only lasted about eight months from her first oncologist's appointment. I would love it if we could give away a trip for two to Ireland. You wanted something meaningful, and that would fit the bill more than a BMW."

Violet smiled. That was a perfect suggestion and one she wouldn't have ever thought of on her own. "That's an amazing idea. I'll get my assistant, Betsy, to call my travel agent and see if they could get us a good deal on an all-expenses-paid trip for two. I know a few people at an airline. Perhaps we could get first-class airfare or a week at a hotel donated. Make it really nice, so the donors will be excited to buy raffle tickets."

This was really coming together and she was excited by its potential. Violet reached out and took Aidan's hand as it rested on her table. The sudden movement seemed to startle them both since they hadn't touched since this morning, but neither pulled away. Instead, he looked at her and smiled. The warmth of his skin chased away the chill she always felt in the air-conditioning of summertime, and the heat in his gaze made her core feel like it was molten inside. She didn't know how she could possibly want him again so soon after last night, but she did.

While she was hopeful to have her apartment back in one piece soon, staying with Aidan wasn't bad at all. The Plaza was nicely decorated with all the amenities of a five-star hotel, but the master bedroom didn't come with a sexy ginger to keep her warm at night the way his apartment did.

A soft tap at the door caused their hands to repel from each other as they both turned to see who was there. She saw it was her long-time assistant as she poked her head inside.

"Yes, Betsy?"

"I'm sorry to interrupt. I just wanted you to know that Mr. Randall is here for your three-o'clock appointment."

"Thank you." Violet looked down at her Rolex and realized the time with Aidan had flown by faster than she'd expected it to. "Well, at least we got a great start on planning. With your first check, you can start renovations on the house. In the meantime, I'll get more of the gala information together for you to look over later this week."

"Okay. This all sounds really great, Violet. There's only one problem I can foresee."

Violet straightened up in her seat. She didn't like the sound of that. She worked really hard with the foundation to ensure that every event went flawlessly. "What's that?"

"You're planning a black-tie affair and I don't own a tuxedo," Aidan said with an apologetic smile.

Even at the peak of his advertising career, Aidan hadn't owned an expensive suit. He had some that were nice—nicer than anything else he'd owned in his whole life—but they weren't even close to the kind of clothes in the windows that Violet was perusing.

Ralph Lauren, Tom Ford, Giorgio Armani…all he could see were dollar signs running through his brain. He shouldn't have said anything to Violet, he knew now. He'd set her on a mission. He should've just shown up at the ball in a black rented penguin suit and no one would've known or cared where it came from.

But Violet apparently cared.

"I think an Armani or Tom Ford is the right style for you," she said aloud as they looked into the windows at the store on Fifth Avenue. "They're trending toward a slimmer fit this season. It will require less tailoring."

Aidan followed her inside the Armani boutique with a dismayed expression on his face. He could hardly afford the food served inside at the restaurant, much less a tuxedo there. That thought hadn't occurred to Violet, however. She surged ahead, eyeballing the displays for just the right look.

It didn't take long for Aidan to mentally check out of the situation. After eyeing a pair of sunglasses he liked and nearly choking at the cost, he leaned against the wall and let his eyes glaze over while she shopped. He focused on her movements as she sauntered back and forth in a tight black pencil skirt that hugged her curves. The sway of her hips was hypnotizing, sending his mind into a full-fledged fantasy that included that skirt up around her hips and a mess of previously folded clothes on the nearby display scattered on the floor.

"Aidan?" she said in a cross tone a few minutes later.

He snapped out of it, realizing it was her beautiful irritated face, and not her ass, that was front and center at the moment. "Yes?"

"I already have a dress to wear to the party," she said. "I came here to help you find something nice to wear and you're not paying any attention to me. I need your input to find something that will work."

"How about you find me a suit with fewer than four digits in the price and I'll wear it?" he challenged. Pushing off from the wall with his shoulder, he strolled over to where Violet was standing with her arms crossed. "I don't know what kind of people typically come to the Niarchos Foundation for help, but I assure you I wouldn't be asking for money if I could lay out four grand for a tuxedo I'll wear one night."

Violet looked at him with concern lining her brow. "This night is important for you, Aidan. You're going to meet the people that will help you make Molly's House a success. They need to have confidence in you, and part of that is looking the part."

"I want to look competent. I don't want to look like I'm skimming from my own charity to line my pockets."

"Think of it this way. A nice, quality suit is a good investment. If you pick the right one, you'll be able to wear it your whole life."

"I'll be wearing it every damn day, Violet, because I'll have to sell all my other clothes to pay for it."

She sighed and twisted her lips in thought. Reaching out to a nearby rack, she pulled a sleeve toward her to glance at the price tag then let it drop. Turning back to Aidan, she narrowed her gaze. "We're getting you a suit. It's my treat. I insist."

Aidan held out his hands to fend off her misplaced generosity. "Oh, no. No, no, no. You are not my fairy godmother, Violet, and I'm not letting you buy me a suit for the ball. Absolutely not. I'll wear sweatpants to the gala before I let you do that." He meant it. It was one thing for Molly's House to be a charity case for the foundation. He wasn't about to be her personal charity case, no matter how badly she wanted to give him a makeover.

"I can afford it. Let me do this for you. As a thank-you for letting us stay with you at your apartment."

Aidan could feel a surge of irritation rise up his neck making him tug at the collar of his shirt. He was regretting mentioning his need of a tuxedo almost the moment he'd said it. The light had come on in her eyes and he knew he was in trouble. "Violet, you have more money than some small countries. I get that. I also get that you are a thoughtful person and you like helping people when you can. But I need you to look at this from my perspective."

"And how is that?"

Aidan crossed his arms over his chest to keep from curling his hands into fists of frustration. "I'm a grown-ass man, Violet. I own my own business. I run my own life. I'm not used to anyone having a say in what I do or how I do it. I brought you along for your opinion. I certainly don't want or need someone picking out my clothes, much less paying for them. Would you have done that for your ex? Treated him like your Pygmalion project? Clean him up so he's suitable to go out in public?"

"Of course not," Violet argued.

"Because he didn't need to be cleaned up, right? He was already the perfect match your parents loved." Aidan shook his head and turned away. He needed to walk away from this before he said something he would regret. "I need some air."

Turning on his heel, Aidan headed for the exit and out onto Fifth Avenue. He pushed through the throngs of shoppers and tourists, hoping that the sounds of the city would block out the pounding of blood in his ears. When he got about a block from the store, he sat down on the edge of a planter and took a deep breath.

A few moments later, Violet sat down beside him without speaking. "I'm sorry," she said at last. "I'm not trying to change you or clean you up, and I don't want you to think that I am."

Aidan didn't say anything. He was too frustrated to answer her right now. He knew he wasn't a clean-cut, upper-class guy like she was used to. He didn't go to prep school or grow up with a trust fund. He went to a small state college on a scholarship and a prayer, trying to mold himself into a new and improved version of Aidan, but in truth, he didn't really like that Aidan. That was why it had been so easy to walk away from the advertising firm. He never felt like he fit in there, something his ex-fiancée did little to help him get through.

"I forget sometimes that people react to my money differently. Some ignore it. Some are more than happy to help me spend it on them or anyone else. Some are almost repelled by it. I try to do the best things I can with my inheritance, and that means helping people when they need it. But the last thing I want to do is use it in a way that makes you feel uncomfortable. So forget it. Buy your own damn suit."

When Aidan turned to look at her, she was smiling. "Fine. I will," he said, matching her smile.

"Fine!" She laughed and turned back to the traffic going by.

"I just need a new suit, Violet," he said after a few moments. "Just a suit. Basic black. Nothing fancy."

"Okay. Can we try again?"

Aidan shrugged. Despite his irritation, he did still need something to wear. "Yeah."

They stood up and when they turned around, they were standing outside of Bergdorf Goodman. "Let's try in here," she said. "They have a variety of brands and even some ready-to-wear pieces that might work."

He reluctantly followed her into the store. They wandered through the displays, but he still didn't see anything that would suit her taste in his budget.

It wasn't until Violet caught a glimpse of a sales associate walking past them. "Excuse me?"

The man stopped and turned to them both with a polite smile. He was wearing a suit that probably cost more than either man made in a month, but that was a perk of working there, Aidan supposed. "Yes, can I help you find anything?"

"Actually, yes. Is there an area where you have any suits or suit pieces marked down? Maybe an end-of-season section?"

"We have a few things. Please follow me." The man with a name tag that said Marcus led them to the back corner of the men's formalwear section where there were a few pieces hanging. "This is all we have marked down in the store."

From Aidan's vantage point, he already knew it wasn't going to work. There was a camel-colored sport coat, a black corduroy blazer two sizes too large for him and a couple dress shirts. This wasn't exactly the type of place to have a sale. Those kind of things would be shipped out to an outlet store or discount retailer, not hanging in plain sight at the flagship Manhattan store. This was Fifth Avenue. It hurt the luxury branding to mark things down. Aidan knew that much from his years in marketing.

Violet looked over the selection and then turned back to the salesman with the sweetest smile he'd ever seen grace her lovely face. She wanted something, and he could tell she was determined to find a way to get it on Aidan's terms.

"I know this is a strange question, but do you ever get suit returns? I know with the custom tailoring you do here it might not happen very often, but I was hoping to find something for my friend. You see, Marcus, we're both involved in a charity organization that's

hosting a black-tie event for some very important donors. As much as I'd love to just pick out the latest style
and let your tailors start measuring him, it's probably
going to be out of our budget."

Marcus listened to her speak, nodding in consideration. "What kind of charity is this for?"

"I'm opening a transitional home called Molly's
House," Aidan chimed in. "It's designed to help alcoholics transition from rehab back into real life by giving them a safe space and the tools they need to cope
with their new sobriety. I'm trying to make a good impression on our potential donors, but the young lady's
taste far exceeds my budget. I understand if there's
nothing in the store that will work for what I need."

Marcus looked thoughtfully over their shoulders
for a moment and then held up his finger. "I actually
might have something." He disappeared into a doorway marked Private and came out a few minutes later
with a black Tom Ford suit bag in his hand.

"This was a custom tuxedo order. We've called the
client repeatedly to pick it up over the last month and
this morning, he finally called back to tell us that he'd
changed his mind about the order. It's a Tom Ford slim-
fit mohair and wool-blend tuxedo. You would need
some additional alterations, but it might work for what
you want."

Aidan watched the man unzip the bag. Inside was
a sharp, black tuxedo with a black satin lapel and bow
tie. He turned in time to see Violet's eyes light up at
the sight of it. He knew from the description alone that
she'd love it. "How much?" he asked. He didn't want

to try it on and have her fall in love with something he still couldn't afford.

Marcus eyed the paperwork attached to the suit bag and did a little mental math. "Normally this is something we couldn't sell, since it was a custom order. We'd either allow one of our employees to use their discount on it or pass it along to the outlet locations, but for you, I think I can make an exception. Would seventy-five percent off make it doable for you?"

Aidan glanced at the paperwork and realized that he was about to get an amazing deal on a designer tuxedo. It was more than he wanted to spend, even then, but the quality was well worth the investment. "Are you serious?" he asked.

Marcus smiled and nodded. "I am. Why don't we take you back to try it on? I'll get one of our tailors to mark it up for you and you can pick it up later this week."

"Okay." Aidan followed him back, leaving Violet in the area outside the dressing rooms.

Once they were alone, he turned to Marcus as he hung the suit in one of the private rooms. "Is this suit really supposed to be marked down that much?"

"Probably not," Marcus said. "But my stepfather is a recovering alcoholic. I appreciate the work you're trying to do, and if I can help you look good doing it, I will."

Seven

"Where are you two headed?"

The following day, Aidan was leaving his building with Knox in his stroller when he ran into Violet coming in. "Hey. I didn't expect you to be off so early today."

"Well, I decided I could stop and take some work home or stay in the office and work until ten. I opted to leave for my own sanity. Are you guys headed out with Tara?"

Aidan laughed. "No, I gave Tara the afternoon off. She mentioned needing to run a few errands. Since I'm off today, I thought I'd take Knox to the park so Tara could do what she needed without hauling the baby everywhere with her."

Violet stiffened and straightened the laptop bag

on her shoulder. He could tell that she didn't like the idea of him having the baby on his own, despite how often he'd interacted with Knox while they'd shared his apartment. "Since you're home early, would you like to join us?" he offered to defuse the tension.

"A trip to the park would be nice," she said, obviously trying not to act like she was afraid of him handling their infant without help. "Can you give me a minute to run upstairs and change?"

"Absolutely. We'll be right here."

Violet went upstairs and returned about ten minutes later, dressed for the park. She'd pulled her dark hair up into a ponytail and put on a pair of tight jeans and a little T-shirt that highlighted her curves. It was casual and clingy, and he enjoyed the look far more than any of the stuffy outfits she seemed to wear at work each day.

They walked a few blocks to the nearest park in a relatively comfortable silence. Once they arrived, they continued around the shady path circling the playground area. Knox was still far too young to play at the park, but Aidan liked the idea of getting him out of the apartment and into what little nature Manhattan provided.

Knox looked up at the canopy of trees and sky overhead and took everything in with wide eyes. He thoughtfully sucked on his Iron Man pacifier, content with his smooth ride in the stroller.

Aidan smiled down at his son, then looked out at the other people around the park. "Nothing but nannies," he pointed out with an irritated edge to his voice.

Violet just shrugged off his observation. "It's the middle of a weekday. Most people are at work and that means a nanny has to take them, or they'd be in school or day care."

Aidan understood the practicality of it, but that didn't mean he liked it. "I get it. There aren't many stay-at-home moms these days. And Tara has won me over, no question. I just worry that these kids are growing up without the kind of parental attention and affection they need to be well-rounded and emotionally healthy adults."

Violet turned to him with a curious cock of her head. "Do you find me to be well-rounded and emotionally healthy?"

Despite the alarm bells going off in his head, he knew he had to answer honestly if he was ever going to convince Violet to raise their son any differently. "Not really. You and your parents definitely have issues. I don't know you well enough to see how that flows into your daily life, but I've already seen evidence of it in our relationship."

Violet stopped walking and planted her hands on her hips. "Like what?"

"Like your drive for perfection in yourself and in others. Your constant unfounded worry that you're not going to make the right decision. I mean, I can tell you that you're the closest thing to perfection I've ever encountered and you won't believe me. You'll only hear your parents' criticisms. I don't understand why their opinion is so important."

Violet sighed and her gaze shifted to a far-off corner of the park. "Their opinion is important because I was always vying for their attention as a child. You're right, I was with nannies over ninety-five percent of my childhood. My parents were always working or traveling or doing any number of things that took them far away from me. I had to be the best at everything I did just so they would take notice of me, but it never seemed like enough for them. I was valedictorian in high school, I went to the college they wanted, I got the degree they wanted, I dated the man they wanted... they still weren't happy. Until the day I walked into Murphy's Pub, I was living a life of their choosing, not mine."

Aidan didn't understand Violet's parents at all and he didn't look forward to the day he'd have to interact with them. They might be Knox's grandparents, but he certainly wasn't going to let them belittle and micromanage his son the way they did with her. "They should be thrilled to have a daughter like you, no matter who you date or what you do."

Violet turned back to him and studied his face for a moment as though she didn't believe his words. He couldn't understand how she could question them.

"Despite what you might think, I don't want to raise Knox the way I was raised. Yes, I have a nanny to help me while he's small, but I have no intention of ever handing my child over while I go globetrotting. I will be there for every day of my son's life. And I want you to be there, too."

Her expression was gravely serious as she looked in his eyes. Up until this point, Aidan wasn't entirely sure that was how she felt. She seemed agreeable enough to including him in Knox's life, but it had only been a couple weeks. They'd just gotten back the positive paternity test results they were both anticipating, and looked over a draft custody arrangement with her attorney. Would she feel the same way months or years from now? When her parents and the rest of Manhattan society found out Knox's father was a poor nobody?

"I mean it," she continued. "Regardless of what happens between the two of us, I want you to be as big of a part of your son's life as you can. Knox deserves that. And you do, too."

Violet reached out and covered his hand with her own as it gripped the stroller handle. Just like at the office, her touch was warm and comforting, reminding him how long it had been since someone had touched him so tenderly. Perhaps since his mom died. His gaze dropped uncomfortably to her hand as he tried not to get overly emotional in the public moment they were sharing.

"Thank you," he said at last. "My father was never around, either. He was always at the bar or sleeping off a bender. I'm not sure whether he opened the bar because he was an alcoholic or if he became an alcoholic because he owned a bar, but the result was the same. He was wasted or hungover most of the time. He never did any of the things a dad is supposed to do with his son. He never even came to one of my ball games in high school. My mom did her best to make up for it, but there was only so much she could do."

"I can't imagine you ever being that kind of father,

Aidan. You've known your son for such a short time and yet you adore him. Anyone can see that. You're not going to cast him aside like your father did to you."

"Did you know that's why I don't drink?"

Violet frowned. "I hadn't noticed that, although it makes perfect sense."

"I can't even tell you what a beer tastes like, only how it smells. I was always too afraid of being like him. I worried one drink would turn into ten and the next thing I knew, I'd be in as deep as he was. I couldn't do that to myself or to my mother. She'd already been through so much with my dad."

"The halfway house will help a lot of people."

"It was my mother's idea, really. Dad tried rehab twice and it worked fairly well at first, but once he came home and went back to work, he'd settle back into his bad habits. Even if he didn't work in a bar he would've had trouble. She always said that he needed more than twenty-eight days. He needed a transitional place to help him adjust to his sobriety in his old, comfortable situations. She hated not being able to stop my father from destroying himself, and eventually that's what he did. He died of liver failure about three years ago. That's why I quit my job at the advertising agency and took over Murphy's."

"Wait. You worked at an advertising agency?"

Aidan frowned. Had he not told her that story? He supposed they had barely scratched the surface in their discussions. "Yeah. I was an advertising executive for about five years after graduating from college. I'd worked on a few successful campaigns for some big accounts and was being fast-tracked at the firm. It was certainly a different life than the one I live now."

"Do you ever miss the work?"

"I hate to disappoint you, but no, I don't. I was trying to better myself and I realized that it didn't make me any happier than I was when I was poor. In truth, I was miserable. Successful and miserable. Running my father's bar isn't the most important or well-paying job in the world, but I like my employees and my clientele. I enjoy going in most days. I like being there when people need someone to talk to. It's a completely different kind of experience each day and I like that."

Violet seemed flabbergasted by their whole discussion. "I don't know why I thought you'd always worked at the bar. Advertising…" She shook her head. "I guess we have a lot to learn about each other."

"We do. I guess it just hasn't come up, but I thought you knew. That's why I've got that nice apartment in Hell's Kitchen. I used my advertising bonuses as a down payment or I couldn't afford to live in it now."

"You own your place? I didn't realize that, either." Violet frowned and Aidan understood why.

"We've done things a little backward, I have to admit."

They turned and started walking back down the path through the park. The more Aidan thought about it, the more he wanted to do things right with Violet. Their relationship was all out of order. They'd had a baby first, then lived together, albeit temporarily. They knew very little about each other's pasts. They might have an emotional connection, but they'd flunk out on *The Newlywed Game*. It was all backward and he wanted to go back to the beginning and have a relationship reset. "I think there's something you and I need to do. Something important."

"What's that?" she asked with a curious expression on her face.

"A real, honest-to-goodness date with food and conversation and getting to know one another. Violet, would you be interested in going out on a date with me?"

This was not what Violet had in mind when Aidan said he wanted to go on a date. She was picturing a nice restaurant, candlelight, maybe a walk through Central Park. The usual. She should've known that with Aidan their date would be anything but the usual. Instead, it was three in the afternoon and she, along with literally fifty thousand other people, was walking into Yankee Stadium to watch a home game against the Pittsburgh Pirates.

It wasn't that she didn't like baseball. She did. The foundation even had seats in the Delta SKY360 Suites that she made use of from time to time, especially when donors needed to be wooed. But it just wasn't what she was expecting when she got asked out. She should've known something was up when Aidan said to be ready at two and to dress casual.

At the same time, the light of excitement in Aidan's eyes made it all worth it. Baseball was important to him. She'd seen the trophy from the state championship he'd won in high school at his apartment. The first gift he gave to his son was a Yankees jersey and a baseball mitt no larger than an orange. She didn't even know they made mitts that small. So coming to see a game was obviously an important experience for him to share with Violet.

She tried to keep that in mind as she stopped at Aidan's side while he looked down at their tickets. Then she realized she could give him a new way to experience the game. "Would you like to go see if anyone is sitting in the foundation box?"

Aidan looked at the section where their tickets were and shrugged with indifference. "I forgot you had those. It's up to you."

Violet tried to hide her disappointment. She thought he would be more excited to get the chance to sit in their swanky private box. "It's awfully hot right now. At the very least we can sit in the air-conditioning and have a private restroom. I thought you might like it."

He nodded. "Our seats are in the direct sunlight. If you're already hot, it might be a good idea to check it out and maybe we can move down closer to the field once the sun sets. Otherwise I will have wasted these thirty-dollar tickets," he added with a smile.

Violet met his smile, hopeful he wasn't offended by her suggestion. In truth, she'd never sat in the regular seats. Her father never let her. He was a big baseball fan. That was half the reason they had the box seats. The foundation was just a good excuse for him to get one. It was one thing he and Aidan would actually have in common if she ever introduced them.

Unfortunately it wouldn't be enough to satisfy her ever-critical father.

So far, as best Violet could tell, nothing he'd acquired on this earth could satisfy her father. Aidan was doomed to failure in that regard, whether he was a crown prince or a Lower East Side bartender.

She didn't want to worry about that today. Today, her parents were in Istanbul, and she just wanted to enjoy her afternoon with Aidan. She led him around the stadium to the stairs that would take them up to the executive boxes.

"Good afternoon, Eddie," Violet said with a smile as she approached the security guard who policed the east entrance to the boxed seats. She brought more than her share of donors to games here and recognized the regular guard. "Is anyone using the Niarchos Foundation box today? I wasn't sure if Daddy had let one of his friends use it or not and I forgot to check before I left."

The large, muscular man with dark brown skin and kind eyes looked down at his tablet and shook his head. "Not today, Miss Niarchos. Will you and your guest be joining us for the game?"

"For a while, I think, until it cools down."

"I'll let the servers know."

"Are there many VIPs up here today?" Violet asked. Sometimes there were actors, politicians or rock stars roaming around these halls and taking in a game.

"More important than you?" Eddie asked with a smile. "Of course not."

Violet playfully smacked Eddie on the arm. "Flattery will get you everything." She turned back to Aidan and took his hand. "Come on."

It didn't take long to reach the Niarchos Foundation box. Just slightly to the right of home plate, they had one of the best views of the park. They went inside, passing the private catering and lounge seating area and approaching the large wall of windows and rows of seats that held over twenty people for each game. When they did big events here, the room would be filled with people munching on platters of catered food and bottles of imported wine and beer. At the moment, the large space was silent and empty.

"It's a shame we don't use this more. Occasionally we auction off use of the box for charity events or bring donors as a perk, but more often than not, it's empty like this. We should coordinate with children's groups like the scouts or contact the Make-A-Wish Foundation to let them use it. It's such a waste."

Violet looked out the window where the two ball teams were still warming up on the field. The stadium seats were pretty full now, so it would be time to start soon. "Well, what do you think?" she asked. "Do you like it? We don't have to stay up here if you don't."

When she got no response, she turned to see Aidan looking wide-eyed and overwhelmed behind her. "Aidan? What's the matter?"

He pulled his gaze away from the stunning view of the ballfield and turned to her. "This is, uh, nice."

Violet frowned. "You don't like it."

"No, no. I mean, it's very swanky. I should be thrilled to get the chance to sit in a private box, knowing how much it costs to reserve one for a game, much less a season. But I don't know…it feels like something is lost. Almost like we're watching it on a television from home. It's impersonal."

A tap at the door was followed by the entrance of a server wearing the standard all-black uniform for the VIP suites. "Good afternoon. Can I bring you anything before the game starts?"

Violet looked to Aidan, hoping perhaps the perks might win him over. "Would you like to order something? They have a full bar, lots of food options…even a sushi chef."

"Are you serious?"

With his Yankees cap pulled down over his eyes, it was hard to read Aidan, but Violet was pretty sure he wasn't impressed with the sushi. "I think we're okay right now, thank you," she said, dismissing their in-suite server.

Once the door clicked shut, Aidan crossed his arms over his chest and chuckled. "Is this where you sit every time you come to a game?"

"Yes," she said. "Although sometimes we go down to the sky bar."

"Where you drink martinis and eat sushi while enjoying America's game?"

He was making fun of her. Violet wasn't used to that. Most people kissed her rear end because of her money. Others just ignored it. But Aidan, he was goading her because of it. "We have this box. Why wouldn't I sit up here?"

Aidan just shook his head. He looked around the

room one last time and held out his hand. "Come on. You're coming with me and you're going to have a real game experience."

Violet hesitated. She wasn't sure why.

"Come on, this is a date and I planned for us to sit in cheap seats, drink sodas and share nachos while we scream at the umpire. I don't want to sit up here in the sterile, fancy place where the rich can avoid dealing with the rest of us."

"That's not why—" she started to argue, but Aidan cut her off.

"Come on, Violet. We're going to start by buying you a Yankees shirt."

Violet took his hand and before she knew it, she was in a section of the stadium she'd never seen before. She was wearing a brand-new Yankees T-shirt blinged out with rhinestones—her requirement—and sitting between Aidan and a family there with their young kids.

He was right. There was definitely a different feel watching the game down here. You could feel the energy of the crowd, smell the roasted peanuts and freshly mowed grass, and actually see the players as more than tiny white blurs. Aidan got them both cold lemonades they drank from plastic cups, then they had hot dogs and shared a huge container of nachos.

When one of the Yankees players hit a home run, she leaped from her seat in excitement with everyone else, loudly cheering for the team. And when the seventh-inning stretch rolled around, she sang "Take Me Out to the Ballgame" with the whole stadium.

By the top of the ninth, the sun had set and bright

lights shone down on them. The game was a blowout and some people had already started to mill out, but she wasn't ready to leave yet. She was full of greasy ballpark food and she couldn't stop smiling at Aidan.

"So what do you think?" he asked her. "Shall we go back up to the VIP seats? Get some sushi?"

She winced at him and shook her head. "No. You were right. This was a lot more fun. I can't believe I've never seen a game from down here. I don't know why my father wouldn't let me."

Aidan's auburn brow went up in surprise. "Let you? You about bit my head off when I even suggested that someone else dictate what you could or couldn't do."

Violet sighed. "My father is different. He's old-school Greek. He didn't really want me to do much of anything but get married to a nice Greek boy and have lots of Greek babies."

"You're just a rebel, then," Aidan said with a grin. "Having Irish babies, eating nachos in the cheap seats…what's next?"

He was right. She was being quite the rebel lately and Aidan was the cause. She liked it. And she liked him. He encouraged her to stretch her wings, broaden her narrow view of the world and live a little. He roused feelings in her she'd never experienced before and she wanted more. More of him, more of the sensations he could coax out of her trembling body. Violet looked up at the VIP boxes and grinned with the wicked idea that came to mind.

"On second thought, I think we do need to make a trip back up to the Niarchos box before we leave today."

"Why? Did you leave something up there?"

She shook her head and leaned in to him to let her soft lips brush against his earlobe. She bit gently at it, feeling a shiver run through his whole body that had nothing to do with the cold. "Ever wanted to have sex in Yankee Stadium?" she whispered.

Aidan pulled away in surprise and looked at her with one deviously arched brow. He studied her face for a moment before a passionate fire lit in his eyes. "I hadn't ever considered the possibility, but now that you mention it…" his arm wrapped around her waist and tugged her closer to him "…abso-frickin-lutely."

He stood suddenly and offered her his hand. Violet accepted, and they made their way back to the VIP box. The desire for him built inside of her with every step they took. Once they were inside the private suite, she locked the door and pressed her back against it.

"Time to score."

Eight

Aidan paused on the sidewalk outside of Violet's building with one piece of luggage slung over his shoulder and another on wheels behind him. Tara and Knox had already gone upstairs, and Violet was taking a bag from the cab driver as he pulled it out of the back of the van.

"Are you sure everything is done right?" he asked again. The contractor had called to tell them this morning that her apartment was done and she could move back in. A day early. Apparently the damage hadn't been as extensive structurally as they thought, so they'd only needed to do cosmetic repairs. He supposed he should be happy for Violet and Knox's sake, but he wasn't. He'd thought he had another day living with them as a family and with one phone call, he was helping her pack.

"Yes, Aidan," Violet said with a sigh that told him she was tired of him asking. He may have pestered her a *few* times since she said they could go back to the apartment.

Who could blame him?

He wasn't ready for things to go back to the way they were before the flood. It had been like a jump start to their relationship. Suddenly they were together all the time in a way that would've taken weeks or months to happen otherwise. He liked waking up to Knox's giggles in the living room and going to bed with Violet in his arms. Sharing meals, taking a grocery shopping trip together. It was the simple things that he enjoyed the most.

It was almost like they were…a family. A real family, not that coparenting thing they'd agreed to with her attorney.

Violet set down the bag on the sidewalk and turned to him. "We're not leaving the country, Aidan. We're just moving back across town. You know where to find us." She planted a kiss on his lips and patted his cheek reassuringly.

"I know that." And practically, he did. He just didn't like the idea of it. He wanted to keep his family together, but he was afraid he'd scare her away if he said something like that aloud. It was too soon. And yet he felt certain about it. More certain than he had ever felt with Iris.

Just then, Aidan turned and noticed a man coming down the sidewalk waving at them. Or presumably to Violet since Aidan had never seen the man before.

."Violet? I think that guy wants to talk to you."

She took a step back from him and turned, her happy expression crumbling when she saw the man coming closer. "Damn it," she swore. "I've been back here for five minutes and he's shown up already."

"Violet!" the man shouted as he approached before Aidan could ask who it was.

He had a pretty good guess. The man was wearing a fancy suit and a smile that came across to Aidan as extremely insincere. Like a car salesman. The kind who sold Jaguars, perhaps, but still a car salesman. Especially when he brushed past Aidan without a second glance and placed a hand on Violet's upper arm.

"There you are, dear. I've been looking for you for days, but no one answered when I knocked."

Violet pulled away from his touch. "I haven't been home this week, Beau. My apartment flooded and they've been doing renovations for the past few days."

"What? Flooded? Why didn't you call me to deal with all of this?"

Violet looked irritated, frowning as she planted her hands on her hips. Aidan couldn't fathom how a man who had been engaged to her at one point would be so clueless about how she responded to him.

"Why would I call you? We're not together anymore. We haven't been a couple for six months. And besides that, I can handle this on my own. I don't need you to come and deal with things for me."

"Of course you could, my pet, but where have you been all week?" Beau asked, ignoring that it wasn't his business and Violet didn't seem interested in talking to him.

"She's been staying with me," Aidan interjected. Beau had already touched Violet without her permission, used pet names, questioned her competence and completely ignored Aidan's presence. It was time for all of that to change.

Beau finally turned toward him as though he'd just noticed Aidan standing there. "Oh. I thought he was your cab driver."

Aidan started to tense for a fight, but a cautioning hand from Violet stopped him. "Quit being so rude, Beau. You knew full well that he was here with me. I'm not going to just stand here while you show up unannounced, question everything I do and then be disrespectful to my guest. Why don't you tell me what it is you want so you can go and I can finish moving back upstairs?"

Beau turned to Aidan with a disgusted look, as though he were somehow responsible for Violet's new backbone. "I just wanted to say hi and see how you were. You haven't been returning my calls."

"Hi. I'm fine, thank you. And I haven't returned your calls because we're not dating any longer."

"I know we're not but—"

"No buts, Beau. I made it very clear when the paternity test came back, but you and my parents don't seem to want to listen. So here's what you need to know— I'm seeing someone else now. End of story."

"Him?" Beau said with a thumb jerked in Aidan's direction.

"Yes," she answered matter-of-factly.

"And just who is he, huh?"

"Knox's father." Violet said the words proudly, startling Aidan.

So far, she'd seemed fairly hesitant for people to know about their relationship, especially where Knox was concerned. He understood that things were new between them, and that she wanted to feel more comfortable before the world poked its nose into their business. Apparently she was feeling more comfortable. Or at least angry enough with Beau overstepping in her business to want to throw that factoid in his face.

"I thought you didn't know who his father was."

"I didn't know. If I had, I certainly wouldn't have led you and everyone else on the entire nine months. But I've gotten some of my memory back from that lost week."

"Some? Not all of it?" Beau asked with a concerned furrow of his brow.

"No, not all of it. Just the part where I met Aidan. We've since reunited. That's all of my business you're going to be privy to from here on out."

Beau's worried expression faded as he crossed his arms over his chest. "Do your parents know about… *him*?" The word almost seemed to taste bad in his mouth as he said it.

It made Aidan want to glance down at what he was wearing to see how bad he looked. He had on nice jeans and a fitted T-shirt with the name of his bar on it. He certainly wasn't dressing up to haul her stuff back to the apartment. And yet her jerk of an ex seemed to think he was less than worthy of Violet.

Maybe so, but her opinion was the only one that mattered. At the moment, she seemed to think he was good enough. She didn't seem the slightest bit embarrassed to announce who he was and that they were dating. He was surprised, especially considering that someone like Beau could take that information straight to her parents or family friends.

"Not that it's any of your business, but no, I haven't spoken to my parents about it yet. They haven't been stateside in a while. But I will when they return. And if you rush home and tell them, Beau, I will make your life extremely difficult, do you understand?"

For a moment Beau's macho demeanor seemed to crumble a bit under Violet's threat. Then he recovered and shrugged it off. "Like I want to spend my precious time gossiping about who my ex is sleeping with. If it's not me, I really don't care. Call me when you regain your senses," he said, turning to walk away without giving Aidan a second glance.

Violet and Aidan both stood together watching Beau stroll casually down the sidewalk, disappearing into a crowd. "That guy is a piece of work," Aidan noted. "If you weren't dating me, I'd question your taste in men."

"I'd question my taste in men, too, except I didn't really choose Beau. We grew up together and it was always just sort of expected that we would get married one day. If I'd been born a hundred years earlier, our marriage would've been arranged. Now, my parents just used social pressures to get us together."

"I don't know why they'd want you with that jerk."

Violet lifted the handle of the bag and started toward the door of her building. "I guess because our families are old friends, we're around the same age, he's from a good family, and of course, he's Greek. They're not good reasons, but they're reasons. I've always said we were better on paper than in real life."

Aidan just shook his head and followed her inside. "Well, if I was your father, the most important thing to me would be how he treated you. And considering the state you were in the night you came into Murphy's, I'd say he wasn't treating you well at all."

Violet paused in the marble and brass lobby and turned to him. "Did I tell you anything that night? Like I just told Beau, I still don't remember everything about that week. Just you. I don't know why I was upset or in the bar that night."

Aidan realized they hadn't really discussed her memory loss in quite a while. At first, he'd considered it a convenient excuse, but the way she spoke about it now, he was more convinced that she really had lost her memory. "You didn't say. Actually, what you said was that you didn't want to talk about it. Just that your boyfriend was, quote, 'a dick' and you wanted to forget about everything for a while."

Violet rolled her eyes and turned toward the elevators. "Be careful what you wish for, huh?"

The apartment was in fine shape. If it wasn't for the faint smell of drying paint, Violet almost wouldn't be able to tell anything had happened in her kitchen.

Knox went down happily for his afternoon nap while Violet, Aidan and Tara worked on unpacking their suitcases. Violet started a load of laundry and then she and Aidan settled on the couch in the living room with glasses of iced tea.

"That guy was a real ass," Aidan said. Even though over an hour had passed since Beau walked off, they both knew exactly who he was referring to.

Violet was well aware that her ex-fiancé was an ass. He may not have deserved Violet cheating on him and having another man's baby, but he wasn't the right man for her by any stretch of the imagination. "I know. He does have moments where I can see the guy that charmed me in college, but they became few and far between as we got older. What scares me the most is that I almost married him. I was quite upset at first when I realized I was pregnant, because I knew what it meant for me. Things had been great with Beau since my accident, but I knew it wouldn't last. Being pregnant meant my chance to walk away from the relationship was over. Having his baby meant getting married. End of story. At least as far as our family and friends were concerned.

"I delayed the wedding by insisting I wanted to wait until after the baby was born. Everyone thought I was just being vain about looking thin on my wedding day, but the truth was that I was looking for any reason to put it off. Then Knox arrived in all his redheaded glory and saved me from having to go through with it. I insisted on a paternity test even though Beau was pushing to be put on the birth certificate and have the baby take his last name. I refused. Something hadn't felt right, and when the results came back, I knew what it was at last. But if Knox had taken after me with dark hair and eyes I might never have questioned if Beau was his father and married him."

She shook her head, shaking off the shudder that ran through her at the mere thought of being Mrs. Beau Rosso. Her pregnancy had been such a confusing time for her, although she'd never spoken to anyone about her concerns. She'd blamed it on the accident at first, but still, she'd questioned it. She'd lain in bed at night looking at her gigantic engagement ring, feeling Knox move in her belly and wishing she knew why it didn't feel right. Something had bothered her about Beau since the accident and she couldn't put her finger on what it was. She'd hoped that the return of her memory would solve the question, but the answer hadn't popped up along with all her memories of the time with Aidan. Amnesia was an incredibly frustrating illness, like having a word on the tip of your tongue but being unable to voice it.

"I almost married the wrong person, too. It happens more than you'd think. I guess we're just lucky we figured it out before we took the plunge."

Violet turned to look at Aidan in surprise. He'd never mentioned a fiancée before, but then again, they hadn't spent much time rehashing their old relationships aside from the thing with Beau. "May I ask what happened?"

Aidan sighed and propped his head in his hand.

"Do you want the long version of the story or the short version?"

"The long version." She sensed some underlying animosity in Aidan and she didn't know where it came from. He didn't really seem to like people with money and took a lot of offense to how much Violet had. His attitude certainly wasn't the result of anything she'd done, per se, but she could feel it sometimes. She wondered now if this wasn't where it originated.

"Back when I was working at the advertising agency, I started seeing a woman named Iris. She was a corporate attorney I met at a party. We were together for about three years before I decided to propose. I knew she had particular tastes—by that I mean expensive ones—but at the time I didn't mind. I was trying to better my situation and in my mind, part of that was dating a high-class girl with high-class tastes. I could afford to indulge her, and buying her things made her happy. I thought that was just how it worked. My mistake was thinking that our relationship was based on more than that."

Violet felt her stomach start to ache. She already knew how this story would end because she'd met Iris before. Not his Iris, but women like her whose loyalty to a relationship lasted only as long as the money did. When it dried up, they went in search of a new source.

"Anyway, so when my father died and I decided to quit my job in advertising to run Murphy's, I was stupid enough to think that Iris would stand by me. She didn't. In fact, she called me a damn fool and left me almost immediately for one of the senior partners at my advertising firm. It all happened so quickly, I had to wonder if she hadn't been seeing him long before all that happened."

"That's awful," Violet said, even knowing what was coming. Breaking up with Aidan was one thing but throwing it in his face like that was just cruel. A woman like that didn't deserve a man like Aidan. It made Violet wonder if even she was good enough for him. After all, she'd cheated on Beau with Aidan, hadn't she? It was completely out of character for Violet, and it frustrated her not knowing or understanding why she'd done it, but Knox was proof that she had. In that case, was she any better than Iris?

"How can you do that to someone you're supposed to love?" she asked instead. Perhaps her lukewarm feelings for Beau had been the cause of her infidelity. They had been arguing a lot at the time.

Aidan shrugged and sipped his tea thoughtfully. "She loved money more than me, I guess. Iris wouldn't even give me the engagement ring back after she broke it off, even though she knew I needed every penny I could get to bail out the bar. I should've known how screwed up her priorities were, but I find a lot of people in this town think just like her. The more they have, the more they love it. Need it. Are willing to do anything for it."

Violet didn't like the bitter tone his story had taken even though she understood why he would be upset. "I don't know that that's true. There are rich and greedy people everywhere. It doesn't mean everyone is like that, though."

"Isn't it true? I'll admit I'm jaded when it comes to rich people, but I have reason to be. With guys on Wall Street like Beau willing to do anything to turn a buck… Pharmaceutical companies willing to let my mom die because she couldn't afford their jacked-up prices on medication… Beau was even willing to claim a child he knew wasn't his just to…"

Violet sat at attention in her seat. "Just to what?"

Aidan shrugged. "I don't know. Maybe I'm wrong and he loved you and the baby no matter what. But my experience leads me to believe that he'd accept just about anything you threw his way if you'd marry him and he could get his hands on all your money."

She'd worried about that. It had always been a factor in the back of her mind whenever she dated anyone. Most men in her social circles knew how much she was worth, at least within a couple hundred million. Somehow, she'd hoped that growing up with Beau had negated that. She'd hoped his affections for her were sincere. And yet, when Aidan said the words out loud, she knew it was true. Beau wanted to land the billionaire heiress. He kept coming back around no matter what she did because he really didn't care what she did. He probably didn't even love her. He just wanted the lifestyle—the prestige—being her husband would provide. He and his family were well off, but not ridiculously rich the way the Niarchos family was. Marrying her would afford him private planes and yachts and going his whole life without working a day if he didn't want to. Love and mutual respect had nothing to do with it. That was not what she wanted her marriage to be based on.

"You might be right about Beau. And about Iris. We obviously aren't the best at choosing romantic partners. But I refuse to believe that everyone out there feels the same way. Money and status aren't everything."

Aidan chuckled at her observation. "Only people with money and status would say that. They say money problems are the number-one cause of break ups."

"No, I'm serious," Violet insisted. "Beau was all wrong for me. I know that now. But all my parents saw was a successful guy from a good family and they looked the other way at all his other flaws. While it's nice to be financially stable and well known in the community, it isn't the most important thing in a relationship. If it were, rich people would never divorce and they do all the time."

Aidan looked at her curiously. "So what do you think is the most important thing?"

Violet had thought about this a lot since she'd broken things off with Beau. She didn't want to make the same mistakes next time, so she'd really tried to identify what she wanted in a partner. "Chemistry and attraction can draw you together, but relationships need a solid foundation to last," she began. "That takes mutual trust, respect and caring for one another. You have to be able to count on your partner to be there when things get hard. To stand by your side when you lose the money and status like you did to run your father's bar. Those things, to me, are far more important than the other stuff. That's what I'm going to look for if I ever decide to get engaged again."

He leaned toward her with a smile that made her stomach flutter. "You mean a poor schmuck like me actually has a chance of winning the heart and hand of a rich, successful and beautiful woman like you?"

There was a light of jest in his eyes as he said the words, but she knew that inside, he wasn't kidding. Violet's chest ached at the thought that Aidan believed he wasn't good enough for her somehow. Why had he put her on a pedestal like that? It made her want to throttle Iris for making him feel like he was unworthy of her love.

"Of course you do," she said, reaching out to take his hand and squeeze it gently. The heat of his touch warmed her blood, making her suddenly flush in the relatively cool apartment. "I wouldn't have gotten involved with you once, much less twice, if you didn't have a chance. I'm not the kind to take physical connections lightly."

Aidan's gaze searched her face for a moment, and then he nodded, pulling his hand away from hers. "I'll keep that in mind," he said. "I'd better get going. Tonight is my last night off until the gala on Saturday. I've got a lot to get done before then."

They both stood, and Violet followed him to the front door. She understood he had things to do; she did, too, and yet, she hated the thought of him leaving. Normally, she was the kind of woman who liked having some alone time even in a relationship, but she found herself fighting the urge to fling her arms around his neck to keep him from going. She wasn't ready yet.

How had she gotten so attached to Aidan so quickly? In all the years she was with Beau, she'd never felt this way. "Stay," she said in a soft voice before she could overthink it.

He looked at her curiously with his hand on the doorknob. "After almost a week together, I thought you'd be sick of me by now."

"Me, too," Violet said with a smile. "But surprisingly, I'm not."

His hand dropped from the doorknob and he moved it to rest on her hip. He came in close to her, warming her body and wrapping her in the cocoon of his alluring scent. She wanted to press into him and pull him into her bedroom. She wasn't sure how she was going to fall asleep without him in the bed beside her.

Violet pressed her face into his neck, feeling the warmth of his skin and the thrum of his pulse against her lips. "So stay," she whispered in his ear.

"Okay. You've twisted my arm."

Nine

The rest of the afternoon passed painfully slowly. Once Violet convinced Aidan to stay the night, it was a countdown to having him in her arms. She'd gotten used to falling asleep beside him and waking up with his scent on her pillowcase. They weren't keeping their relationship or Knox's parentage a secret from Tara any longer, but they weren't flaunting it in front of the nanny, either. That meant if Violet wanted a soft, slow kiss or a good hug, she had to wait for bedtime.

Although the kitchen was repaired, most of the cabinet contents were still in boxes in the dining room. Aidan ordered Chinese delivery while Violet fed Knox some baby cereal and mashed-up banana. The banana—at least what made it into his mouth—was a hit.

At bedtime, Aidan took his opportunity to put his

son to bed. Violet watched from a distance as he went through the nightly routine he'd picked up from her while they'd stayed with him. A new diaper, pajamas and then a quick rock in the rocking chair together to settle Knox down. Sometimes Violet would tell Knox a story or sing him a song. When he was a little older, she would start reading to him. Aidan regaled his son with a story about the Yankees triumphing over the Phillies in the 2009 World Series. Knox lay in his arms, enthralled the entire time.

Watching the two of them together always turned her heart into butter. Violet wasn't entirely sure what it was really like to have a father—at least one who was involved in her life. Her bedtime had always involved a nanny, and if her parents were in town, perhaps a kiss on the forehead from her mother. But bedtime stories, baths and lullabies were not something she associated with her parents. Her father cared for her in his own way, but he just wasn't the demonstrative type. Her grandfather Stavros hadn't been the kind, either, although he'd warmed up to being a grandfather by the time she was born. Maybe someday her dad would soften with Knox, but when she was a child, it was likely all he knew how to be—firm and distant.

Violet knew that Aidan's father had problems drinking throughout Aidan's childhood, so it was possible he wasn't much of a hands-on father, either. The difference was that Aidan didn't use that as an excuse to be cold with his son. Instead, he went over and above, making sure he did better for Knox than his own father had done for him.

She appreciated that more than she even realized at first. Watching them together, she thanked her lucky stars for the twist of fate that brought her and Aidan together. She knew that even if Knox had been Beau's son, it wouldn't have been like this with him. He hadn't really been involved throughout the entire pregnancy. He blew off an ultrasound. Moped through the baby shower because he'd had to cancel a standing racquetball match for it. The idea of having a son appealed to him, but not the reality of it.

Aidan had a son dropped into his lap out of nowhere and he'd recovered beautifully. She got the feeling that going through her pregnancy with him would've been different, as well. Would he have rubbed her swollen ankles and gone out in search of her latest food craving? Probably so. Because he seemed to care about the people in his life. To Violet, that was more important than all the other things Beau supposedly had to offer her but Aidan didn't.

Knox nodded off in his father's arms. She watched as Aidan gently stood up, walked his son over to his crib and got him settled in.

"He's out cold," Aidan whispered when he turned and saw her watching him from the doorway. "How did I do, Mama? Did I pass the bedtime test?"

Violet smiled. She hadn't been watching him with that in mind, but she appreciated that he was trying to do everything right. "With flying colors."

"Do I get a reward for a job well done?" he asked with a devious arch of his brow.

"I think that could be arranged." Violet took his

hand and led him across the hallway to her bedroom. Once inside, she shut her door and then pushed Aidan backward until he was sitting on the edge of the bed. With her gaze fixed on his, she slowly lowered herself down to her knees in front of him.

"Are you ready for your reward?" she asked with a coy smile.

"Oh, yeah."

Violet took her time, running her hands up and down his legs and stroking his thighs through his jeans before moving to his fly. She unbuttoned it and ran down the zipper, feeling his body tense beneath her touch. He helped her tug his jeans and black boxer briefs over his hips and down his legs. They went into a pile along with his shoes and the rest of his unnecessary clothes.

She'd barely touched Aidan and yet once he was naked, she realized he was already primed and ready for her. As she reached for his exposed desire, she heard his sharp intake of breath. He continued to hold his breath as she wrapped her fingers around his firm heat and gently stroked him until he let out a ragged burst of air from his lungs.

"Violet," he whispered with his eyes squeezed shut.

Feeling emboldened by his response, she brought him to her lips and enveloped him in the moist warmth. Aidan groaned aloud as she moved up and down the length of him, teasing at him with her tongue. He buried his fingers in her dark hair and bit at his bottom lip in an apparent effort to stay quiet.

Violet was determined to make that difficult for him. It was a reward, after all.

Working him over with her hands and mouth, she increased the pace until he was gritting his teeth. "Okay," he said, reaching out to grasp her wrist and still the torturous movements. "That…is about all I can take of that unless you want Tara to know way too much about us."

Violet giggled, but relinquished her hold on him. "I'm sorry," she said in a pouty voice that proved she was anything but sorry.

"I bet you are." With one quick tug, he pulled her up off the floor, and she landed in a sprawled position on top of him. He held her tight to him even as she wiggled and tried to right herself. "Oh, no. You've had plenty of fun. It's your turn to shout," he said.

Rolling across the bed, Violet found herself on her back with Aidan pinning her arms to the mattress. He shifted his grip until he was holding both wrists in one of his massive hands over her head. He straddled her hips, using his free hand to push up her shirt. He shimmied it over her head and shoulders, leaving it tangled around her wrists. He unsnapped the front clasp of her bra and pushed the lacy blue cups out of his way to expose her tight, rosy nipples.

Violet gasped silently as he cupped her left breast in his hand and drew her into the warmth of his mouth. He sucked hard on her nipple until she squirmed and arched her back toward him. She was completely at his mercy now and not being able to move her arms made her feel even more vulnerable to him.

She liked it.

When he did finally let go, it was so he could slide

her jeans and panties down her hips. With those gone, she used her newfound freedom to pull his face back down to her so she could kiss him at last. His lips collided hard with hers, matching the intensity that was building between them both. It had been less than a day since they'd shared a bed and yet it suddenly felt like weeks. Like Violet would be consumed by her need for him if she didn't have him right now.

Aidan seemed less inclined to rush tonight. Even as he kissed her, one hand roamed over her skin, eventually seeking out the heat between her thighs. He stroked her, dipping his fingers inside and rubbing the heel of his palm against her sensitive flesh. His mouth on hers muffled her cries as he made slow circles guaranteed to make her climax.

And climax she did. Her whole body was shaken with the pleasure that radiated through her. She'd never come so fast and so intensely before, but it was as though Aidan had mastered her body. She tore her mouth away from his to suck in a cool lungful of air and gasp with the force of her orgasm.

As she lay there, nearly incapable of moving, Aidan sought out a condom and returned to her side. As they came together, she felt her body responding to him again and Violet noticed a difference in their lovemaking. It had only been a week since they'd first come together at his apartment, and yet the newness had given way to the familiar and easy. Not that it was boring by any stretch, but that there was experience behind every touch and taste of each other's bodies. He knew exactly how to move and how to touch her to make her respond.

Violet had never been with a lover who focused on her pleasure the way he did. Even tonight, he had taken his reward and twisted it into an experience to satisfy them both. He didn't just give lip service to her needs, he genuinely prioritized them, just as he prioritized her in every aspect of his life.

Even as he groaned her name into her neck and held her body tight to his, she couldn't help but think of how special he made her feel. Like she and Knox were a priority in his life. Not his business or his money, his reputation or even himself. She'd never been loved like that before.

Is that what it was? Love?

If that was what she was feeling, Violet had never truly been loved by any man she'd been with in the past. At least not loved body and soul the way Aidan seemed to. He hadn't shared his feelings with her and she hadn't shared hers with him, but he certainly made her feel cherished and appreciated in a way that made her want to give a voice to her feelings.

She *was* in love with him.

It wasn't something she'd really thought about before tonight, but the truth of it was clear. Their time together had been brief, but her heart and mind both knew what they wanted. They both wanted him.

She was absolutely, totally in love with Aidan.

The warm feeling in the center of her chest spread through her whole body. Like some kind of emotional floodgate opening, she felt the heat build up into an unexpected second release. When it exploded inside of her moments later and Aidan gave in to his own pleasure, she found herself on the verge of happy tears. She wanted to hold him, to hang on to this moment and cherish it forever.

A part of her wanted to tell him how she felt right then, but her logical side overrode it. It was one thing to fall in love quickly, another to announce it and have the timing be bad. Aidan might not be as in tune with his emotions. He might need more time to realize that what they had together was special and rare.

As he collapsed off to her side, the cool air danced across her damp, exposed skin, bringing a chill. She rolled against Aidan's side and snuggled into the nook of his arm. She felt safe and protected there, like everything outside of her apartment couldn't get to them. Things like her parents' disapproval.

Violet knew that was a discussion that needed to be had, and soon. But not tonight. Her parents were still in Eastern Europe somewhere and she wanted to enjoy this moment with Aidan. An unexpected sinking feeling in her stomach followed that thought, making her cling more tightly to him.

As though the moment wouldn't last much longer.

The following morning, Aidan went back to his apartment to get ready for work. He wasn't opening today, but he wanted to head out to his mom's house to grab something before his shift was supposed to start.

Last night with Violet had made him start thinking about things he hadn't really considered before. They hadn't been together as a couple long, but getting up in the morning to return to his place was a painful reminder that their cohabitation had been a temporary thing. With her kitchen fixed, Violet was back home. That meant everything he'd gotten used to so quickly was over. Yes, he had a standing Sunday afternoon date to see Knox, but there was nothing to say that he had a standing date with Violet.

Yes, he was happy to be Knox's father, and involved in his life, but he wanted more. As impractical as it might seem, he wanted them to be a real family. One that woke up together and shared breakfast before starting their day. One that went on trips to the park and the ball field. Who cheered together for Knox's T-ball team. Who went on family vacations and took cheesy photos together that they would frame and hang on the wall of their home.

Walking up the front steps of his mother's house was a cold reminder that they didn't share a home. Not in the same way his parents did. Their marriage had been anything but perfect, but his mother had loved and cared for his father until the end. They had built a home and family together in a way that Aidan longed for.

But would Violet ever consider something like that? A real family? A marriage? Marriage hadn't even come up when he found out about the baby, and for good reason. If she did agree to marry him, it would be because she wanted to, not because she felt obligated to because of Knox and the societal pressure to marry his father.

That was both encouraging and frightening because he didn't know which way it would go. He wanted Violet to say yes. His feelings for her were still new and uncertain in his mind, but his feelings about the three of them were clear. No matter what she might say, he felt compelled to give it his best shot.

Inside the house, he stopped at the bottom of the stairs. Aidan had avoided going upstairs. More specifically, he'd avoided cleaning out his mother's bedroom. Right after she'd succumbed to her pancreatic cancer, it had been too painful to go through her things and give them away. Really, there wasn't a rush. It hadn't mattered until now if they sat and collected dust or got boxed up.

But with the money from the foundation and the charity event coming up, his administrator and first round of tenants would soon be moving in and Molly's House would become a reality. That would require a good bit of work on Aidan's part.

Most of the clothes and miscellaneous items would be donated to a shelter or charity. Probably to St. Vincent de Paul. The furniture that was good enough to stay would be used for the new residents along with items for the kitchen. Most of the people who would be moving in wouldn't have anything but a bag of personal effects for the temporary stay.

Anything that fell in the bucket of a family heirloom would go to his apartment. There wasn't much, but he knew there were a few things his mother took special care of. Knox would inherit plenty from his mother's family he was sure, but Aidan wanted him to have some things from his side, too. It would be hard to compete with a couple million or so dollars in a trust fund, but a silver pocket watch that belonged to

Knox's great grandfather might be a special keepsake for him to have one day.

He forced himself up the stairs to the bedroom his parents had shared for his entire life. Everything was just as he remembered it, only covered in a light layer of dust and neglect. The room still held the faint scent of his mother's favorite rose perfume. Just catching a whiff of it in the department store was enough to bring tears to his eyes. Here was no different.

Looking around, he realized there was a lot to go through, but today, there was only one thing he was concerned about finding—one thing he didn't dare lose in the shuffle.

He strode across the room to the old oak dresser and the jewelry box standing on top of it. In it, he knew he would find his grandfather's watch, his mother's good pearls, a medal he'd earned in Boy Scouts and a couple other little pieces she'd cherished over the years. That included her engagement ring.

Aidan hadn't wanted to take it from her. He was just as happy to bury her with her jewelry, but she had insisted on it. Her wedding ring was enough, but the engagement ring was special. It had belonged to his great-grandmother on his father's side and was given to his dad when he wanted to propose. It was family and history and she'd wanted Aidan to give it to his future bride, not to let it rot with her corpse under the earth.

He'd finally relented, bringing it upstairs and putting it in her jewelry box for safekeeping. He'd still held on to the hope that she would recover, come home and want to put her ring back on. That, of course, hadn't happened. So the ring had sat there with everything else over the last year.

He found the old satin-covered box just as he'd left it. It was the original container, worn and fragile, easily eighty years old. As he opened the tarnished hinge, his gaze fell upon the familiar ring he'd seen on his mother's finger nearly every day of her life.

Aidan didn't know much about rings or diamonds, but his mother had told him it was an art deco ballerina-style setting. He supposed that was a fancy way of saying it was a center stone surrounded by smaller diamonds radiating out around it like a sun or a ballerina and her tutu. All he knew was that it was beautiful and his mother had cherished it.

If it hadn't been an heirloom, he doubted his father would've ever been able to afford a ring like this. Aidan probably couldn't afford to buy one in this style, either. He couldn't stroll into Tiffany & Co. and drop six figures on an engagement ring like Violet probably expected to receive one day. Like Beau had probably already given her last year. But he could offer her this.

If she'd accept it.

He wasn't certain how she felt about him. Or even how he felt about her. But he knew he wanted to be around her and Knox every day of the year. Not just Sunday afternoons and alternating holidays. He wanted to wake up to Violet in his bed and he felt like if he didn't step up now he would miss his chance. Violet was easily one of the most eligible women in Manhattan. Even if Beau was out of the picture, and it didn't seem like he was ready to go quietly, someone else might come along.

If he wanted Violet, he needed to let her know before she found someone who would fit more easily into her life and her family.

The idea of someone else taking his place made his blood boil. He wasn't that great with feelings, but he knew that meant something. And if that something meant he needed to ask her to marry him, then he would ask her to marry him and hope for the best.

Holding the ring up to the light, he twirled it between his fingertips to watch the colors dance. It would look beautiful on Violet's hand.

Taking a deep breath, he put the ring back in its box and headed downstairs. Soon, he told himself. Soon.

Ten

"The turnout for the event is amazing."

Violet stood at the edge of the ballroom with her assistant, Betsy, as they admired the crowd. She was right. Betsy had worked for the Niarchos Foundation long before Violet was in charge and knew a successful event when she saw one. They'd had one of their highest RSVPs ever for the charity gala and she was pleased to know it was all going to benefit Aidan and Molly's House. The band was great, the dance floor was filled with people, and more in their finery and masks were showing up every second.

"I do have a question for you, though," Betsy added.

"What's that?" Violet eyed the crowd, looking for Aidan, but she hadn't spotted him yet. She was anxious to see him in his new tuxedo. He looked damn sexy in his snug jeans and tight-fitting T-shirts, but there was something about a man in a great tux that brought all her James Bond fantasies to life.

"Your parents. I noticed they aren't on the guest list for tonight."

She pulled her attention back to her assistant, curious as to her line of questioning. "And?"

"And," Betsy said, "this is their foundation. We usually invite them to all the events."

"I think they're in Romania," Violet said dismissively. "What's the point in sending them an invitation when it's just going to stack up with the rest of their mail? We're trying to raise money, not spend it unnecessarily."

Betsy was a woman in her late fifties who rarely took nonsense from anyone. As she looked over her tortoiseshell glasses at Violet, her pointed expression made Violet think that perhaps she'd protested too much. Yes, they typically invited her parents. But typically, her lover and father of her child was not also at the event. There was no way they could look at Aidan and Violet together and not at least suspect that he was Knox's father. Even with a mask on, his hair would give him away.

That would open up a can of worms best left sealed for now. She hadn't told them about Aidan yet and she wasn't ready to. He had enough on his plate at the moment without being subjected to the scrutiny of the lovely Mr. and Mrs. Niarchos. They certainly didn't need the truth blowing up at a black-tie fundraiser with every important person in Manhattan watching with interest lighting their bloodthirsty gazes.

"Well, I hope you're telling me the truth, because your parents got home from Romania yesterday afternoon."

Violet stiffened and began nervously fidgeting with her Cartier diamond bracelet. "Oh, did they? They're not that great at keeping me up to date with their itineraries."

"Yes, your father came into the foundation yesterday after you'd left for the day. When I mentioned the gala, he seemed surprised to hear about it and that's when I realized they weren't on the guest list."

There was no suppressing Violet's expression of wide-eyed horror as she turned back to Betsy. "Betsy, is Father coming tonight?"

Betsy bit at her lip as though she were hesitant to say the words aloud. "He is. Both he and your mother are planning to come. But I didn't know you didn't want him here or I wouldn't have said anything to him. I thought it was just an oversight. There's nothing I can do about it now."

"It's not that I didn't want them to come," Violet said, hoping her shocked reaction wouldn't get back to her parents somehow. "I'm just avoiding having an important conversation with them and I don't want to do it here, tonight."

"About Mr. Rosso?"

Violet blinked a few times in confusion. What did her ex-fiancé have to do with any of this? "What makes you think this has something to do with Beau?"

Now Betsy looked as though she wanted to disappear into the velvet drapes behind her. "Because they're

bringing him with them tonight," she said in a voice
so small, Violet almost didn't hear her.

"What?" Everyone nearby heard Violet's sharp response, with several people turning to look their way.
"Are you serious? Beau will be here tonight, too?"

"I'm afraid so. You know how they are. Every time
they come back into town, they ask me if Beau has
come around the office or if you two have reconciled.
With the champagne flowing and the slow dancing,
they probably figured it would be a good environment
for romance. They're so anxious to have you and Beau
get back together."

"Yes, I'm aware of that." Violet turned back to the
crowd, this time her eyes seeking out not only Aidan,
but her parents and ex-fiancé, as well. The bottom had
fallen out of her stomach, making it ache with worry.
She took a few sips of merlot to drown the sensation,
but it didn't work.

"Have I screwed up, Miss Niarchos?"

"No, Betsy." Violet used her most calm and prac-
ticed voice. "You had no reason to think it was an issue.
It's my fault for not telling you. I should've known this
would happen anyway. It's my luck."

"Would it help at all if I were to say that you look
lovely tonight?" Betsy offered. "The copper shade of
your gown is stunning with your coloring."

"Thank you, Betsy," Violet said.

It had taken her hours to choose a dress for tonight.
She wanted just the right thing so she would look amazing on Aidan's arm. In the end, she'd opted for a taupe
halter gown that was covered on the top with copper

metallic beading and sequins that faded away down the length, leaving only the draping, sheer fabric from the knee down. The dress had a cluster of copper flowers around her throat, so she'd worn her dark hair up in a messy chignon and opted for only a fancy bracelet and understated earrings to go with it.

She couldn't tell Betsy that she'd chosen the color because it reminded her of Aidan's hair, though.

"Oh, look," Betsy said. "Here comes Mr. Murphy."

The couples scattered from the dance floor as a song ended, revealing Aidan as he strolled toward her. When his light blue gaze met hers, she forgot about all her other worries for tonight. He was always handsome with his strong build and wild ginger hair, but tonight with that tailored Tom Ford tux, she had to remind herself not to stare. Not even the black satin mask he was wearing could obscure how sexy he looked. In fact, it just highlighted his piercing eyes, square jaw and full mouth. She couldn't wait to feel that mouth on her body once again.

He approached with a coy smile that made her core melt and the collar of her gown feel uncomfortably tight. "Good evening, ladies."

"Good evening, Mr. Murphy," Betsy said in a chipper voice. "You're looking so handsome tonight."

Aidan turned to the assistant and took her hand in greeting. "Why thank you. You're looking lovely yourself. Perhaps you'll grant me the honor of a spin around the dance floor later." He lifted the back of her hand to his lips and kissed it.

Betsy blushed crimson from her cheeks to the respectable amount of cleavage her black beaded gown revealed. She quickly brought her mask up to her face to cover it, but it was too late. Violet had never seen Betsy react this way to anyone. It seemed that women of all ages were quick to succumb to Aidan's charms. Violet hadn't stood a chance, really. He was handsome, charming, thoughtful and the sexiest devil she'd ever had the pleasure of sharing a bed with.

No wonder she was in love with him.

"And you are looking stunning tonight, Miss Niarchos." Aidan turned his attention to Violet, taking her hand and kissing it, too.

The warm press of his lips on her skin sent a shiver up her arm and down her spine. The simple touch was enough to make her nipples tighten with anticipation and press eagerly against the silky fabric of her dress. She tried not to squirm, delicately extracting her hand before anyone nearby noticed how their touch lingered.

"And where, pray tell, is your mask? This is a masquerade party, isn't it?"

Violet sighed and reached into her small clutch to pull it out. It was a copper metallic mask, with intricate swirling cutouts. The color perfectly matched her dress, but she'd been too busy worrying about getting the party started to put it on. Pressing it to her face, she tied the satin ribbon behind her head. "Is that better?"

"In truth, not really. Now I can't see your beautiful face. I guess I'll have to settle for gazing into your enchanting eyes."

Violet giggled nervously, worried Betsy would

read too much into their exchange. "You're laying it on thick tonight, Mr. Murphy. Perhaps you'd better use that charm on the potential donors instead of me. I've already given you money."

"Will you excuse me?" Betsy smiled and headed off to the other side of the ballroom where something needed her attention.

Violet gave a heavy sigh of relief once she was gone, although she feared it would be short-lived. "Do you want everyone to know we're together?" she asked.

"I'm being charming. That's what you told me to do. I can't help it if my words sound more sincere when I'm speaking to you. I mean every one. I also mean it when I say that I'd like the next dance with you."

Aidan held out his hand, and Violet knew she couldn't resist it. "Just one," she warned.

"One is all I need."

Aidan led Violet to the already crowded dance floor. He made his way through the couples to the center of the crowd and then turned to pull her into his arms.

She moved into him, gripping his hand and resting her other hand on his shoulder. Even then she was stiff in his arms. She seemed anxious, although he wasn't sure why. The event was going smoothly. Just like everything she did, it was perfect.

He wondered if there wasn't more to it, though. The ring in his coat pocket felt like a hundred-pound boulder pulling him down. It was a constant reminder of what he intended to do tonight, although at the moment, he was rethinking his plan. It felt like a proposal would just pile more stress upon Violet, who was already strung tight as a drum.

"Are you worried someone will see us dancing and think too much of it?"

"Yes and no," Violet admitted. "Just be careful tonight. Betsy just told me that my parents and Beau plan to attend despite me not inviting them."

Aidan's brow knit together beneath his mask. Just when he seemed to think he was making progress with her, she would say something that set them back. "Why didn't you invite them? Don't you usually include them in foundation events?"

"I do. And they attend when they're in town. But tonight was different. I didn't invite them because I didn't..." Her voice trailed off.

"You didn't want them to see us together." Aidan felt a bitter taste rise up in his throat. He knew then that the ring was staying in his pocket tonight, no matter what.

God forbid her rich, perfectionist parents find out she was slumming with someone like him. That had to be why she seemed so adamant about keeping the lid on their relationship. "After everything I told you about my breakup with Iris, I can't believe you're going to stand here and tell me you didn't invite them because I'm not good enough for them to see us together."

Violet's eyes widened, filling the large space cut out of her mask. "No. That is absolutely not why I did it. Don't put horrible words in my mouth like that."

"Then enlighten me," he demanded.

Violet sighed and looked around them at the nearby dancers for a moment. "This isn't about you, Aidan.

You are amazing. You're a great father to Knox. I love every minute I spend with you. This is completely about them. I didn't want to subject you to them until it was absolutely necessary. I've told you how they are with me… I'm never good enough. I wanted to protect you from that. But know that no matter what they say or do, their opinions are their own, not mine."

"Okay. Then kiss me," he challenged.

Violet stiffened in his arms. "That isn't appropriate at a foundation event."

Aidan only shook his head. "Maybe not, but do it anyway. Thumb your nose at the people who say we're not a good match and show them all we're together."

She glanced around the room, anxiously looking for someone. He parents most likely.

"Come on." He captured her chin in his hand and gently turned her face toward his. "Kiss me, Violet. Forget about everything and everyone else and show me how you feel about me."

"Aidan…"

"If you can't do this right here, right now, we might as well stop seeing each other and just stick to coparenting Knox. I'm not going to spend our whole relationship as a dark secret you're afraid of people finding out about."

Violet's delicate brow creased in concern as she studied his face. "You're not my dark secret, Aidan."

"Then kiss me and prove it."

Violet sighed and placed a hand against his cheek. "If that's what it's going to take for you to believe me, then fine. Let the whole world see this."

She leaned into him, reaching up to press her lips to his. He met her halfway, scooping her into his arms and holding her close. Then their lips met, and the world seemed to fade away for a while. There was no crowd, no disapproving parents, not even an orchestra playing nearby. It was just him and her. He wished he could bottle how it felt in the moment so he could remember it when life seemed too complicated.

Or once she was gone from his life forever.

A loud "ahem" interrupted the moment.

Pulling apart, they turned to find an older, well-dressed couple standing beside them. It only took half a heartbeat for Aidan to realize that it was Violet's parents. The woman looked like a more mature version of Violet with more gray than brown in her hair and soft wrinkles creasing her eyes and mouth. She was wearing a sparkling gray gown and easily half a million dollars in diamonds and gray pearls. The man was shorter, rounder and mostly bald, but he had shrewd dark eyes just like his daughter. Neither of them looked happy to find their daughter on the dance floor kissing some stranger.

Violet moved even farther away from Aidan once she realized who had interrupted them. Aidan noticed the move, but now wasn't the time to mention it.

"Mother. Father. You're home early from your trip," she said with a forced smile as she untied her mask.

Aidan noticed there was no warmth between them. No kisses or hugs of greeting after all that time apart. Not even a handshake. Just a polite, verbal exchange. He couldn't imagine having that sterile of a relationship with his parents, even when his father was at the height of his drinking.

Mr. Niarchos didn't comment on his daughter's words, instead turning to Aidan and ignoring her entirely. He studied every inch of him, then sighed heavily as though he recognized the similarities between Aidan and Knox and was less than impressed with the man who must be his grandson's biological father.

"Our invitation got lost in the mail," Mr. Niarchos said with a dry tone that indicated he didn't believe that for a second. "I'm glad we were able to make it anyway, however. Wouldn't have wanted to miss this." He looked from Aidan to Violet with a displeased scowl distorting his face.

"Mother, Father, this is Aidan Murphy." Violet started the introductions with a hint of nerves in her voice. "He's the one starting the Molly's House transitional home in memory of his late parents."

Her mother smiled politely, but her father just continued to stare Aidan down.

"Can I have a moment alone with Mr. Murphy?" her father asked after an awkward silence.

"I'd rather you didn't," Violet said, but her father gave her a stern look that made her confidence shrivel right before Aidan's eyes.

"It's okay," Aidan interjected. He placed a comforting hand on her shoulder, stroking her skin to soothe her and keep him from punching the other man for talking to her that way. "I'll be right back."

He followed her father away from the dance floor to a corner of the room that was more private. Private enough to talk, but not so much that there wouldn't be witnesses if things went sideways.

"I've been watching you two together, son."

Aidan straightened his spine, ensuring he towered several inches over her father, who wasn't much taller than Violet. He might be a billionaire wearing more in gold and designer clothing than Aidan would make in a year, but Aidan wasn't about to be intimidated by him the way Violet was. He didn't have any power over him. "I'm not your son. My name is Aidan."

"You're right. And you never will be my son, you understand? You think I don't know who you are with that bright red hair? The moment I saw you two dancing I knew the truth. But it doesn't matter. You haven't landed your meal ticket."

"Anyone who sees Violet as nothing more than a meal ticket doesn't deserve her," Aidan worked up the courage to say, interrupting him. Violet was smart and strong and a wonderful mother. To reduce her to the balance of her bank accounts was offensive.

Mr. Niarchos scowled at him for a moment and then pointed a stubby finger in his direction. "Her future is with Beau. Someone who understands her and her life, someone who's of the same class and background as her. I don't know you, Mr. Murphy. I don't know if you're a plumber or a taxi driver or what, but I know this—you're temporary in her life. You might be Knox's father, but that won't matter for long. Violet will come to her senses and you will be a footnote in the story of her life, I guarantee it."

Aidan tried to hold as stoic a face as he could while

the older man spewed his hateful diatribe at him. He wanted to fight back, to argue the point with her father, but since a part of him agreed with every word he said, that made it hard. Since the moment he realized that his disappearing lover was billionaire socialite Violet Niarchos, he'd had those doubts running through his mind.

He wasn't after a sugar mama. Honestly, the money was more of a detriment to their relationship than a perk. He already knew he wasn't good enough for her, and he didn't want to deal with the kind of rich snobbery that followed people like Violet around. He would always be judged, always have noses turned up at him, always be accused of using Violet. He didn't need that. He'd had enough of that at the advertising firm where he was one of the few self-made successes among a bunch of spoiled elitist kids.

"You may be right, sir, but that's Violet's decision to make, not yours."

With every ounce of self-control he had, Aidan turned and walked away. There was nothing more to be said between them. Both had made it pretty clear where they stood. Now he had to go or he would say or do something he would regret. Like it or not, that was Knox's grandfather.

It might be his party, but Aidan had had enough for tonight. The rich would continue drinking and mingling without him, he was sure. He had just cleared the ballroom when he heard a woman's voice shouting his name in the hall. He stopped and turned to see Violet rushing after him.

"Aidan, wait!"

He held his ground until she caught up with him. "I'm going home, Violet."

"What did he say to you?" she asked with concern lining her face.

"Nothing I didn't already know."

"Please don't take it personally, Aidan. He wouldn't like any man that wasn't Beau. Father's got it in his head that Beau is the right match for me. And yes, it would be easier to date Beau, but—"

"Easier?" Aidan interrupted. "Is dating me such a hardship? Is slumming at ballgames and eating hot dogs with me so horrible that you'd rather be drinking champagne and eating caviar on a yacht with an ass like your ex?"

"No. Of course not. All I'm trying to say is that it would be easier for us if we were more alike."

"You mean if I was rich, too, so you didn't have to feel self-conscious about your money and the fact that I don't have any."

"No, Aidan. I mean everything. Culturally, religiously, family history… Beau and I come from very similar backgrounds so there's less friction with things like that. We grew up together and went to the same Greek Orthodox church. We just have a lot in common."

"So it's not that I'm poor, it's that I'm poor, Irish and Catholic? Iris didn't even stoop that low. She wasn't much of a shining example of womanhood, but at least she was honest about money being the most important thing to her."

Violet dropped her face into her hands. "You're obviously in a fighting mood and nothing I say is going to come out right in your mind. So go home if you want to. Just know that I don't want to be with Beau, Aidan. I want to be with you. Because I love you."

If Aidan had heard those words at any other moment, his heart might have leaped with joy. But not right now. It just seemed like a bandage over a wound that wasn't going to heal anytime soon. He was a fool to keep beating his head against the wall where Violet was concerned.

"I'm sure you'll buy yourself something pretty and get over it," he said before turning and heading down the grand staircase to the exit of the hotel.

Eleven

Aidan found himself wandering through the streets of Manhattan, unwilling to go home, and unsure of where else to turn. Instead, he'd just walked block by block until his shiny black dress shoes started to rub a blister into his toes. Stopping at a corner light, he looked up and spied the neon sign of a bar he'd heard of, but never visited before.

Crossing the street, he went inside and found it dark and fairly quiet. It wasn't a rowdy sports bar with dozens of televisions blaring or one offering a live band making it too loud to think. It was more the kind of place people went to drown their sorrows and hide away from the world for a while. It was perfect.

The bartender was a balding man in his forties with a graying goatee and bushy matching eyebrows. He nodded in greeting to Aidan and went back to what he was doing. Aidan found a seat at the far end of the bar in a dark corner isolated from any of the other patrons. He climbed onto the bar stool, immediately tugged loose his bow tie and unbuttoned the collar of his dress shirt. That helped lessen the irritating feeling of a lump in his throat that he couldn't swallow.

Now that he was off his feet, he was happy, but sitting still left him alone with his thoughts in a way walking through the city hadn't. A shot or four of whisky would do the trick, he was pretty certain. That would've been his father's solution. It was easy to forget your troubles in a glass until one day your troubles were caused by the glass itself. Tonight wasn't the night for Aidan to start drinking.

"What can I get ya?" the bartender asked as he came up and placed a napkin in front of Aidan.

"Ginger ale," he answered before he could change his mind and get something stronger.

The bartender arched a curious brow at Aidan, but didn't say anything. He just turned and went about pouring a soda in a tall glass of ice. Delivering the drink, he said, "Holler if you need anything," and disappeared.

He was grateful to be left alone. Bartenders had a reputation for being amateur therapists, even Aidan, although his father had a knack for it that he lacked. Most of the bartending community enjoyed that part of the job and sought out the customers who looked like they needed to chat. He probably could use someone to talk to tonight, but he wasn't ready. Not yet.

Instead, he sipped his ginger ale and stared intently at the wood grain of the bar top. The longer he sat, the heavier the engagement ring felt in his coat pocket. Finally, he took the box out and set it down next to his drink. Opening the hinge, he lifted the ring and twirled it thoughtfully between his fingers. Even in the dim light of the bar, the diamonds sparkled brilliantly. It was beautiful, just like the woman he'd intended to give it to tonight.

He was a fool to have even thought that was a good idea. Spending that week living together had tricked him into believing they could pull a relationship off in reality. And maybe they could. But proposing to Violet? A gorgeous billionaire who could have any man she wanted? Just because she'd chosen Aidan for a one-night stand didn't mean she would choose him for a husband. She probably wouldn't have chosen him for her son's father if that was a decision she'd gotten to make.

Hell, he should consider himself lucky that her parents showed up and everything went wrong before he worked up the nerve to ask. He'd probably still end up in this bar, miserable and alone, but at least he'd saved himself the embarrassment of her turning him down in front of everyone at the masquerade party.

Because she would've said no, right?

Of course she would've. What did he have to offer her? That day when they ran into Beau, she'd made a big deal about how there were more important things in a relationship than success and money. But did she really mean it? She said she loved him, too, and he

didn't know if he could take her declaration for truth,
either. She was desperate to keep him from walking out
on her, nothing more. He couldn't imagine she could
take her father's side and then say something like that
and mean it.

Then again, if he had truly listened to what she said
with his brain and not just his ears, maybe he would've
interpreted things differently. The argument had played
in his mind a dozen times like a looping viral video.
He realized now that she'd never said he wasn't good
enough or that she would choose Beau over him as her
father wanted. Just that her father had a point about
them being different and how it could make a relationship harder.

That was true. They were different in every way,
not just where money was concerned. And yes, that
meant they would face challenges as a couple. They
would have to have discussions like what religion to
raise Knox in or whether or not he went to a swanky
private school. But he loved her. And he loved his son.
He wanted them to be a real family. If she truly loved
him the way she said she did, they could make their
relationship work.

If he hadn't ruined it all by throwing her love in her
face and stomping off.

"Normally, I try to mind my own business, but it's
not very often that a guy in a tuxedo with a diamond
ring and no girl wanders into a place like this. Especially one throwing back ginger ales like there's no
tomorrow."

Aidan looked at the line of empty soda glasses in

front of him and smiled at the bartender. "I'd have to ask, too," he admitted. "I run a bar, myself."

"What are you doing here, then?"

That was a good question. He'd considered going to Murphy's. He'd even walked past it at one point. "If I went into my own bar, I'd end up working on a rare night off. Tonight I have other things on my mind."

"Like woman troubles?"

"You could call it that." Aidan looked at the ring, and then slipped it back into the box. "Are you married?"

"I was."

"Divorced?"

The bartender shook his head. "I'm a widower."

Aidan straightened up in his seat, suddenly feeling guilty for moping around when others had bigger problems than he did. "I'm sorry."

"Don't worry about it. It's been ten years now. I wish I could say I've gotten over it, but that would be a lie. I'm just getting better at talking about it."

"Was she sick?" For some reason, talking about the bartender's problems was easier than worrying about his own at the moment.

"No. It was an accident. One moment we were arguing about something stupid, and the next, she was gone."

Aidan could see the lines of regret etched into the man's face. Even a decade later, losing his wife seemed to haunt him.

"We were always arguing about stupid stuff," the bartender continued. "Her parents never liked me, so they were always causing trouble in our relationship by putting her in the middle. She was constantly trying to keep the peace, but I didn't want peace, I wanted her to side with me. The stress would build up until we would just pick at each other over little things. It all seems silly now."

After the night he'd had, Aidan could understand the issues the bartender had with his in-laws. "Why didn't her parents like you?"

He shrugged. "Name a reason and you'd probably be right. They didn't like anything about me. I wasn't educated and I didn't have a career with a future. My family wasn't the greatest. I didn't kiss their rear ends whenever we were together. They never seemed to care how much we loved one another or how well I treated her. She was my world. But after all these years, I've finally realized that basically anything I did would be wrong because no one was good enough for their only daughter."

"I can understand how that is. My… Violet…is an only child. Her parents have very high expectations."

The bartender nodded. "In the end, none of that mattered, but I didn't know it. I could never see what was the most important—that she loved me. That should've been my sole focus. Not all that other stuff. Instead of arguing with her, I should've been holding her tight. I should've been appreciating every precious moment I had with her, because I didn't have that many left."

Aidan wasn't sure what to say, but he knew that the thought of losing Violet permanently made him ill. Or maybe it was the four ginger ales he'd gone through since he arrived. Either way his stomach ached as he thought about living his life without Violet in it. Raising Knox without her. He knew he never wanted to know what that would feel like.

And yet, he'd walked away from her tonight and threw her love back in her face like a fool. What had he been thinking?

"Listen, I don't know what's going on with you and your intended. But I know this much—when you find the person you love, and who loves you, you've got to hold on to it. It isn't every day that you meet the person that makes you feel complete. When they come along, you've got to focus on what's truly important because that other stuff is just noise. What her parents think, what society thinks…it doesn't matter. Unfortunately, most people don't realize that until they lose that person for good. I know I didn't. And I regret it every single day of my life."

Aidan already felt an unbearable amount of regret swirling in his gut. He couldn't stand the thought of living with a lifetime of second-guessing himself. Reaching into his wallet, he pulled out enough for the soda and a hefty tip. The guy had earned it tenfold. "Thanks for the advice. I really needed that pep talk."

"No problem. You don't want to be like me. You've still got the chance to make things right with Violet. Don't waste the opportunity you've been given."

Aidan slid off the bar stool with a new sense of purpose moving his feet. He was going to get a cab back to his apartment and once he was there, he was going to figure out how to fix this mess.

He loved Violet. He just hoped she still felt the same way about him.

Violet looked at the paperwork on her desk but couldn't get her eyes to focus on it. It had been that way for the last week, since Aidan walked out of the masquerade ball. She wasn't able to erase the image of his face as he said his hateful words and walked away.

She'd deserved some of it, she was sure, but she never imagined he would throw her love in her face like that. Violet didn't agree with her father; she was just trying to explain where he was coming from. Opposites did attract but in the long run, they made for a challenging relationship. She and Aidan had little in common aside from their son. She wasn't holding that against him, it was just a fact.

It didn't make her love him any less. It meant that maybe it wasn't enough. Perhaps being coparents and nothing more was the right answer for them.

She only wished she could convince her heart of that.

A tap at the door interrupted her thoughts. "Yes?"

Betsy opened the door with an apologetic look on her face. "I'm sorry to disturb you, Miss Niarchos, but Mr. Rosso is here to see you."

Her stomach sank in her belly. She'd hoped for half a moment that it was Aidan, not Beau, waiting to see her. "Tell him I'm busy. He'll have to call and get time on my schedule."

"I did, but he is quite insistent that he see you right now."

Violet sighed. Beau was like a stubborn ox. He wasn't going to leave the office until he got what he wanted. "Fine. But interrupt us in ten minutes with an urgent call."

Betsy nodded and a moment later, Beau strolled through the door. He looked just as cocky as ever in his pinstripe suit, slicked-back dark hair and knowing smile. He strolled arrogantly across the room to her desk with his hands buried in his pants pockets.

With every step closer he took, she found it harder to believe that she'd almost married Beau. Yes, her father was right when he said that things would be easier with Beau. At least on the surface. But at the moment, the idea of dating Beau again made her feel very unsettled.

"Violet, I'm disappointed," Beau said.

She arched her brow as she looked up at him from her office chair. "Dare I ask why?"

"No kiss? Not even a handshake?"

Violet put out her hand to shake it and he brought it up to his lips. She squirmed out of his grip and buried her hand beneath her desk. "What can I do for you, Beau? I'm very busy today."

Beau unbuttoned his coat and sat down in her guest chair. He sprawled out, making himself more comfortable there than he should. "Well, I missed out on seeing you at the gala the other night. I got hung up in traffic and by the time I arrived, your parents told me you'd already left."

"I wasn't in the partying mood." And that was true. After Aidan walked out, she couldn't bear to go back into the room and face her parents. She knew she would do or say something she would regret. She hadn't wanted to hurt Molly's House's chances by tainting the event with scandal, so she'd turned it over to Betsy and called it a night.

"So your parents said. They said you'd had a fuss with Knox's father and encouraged me to come see you."

"Why? So you could swoop in and save me?"

Beau just shrugged. "Maybe. I thought perhaps you'd had a taste of what was out there and you'd come to your senses about our engagement."

"'Come to my senses'?"

"Well, yeah. We're good together, Vi. Everyone seems to know it but you."

"I'm not so sure I agree with that sentiment." Beau was hardly a perfect boyfriend, something her parents never seemed to understand. Perhaps their own relationship was so flawed they didn't notice the difference.

Violet hadn't noticed the difference either until she'd spent the last few weeks with Aidan. It wasn't just that he was a good man and a great lover, but he was a great father. The kind of father Beau would never be. There were so many things that she and Knox would miss out on without Aidan in their life. Beau couldn't compete as a father. He wouldn't play sports with Knox or take him to Yankees games. He couldn't even pick up the baby without him howling.

"I don't think you're in a position to be so choosy, Violet."

"Choosy?"

"Yes. I'm being the bigger man here. Overlooking your infidelity and raising Knox as my own son is a big offering on my part. Not many men would be willing to do that. I'm willing to marry you, Violet. I'm willing to forgive your little dalliance and move our relationship forward."

Violet narrowed her gaze at Beau and suddenly, something about his words felt familiar. Little dalliance. *Dalliance.* That wasn't a common phrase and yet it seemed like she'd heard it recently.

Then, just as when Aidan had walked into her office that first day, a wave of missing memories rushed over her. All this time, she'd wondered why she'd ended up in Murphy's Pub that night. Going out alone looking for tequila and oblivion was not her modus operandi. And yet she had. When her memories had returned about her time with Aidan, this was the one piece that had remained out of her reach.

She'd convinced herself that maybe they'd had one of their usual fights. They argued more than she was comfortable with, usually because Beau was staying out late or doing things that led her to believe he wasn't ready to settle down. If she hadn't gotten pregnant, she never would've agreed to marry him.

And if she had remembered what she knew now, she would've punched him in the face instead.

"You bastard," she said in her coldest tone.

Beau's eyes widened in surprise. "Excuse me?"

"How could you let me go all those months believing you, planning our wedding, when you knew the truth?"

"The truth about what? That you were having someone else's baby? I didn't know that. I thought it was mine. How was I to know you'd banged some bartender? I thought you were faithful."

She had to admit Beau was good. He was going to stick with his lie because he thought she still didn't remember. "I meant the truth about you and me. Because I *was* faithful, Beau. When I so-called 'banged' that bartender, we had broken up because I caught you in bed with that sneaky little cow Carmella Davis."

The previously suppressed image was suddenly incredibly clear in her mind. Her apartment. Her bed. Her boyfriend. Blonde and buxom Carmella completely naked and taking Beau for a ride… They'd fought, he'd argued it was just a *little dalliance*, nothing serious, and she ran out, wandering the streets distraught until she ended up in Murphy's Pub.

"I don't know what you're talking about, Violet."

She planted her hands on her desk and pushed herself up to glare at him from above. Her cheeks were flaming hot with anger. "When I lost my memory in the accident, it must've been a godsend for you. You'd lost your billion-dollar meal ticket through your own stupidity and got a reprieve because I forgot about the whole thing and you could just continue our relationship like nothing ever happened."

This time Beau had the good sense to keep his mouth shut.

"You rushed to my bedside at the hospital. Held my hand. And all the time, thanking your lucky stars I didn't remember what happened with you and Carmella. But the doctors said I would get my memory back eventually. Weren't you worried about that?"

"Not really." He shrugged arrogantly. "When you turned up pregnant, I figured it was mine and I was in the clear no matter what. If you hadn't insisted on getting your pre-baby body back before we got married, I would've had you locked down long before your memory returned. Then that little redheaded brat popped out of you and ruined all of my plans."

"That's it." She pointed one finger angrily toward the door. She was a patient person, but she was going to go full mama bear on his ass if he didn't leave soon. "Get out of my office."

"Violet—" he started to argue.

"No. End of discussion. I mean it, Beau. I want you out of my office and out of my life. For good. I don't ever want to see you here, at my apartment, or kissing up to my parents. I want you gone."

She held her arm stiff, pointing toward the door with a stern expression on her face until he relented. With a low growl of irritation, he pushed up from his chair and marched out without another word.

As the door to her office slammed shut, Violet breathed a sigh of relief. Beau was gone and even he wasn't stupid enough to come back and keep trying after this. It was over. Her parents would just have to learn to live with disappointment. That was all she was to them anyway. The difference was that now, she no longer cared.

Violet was in love with Aidan and she wanted to be with him more than anything. She just had to convince him that she meant it.

Twelve

The front parlor of his mother's house felt empty without all the knickknacks and doilies to protect the furniture no one was ever allowed to use. Now the room housed a large thrift store desk, a bookshelf and a file cabinet. The space had been christened as an office for the administrator Aidan had hired to manage Molly's House. Ted was five years sober himself and had agreed to manage the house and its tenants for a small salary in addition to room and board at the house.

So far, Ted had been great. Not only would he be good as a mentor to the people staying here, but he previously worked in construction and was helping Aidan fix things around the house. There were so many little things that needed to be taken care of and Ted was tackling them as quickly as they were added to the list.

While Aidan had every intention of going to Violet and apologizing right after his conversation at the bar, things hadn't worked out that way. Monday morning when he'd gone to the foundation to try to talk to her, he found she wasn't in the office. Instead, he'd been greeted by Betsy, who'd been kind enough to act as though nothing had happened at the masquerade party. She'd happily handed him a flash drive with the database of gala attendees and a huge check with his cut of the proceeds from the successful event. Thankfully, the little scene they'd caused with Violet's parents hadn't hurt the charity's chances. He was grateful for that. Betsy had also promised to let Violet know he'd come by to see her and to call him when she had a chance to talk.

While he waited for her call, he'd been focused on getting the ball rolling with Molly's House. First, he'd put his assistant manager in charge of the bar and took off a week from Murphy's for the first time since his dad had died. Making the most of it, he had been at the house 24/7. He'd bought supplies and some basic furniture and linens for the bedrooms and baths, paid a cleaning crew to come in and brought Ted on board. They were close enough now to opening that Ted was reviewing applications for their first tenants from the nearby rehab center.

It had taken up more of his time than he'd expected, but he decided that a cooling-off period never hurt anyway. Tonight, when he got done here, he was going to Violet's to spend his previously scheduled time with Knox. Since she hadn't called, Aidan wasn't entirely sure how receptive she might be to his apology, but he figured that was as good a time as any to talk to her. Even if they didn't repair their relationship, they at least had to be cordial enough to manage caring for Knox together. Tara had taken to going out during his visits, so they'd have the evening to themselves to chat.

He just wished he wasn't so damn nervous about it.

"Hey, Aidan?"

He placed the plastic floor mat beneath the desk for the new office chair and looked over at his office administrator. "Yeah, Ted?"

"There's someone here to see you."

That was unusual, but okay. "Send them on back for me." Aidan rolled the chair up under the desk and straightened out some of the computer cords running to the power strip.

"Aidan?" a familiar woman's voice said.

Looking up, Aidan spied Violet unexpectedly standing in the entryway. He straightened up from where he'd been crouching and dusted his hands off on his jeans. "Hey there. I, uh…wasn't expecting to see you here. I thought I was coming to your apartment tonight." It was a long trip out to the house, and she'd never even visited before. That made him instantly anxious when he coupled it with the lines of uncertainty on her face. "Is everything okay? Is Knox all right?"

"He's fine," Violet assured him. "I suppose I could've brought him here with me this afternoon, but Tara was about to give him his lunch and I didn't want to mess up his routine. He gets so crabby when he's hungry."

"He takes after me in that," he said with a smile he hoped would make him feel less awkward. It didn't. Aidan still didn't understand why she was here, if nothing was wrong with the baby. She could've texted or called about most things and saved herself the trip. What could she possibly have to say that needed to be done in person?

"Do we need to reschedule tonight?"

"No. Tonight is fine. I just…" She hesitated with her dark gaze dropping to the hardwood floors he and Ted had recently refinished. "I didn't want to wait to talk to you. I've already waited too long, but things got busy at the foundation this week."

Aidan frowned. He didn't like the way she said that. It felt way too ominous for his taste. "Do you want some coffee or something?" he asked to prolong the discussion. "I've put in a Keurig for the kitchen. Recovering alcoholics drink a lot of coffee, I've been told."

"Um, sure." She followed him through the house to the kitchen. She waited silently while he made them both a cup of coffee, and then they sat down together at the old kitchen table.

"I've eaten thousands of bowls of cereal sitting at this table," he said, hoping he didn't sound like he was nervously rambling even though he was.

Violet chuckled, warming her hands on the mug of coffee and gathering her thoughts. "This is a great old house with a lot of important history for you. I think it's perfect for your vision for Molly's House. I don't know why I haven't been by to see it sooner. I can't wait to see how it all turns out for you."

"Is that why you came out today? To see the house?"

"No. I'd actually gone by Murphy's first thinking you would be there and the bartender told me you'd taken the week off to focus on the house, so I came here instead. I wanted to see you today so I could tell you that I'm sorry."

He almost didn't know what to say to that. He'd had every intention of apologizing to her, and yet she'd come all the way out to the Bronx to apologize to him. "What are you apologizing for? I don't understand."

She sighed and shook her head, her gaze never leaving her mug. "I'm sorry for not standing up to my father at the gala. I should've spoken to them ahead of time about finding Knox's father. Instead I just avoided the whole situation for as long as I could and ended up putting you in the crosshairs."

"You couldn't have anticipated how your father would react."

"He's really predictable, like a stubborn old mule. You were worried that I was ashamed of you that night, but that was never the case. I was worried about my father seeing us together and sticking his nose where it didn't belong. Of course, that's what he did. I never should've let him pull you aside to bully you because it wasn't his place to tell you anything. I should've protected you from him. And even if I couldn't stop him, I needed to stand up for myself and for our relationship and tell him once and for all to stay out of my love life. But I was a coward and I ended up hurting you instead. I managed to drive you away when all I wanted in the world was for you to stay."

Aidan was thrilled to hear her say those words, but he tried to keep his cool for now. She seemed to have a lot she wanted to say and he was going to let her get it all out. "It's been almost a week since the gala. What prompted this revelation?"

Violet looked up from her coffee. "Beau came by the foundation yesterday and I ended up getting the last piece of my lost memories back. All this time, I'd felt guilty for cheating on Beau. My parents kept insisting that he must really love me to overlook it and raise Knox as his son, but it never felt right. Now I know why. I'd come to Murphy's that night because I came home and found him in bed with someone else. I broke up with him and ran out. I didn't cheat on him. He cheated on me, then when I had the accident and forgot, he just continued on with our relationship as though nothing had happened."

"Wow," Aidan said aloud, although he wasn't entirely surprised. Beau had an underlying sleaziness that had bothered him the moment they met outside her building. "I'm sorry he hurt you, Violet. I wish you had told me exactly what happened that night at the bar, so I could've told you sooner. It would've still been a year too late, but you would've known before yesterday."

She smiled softly. "It's okay. The timing worked out. He was trying to talk me into giving us another shot— probably at my father's prompting—and the memories returning at that moment helped me put an end to it for good."

It was all an interesting story and he was happy her memory had returned, but Aidan wasn't quite sure why she was telling him all of this. Beau being gone didn't necessarily clear the way for them to be together. He wasn't the only obstacle. "I'm glad for you," he said instead.

"That really isn't the most important part, though. While I was talking to Beau, listening to him tell me about how we needed to give it another try, even before my memory came back, I realized that I didn't want to give it another try with him. Despite everything that should make our relationship work, there were critical pieces missing. Pieces that only you have ever provided. You're Knox's father. Not just biologically, but you have taken on the role fully. You're involved with him now, even when he's tiny, so I know how wonderful you'll be with him when he's older. Beau would never be that for Knox. My son was always more of a…complication for Beau."

While he was pleased to hear he was meeting her expectations in the parent department, it wasn't what he wanted to hear right now. He wanted to know that she wanted him to be in her life for her sake, not just for Knox. "Is that it?" he asked.

"No. I'm just getting started. Of course I don't just want a father for Knox. I've realized that I want you, too. No, not even that. Of course I want you. That didn't come out right. I want to be with you, regardless of what anyone else says or thinks or wants for my life." Violet reached out and covered his hand with her own. "I love you, Aidan. And not because you're my son's father. I would want you in my life even if I hadn't gotten pregnant that first weekend."

Aidan was stunned speechless. He wasn't quite sure how to even respond to that. It was everything he'd hoped she'd say and yet the idea of it scared the crap out of him. Although he knew he had feelings for her, and she'd said she loved him, a part of him didn't truly believe it could be true. Could a woman like Violet ever truly love someone like him? He was afraid to believe her.

"What about the things you said at the party? About how different we are. How things would be easier with someone like Beau? Someone that shared your culture and background. Nothing has changed in that department."

"And I don't expect it to. Love isn't easy. I've realized that even with all those things going for Beau, loving him after everything we've been through would still be hard. It would be more work to forgive and trust him than any obstacle the two of us would ever face. It might be work for us to navigate, but it can also be fun and exciting for us to learn about each other. I don't want us to be alike. I just want us to be together. And happy. Do you think you could be happy with me? And with Knox? To have our own little family?"

Aidan felt his chest tighten at the mere thought of having a real family with Violet. Childhood memories of Christmas and Easter, first days of school and Friday night cheese pizza, all came back to him. Having all of that for Knox, and sharing it with Violet, was the most amazing thing he could think of to happen in his life.

There was just one thing left to do.

* * *

Aidan had been unnervingly quiet throughout their entire discussion. He asked a few questions, but for the most part, had sat with his coffee and listened quietly while she cut open her chest and laid her heart out on the table. She had come here knowing that he might not be receptive to what she had to say. She was prepared for that, and yet, had hoped desperately for him to leap out of his chair, scoop her into his arms, declare his love for her and kiss her senseless.

When Aidan finally did move, he stood up with a stoic look on his face. "Would you excuse me for a minute?"

She nodded and watched him disappear into the living room and go up the stairs. She wasn't sure what was upstairs that he had to go there right now, of all the times, but she did her best to sit patiently and not overreact.

Even then, she felt tears of disappointment start to well in her eyes. She asked him if he wanted to have a life with her, told him that she loved him, and he just got up from the table and walked away. That was not how she imagined this moment going.

But then Aidan returned a few minutes later with something small clutched in his fist. "I'm sorry about that. I had to go get something important. It couldn't wait."

Violet sniffed back her tears, hoping they were premature. "It's okay. Take all the time you need. I know I've dumped a lot on you at once."

He nodded. "I know. But it's okay. I've spent the

last week going over the gala and really, every moment we've ever had together. I've been trying to figure out what I could say or what I could do to convince you to give us a chance. A real chance. If we're going to be a family, there can't be any more secrets. If you love me, you love me when your parents are around. You love me when we meet some of your fancy friends and have to tell them I run a bar for a living."

"I do," she said, pushing up from her chair. "I love you all the time, no matter what we're doing or who we're with. I always will. I sat my parents down and told them that last night."

"What did they say?"

Quite a bit, but she would spare Aidan the details. "My father threatened to cut me out of the will."

Aidan's eyes widened. "Oh, no."

Violet just shrugged. "That doesn't matter to me. All my money came from the trust fund my grandfather set up for me when I was born. I don't need my father's money. I think he was just blustering to get his way. He's got to get used to not having a say in my life any longer. I'm almost thirty. It's well past time."

Aidan smiled widely. "I'm glad you said that because there's something I want to give you. To tell you the truth, I had this with me the night of the gala, but I didn't feel like the time was right. And then…well… I thought it was better that I hadn't."

Violet's eyes zoomed in on the object in his hand. She knew exactly what that was now. It was a jewelry box. It was unmistakable. She felt her heart start to race in her chest. Could it really be what she thought it was? Would she be able to hide her disappointment if it were just a pretty necklace or a pair of earrings?

"The two of us are different, but I think it's a good thing. The only thing that's ever worried me was that we're never going to be financial equals. I would say that there are few men on the planet that ever could be. And since Mark Zuckerberg and Bill Gates are already taken, there's even fewer than that in the world to win your heart. It's not easy on a man's pride to be in that kind of a situation, but there's no way I can ever catch up to you, so I'll need to make peace with that. I didn't realize how much it bothered me until I realized that I loved you."

Violet held her breath. He'd never said those words out loud to her. She'd said it at the party and several times today and he hadn't yet responded in kind. A wave of relief washed over her. He loved her.

Even as that worry faded, a new kind of anxiety built inside of her. Was this really the moment she was waiting for? Despite being engaged to Beau, she'd never had the proposal moment most girls dream of. When she'd discovered she was pregnant, he'd said, *I guess we should get married, then*, and they'd gone to Tiffany & Co. to pick out a ring. Violet didn't expect perfectly timed fireworks and a gospel choir, but it was not exactly a romantic and heartfelt proposal, either.

"You may not know this about me, but in a lot of ways, I'm an old-fashioned kind of guy. I would've done the right thing and offered to marry you the moment I found out about Knox if I'd thought for a second you were interested in that. And later, when you and I got closer and I decided that I wanted us to be a real family, that I wanted us to get married because I loved you and wanted you in my life forever... I had new worries aside from whether or not you would say yes."

Aidan held up the box in his hand, which was still frustratingly closed. "It bothered me that I could never afford the kind of ring that other men might be able to offer you. Because you deserve it, Violet. You deserve the biggest, sparkliest diamond ring that Harry Winston could make. And I couldn't give you that."

She wanted to tell him that it didn't matter what kind of ring it was or if there even was a ring. It might be a status symbol to some women, but Violet wasn't like that. The ring Beau gave her was nice, but it was clunky and heavy on her hand. She would be relieved to have something that was simpler to wear and she hated that he was agonizing over a moment that should be special and simple in its own way. She wanted to shout out that she wanted to marry him before he even asked, but she held her tongue. She did want to marry him, but she wanted him to say what he needed to say.

"I realized that the best thing I could offer you, aside from my heart, my love and my devotion to you and our son, was something that was important and special to me. Sentimental value is priceless."

Aidan opened the box at last. Inside was a diamond ring just as she'd hoped, making her heart flutter with excitement. The round diamond was set in platinum with a sunburst of diamonds radiating from the center. It was art deco in style, probably from the 1930s, making her wonder where he'd found such a beautiful antique ring.

"This ring belonged to my mother, and my paternal great-grandmother before her. When my mother got sick, she insisted I keep the ring and just bury her with her wedding band. She told me that one day I would meet a woman special enough to wear it, and thankfully, she was right. You are special to me in so many different ways, Violet. You're smart and beautiful and an amazing mother. It makes my heart hurt to think of waking up every morning without you by my side."

Violet's heart was pounding so loudly in her chest she could barely hear what Aidan was saying. All she did know was that he hadn't yet asked the critical question she was desperate to say yes to. Even then, he stood with the ring in his hand, looking at her expectantly.

"And?" Violet asked.

Aidan looked at her with a confused arch of his brow. "And…?" Then his eyes widened in surprise. "Oh! I forgot the most important part, didn't I?" He dropped down to one knee on the worn linoleum floor of his mother's kitchen. "Violet Niarchos, I love you so much, it hurts to breathe when you're not near me. I know that I'm not perfect, and I never will be, but I'm willing to spend the rest of my life trying to be the kind of man you deserve. Will you do me the honor of being my wife?"

Finally.

"Yes!" Violet shouted.

Aidan's hands were shaking as he took the ring from

its velvet bed and slipped it onto her finger. It fit beautifully, sparkling in the afternoon sunlight. It wasn't too bulky or too heavy. And knowing it was a family heirloom passed down made it all the more special. It was absolutely perfect.

He squeezed her hand and stood up, pulling her into an embrace. Violet wrapped her arms around his neck, tugging him tight against her. When his lips found hers, she drank in the taste of him, so thankful she had a second chance to kiss the man she thought she might've driven away forever. She never wanted to let go and now she knew she wouldn't have to. He was hers and she was his.

Forever.

* * * * *

TANGLED VOWS

YVONNE LINDSAY

To the awesome team at Harlequin who shine my ideas and my words to a high polish and who dream up titles when I cannot and who create amazing covers for my readers to love and who take care of all the behind-the-scenes stuff I don't even know about—thank you.
I wouldn't be where I am without you all.

One

"There's been a terrible mistake."

Yasmin Carter froze—poised in her wedding finery at the end of the royal blue carpet leading to the altar. She stared at the man who had just turned to face her. Ilya Horvath, heir apparent to the Horvath empire, CEO of her biggest business rival.

Her groom. The one she was meeting for the first time today.

Her eyes skimmed the small gathering of guests flanking the aisle. Their expressions registered varying degrees of dismay and shock at her words. She forced her gaze back toward Ilya. He did not look surprised...or amused. In fact, he looked annoyed.

Well, that was fine with her. She was pretty annoyed, too, right now, and she'd tell the Match Made in Marriage people at the first opportunity. When her office manager, Riya, had brought the matchmaking business to her attention, it had appeared to be a solution to her current busi-

ness woes. Cost aside, she had stood to gain more if she
went through the type of arranged marriage at first sight
offered by Match Made in Marriage than if she remained
single. She'd endured the psychometric testing and the interviews with the end goal in mind—securing an exclusive deal to handle Hardacre Incorporated's corporate and
family travel for the next five years. The company was a
well-known motivational and business coaching enterprise
that worked all over the country. That agreement was the
golden treasure that would pull her small charter airline
out of the red and back into the black—so she'd signed the
detailed contract that stipulated she must stay married to
her stranger-husband for at least three months without a
second thought. But contract or no contract, this wedding
simply could not happen.

She should never have entered into this ridiculous
scheme to save her business, but her inside source had
warned her that the owner's wife would never allow her
husband to do business on a regular basis with a beautiful,
young, unmarried woman. Wallace Hardacre had a wandering eye but was known to leave married women alone.

It had seemed so simple. To seal the deal, she needed
to be married. She knew she had everyone else's quotes
beaten on price. And it wasn't as if she didn't want to
marry Mr. Right someday. She absolutely did. It was just
that with running the company and all the hours that took,
she didn't have time to form quality relationships with
men.

Her gaze caught and meshed with Ilya's for just a moment and a shiver ran through her. Not of apprehension,
exactly—something more primitive than that. But it was
enough for her to be certain that this whole thing had been
a mistake from the start.

Ilya Horvath might look as though he'd stepped from

the pages of *GQ* but there was no way she could consider marrying him.

Physically, of course, he was perfect. Tall, with broad shoulders filling out his suit to perfection and a light beard wreathing his jaw, he was—in a word—gorgeous. Attraction rippled through Yasmin's body, making the corset beneath her strapless bodice suddenly feel a hundred times tighter than when Riya had hooked her into it this morning. Yasmin clamped down on the sensation and forced herself to take a breath, reminding herself that mentally, emotionally, socially and fiscally he was all wrong for her. No, she couldn't do this to her late granddad's memory—not to the man who'd taken her in and raised her when her parents had dumped her on him so they could continue to pursue their adventures rather than face up to adulthood and responsibility. She couldn't marry the man whose own grandfather, her granddad's best friend, had stolen and married the woman her grandfather loved. Attraction was all very well and good, but not when two families had been feuding for as long as theirs had.

"There's definitely been a mistake," she repeated, more firmly this time.

She bent and gathered the fullness of her layered organza gown, completed a swift one-eighty and exited the ballroom as fast as her feet, clad in intricately beaded slippers, would carry her. There was total silence for a few seconds, then the room broke out in a clatter of noise that followed her down the wide corridor.

Yasmin didn't know which way to go as she headed into the resort's foyer. To the elevators and back to the luxurious honeymoon suite where she'd gotten ready this morning or straight out the front door and hope there was a cab waiting there? It was a long way from here in Port Ludlow, Washington, to her home in California. The fare would be—

"Yasmin!" a woman called from behind her. "Please, wait. We need to talk."

Yasmin turned to face the petite, elegant older woman now approaching her. Alice Horvath—the woman responsible for the bitter rivalry between the Carters and the Horvaths these past sixty-plus years.

"There's nothing you can say that will make me change my mind," Yasmin said firmly.

"Just give me a moment of your time." Alice put a gentle hand on Yasmin's arm. "Please? It's important."

"Look, I—"

"Perhaps up in your suite would be best, more private." Alice began to steer Yasmin toward the elevators.

The adrenaline that had surged through Yasmin's body at the sight of her intended groom began to abate, leaving a dragging lethargy in its wake.

"Fine, but you, of all people, should know you're wasting your time if you're going to try and persuade me to marry your grandson."

The older woman gave her a sweet smile in response but said nothing as they rode the elevator up to the honeymoon suite. Yasmin was surprised when Alice produced a key card that opened the door.

"Forgive me the intrusion," Alice said, closing the door behind them. "I was merely holding the key for Ilya until after the ceremony."

Yasmin didn't know what to say or where to look, so she opted to plunk herself down on one of the sofas in the sitting room. Alice gracefully seated herself opposite.

"You have a right to know what's going on."

Damn right she did. Yasmin tightly squeezed the bound stems of her bouquet of pale pink roses and gypsophila to stop the trembling that had begun in her fingers and now threatened to travel up her arms and take over her entire body.

"Let me be frank with you, my dear. When you applied to Match Made in Marriage I immediately knew you and my grandson were compatible. I didn't need the specialist tests to assure me that you and Ilya would very much be a perfect match."

"I beg your pardon? You work with Match Made in Marriage? Are you telling me that *you* make the matches?" Yasmin replied in stunned surprise.

"It's not widely known, of course, and we do take the tests and interviews into consideration, but more as a confirmation that I'm on the right track with my couples. Trust me when I say I've always had a knack for these things. Once I retired from the family firm it was purely common sense to turn my little talent into a business. When my grandson told me he was ready to marry and settle down, it was only natural he would turn to me, but I didn't expect to find the perfect match for him so promptly. I have to say, getting your application was quite the surprise."

Alice Horvath looked at the beautiful but clearly confused and angry young woman sitting opposite her and wished things could have been different between their families. That the painful rift between best friends hadn't formed when Jim Carter and Eduard Horvath both fell in love with her and, eventually, fallen out forever when she chose Eduard for her husband. But this was her chance to make things right—to heal the wounds of so long ago and to put this stupid feud to bed once and for all.

If only she could persuade Yasmin to go ahead with the wedding.

She drew in a breath and chose her words carefully. If there was anything this young woman seemed to have a grasp of, it was business. Oh, yes, Alice knew that Carter Air was struggling. She also knew that Yasmin, despite having come up with the hefty commitment fee, could not afford to break the terms of the marriage contract she'd signed or attempt to sue Match Made in Marriage to get out of it.

Alice sighed softly and composed herself.

"I repeat, matching you and Ilya is no mistake. The two of you are perfectly suited to each other and are fully compatible when it comes to your values and your hopes and dreams for the future. I have every faith that you belong together and that you could make a long and very satisfying marriage."

"But—"

Alice raised a hand. "Please, allow me to finish. There comes a time when the past has to be put behind us so we can look to the future. This is your time. I know that there's been a great deal of bitterness between our families, that your grandfather and my Eduard ceased to have a civil word to say to each other after…" Alice blinked away the emotion, the weakness she couldn't afford to show. "Suffice it to say that bitterness has tainted too many lives for far too long."

"It's not just a family feud, Mrs. Horvath—"

"Please, call me Alice," she interrupted. "And, yes, I know it goes deeper than that. But I urge you to reconsider and to return to the ceremony. Everyone is waiting."

"I can't do it. I can't go against everything I've ever been raised to believe. I can't marry the man whose business is trying to put *me* out of business. I owe it to my staff and to my grandfather's memory to walk away from this. I want to invoke the exit clause in my contract early. Ilya and I are incompatible on far too many levels."

Yasmin's gray eyes flashed with emotion, reminding Alice so much of Yasmin's grandfather.

"Ah, my dear. So often pride comes before a fall. Your beloved grandfather aside, you owe it to your staff to go through with this. Let's be honest. You're not in the best position financially, are you?" Alice paused to let her words sink in. To ensure that Yasmin was aware that she knew exactly what the younger woman's situation was right now. "The figures you provided as proof of your monetary position were inflated, to put it kindly, and before you ask, yes, we checked."

Yasmin began to protest but Alice cut her off.

"You gave us every right to examine your financial situation when you signed the contract. Let's be quite honest with each other. We both know you can most certainly do without the negative public fallout of walking away from your contractual obligations, not to mention the financial fallout from attempting to break your contract with Match Made in Marriage. I know you took out a loan to fund your application. A loan secured by the assets of Carter Air, I believe?"

She watched Yasmin grow pale as her words sank in.

"You're threatening me with ruin? Really? All to *make* me marry your grandson?"

"Sometimes, my girl, the ends justify the means. Don't you think your future happiness is worth it?"

"So you want me, specifically, to marry Ilya. Why?"

Alice studied Yasmin, her ashen face, her clear gray eyes, the set of her pretty mouth and the proud posture as she fought a battle she couldn't win. She recognized the girl's spirit; after all, hadn't she been just such a young woman once? And Alice was no different now. She still fought hard for what was best for everyone she loved. This was important and she was convinced, beyond a doubt, that Ilya and Yasmin belonged together. She wouldn't have made this match if she hadn't known, deep in her bones, that they were right for each other. That "knack" she'd mentioned earlier—it had manifested early in her life. A knowing that some might call mumbo jumbo and others prescience. Whatever it was, it was her gift and she only used her gift for good.

Alice loved her eldest grandson, the son of her first-born son, more fiercely than she'd ever believed possible. This woman was the key to his long-term happiness—she knew it as surely as she knew she'd made the right decision when she'd chosen Eduard Horvath for her husband. As surely as she'd known every one of the matches she'd engineered was right. She only hoped Yasmin would come to see that, too.

"I love my grandson dearly, but he works too hard and, deep down, I don't believe he's happy. You, whether you realize it or not, hold the key to his future happiness. I wish nothing more than to see him and his bride happy together. It's as simple—and as complicated—as that." Alice flicked an invisible speck of dust off the sleeve of her impeccably tailored jacket. "Now, shall we return? We both know you can't afford not to let this wedding go ahead."

"But what about the clear conflict of interest? Ilya is my business rival. How are we to manage that?"

"That is something you will need to work out together."

"No, that's not enough for me. I need to know that the Horvaths will not interfere with Carter Air. Ilya's company has either bought or driven out of business every other small charter company at the airfield. I will not let that happen to Carter Air. I made a promise to my grandfather that I would keep his legacy safe."

Alice nodded and gave Yasmin a small smile of compassion. "Dear girl, I know you loved your grandfather dearly. For all his bluster and noise, he was a man who cared deeply. But sometimes promises made in the heat of the moment should be broken. Is Carter Air truly your passion, or are you merely holding onto an old man's dream... and his bitterness?"

"How dare you say such a thing? His bitterness? You dumped him! In fact, you didn't even have the decency to

tell him yourself at the time. He had to read your engagement notice in the local paper."

Alice felt a pang in her chest. "It was for the best."

"You'll have to forgive me if I disagree." Yasmin got
up from the sofa and began to pace the floor, the layers of
her gown swirling around her like a cloud.

"Fine, I know I can't afford to break the contract. I'll go
ahead with the wedding, but on one condition."

"And that is?"

"That our companies remain as two separate entities
and Ilya and I never discuss business."

Alice rose and went to stand in front of Yasmin. "Your
businesses are a big part of both your lives. Not being able
to share and discuss your day's work, your challenges and
successes, means you'll only be sharing half a life together.
Are you sure this is a wise decision?"

Yasmin's eyes darkened and her mouth firmed into a
straight line before she spoke.

"It's the only way. If he won't agree to it then the wedding is off and you will release me from my contract with
no penalty because while it would definitely harm my
business if it was to be widely known I broke my contract
with you, wouldn't the same be true for Match Made in
Marriage? After all, Ilya is *your* grandson. In itself that
would raise eyebrows if your involvement in this was made
public, wouldn't it?"

Alice had to admire the girl's mettle. She inclined her
head slightly. "And you'll accept my grandson's word that
he will honor your request? I'm sure you've heard that his
word is his bond."

Yasmin nodded.

"Fine. I will discuss it with my grandson."

"I have to say I'm surprised at how well you're coping,"
Valentin Horvath leaned over and whispered in Ilya's ear.

"After all, it's not every day a man is rejected by his bride on first sight. Maybe I'm biased, being family and all, but I didn't think you were *that* ugly."

Ilya clenched his jaw and deliberately counted to ten before answering his cousin, who also happened to be one of his closest friends. Valentin headed up Horvath Pharmaceuticals in New York and was generally more serious in nature than his younger, more carefree brother, Galen.

"It's only to be expected that she would be nervous."

"And if she doesn't return?" asked Galen.

"She'll return."

"With Nagymama frog-marching her from behind, no doubt," Valentin said, using the family's Hungarian nickname for their grandmother.

Galen stifled a laugh. "Can't say I've seen Nagy move quite so quickly in the past few years."

"Protecting her investment, perhaps," his brother replied archly. "You know how personally she takes her matches."

Ilya rolled his eyes. Family ribbing was all very well and good—to be expected under the circumstances—but he was getting impatient. Where the hell was his bride?

He'd recognized Yasmin Carter the moment he'd turned around. So many thoughts had crossed his mind, the first being how stunningly beautiful she was in her wedding gown. Who knew that beneath the flight suits or jeans and a T-shirt he'd seen her wearing at the airfield, she could be so incredibly feminine, or so vulnerably fragile. That first glimpse of her today had appealed to an instinct his family constantly teased him about—his need to protect and provide for those he cared for. He hadn't expected to feel that for his bride immediately, but he had—deeply and viscerally. His response had made him want to follow her when she'd turned and left after her awkward pronouncement. It was only his grandmother's hurried whisper that she would deal with it that had prevented him from chasing Yasmin as she'd bolted from the room, even though every cell in his body had called on him to do so.

He looked at his watch again and fought not to start tapping his foot in impatience. The women had been gone twenty minutes now.

"The natives are getting restless," Valentin observed as he cast his eyes over the assembled family and friends who'd been able to make it on short notice. "It's a good thing you have the champagne flowing, Galen."

Galen was the head of Horvath's hotel and resort chain. He'd automatically switched into damage control mode the moment the wedding had gone off the rails. Ilya refused the offer of a waiter passing by with a tray of beverages. He needed a clear head today.

A movement in the doorway attracted his attention and he started toward his grandmother before anyone else noticed her.

"Is Yasmin all right?" he asked as his grandmother tugged him into the hallway.

"You recognized her?"

"Of course I did. While I'm left wondering what madness possessed you to match her to me, I've learned to trust you. But does she? She's more skittish than I would have thought."

"And so you ought to trust your grandmother. I only ever have your best interests at heart," Alice said, patting him fondly on the cheek. "We have a small problem."

A small problem? He would have thought his bride running away from the ceremony was a bit more than that.

"She has a stipulation if the wedding is to proceed," his grandmother continued.

"And that is?"

"She's very protective of Carter Air. She will go ahead with this, provided that you two never discuss business together and that your companies remain two separate entities. Therefore, no mergers, no buyouts, no sharing of information."

"And that's it?"

In the grand scheme of things, it was nothing. Of course she'd want to protect her company. And though their families had bad blood between them, he wasn't interested in Carter Air as a takeover target and didn't wish Yasmin ill beyond the usual competition in the industry. It wasn't his style. He'd never understood why the cold war that had raged between his grandfather and Jim Carter, Yasmin's grandfather, had been carried on for generations. Ilya didn't believe in holding grudges. But even so he did wonder if his grandmother had some other ideas cooking beneath her halo of perfectly coifed silver hair.

"You agree, then?"

"Of course I agree, Nagy. Show me where to sign and I'll sign."

He saw relief in his grandmother's blue eyes. "Thank you, my boy. I think it's best if we keep this a verbal agreement for now, don't you? We don't want anything to muddy the waters should circumstances change, and thanks to your exemplary reputation, Yasmin is prepared to accept your word. Now, go back inside and wait."

"We're going ahead?"

"We most certainly are."

Two

Yasmin fought the overwhelming sense of déjà vu that assailed her as she approached the double doors to the ballroom. This was it, her wedding day. She was actually going through with it. And now, hopefully, her problems would begin to fade away. Her business problems, at least. As for her personal ones, well, that was another story.

She hovered at the end of the carpet, sensed a movement at her side. Ilya.

"Yasmin Carter, will you marry me?" he asked, offering her his arm so he could accompany her down the aisle.

She looked up into his denim-blue eyes and saw only reassurance there. Strange that in business they were such fierce rivals, yet here he was offering her comfort, companionship. Marriage. It shouldn't have made sense—she barely knew the man—but in this moment he was the key that would hopefully unlock the door to her future.

"Yasmin?"

"Yes, I will marry you," she said in a voice she'd hoped

would be firm and decisive, but that came out husky and with a faint tremor.

"Shall we?" He nodded toward the aisle.

She tucked her arm in his and together they walked slowly down the aisle toward the celebrant.

The ceremony itself passed in a blur. She supposed she said the right things at the right time, because before she knew it, Ilya was putting a blindingly brilliant wedding band on her finger and the celebrant was pronouncing them husband and wife.

Ilya leaned toward her. *Oh my, he's going to kiss me!* she thought, her heart kicking up to double speed in her chest. Unsure of what to do, she stood there, watching him come toward her with a twinkle in those intriguing eyes and an expression of humor mixed with determination on his face.

As he drew closer Yasmin felt his warmth and took in the scent of his cologne, the tang of pine with an underlying hint of sandalwood. And then his lips touched hers. Sensation rippled through her whole body and her breath caught in her throat. Time stopped. All that existed was the sensation of his kiss. And then, just like that, it was over. Too soon and yet not soon enough.

As he pulled away, there was a polite smattering of applause together with whoops and hollers from Ilya's groomsmen. He might not be touching her right now, but every nerve in her body continued to party as if he still kissed her. It was madness and it was wonderful all at the same time. A roaring sound filled Yasmin's ears.

Her new husband leaned forward and whispered, "Breathe, Yasmin."

She took in one shuddering breath and then another before turning to accept congratulations from the few members of her staff—pretty much her only friends these days—who'd made it to the wedding. All the while she tried to come to terms with the avalanche of emotion that swept her along on its tumbling course. She was married. To Ilya Horvath. And the man was dangerous.

One kiss had scrambled her synapses. One. That's all it had taken. Was she so weak? So starved for male attention? Yasmin looked across at Ilya, her *husband*, and the tingle of desire he'd ignited in her dialed up a few notches. She felt a flush warm her cheeks as he turned from the person congratulating him and his gaze met hers. Yasmin swiftly averted her eyes.

Alice Horvath stood before her. Were those tears in the older woman's eyes? Surely not. Before Yasmin could say anything, Alice stepped closer.

"Congratulations, my dear, and welcome to the family. You're one of us now."

Alice pulled Yasmin into a firm hug, holding her close for several seconds before letting her go. Her words, however, settled into Yasmin's mind like a rock sinking in quicksand. Before she could reply, Ilya was back at her side.

"The photographer would like us to himself for a while. Nagy, will you excuse us?"

Yasmin wasn't sure how Ilya managed it, but within moments they were in the beautiful gardens overlooking the marina. She'd been excited when she'd learned that due to California's requirement that the couple apply for their license together, their wedding would instead take place in Washington State, where they could show up to apply separately, which satisfied the Match Made in Marriage condition of bride and groom first meeting at the altar. She'd always loved the area, with the trees, mountains and Puget Sound. The resort was as picturesque and breathtaking as she'd hoped, and the sounds of rigging clanking on the boats berthed in the marina peppered the sea-scented air.

"Are you okay?" Ilya asked. "You looked as if you could benefit from a breath of fresh air."

"I'm fine, thank you, but you're right. It's good to be away from the circus. I didn't know it would be so…"

"Overwhelming?" he said in a voice that sounded like he understood exactly how she was feeling.

She looked up at him. She was not a short woman, but in her flat-heeled slippers, he was a good head taller. "Yeah, overwhelming."

And she didn't just mean the ceremony. It was him— everything about him was more than she'd expected. Of course, she'd seen pictures of him. Even been in the same room with him a time or two when they'd attended aviation industry functions. But she'd never in a million years imagined being his wife. She dropped her gaze to his hands. He held a bottle of French champagne and a single glass. When had he grabbed those? she wondered as she noted his long fingers and how gracefully he poured the wine.

"Here," he said, handing the flute to her. "This might help."

Her skin was peppered with goosebumps—as if he'd touched her already, as if he'd traced those smooth fingertips across the swell of her breasts and lower, ever lower. Inside her corset she felt her nipples harden. A tiny gasp of surprise escaped her as a spear of longing arrowed straight to her core. Was this what Alice had meant when she said they belonged together? Did the woman have some kind of insight into the chemistry that attracted one person to another? The chemistry that made Yasmin feel as though she had about as much chance of avoiding her attraction to Ilya as an iron filing did a magnet?

She ripped her gaze from his hands and accepted the glass, lifting it straight to her lips and downing at least half the champagne in one gulp. The bubbles fizzed and danced along her tongue and down her throat, much as her blood danced more and more heatedly through her veins the longer she was around him.

This wasn't what she'd expected. This instant, engulfing need for a man she barely even knew, yet was now wedded to.

"Thirsty?" Ilya asked, cocking one brow.

A flush of embarrassment stained her cheeks, making her feel even more flustered.

"Something like that," she muttered and took another, more delicate, sip.

Before she could ask him why he didn't have a glass himself, the photographer and his assistant joined them. Yasmin took in as deep a breath as her corset would allow, grateful for the distraction.

The next hour passed in a blur of directions, unnatural poses and equally unnatural smiles. By the time the photographer called for one last pose, she'd drank far more of the bottle of champagne than anyone who'd skipped both breakfast and lunch out of nerves had a right to.

"Okay, people. How about a bit of passion?"

"He does know we only just met today, doesn't he?" Yasmin said to Ilya through gritted teeth. "We don't even know each other."

Ilya's arm slipped around her waist and he stepped in closer. "I think we can produce a reasonable facsimile of the feeling, don't you?"

He lowered his face to hers, his lips hovering a hairs-breadth away from her mouth. She could see the silver striations that radiated from his pupils and the rim of dark blue around his irises. He really had the most beautiful eyes she'd ever seen. His hand was strong against her back. Supporting. Warm. The warmth seeped slowly into her skin. A shiver ran up her back in total contrast. He might essentially be a stranger to her, but he affected her on a level that intrigued and frightened her at the same time.

His breath was a mere whisper against her lips, his gaze intense as he looked into her eyes. Involuntarily she raised her hand to cup his cheek, her palms tingling as she felt the bristles of his neatly trimmed beard against her fingertips. Her lips parted on a sigh and her senses primed themselves for that moment when their lips would touch.

"Perfect!" the photographer exclaimed joyfully, breaking the spell. "Now let's go back inside for some group shots and the cutting of the cake."

Yasmin blinked and let her hand drop to her side. Her other hand still clutched her bouquet in a death grip. What had nearly happened there? She wasn't sure if she was grateful for the photographer's interference or maddened by it. She shivered again. Even though it was early fall, and the day had dawned sunny and mild, clouds were gathering in the sky and the temperature had dropped markedly.

"Here, you're cold. Let me put this on you."

Before she could protest that they'd be inside soon, Ilya had stripped off his jacket and was draping it over her shoulders. The heat of his body transferred from the silk lining to her skin, leaving her feeling overly sensitive. A few drops of rain fell on his white shirt, rendering it transparent where they hit. She caught a glimpse of a dark nipple behind the fine cotton, felt a clench of need so intense it made her stumble as she started to move forward.

Ever the gentleman, Ilya steadied her. The photographer's assistant rushed toward them with a massive white umbrella that Ilya accepted and held over them both. He guided her toward the doors leading to the main reception room. As soon as they were inside, she pulled off his jacket and thrust it toward him.

"Thank you. I don't need this now."

"It's okay to accept a little help from time to time."

"Said the man who has never had to ask for help from anyone, ever."

She smiled to soften her words but her meaning hung in the air between them. He had been born into a life of privilege. Certainly the privilege had been created by the hard work of previous generations and, she knew well, of the current generation, too. But had he ever truly wanted for anything?

"Besides," she continued, "you'll need to look your formal best for the reception."

He said nothing but shrugged the jacket back on. The resort's wedding planner hovered at the inner doors to the reception room.

"Are the two of you all ready?" she asked with an encouraging smile.

"As ready as we'll ever be, right?" Ilya replied with a crooked smile in Yasmin's direction.

She nodded, desperately trying to ignore the ridiculous sensations that poured through her. Anyone would think she was a sex-starved crazy woman if they knew how easily he sent her senses into overdrive. *And aren't you?* a little voice teased from the back of her mind. Okay, sure, she hadn't had a date in, what? Two years? And as for sex, well, it had been even longer. That didn't mean she had to melt like an ice cube on hot tarmac in the middle of July with just one look from him. Besides, he didn't appear to be similarly afflicted, she realized with a burst of chagrin. From now on she'd keep her ridiculous reactions very firmly under control. It couldn't be that difficult, could it?

Ilya observed his new wife with amusement. She was working hard to hold herself completely aloof, and yet the endearingly pretty flush of pink on her cheeks and her chest suggested she was just as attracted to him as he was to her. It would prove to be an interesting marriage, he decided. But would it be one that endured? His grandmother seemed to think so. He had yet to hear her reasons as to why, but Ilya knew that he and Yasmin at least had flying in common. The fact that they flew in direct competition with each other was another matter entirely.

Her gray eyes darted from one group of people to the next as they circulated through the room after the announcement of their arrival. He'd felt her entire body go rigid as they'd been introduced as Mr. and Mrs. Horvath.

"I'm not taking your name," she whispered fiercely as they finally settled at the head table.

"I didn't expect you to," he said to defuse her irritation. But mischief prompted him to add, "Would you prefer I took yours?"

Surprise chased the exasperation from her face. "Seriously? You'd do that?"

"If it was important to you," he answered sincerely. "I want this marriage to work, Yasmin. I don't yet know your reasons for entering into it, or why we've specifically been matched together, but I'd like to think the experts got it right and that we can make an honest go of this. I want a future that includes a family with the kind of companion I can't wait to see, whether it's when I wake or just before we fall asleep at night."

He hesitated. Was that too much, too soon? Judging by the startled expression on her face, perhaps it was. He'd surprised himself with that declaration, too. Still, he was the kind of guy who said what he wanted. He didn't hold with beating around the bush, and it was true. He wanted a family of his own. A wife who would be his partner in all things.

The reception continued with speeches interspersed between courses of the meal. He noticed she barely touched her food. And only one person stood up to speak for Yasmin. A woman Ilya recognized from the airfield—Yasmin's office manager, he recalled—who sat in her colorful sari at a table with a handful of others from Carter Air. His wife had no family here, he realized in surprise. He knew the grandfather who'd raised her had died a few years ago, but why hadn't her parents come today? Was their absence a sign of something deeper missing in her life? Did her reason for marrying stem from a need to create a family of her own?

He knew part of his reason in approaching his grandmother for a bride came from his wish to continue the family tradition of handing control of the corporation over to an heir or heirs. But finding the right woman had eluded him. He'd been engaged once, in college, but that had ended disastrously.

Ever since his father's death when he was sixteen, and his mother's subsequent withdrawal from parental duties as she went on a new quest to find love, he'd missed that feeling of being a piece of a small, tight-knit family unit. Yes, he'd had his grandmother, his aunts and uncles and cousins, but it wasn't the same as what he'd lost and what he craved to be a part of again.

He looked at Yasmin and felt a pull of sympathy. Her family life hadn't been much better. Ilya had met her irascible grandfather once and was surprised that Jim Carter and Eduard Horvath had been such great friends many years ago. They couldn't have been more different, from what Ilya could tell. His late grandfather had been a charismatic and driven man who always had an eye to the future and to expansion. He had lived, laughed and loved hard. On the flip side, Jim Carter had been quieter, withdrawn even, and his reluctance to embrace change had set Carter Air back in many ways. While his work ethic had never been in question, he'd lacked the vision and the willingness to expand and adapt to new horizons the way Eduard had. Their very differences had been what had made them such a great team until they'd fallen out over his grandmother and become enemies.

Yasmin, it seemed, had her own way of doing things

with a liberal dose of her late grandfather's caution sprinkled in. Ilya knew one thing for certain—she was a damn fine pilot. He'd seen her in her vintage Ryan PT-22 Recruit at airshows and she'd taken his breath away. The Ryan had a reputation as an unforgiving aircraft but she handled hers as if it was a simply an extension of herself. Which made her an intriguing package, indeed, and begged the question: How many more layers would he uncover as he got to know his unconventional bride?

Three

Ilya leaned over and murmured in Yasmin's ear, "Everyone seems to be enjoying themselves."

Yasmin nodded, trying to ignore the frisson of awareness that tracked down the side of her neck as he spoke.

"Everyone except you," he added dryly.

"I'm fine," Yasmin insisted even as she clenched a fist in her lap.

She might be fine, but she hated being the center of attention like this. As if she was on display for approval by every member of his family. His cousins seemed nice enough, but she sensed a lot of confusion and perhaps even some veiled hostility from some of their parents' generation. And then there were the questions—like, where were her parents? Didn't they approve of her marriage?

Truth be told, she hadn't even been able to get hold of them to let them know about the wedding. They were somewhere in the wilds of South America the last she'd heard—chasing whatever dream they'd come up with this time. A traditional life filled with predictable choices was definitely not for them. Who knew? Maybe they would have approved of her adventurous approach to marriage, although she doubted it. Her father had tried to fit in to the mold her grandfather had cast for him but the two men had never been close, and in the end her father had left Carter Air, following his dreams with the woman he fell in love with and only returning long enough to leave his daughter in his father's care so she'd have stability and regular schooling.

She was grateful to her parents that they'd done that for her, even if her granddad had not always been the easiest man to live with. The transient life was definitely not her thing. She was more like the old man than she liked to admit—needing order, consistency, control. All of which had made today very hard to handle.

Ilya interrupted her thoughts. "Let's get out of here."

She turned to face her husband. "Can we do that?"

"I don't see why not. It's our wedding day. We can do whatever the hell we want, can't we?"

He held out a hand and she took it. His fingers closed around hers and he gently tugged her to her feet. Was this when their marriage would truly begin? In the honeymoon suite upstairs overlooking the marina and Puget Sound? Her stomach tightened into a knot of anxiety. As powerful as her attraction to him was, she knew she wasn't ready for this. Wasn't ready for *him*.

They managed to slip through one of the French doors to the patio outside. The earlier rain had passed, leaving the evening air damp and cold, heavy with the scent of woodsmoke. Ilya hastened to drape his jacket around Yasmin's shoulders again. She was grateful for the warmth as she followed him across the patio to another door that led to the hotel's main foyer.

"You know your way around," she observed. "It was

all I could do today to negotiate my way from my room to the wedding."

He flashed her a smile. "You probably had other things on your mind."

Yasmin tried to ignore the way his smile made the corners of his eyes crinkle. It made him look even more impossibly handsome and made her wonder anew just how they were going to approach this first night together. She doubted she would have been as nervous had her husband been anyone other than the man standing before her now.

She squared her shoulders and took a deep breath.

"Let's go do this, then," she said with all the enthusiasm of an unrestrained wing walker heading into a double barrel roll.

Ilya laughed. "You don't need to sound quite so keen," he commented, as they headed to the elevators.

"I'm sorry," she said, blushing furiously. "I've never done this before. I'm not quite sure what the protocol is."

"It's okay," he assured her, his voice deep and even. "It's been a difficult day. Certainly not what I expected."

"What did you expect?" she asked as they stepped into the elevator.

"Not you, that's for sure. Not that I'm complaining," he added hastily.

"Well, I wasn't expecting you, either, if that's any consolation."

"Yeah, I think that was pretty obvious by your reaction," he teased.

Yasmin felt her lips tweak into a smile. It was the first genuine moment of humor she'd appreciated all day.

"You have a beautiful smile," Ilya commented as the doors swished open and they stepped out on her floor.

Their floor, she reminded herself. And just like that, the butterflies were back in her stomach and commencing an aerobatic maneuver. She suddenly wished there had been some kind of handbook issued explaining what happened next. Her smile died as the little voice in the back of her head told her she was an idiot. It was their wedding night. What did she think would happen next?

They reached the door to the honeymoon suite and Ilya produced a keycard from his pocket.

"My cases were brought up here during the reception," he said as they walked inside the beautifully appointed room. "I told them not to unpack."

"Not to unpack?" Yasmin repeated. "Aren't we supposed to be honeymooning here?"

"Did you particularly want to? I'm happy to stay if that's what you prefer but we have other options. We could disappear to Hawaii or even hide out at my home overlooking Ojai. The choice is yours."

Yasmin considered his words carefully. As much as she loved Washington, she felt like a fish out of water here with Ilya. Perhaps if she was back in California, in more familiar surroundings, this unusual marriage of theirs might begin to feel more usual.

She looked around the sumptuous suite where she'd felt like an outsider from the moment she'd arrived. She wasn't used to this world of wealth and glamour.

"No," she answered simply. "I don't want to stay here."

"So which is it to be? Hawaii or back to my place?"

He made it sound so simple. But then again, in his world, maybe it was.

"Let me change and pack."

"Do you need help?"

She was on the verge of refusing when she remembered the dress's multitude of hooks and eyes that Riya had helped her with.

"Thank you," she answered, turning her back to him. "Perhaps if you could undo the hooks for me?"

She heard his indrawn breath before he answered. "Sure. They look tricky. Let's see what I can do."

Yasmin braced herself for his touch. And there it was. He tucked his fingers into the top of her bodice and deftly worked the hooks and eyes apart. His hands were warm—didn't the man ever feel cold? She held the front of her dress against her.

"You're wearing a corset," he said as the back of her dress parted to reveal her undergarments. "Can you manage that on your own?"

Yasmin closed her eyes a moment. Having him undress her was proving to be sheer torture. "Perhaps if you can just undo the first few inches? I can manage the rest."

Ilya didn't answer. Instead, she felt his hands at her back again as he slowly worked his way through the fastenings. Yasmin dragged in a deep breath as the corset loosened and took a step forward.

"Thank you. I'll take it from here."

There was a tightness to her voice she couldn't hide and her heart hammered in her chest like a trapped bird. Curiosity pricked at the back of her mind; she wondered what it would be like if she turned around to face him. If she let her hands drop from where they held her bodice and just waited to see what would happen next. Fire raced along her veins again, licking tiny flames of need into aching life.

"Take your time," Ilya said. "I'll be waiting for you right here."

She felt him step away from her, heard the sound of leather creaking as he settled into one of the easy chairs. Yasmin forced herself to walk steadily to the bedroom. Once inside she closed the door behind her and released the breath she hadn't realized she was holding. She shook with reaction, fine tremors rippling through her body. If he hadn't withdrawn from her, she would have done it—she would have turned around.

She'd never been that kind of girl. Never one who followed her impulses. All her life she'd been focused and hardworking. She knew the consequences of not completing things to her best ability—knew, also, the rewards that came with achievement. So what had come over her that she was prepared to put all that aside and virtually throw herself at the stranger who waited on the other side of the door? The stranger who was her husband, she reminded herself. Did that make it right? She doubted it.

Yasmin let the gown fall to the carpet in a whoosh of expensive fabric, the hand-sewn crystals on her bodice winking at her reproachfully as she stepped out of the gown and toward the bed. Her hands worked feverishly on the final hooks securing her corset as she kicked off her slippers. When she was finally free of the garment, she let it drop to the floor, too. She rushed into the bathroom and turned on the shower, then shimmied out of her stockings and lace underpants.

Warm water coursed over her, flattening her short-cropped hair to her skull and washing her body free of the tension that gripped her. She wasn't that blushing bride who'd so intently embarked on this morning's adventure. That person had been a dreamer, not the doer Yasmin had always prided herself on being. And the man waiting for her outside the bedroom? He was beautiful and appealing and all of the things that made her body react with unseemly eagerness. But he was also the enemy, and she'd do well to remember that.

Ilya began the final approach, relieved to see the helipad next to his house in the hills overlooking the Ojai Valley coming up ahead in the darkness. Yasmin sat next to him in the cockpit—silent, watching, stifling a yawn every now and then. He knew how she felt. The day had been exhausting, but they were nearly home.

They'd barely spoken since leaving the hotel. She'd taken longer than he expected to pack, and the woman who'd eventually emerged from the bedroom, dressed in long, dark pants, a cream linen blouse and battered leather flying jacket and wearing no makeup, had been a far cry from the bride he'd begun to undress.

His hand clenched on the controls, his fingers tingling as he remembered what it had felt like to undress her—how soft her skin was, how enticing her scent as they'd stood so close. It had taken every ounce of his considerable control not to lower his mouth to the curve of her neck where it flared into the feminine line of her shoulder. But he hadn't wanted to frighten her. If this marriage of theirs was going to work, he'd take it as slowly as she needed. He had a feeling it would be more than worth it.

He wondered what had brought her to Match Made in Marriage and made a mental note to check with his grandmother. Or maybe he should ask his wife. From now on, in all things she should be his first port of call, shouldn't she? In all things but their businesses.

Following the directions of the staff member marshalling him from the ground, he landed the chopper on the helipad.

"Welcome home, Mr. and Mrs. Horvath," Pete Wood, head of his air crew, said as he came forward to open the chopper door on Yasmin's side. "Watch your head, Mrs. Horvath."

"Call me Yasmin, please," Ilya heard his wife say tightly as she unlatched her harness, took off her headset and stepped down from the chopper.

He fought back a small smile. It gave him a surprising sense of pride to hear her called Mrs. Horvath. His wife. It sent a pulse of something powerful through him. As though he was a part of something new and exciting and uncharted. And in many ways, he was. He'd never been married before—hadn't even lived with a woman—which made the rest of his life with Yasmin pan out ahead of him as very much the great unknown.

How hard could it be? he reassured himself as he completed his shutdown procedures and then removed their suitcases from the rear of the chopper.

"Thanks for coming to marshal us in, Pete."

"No problem, sir. Congratulations on your marriage, both of you," Pete said with a beaming smile in Yasmin's direction.

She ducked her head shyly and a slight smile curved her lips. Ilya had noted that reticence around his family, too, and wondered if it had been just them. It looked as though she was like that with everyone—everyone connected with him, at least.

"Can I take your bags for you, Mr. Horvath?"

"No, it's okay, Pete. You head on home now."

Pete tipped his cap to Ilya. "Call me if you need me."

Ilya gave him a smile. "I'm officially on honeymoon. Hopefully I won't need to call you again until I'm back at work in two weeks' time."

"Sure thing, boss. Happy honeymooning."

Ilya walked over to Yasmin, who stood on the outer perimeter of the helipad. Behind him he heard Pete start the helicopter back up.

"If you don't want to be blown about, we'd better start walking toward the house. We'll take that path there," he suggested, nodding toward a path off to one side lined with garden lights.

"Are we stranded here?" Yasmin said, her eyes not straying from the helicopter.

"Does that bother you?"

"Should it?"

Ilya laughed. "No, it shouldn't, and no, we're not stranded." He gestured to the multicar garage off to the side of the house they were now approaching through the garden. "You can take your pick of vehicles in there should you feel the need to flee."

"Flee?" She arched a finely shaped brow as she looked at him. "What makes you think I'd want to?"

"Oh, perhaps the way you're twisting the strap of your bag."

She looked down at her hands. "I'm just nervous. Like I said before, I've never done this."

"Nor have I," Ilya assured her swiftly. "So let's agree to remain open with each other about how we're feeling, okay? Let me know, so I can relieve your nerves. Well, here we are."

Ilya approached the portico of his home. He'd fallen in love with the Mediterranean-style property nestled on forty acres of land the moment he'd seen it. It was a half-hour drive from the airport and Horvath Aviation—less time, of course, if he took a chopper—and now he'd get to share it with Yasmin. He set the suitcases down and pressed a finger on the reader at the front door before pushing the double doors open to reveal the entrance.

"Welcome to our home, Yasmin."

She started to move forward but he stopped her with a hand on her shoulder. "Allow me," he said and stepped closer to swing her up into his arms.

She stifled a squeak of surprise and hooked her arms around his neck as he crossed the threshold. She felt ridiculously light in his arms, but the press of her body against his had all the impact of a jumbo jet blast when it came to his senses. One hand curved around her ribcage, just beneath her breasts. Oh, yes, for all her slenderness she had curves, all right. What would she do if he followed tradition even further and kissed her again?

The brief peck on her lips after their ceremony had been both a tease and a torment for him. The second he'd felt her lips beneath his he knew he wanted to explore her further, but with a room full of family and friends looking on, he'd been forced to acknowledge there was a limit to what was acceptable in public. Even now that they were alone, her obvious apprehension about the day meant he would have to take things slowly, he reminded himself, as he set her back down on her feet again.

But then she shifted and leaned closer to him. His arms closed around her, pulling her against him, and he lowered his mouth to hers.

He felt a shock ricochet through him as her lips parted beneath his. She might be slight, but oh boy, did she pack a punch when it came to kissing. For a moment all Ilya could think of was the sweet taste of her, the softness of her lips, the texture of her tongue as it swept against his. He deepened the kiss, taking his time to relish the moment, to relish her. If this was a sign of things to come, they had a great deal to look forward to. She made his head swim with need, or maybe it was the blood heading to other parts of his body that made him so lightheaded.

He drew her lower lip between his teeth, sucking on it gently before tracing its fullness with his tongue. He wanted to do that all over her body. From her gorgeous, beautiful mouth to her breasts and lower. Just thinking about following his instincts left him aching with need—to pick her up again, take her upstairs to his bedroom and show her exactly how good their marriage could be.

But he felt her hesitation, that infinitesimal withdrawal. With the greatest reluctance he pressed one final kiss against her lips then let her go, steadying her on her feet as he did so. Yasmin's eyes were bright and her cheeks flushed.

Ilya walked to the entrance and picked up their suitcases, bringing them inside and closing the large wooden front doors behind him.

"Do you want the full tour now?" he asked. "Or would you rather wait until the morning?"

He watched her as she looked around the entrance and past it to the formal dining area and living room before turning back to face him again.

"I didn't expect your place to be so big," she said. "All this for just one person?"

"Well, when I bought it a couple of years ago I kind of had a vision of filling it with a family." He still had that vision and it grew sharper and clearer with every moment he spent in her company, even if it might be too soon to be thinking along those lines just yet. "How about you? Have you always wanted kids?"

"Yes," she answered emphatically. "Like you, I grew up an only child, but I didn't have cousins to fulfill a pseudo-sibling role as I understand yours did. I always swore that if I ever had children I would have more than one. I guess that's one of the reasons we were paired."

He breathed an inward sigh of relief. Some of his relationships had failed in the past because the women weren't at all interested in starting a family. It was vitally important to him that Yasmin be on the same page.

"So, the house—do you want to see more now? Maybe pick out a nursery?" he teased.

"It's probably a little too early for that," Yasmin answered with a chuckle. She stifled another yawn. "I'm sorry. Perhaps we can wait on the tour until morning."

"Sounds good. I'll show you your room. Follow me."

He led her up the stairs and a short way along a landing. He stopped outside the door to a guest bedroom and opened it. He gestured for her to precede him in and set her suitcase down on the blanket box at the foot of the large sleigh bed.

"You should be comfortable here. There's an en suite bathroom and my housekeeper will have stocked everything you need in terms of toiletries."

"We're...um...we're not sharing a room?"

"Not yet. Unless you'd like to?"

"I..." Yasmin's voice trailed off again.

"It's okay. I think you'd probably prefer that we get to know each other a little better before we take that step."

The words tripped glibly off his tongue, but inside his body protested strongly. He'd like nothing better than to whisk her down the hall to the master suite, lay her gently on his massive bed and show her exactly how well he wanted to get to know her. But the relief that spread across her face was about as effective as a cold shower.

"Thank you, I appreciate it."

"That doesn't mean I can't wish you a good-night, though. Sweet dreams."

Before she could say another word, he bent to kiss her gently, sweetly on her lips. He felt her lean toward him, but this time, rather than lose himself in the caress, he forced himself to keep it brief—to pull away and to leave them both wanting more. If he had to go to bed in a state of torment, then so could she. It was only fair.

He hesitated in her doorway on his way out. "My room is just down the hall if you change your mind."

And with that parting comment he left her alone.

Four

It took Yasmin longer to get to sleep than she'd expected, considering how exhausted she'd been when Ilya had left her. But weariness aside, his kisses had fired up her imagination and as she lay between the cool crisp sheets of her lonely bed she couldn't help wondering what her wedding night could have been like if she'd just been brave enough to reach for him after that sweet goodnight and beg him to show her more.

She had no doubt he would be a consummate lover. From what she could tell, the man was incredibly accomplished in all that he did. And now she was married to him. She had the rest of her life to discover just how skilled he was. If they went the distance.

The next morning she rose and went downstairs, following the sound of a blender to a large kitchen. Ilya stood at the granite kitchen counter, oblivious to her entry. She took a moment to watch him—to appreciate the way his Henley hugged the muscles of his shoulders and skimmed his pecs. A decrepit pair of jeans hugged his hips and she felt that all too familiar tingle through her body as she noticed how the denim had faded in certain areas. The blender stopped and Ilya looked up, a smile creasing his face as he saw her hovering in the doorway.

"Good morning," he said. "I hope you slept well."

"Thank you. I did, eventually."

Yasmin perched on one of the bar stools that lined the counter and watched as he poured two smoothies into tall glasses. Ilya pushed one toward her.

"I figured if we were so perfectly matched, you'd prob-ably like one of these for breakfast," he said with a crooked grin. "But if you'd prefer bacon and eggs, I can do that, too."

"No, this is fine. I don't usually have breakfast anyway."

"Well, you'll need the energy for what I've got planned this morning."

"Oh?" She looked up at him, raising one brow.

"I love the way you do that," he said, reaching out and stroking her brow with a fingertip.

The sensation of his skin against hers made her hand tremble and she set her glass down on the counter with a sharp click. Ilya laughed and turned his attention to his smoothie, downing most of it in one gulp.

"And what is it you have planned for the morning?" Yasmin asked, picking up her glass again and taking a sip. "Oh, that's good," she exclaimed in surprise. "What did you put in it?"

"First question first. We're going for a hike. Have you got hiking boots or something suitable in your suitcase? If not, we can do something else. As to the smoothie, that's a closely guarded secret," he said with a sly wink. "One day I might let you in on it."

She chuckled. "Well, in the meantime I shall just ap-preciate your culinary expertise. And, as to shoes, I have something suitable for a hike. What time do you want to head out?"

"Probably in half an hour or so. Think you can be ready by then?"

"I was born ready," she answered, finishing off her smoothie and hopping down from her seat.

"Good to know," Ilya responded.

His voice was deep and reverberated through her in a way that sent her senses scrambling. She had the distinct feeling they were speaking along completely different lines. Yasmin took her glass over to the sink and rinsed it out. It was easier to fake being busy with something than it was to acknowledge exactly what kind of an effect her new husband had on her.

"This is a nice kitchen," she said, striving for more neutral conversational territory. "Did you have it installed or did it come like this when you bought the house?"

"I bought the house pretty much as you see it," he said. "With the exception of the furnishings and art. Why don't I show you the rest before we head out?"

She nodded and followed him as he led the way out of the kitchen and through to a casual sitting area. A massive television dominated most of one wall.

"Wow," she exclaimed. "All you need is a cooler in the side of your chair and you'll be living every man's dream, won't you?"

"Hey, when I watch the air races I want to feel like I'm in them, not just a spectator."

"I understand. Although nothing quite beats the real thing."

"Speaking of which, are you going to take me up in your Ryan anytime soon?"

"I heard you don't like being a passenger—that you prefer to hold on to the controls yourself."

She said the words lightly, but she understood them

on her own level. She'd spent years side by side with her grandfather restoring the Ryan to flying condition and had worked really hard to earn her rating to fly it. No one took that plane up but her.

"Where did you hear that?" Ilya asked, his brows drawing into a straight line.

"Oh, it's pretty common knowledge around the airport. You know how people talk."

"What else do they say about me?" Ilya asked, moving closer to her.

She could feel the heat that emanated from his body. It was like a magnet, drawing her closer. She nearly always felt cold, but with him around, she doubted she'd ever need an extra layer again.

"Oh, that you're a hard worker and a reasonable boss."

"That's it?"

"Hey, you wouldn't tell me what was in the smoothie, so I'm not sharing all my secrets. A girl's got to hold something back, right?"

He laughed again and Yasmin felt her lips kick up in an answering smile.

"So I'm an overbearing pilot, a hard worker and a *reasonable* boss."

Her grin widened at the chagrin with which he said the word *reasonable*. "I never said overbearing. But if the shoe fits…?"

He reached out to catch her shoulders with his hands. Heat seared through her top and penetrated her skin. Her heart rate kicked up a notch. Was he going to kiss her again? Part of her hoped he would, while the other… The other part wasn't ready to face the tumult of sensation he set off in her. It was a weakness she needed to learn to shore up, and swiftly, if they were to remain on an even playing field when it came to this marriage. She had too much to lose otherwise.

To a lot of people, marrying sight unseen just to save her business was an extreme measure. Heck, even to her it was extreme. But to win the Hardacre contract, she had to be married. It was as simple as that. It was frustrating that, in this day and age, her business was held hostage by Wallace Hardacre's wandering eye and his wife's jealousy. But if getting married meant she'd win the five-year exclusive contract ensuring her company had the income stream to not only keep it afloat but eventually allow it to expand and create more jobs, she was prepared to do it.

All she'd had to do then was find a husband. Fast. She'd just never expected that husband to be Ilya Horvath.

Ilya snapped his fingers, dragging her out of her reverie.

"Earth to Yasmin. I feel like I lost you there for a moment."

She forced a smile. "Sorry, just thinking about my grandfather," she fibbed.

"I never met him but I heard he was a wizard mechanic. Not an aircraft engine he couldn't fix, right?"

She nodded. "Yeah. He was always better at mechanics than people."

"Was it hard growing up with him?"

"Yes and no. Obviously I missed my mom and dad. They'd cruise by when they were in the area, still do occasionally. But Granddad gave me stability, which I didn't have with them. And he taught me the value of silence."

"Is that a hint?"

"Oh, heavens, no. Not at all. It's just some people seem to need to fill a silence with noise, rather than simply letting the silence fill them for a change."

Ilya nodded. "I think I know a few people like that. Come on, let me show you the rest of the place, then we can head out in the hills."

* * *

She was fit and strong, Ilya thought appreciatively as they reached the crest of the hill that would afford them the best view across the valley. And she didn't complain, either.

"That was quite a climb," Yasmin said, as she stopped and put her hands on her hips.

Her breathing was only slightly labored and she'd barely broken a sweat even though the temperatures had begun to climb into the seventies very soon after they'd started hiking.

"It's worth it for the view," Ilya commented as he came to stand beside her.

And he wasn't just talking about the stunning Ojai Valley vistas, either. The woman standing next to him was a picture of perfection. She glowed with natural good health and vitality, a far cry from the kinds of women who moved in his circles. At the back of his mind he couldn't help but feel there was something familiar about her, too. But of course there had to be, he told himself as he turned his gaze from her to the valley that spread before them. They worked at the same airport. They'd both been fed stories of how their families had been friends then feuding rivals. They knew of each other, even if they didn't actually know each other. Even so, the little niggle persisted that he knew her from somewhere else.

"You were so lucky last year's fires missed your home," Yasmin said, looking around at the flora fighting to regenerate on the hills around them.

"I was luckier than a lot of people."

"Your property looks like an oasis from up here," she commented.

"It certainly feels like it after a hard day in the office."

He heard her breath hitch. "We agreed not to talk about work, remember?"

"Right. My mistake."

He clenched his jaw. It had only felt natural to mention work. After all, it had taken up more than half of every day of his adult life. It was going to be harder than he thought to compartmentalize things, to exclude her from what was essentially the core of his world. But then again, he reminded himself, in time she would become the core of his world—wouldn't she?

A tiny animal sound came from somewhere behind them.

"Did you hear that?" Yasmin asked, looking around.

"Yeah. There it is again."

Ilya walked cautiously toward the source of the noise, wary in case the animal was unfriendly. Yasmin showed no such care. She pushed past him into the undergrowth.

"Oh look, it's a puppy. The poor baby."

She scooped the mess of dirt and multicolored fur up into her arms and cradled it to her. The puppy whimpered.

"Is he hurt?" Ilya asked, stepping forward.

It maddened him that people could be so cruel as to abandon their animals, and this one looked very definitely abandoned. The puppy bore a narrow blue collar, which hinted that at some stage it had had an owner who cared enough to buy it one. There was a road that passed not too far from this point. It had probably been dumped along there. Possibly even thrown from a passing car if the grazes on his paw pads were anything to go by.

"Not too badly, I think. But he'll be thirsty, poor baby. I wonder how long he's been up here."

Ilya poured some of the water from his bottle into the palm of his hand and offered it to the puppy. The animal weakly lapped it up. The little guy was probably dehydrated. Ilya kept adding a little trickle of water until the puppy stopped drinking.

"What are we going to do with him?" Yasmin asked, stroking the puppy's grubby head.

"I guess we'll take him to the vet to be checked out and maybe see if he was stolen before he was dumped. There might be someone missing him. If he was stolen we'll know more."

"And if he wasn't?"

She looked at him with such an expression of yearning in her eyes that it made him wish he could grant her every wish.

"Then we'll keep him."

"I've never had a dog," she admitted, pressing a kiss to the top of the puppy's head and earning a sloppy kiss in return. "But I've always wanted one."

"First, let's get him to the vet."

Ilya put out his hands to take the puppy from her. The animal really was a sad little bag of bones and hair. Ilya only hoped that it didn't have any underlying problems. He could see that Yasmin had already lost her heart to the little guy. He didn't want to see it broken if the puppy had to be euthanized. It didn't matter how much money it took, he decided. They'd be bringing this little one back home.

Five

When Yasmin and Ilya returned from the vet, they were both covered in grime from the puppy. They'd left him for a thorough checkup and to be rehydrated. The animal wasn't microchipped and didn't appear on any lost pet registers so it didn't look like he could be returned to his owners. Not that they deserved him if they had been the people who dumped him in the first place, Yasmin thought with a surge of anger.

She'd been pleasantly surprised by Ilya's reaction, though. She'd seen a side of him she hadn't known existed before today. Everything she'd ever heard about him in the past had pointed to his being an overentitled, calculating person. Not someone who could show so much compassion to an abandoned animal. And certainly not someone she would ever have seen herself married to, let alone potentially happily married to. She didn't want to admit she could be wrong about him—after all, once she made up her mind, she didn't usually waver. But she needed to form her own opinions of the man she'd married, and so far he was shaping up to be very interesting, indeed.

"I don't know about you, but I feel like I could do with another shower," Ilya said, closing the front door behind him. "But before we do that, let's get you into the biometric security database so you can come and go as you please."

He invited her to the keypad and pressed a few buttons before asking her to put her finger on the sensor.

"There, that's all done."

"And in a power outage?"

"Battery backup."

"And if that fails?"

"Generator."

She pursed her lips. "Do you always think of everything?"

"Contingency plans are my thing."

"Is there a particular reason for that?"

"I don't like being caught unprepared. It happened once in my life and I swore to always be primed for whatever could happen next from then on."

"Sounds serious."

"It was."

Yasmin looked at Ilya—saw the shadows that passed through his eyes.

"Do you want to talk about it?" she prompted gently.

"Not really, but you deserve to hear it from me rather than secondhand from anyone else. In fact, I'm surprised you don't already know."

"About what?"

"The day my father died." Ilya sighed and rubbed his fingers over his beard. "I was sixteen and he was giving me a flying lesson. He just died. Right there next to me. His head dropped forward, he stopped breathing and his heart stopped beating. Just like that. One minute we were talking, the next he was gone. I couldn't do a single damn thing to help him. Even if I'd known CPR, it wasn't like I could start it right there in the cockpit. I had to land as quickly as possible to give him a chance, so I radioed for help and they talked me down."

"Oh, no. That must have been terrifying for you."

"I'd done a couple of landings before, so while it wasn't the best of landings, we got down safely. But it was too late for my dad. They said he suffered catastrophic heart failure and there was nothing that I could have done."

Silence fell between them and Ilya shook his head.

"Anyway, that was nearly twenty years ago. It's well and truly in the past and it's part of the reason why I like to be prepared for any eventuality now."

"I'm really sorry about your dad, Ilya."

He looked at her, his intense blue eyes piercing her as if he could see through all her shields to the genuine compassion she felt for his loss.

"Thank you." He gave her a bittersweet smile. "You know, most people, when they hear what happened, focus on the flying and on how I got the plane down. Very few actually remember I lost my father that day."

Yasmin tried to ignore the tug in her chest. "Well, I don't think anyone could ever accuse me of being like most people."

"You're not at all like I expected."

"That makes us even, then," she answered as lightly as she could. Before he could reply, she started up the stairs. "I'm going for that shower you suggested."

She felt his eyes boring into her back, as if he was reassessing her in some way. It made her wonder exactly what he had expected when he realized she was to be his bride.

In her room, Yasmin gathered up some clean clothes and went into the bathroom. His housekeeper had been in already and changed the towels. The woman had to be a ghost because Yasmin hadn't met her yet, but she could certainly tell where she'd been. She put her things on the vanity and reached to turn on the shower. Her wedding ring caught the light and the diamonds sparkled brightly.

Unused to wearing jewelry, Yasmin was surprised at how quickly she'd become accustomed to the ring. It wasn't something she would have picked for herself but she certainly wasn't averse to wearing it. The design was very low profile, so it wouldn't catch on anything, and the baguette and round diamonds that crested the top of the platinum setting appealed to her hidden sense of whimsy.

She quickly disrobed and stepped into the shower, rinsing away the perspiration of the morning and the grime she'd picked up from the puppy. She wondered how he was doing. The poor thing had been so very listless but the vet, apparently another of Ilya's cousins, had been reassuring and said she expected him to make a full recovery in a few days' time.

Yasmin lathered up some soap and stroked it over her body, remembering just how gently Ilya had held the pup when he'd taken it from her on the walk back to the house. His hands fascinated her. Broad but with long tapered fingers, they contained such strength and capability. What would it feel like when he touched her intimately? she wondered.

Her pulse kicked up a beat and her insides tautened on a swell of desire. Only time would tell—if they lasted that long—she told herself as she switched the spray to a cooler setting and rinsed off quickly before drying and dressing herself again. There was still the incompatibility clause to contend with, although based on this morning's adventure, they seemed to be getting along okay.

But one morning did not a marriage make, she reminded herself firmly. She grabbed her cell phone from her bedside table and quickly checked her email, flicking through the congratulatory messages from her colleagues at Carter

Air. There was one there from someone she didn't know. *Strange*, she thought as her finger hovered over the message, debating whether to open it or send it to spam. Curiosity got the better of her and she opened the unread message.

You had no right to marry him.

A sick feeling lodged in Yasmin's throat. Sheer instinct made her press Delete but then she went into the trash file to find out who had sent it. The sender's address was linked to a widely used email provider and there was nothing in the moniker attached to it, *hisgirl*, that rang any bells. Yasmin hit Delete again, removing the message from her email server completely. It was just some sicko with nothing better to do, she told herself as she returned downstairs and put the correspondence to the back of her mind.

She found Ilya out in the loggia by the pool. Grapevines, laden with bunches of plump fruit, grew over wooden rafters that sheltered the area. He rose from a chair as she approached.

"I just made a call to Danni. She tells me the puppy is on a drip with dextrose and he's already starting to look more alert."

"Oh, that's great news. Thanks for checking up on him."

"No problem. I thought you'd want to know. Danni said she'll give me an update this evening. By tomorrow she thinks he might be able to take a bit of food."

"And then can we have him?"

"That'll be up to her."

"Of course," Yasmin was quick to agree. "He's getting the best care possible, which is just as it should be."

"I'm surprised you never had a pet as a kid. You seem very invested in this one."

"Granddad wasn't keen on animals. Just another mouth to feed, he always said."

* * *

Ilya looked at her in surprise. Was that how old man Carter had thought about his granddaughter, too? When her parents had left her with him, had she just been another mouth to feed, or had he genuinely loved her?

"Speaking of feeding, Hannah has made us some lunch."

"Hannah? Is that your housekeeper?"

"Yes, she thought she'd remain scarce while we're still on honeymoon."

"She needn't stay away on my account."

Ilya laughed. "Sick of me already?"

"That's not what I meant," Yasmin protested.

"Just teasing you. You're going to have to get used to that."

"I'm not used to teasing, period. Anyway, I reiterate, she doesn't have to skulk around avoiding us."

"When you get to meet her, you'll know that Hannah never skulks," he said on a chuckle. "She just thought we'd benefit from time to get to know each other. She'll pop in every few days, freshen up our supplies and do a bit of housework."

"I can do housework. I don't expect to be waited on."

"Not even by your husband?"

To his surprise, Yasmin's cheeks grew flushed.

"Not by anyone," she said firmly.

"That's a shame, but you're going to have to get used to it because I've been appointed your waiter for this afternoon. Take a seat and I'll go get lunch."

"I can help."

He walked around behind her and put his hands on her shoulders, guided her to a chair facing the pool and gently pressed her into it.

"I've got this. Just relax."

Yasmin choked out a laugh. It had a slightly bitter ring to it. "I'm not used to relaxing. I'm more used to working."

"Everyone needs a break," he said lightly. He wasn't going to be the one to point out that she'd brought up work this time. He hated that they had to walk on eggshells around the topic. The longer he thought about it, the crazier it seemed. But then again, they were business rivals, which was going to make this a very interesting marriage all around.

He removed the lightly grilled salmon from the oven, divided it into two equal pieces and plated it. He set the plates on a large tray, then added a bowl of salad together with a small jug of lemon-caper sauce for the salmon before taking it all outside.

"That looks good," Yasmin commented with a great deal of interest as he approached.

"Trust me, Hannah is an incredible cook. I'd be half the man I am today without her," he answered with a smile. "How about you serve up our salad and I'll go get us drinks."

He went back to the kitchen and grabbed the ice bucket, together with two glasses and a particularly good German Riesling he'd been saving for a special occasion. Returning to the table he pulled the cork and poured two measures of wine. He gave one glass to Yasmin then held his up in a toast.

"To us," he said simply.

She hesitated a moment, her eyes not quite meeting his, but then she seemed to come to a decision and she clinked her glass against his. "Yes, to us."

For some reason her response made him relax. He hadn't even realized he'd been on tenterhooks until he'd waited those extra few seconds. He took a sip of the wine. It shouldn't matter so much already, but he wanted to be fully invested in this marriage. He had told his grandmother he was ready for it, ready to commit to one person for the rest of his life, and according to her she'd found him

The One. He was the kind of guy who, once committed, gave it his everything. Was Yasmin ready for that? Ready for him? Maybe if he understood her reasons for entering into their match he could be sure they were completely on the same page, but until then he knew he'd be holding a piece of himself back.

He'd been hurt. He'd believed his ex-fiancée had loved him the same way he'd loved her. That she'd wanted the same things. But in the end it had turned out that she was a fake, and not only a fake but a cruel one into the bargain. He didn't want to make that same mistake again. It had made him wary of relationships, of trusting anyone outside of the tight-knit circle of his family.

Could he trust Yasmin?

Six

Yasmin continued to swim against the tide of the pressure jets in the pool. Her arms and shoulders were beginning to burn but she had to rid herself of the frustration and tension that had become her companion over these past few days.

There'd been another email since the one a few days ago. Again, she'd been tempted to delete it unread. Again, she'd opened it. The message had been succinct.

Leave him!

Yasmin had the strong feeling that *or else* was implied. She wondered who the heck *hisgirl* was. Clearly someone who thought they had a prior claim on Ilya. Well, that someone could take a long walk off a short pier. Which made Yasmin realize she felt oddly proprietary about her husband of only a few days.

Yesterday, they'd visited the puppy at the vet's, and he was coming along quite literally in leaps and bounds. His stomach was taking a while to adjust to solid food again so Danni was taking an extra day or two just to ensure he was one hundred percent before releasing him. Ilya and Yasmin would initially foster him, then hopefully become his full-fledged owners if no one came forward to claim him soon.

Watching Ilya with the puppy really tugged at her heart-strings. This big man who had such a powerful reputation in the aviation world was an absolute pushover when it came to the puppy. It seemed as if Ilya wore a different face for each different situation he found himself in, which made her wonder about the face he showed her.

He'd been solicitous toward her, but since the night of their wedding he'd made no further move to touch her or kiss her again, and quite frankly, it was driving her crazy. Her nights had been peppered with dreams of the two of them, limbs entwined, lips fused in passion—and unful-filled demands had woken her every morning, leaving her seething with frustrated need.

She'd had sex before. Quite liked it on occasion. But she'd never missed it when she hadn't been in a relation-ship with someone, partly because she could always throw herself into her work. And she'd certainly never suffered from this level of torment before. Nor had she ever found herself sizing someone up—in this case, her husband—and wondering about how the play of his muscles would feel beneath her fingertips or her tongue. Or wondering at the shape of his butt as he bent to remove some plate of deli-ciousness from the oven for their evening meal together.

Hence the swimming. Between that blasted email and her unrequited sexual needs she had to find release some-where. She didn't want to spend all her time mooning over her husband's all-too-few masterful kisses or the shape of his body. Well, maybe she did, but it wasn't going to help her any, was it?

Her muscles screaming, she did a flip turn, slowly swam to the opposite end of the pool and hauled herself up onto the edge.

"I was beginning to think you'd developed fins and gills," Ilya said from above her.

She lifted her head and looked up. Her mouth dried instantly. He was wearing a pair of swim shorts that exposed his long, tanned legs, and above the waistband all she could see was an expanse of skin and muscle.

"Gotta get my exercise somehow," she muttered, accepting a towel from him and averting her gaze as she dried off.

"Our daily hikes not enough for you? Maybe I need to set a more challenging pace," he teased.

He sat down beside her on the edge of the pool and dangled his legs in the water. Her skin was cool from being in the water for so long and she could feel the heat coming off him in waves. How was it that he was literally so hot? It was like his internal thermostat was constantly set on high. Her one-piece suit clung to her body like a second skin and she felt her nipples tighten against the wet fabric.

"It's okay," she said. "I enjoy the walks."

"Me, too. You're good company."

"Just as well, huh? It would make life difficult if we didn't get along."

Ilya propped himself up on his arms and turned his face to the sun. With the light streaming over his body, he looked like a gilded warrior god of ancient times. Yasmin felt that all-too-familiar tug through her body, that clench deep in her core.

"I've been meaning to ask you something," he started and straightened to look her in the eye.

Yasmin felt a frisson of wariness. "And that is?"

"Why did you apply to Match Made in Marriage? After all, you're a good-looking woman who runs her own business. I haven't seen any evidence of unusual traits or habits that would be majorly off-putting to anyone."

"Majorly? Oh, so you think I have some minor off-putting traits?" she asked on a laugh.

"You know what I mean. Getting to know you is interesting. Like, I never realized you were such a nerd at school."

"I never told you I was a nerd."

"No, but this morning while we were on the trails you did tell me about winning the science prize and the math expo and—"

"Okay, so I was a nerd."

"And you're very good at dodging a direct question."

She was about to protest when she realized that was exactly what she had done. She looked down to the end of the pool.

"I should turn the jets off."

"And there you go again. It's okay. They can stay on for now."

"Fine. In answer to your first question, I went to Match Made in Marriage because I didn't trust myself to find the right guy for me."

That was partially true, at least. Her own track record with men was not the best. It didn't help that she'd never really considered what she wanted out of a relationship. That, combined with her reluctance to allow people to get close to her and really share her life, tended to send her beaus away in frustration. People didn't like being shut out all the time. And she'd thought Match Made in Marriage would be safe, especially with its out clause if they turned out to be incompatible. Of course, if she'd known Alice Horvath was behind the matches she probably wouldn't have approached them at all.

"How about you?" she asked.

"I guess my reason was similar. I trusted Nagy to find the right woman for me."

"I heard you guys call her that. What is it? Russian?"

"No, Hungarian. My great-grandfather was a scientist and lecturer. Prior to the outbreak of World War II he began to grow uneasy about what was happening across Europe. He decided to move his family out of Hungary and to the States. Even though she was mostly raised here in California, my grandmother still clings very much to the old ways. More so as she grows older, I guess."

He fell silent for a bit then spoke again. "Do you think Nagy got it right, pairing us?"

"It's early days, but we're not an abject failure yet, are we?"

"No. So, why now? What made you decide this was the time you wanted to get married?"

Boy, he was like a dog with a bone on the subject, wasn't he? Yasmin raked her mind for a suitable response. There was no way she'd tell him that she had to marry now because of the Hardacre contract. Had Horvath Aviation pitched for the same business? How would Ilya feel when she won it out from under him? she wondered. Especially if he knew he'd handed it to her on a platter by marrying her. *You haven't got the contract yet*, she reminded herself.

In answer to his question, she shrugged. "What can I say? I'm thirty-two years old. Yes, I know that's still young but, like most people, I want a family and stability. Now felt like the right time."

She paused before she inadvertently let too much out. Her current stability hinged on the Hardacre contract but she couldn't let Ilya get a whiff of that information. She let out a breath before continuing, knowing she'd have to dig deep into a part of her she kept hidden, even from herself, if she was to satisfy Ilya's curiosity.

"I didn't have the most traditional of upbringings. I knew I had someone who loved me, even if Granddad wasn't the best at showing it. But I have to admit to having had some envy for the other kids at school. The ones whose parents came to sports days or helped in class. Some of the kids used to complain about it, that their parents were always right there. They had no idea how lucky they were. It just seemed so *normal*, y'know?"

"And being brought up by your grandfather made you different among your peers, didn't it? That and the fact you were such a nerd." He smiled and leaned over to bump shoulders with her, taking any imagined sting out of his words. "I get it. I never thought about things that way. I mean, my parents didn't show up at everything but they put in an appearance when it mattered enough to me to ask them to. Until my dad died, anyway."

Yasmin drew her knees up to her chest and wrapped her arms around them. "Granddad was always sparing with his approval, but it didn't stop me working hard to earn it. In its own way, that set me up for life. You can't always expect sunshine and lollipops, right? You need to learn to roll with disappointment and get up and just keep going."

Ilya listened to Yasmin and felt a pang of sympathy for the child she must have been growing up. He knew Jim Carter had been a cantankerous old bastard, but not to show encouragement to a little girl trying to find her place in his life? That was downright mean. Ilya's children would never doubt that he was behind them in whatever they chose to do. And, yes, while it was his dream that they would follow him into Horvath Aviation, as he had done with his father and he with his father before him, Ilya certainly wouldn't force them to do it. Encourage them, maybe, but force them? No.

"What about you, Ilya? What made you use your grand-mother's service? I could use the same argument you did. It's not as if you're all that ugly or anything."

He could recognize deflection along with the best of them. Yasmin was obviously uncomfortable being the topic of discussion. If he was going to earn her trust and get down to the layers that really made up the woman, he was going to have to give a little of himself, too. He swallowed. Opening up to someone who was essentially a stranger, even though the license said they were married, didn't come easily. Growing up a Horvath had taught him to be careful around people, especially those who thought he was an easy meal ticket because of his family's wealth. The one time he'd let his guard down... No, he didn't want to waste this beautiful day thinking about past mistakes.

"Thanks for the compliment," he responded lightly. "I guess my reasons are the same as yours. I'm thirty-five. Again, not old, but I'm ready for the next stage of my life. I'm ready to be part of a partnership and all that brings—including children. Family is really important to me." He barked a humorless laugh. "*Everything* to me, to be completely honest with you. I just want the chance to do it right the first time. And people can be so fake. The lines are so blurred now it's hard to tell who's being real and who isn't."

Yasmin's face was set in serious lines and she looked as if she was about to say something, but she was distracted by a notification tone from her cell phone sitting on a nearby chair.

"Will you excuse me? I'm expecting this."

"Sure."

Ilya slid forward on the pool edge and allowed himself to slip into the water. It was a bit of a comedown—having bared a piece of his soul only to be interrupted by an incoming message on her phone. But, he reminded himself, it was early days yet.

He sank down in the water, letting the silky softness of

it close over his head and caress his skin before he popped
back up to the surface. He slicked his hair back off his forehead and looked across at Yasmin, who was standing by
the chair. Nope, the water definitely wasn't cold enough,
he thought as he let his gaze roam from her bare feet and
up her long, slender legs. Even though she wore a modest
one-piece suit, there was no mistaking the lean muscles
of her body. The woman looked after herself, there was
no denying it.

His gaze traveled over the gentle swell of her hips, to
her narrow waist and then upward to where her swimsuit
cupped her breasts. His mouth went dry and he dunked
himself again, feeling just a little disgusted with himself
for staring at her like some horny schoolboy. This time
when he surfaced he realized she was still standing in the
same position but something wasn't right. Yasmin had her
phone in hand and was staring at the screen with a stricken
expression on her face.

"Everything okay?" he asked, pulling himself up onto
the edge of the pool and getting up to check on her.

Yasmin put her phone face down on the table and looked
up at him, swiftly composing her features.

"Why shouldn't it be?"

He noticed she didn't answer his question. "You looked
upset. Is there anything I can do?"

"You can do?" she repeated before shaking her head.
"No, it's nothing. Really."

"It didn't look like nothing. If you want to talk—"

"Really," she emphasized. "There's nothing wrong. Go,
have your swim. I think I'll go upstairs and get changed."

He watched her grab her phone and retreat—there was
no other word for the way she left the pool area. There
had been something on her phone that had bothered her,
he knew it as surely as he knew the maximum fuel uptake
of every aircraft in his fleet. And, like the man who knew

his business inside and out, he wanted to know Yasmin inside and out, too.

Eventually he'd find a way to break through the barriers she had around her. It wouldn't be easy, but something told him that if he persevered, it would be worth it. But first he needed to earn her trust. And that might be the hardest thing of all.

Seven

Yasmin couldn't get to her room fast enough. The moment she was upstairs she secured her door and opened the email. And there it was. There were no words, no subject header. Just that photo.

A shudder ran through her body from the top of her head to the soles of her feet. She'd believed that dreadful night was behind her. That no one had any further cause to hark back to what she'd done. Oh, sure, she had behaved under extreme pressure. And her desperation to be included in the sorority made up of all the cool girls had been the catalyst for what would lead to her greatest shame.

Why would anyone hold on to something like this? And why bring it up now? She'd changed universities; she'd moved back West; she'd severed all ties. In fact, the very thought of coming face-to-face with anyone who had been there that night, egging her on to drink another shot every time she got a question wrong in that stupid quiz they made her and the other pledges take, was unfathomable.

Bile rose in Yasmin's throat as she looked at the photo. She looked just like any other college girl having a good time, but even though she'd already been feeling the effects of the vodka shots, she'd been horribly uncomfortable posing with the sex toy someone had thrust in her face that night. But her desire to win at any cost had seen her outlast her fellow pledges and the challenges had just kept on coming. She'd fulfilled that challenge, and the next one, and the one after that, but by the time they'd made her enter the lake and swim out to the pontoon, blindfolded, she'd also been highly intoxicated. The alcohol in her system, the cold of the water and her sense of disorientation at being blindfolded had combined in a perfect storm that had led to her losing consciousness before she could complete the challenge.

She had no idea who'd rescued her from the water, or who had called the ambulance that had taken her to the hospital where her stomach had been pumped and she'd been rehydrated and treated for hypothermia. She did remember the letter she'd received from the sorority, though. The one saying that, on reflection, they felt she wasn't the caliber of student they were looking to have join them.

It had been hard, going back to class and facing the pitying looks from some of her peers. Worse was the outright laughter from others. These people had seen her at her worst, at her most desperate, her most vulnerable—and she knew she couldn't continue at college in that environment. At the end of the semester she'd transferred back to California and completed her education closer to home. Her grandfather had never questioned her choices; he'd been only too pleased to have her close again. His health had begun to fail, and his reluctance to follow doctor's orders and make simple changes in his lifestyle aggravated existing conditions. And, as soon as she graduated, she'd gone to work with him full-time.

She'd honestly believed that what had happened out East was behind her, but now it appeared it wasn't. Even though it was more common now to report extreme hazing incidents for the cruel bullying they were, back then she'd been so ashamed of her own desperation to be one of the "in" crowd, and what she'd been prepared to do to be accepted, she'd never made a report to the campus authorities or the police. And now it was coming back to bite her.

It seemed obvious that her marriage to Ilya had triggered this, but who was behind the *hisgirl* email address? What did they hope to gain? Worse, what would happen if this photo, and potentially others—because she knew there'd been a lot of people taking pictures of her that night—were shown to anyone else? Anyone, for example, like her new husband, her employees—or the Hardacres? She'd lose all her hard-earned respect from everyone.

Yasmin hadn't responded to any of the emails she'd been sent so far. She hadn't wanted to engage with whoever was behind this, but she had far too much riding on getting that Hardacre contract. She couldn't afford to let anything derail her plans. Her finger hovered over the reply icon on her screen, but she let her phone drop onto her bed. If she didn't answer, maybe they'd give up and leave her alone. And if they didn't? Would she have to bring this to the attention of the police? There was no actual threat in so many words. Could the police even do anything? She hadn't wanted to bring the whole sorry incident to the police all those years ago and she certainly hadn't changed how she felt about that now.

Yes, she was doing the right thing, she told herself as she grabbed a change of clothes and went into her bathroom. Right now, ignoring *hisgirl* had to be the best option. After a quick shower, Yasmin left her phone where she'd tossed it and returned downstairs.

Ilya was stretched out on a sun lounger by the pool.

His body was strong and tanned and healthy with altogether too much flesh on display for her peace of mind. For a second Yasmin wondered what it would have been like to become involved with him outside of the hothouse atmosphere of their arranged marriage. Would they have found compatibility with each other had they met like a regular couple? She mentally shook her head. It was unlikely they'd have interacted at all, except in the most formal manner. Being competition for each other in their field of business, they had everything in common and yet were poles apart at the same time.

And now they were married and had to stay that way until she at least won her contract and saved Carter Air from oblivion. Her gut twisted at the thought of losing her company, but at the same time she hated that it had come to this. That she'd entered into a marriage contract with someone who appeared to be approaching their relationship with every intention of this being a forever thing. And, to be honest, that had been at the back of her mind, too. She hadn't been entirely lying when Ilya had pressed her for her reasons for using Match Made in Marriage, but she certainly hadn't given him the full truth, either.

Being purposely deceitful sat uncomfortably on her shoulders—but, she reminded herself, sometimes you had to walk a fine line.

And if her husband had been anyone other than Ilya...?

She swallowed against the lump that rose in her throat at the thought that right now she could have been on honeymoon with another man. She couldn't fool herself. She doubted very much that another man would appeal to her on the same level Ilya did. He was everything she would have looked for in a husband—if he hadn't been her rival. If their families didn't have that yawning rift between them. If his grandmother hadn't broken her grandfather's heart and made him eventually settle for marriage with a woman he didn't love enough, breaking her heart in the bargain.

But Yasmin was married to Ilya. To the beautiful man right here in front of her. He took off his sunglasses and looked at her now with his sexy, blue eyes in a way that made her feel as though she was wearing nothing at all. He gave her a welcoming smile.

"I was beginning to wonder if you'd decided to take a nap."

"Naps are for old people," Yasmin snorted.

She sat down on the edge of the lounger next to his. The evening sun felt warm through her clothes and on her bare arms and legs.

"Oh, I don't know. Sometimes they're called for. Like those times when you've expended a whole lot of energy and need to restore."

A whole lot of energy? Somehow she didn't think he was talking about their morning hikes in the hills. Her skin prickled.

"I'm going to grab a glass of juice," she said, getting back to her feet. "Can I get you anything?"

"Maybe a beer?"

"I'll be right back."

Yasmin avoided looking at him as she went into the kitchen and got their drinks. But she couldn't erase the image of his near-naked body imprinted on her retinas. Ilya Horvath dressed was hard enough to deal with, but undressed? Her hand shook, making her spill a little of the juice onto the countertop. She cursed under her breath as she reached for a cloth to wipe up the spilled liquid. They didn't even have to be in the same room and she was a mess about him. Something had to give. Maybe she needed to rid herself of the itch that crept under her skin on a daily basis. Maybe she needed to take him up on that offer to share his room when she was ready.

Was she ready? Could she take that step? While it would no doubt assuage some of the perpetual hunger for him that simmered through her body, would it provide relief or would it do more harm than good? Would it cement this orchestrated relationship they had, or would it just make things a whole lot more complicated?

There's only one way to find out, nagged that pesky voice at the back of her mind.

She ignored it and snatched up their drinks, taking them back out to the patio. She put Ilya's beer on the small side table next to his chair, careful to avoid accidentally touching him. Right now she felt so tense with anticipation that she worried what a single touch from him might do.

"Thanks," he said, reaching across for the drink and taking a long pull. "Ah, that's great. Nothing like a cold beer on a hot evening when you've got nothing else to do."

Yasmin sipped her juice, relishing the cold sweetness but wondering if she shouldn't have added a shot of something alcoholic just to take the edge off her nerves. Unfortunately, that brought her back to thinking about the photo she'd just received. It had been years before she'd trusted herself enough to touch alcohol again, and she'd always been a moderate drinker. Now Ilya had her thinking about having a drink.

The man couldn't be good for her. They'd been married a week and already she couldn't get him out of her mind. Going back to work would be a welcome panacea, but that wouldn't happen for another week. She had thought the two-week honeymoon was a good idea at the time. An opportunity to spend time with her new husband and get to know him better.

Know him in the biblical sense? She took another, longer sip of her drink. This was getting ridiculous. Maybe she should just sleep with Ilya and get it over with.

"A penny for your thoughts."

Yasmin felt a blush creep into her cheeks. "Not even worth a penny," she answered dismissively.

"Or you just don't want to tell me," he responded with a little smirk. "I was thinking we could go out for dinner tonight. Maybe the tapas restaurant in town."

A restaurant? That would be good, she thought, nodding in agreement. At least there they would be surrounded by people and maybe, just maybe, she'd stop thinking about how sexy her husband was and what the heck she was going to do about it.

"That sounds great. Would you like me to make the booking? I'm happy to drive us."

"I thought we'd take a car service. That way we can both have a couple of drinks."

And her inhibitions would fly out the window, she thought ruefully. But then, maybe it was time she let them and learned to let go a little. For so long she'd lived such a structured, self-disciplined existence. Get up, work hard, go to bed and then do it all again. Her entire adult life had been one long treadmill of doing the same thing all the time. Working for the greater good of Carter Air and her employees. So why shouldn't she let her hair down and live a little? Especially with a man she was married to.

"Okay," she said, before she could change her mind. "That sounds nice."

Nice? What was she thinking? She wasn't quite sure she was ready to handle this, but then again, she'd never know until she tried, right?

It was late and Ilya couldn't sleep a wink. Dinner had been incredible. The tapas restaurant was always good but somehow sharing the platters with Yasmin had given him a new appetite and enhanced the flavors more than ever.

He'd never met anyone like her before. She was that incredibly perfect blend of beauty and intelligence. And all his life, she'd been living only a short distance away from him. If it hadn't been for that stupid feud between their families, would things have been different? Would they have ever come together under different circumstances, courted like a normal couple and done all the things a regular couple did?

Things like make love under a moonlit sky until they both drifted to sleep in sated exhaustion?

He shifted uncomfortably in his bed. Being around Yasmin was proving very uncomfortable. Not being around her was even worse. Ilya flopped over onto his other side and willed himself to relax, but that was easier said than done when he was once again going to bed with an unrelieved hard-on.

What would she have done, he wondered, if he'd stroked the fine skin of her lightly tanned arms the way he'd wanted to at dinner, or if, when the car had dropped them home, he'd reached over and planted a kiss on the exposed nape of her neck? Would she have shivered in delight? Would she have turned and met his passion with an answering kiss of her own?

He huffed another sigh of frustration. Wherever his thoughts were leading, it was irrelevant. Until Yasmin was ready to come to him on her own terms, he wasn't going to push her. There was still that fragile insecurity beneath the assured surface that she presented to him each morning at breakfast. He wasn't sure why the insecurity was there, or what had created it, but he certainly wasn't going to make it any worse. He could be patient along with the best of them. Even if it just about killed him.

A sound at his door made him stiffen. He opened one eye a crack and detected the svelte silhouette of his wife as she came into the room. Ilya congratulated himself on sleeping with the drapes open, because the weak moonlight provided just enough illumination for him to see his bride step carefully across the room.

She hesitated at the edge of his bed. For a moment he thought she might turn and walk back out as silently as she'd walked in. She'd been incredibly stealthy. If he hadn't been awake and facing the door, he probably wouldn't have heard her arrival. But here she was. An arm's length away. Ilya found himself holding his breath, wondering what she was going to do next.

He didn't have to wait long. Yasmin obviously had made her decision. She reached for the top sheet and slid under it beside him. His body went into overdrive. His every instinct urged him to pull her into his arms and to fulfill the fantasies that had plagued him since he'd left her alone in her bedroom on their wedding night. But he was stronger than that. She could be here for a myriad of reasons—none of them having anything to do with the desperation raging through him right now.

How did a gentleman react in a situation like this? What did he do, or say?

"Bad dream?" he asked gently.

He felt, rather than saw, her shake her head.

"No, nothing like that," she answered. Her voice was husky and she swallowed. "I… I thought it was time I took you up on your offer. I changed my mind about sleeping alone. Are you okay with that?"

Eight

Was he okay with that? *Hell, yes!* He wanted to punch the air and shout out loud.

"Are you certain?" he asked instead.

"I haven't been able to think about anything else. It's…" She hesitated.

"It's…?" he prompted.

"Driving me crazy."

"I have to admit to being a little crazy, too. It's a weird thing, this marriage of ours, isn't it?"

He heard her sigh in the semidarkness. "It really is."

She fell silent beside him. Her body was rigid with tension. Maybe he should have acted on his first instinct after all—gentlemanly conduct be damned. But then he felt her move toward him. Felt a tentative touch of her hand on his shoulder. He reciprocated, letting his hand rest on the curve of her hip. She was wearing some kind of silky slip, and as he stroked her it moved beneath his palm like a luxuriously delicate barrier between them. But as good as it felt, he wanted to feel *her*.

He pushed the fabric higher until he touched bare skin. She wasn't wearing any underwear and the knowledge sent a bolt of heat straight to his groin. His hand shook as he stroked her, pushing the slip higher, feeling the dip of her waist, the shape of her ribs, the curve of her breast. Her breath hitched as he touched her there, as he cupped her fullness and let his thumb drift across her tight nipple.

Her skin was hot, as if she burned with the same need he did. Ilya shifted in the bed so he had better access to her and bent his head to her breast, taking his time kissing and licking a path from the underside to the budded peak. He wished he could see her more clearly. Drink in her beauty, the color of her skin. But like this, in the dark, his other senses became more attuned to her. To the sighs and gasps she made as he caressed her body. To the scent of her—not just the light summery fragrance she wore, but the scent of her body—her desire.

It was a powerful aphrodisiac, the knowledge that she wanted him that much. He continued to lavish attention on her breasts while letting his hand trail down over her taut stomach and lower still. She was obviously the kind of woman who took her personal grooming to the next level, he realized as he felt the tiny neat patch of body hair nestled there. He groaned. Ah, what he wouldn't do to see that. But there was time. Hopefully tonight would be the first of many such nights where they could explore each other, touch and taste and revel in each other's bodies.

His fingers dipped a little lower, to the molten core of her—slick and soft and, oh, so very tempting. She moved beneath him, a groan coming from her that spoke to how ready she truly was. He let one finger slip inside her and felt her tense and shudder against him.

"You like that?" he asked.

"Oh, yes," she sighed on a quiver of breath. "Don't stop, please."

"Well, since you asked so nicely."

He repeated the movement, this time easing two fingers inside her and curling them to stroke her. Her hips lifted from the bed and she tightened around his fingers again. Keeping his movements small and slow, he continued to caress her, all the while trailing a line of kisses down the center of her body. The scent of her was hot and musky, and yet enticingly sweet, as well. He nuzzled against her mound, pressed a kiss there, then used his tongue to find the pearl hidden in her folds.

Yasmin's hands caught in his hair, holding him to her as he worked his tongue in patterns against her clitoris. Beneath him he felt her body grow more and more tense. It was time. He increased the tempo of his fingers, closed his mouth around her bud and suckled her.

She climaxed on a keening cry, her body shuddering as she came around him, beneath him. It was all he could do not to come himself, such was the force of her orgasm. Instead, he held onto the last shred of his control, determined to make her enjoyment last. His pleasure would come later and be all the better for it.

Ilya slowed his movements, pressed a lingering kiss against her and withdrew his fingers from her body.

"I know this probably comes across as cliché," she said, her voice just a little shaky. "But wow."

Ilya laughed, loving the fact that she could make a joke at a time like this.

"I've yet to meet the man who wouldn't find that a compliment," he admitted, still smiling.

He lay down next to her and pulled her closer to him.

"I meant it as one," she answered, pressing a kiss against his shoulder. "And now, it's your turn."

"There's no need—"

"Shush, there's every need. I'm all about equal opportunities. Aren't you?" she teased.

She nipped him and the sensation of her teeth against his skin sent another jolt of desire crashing through him. He'd be lucky to hold on another minute, let alone for as long as she planned to torture him. And torture it was. Sweet, delicious, sensation-filled torture as she explored his body with her hands, her lips and her tongue.

Every now and then her hand would drift close to his groin and brush against his penis, making it twitch involuntarily. His balls were so tight they ached, and the pleasurable pain of it nearly drove him to distraction. Tremors began to rock him as she worked her way down his body, as her teeth scraped over the sensitive skin at the V of his groin. If she was going to do that somewhere else, he—

She did. Ilya clenched his fists in the sheets beside him, allowed his body to ride the wave of sheer unadulterated pleasure that threatened to swamp him. Her fingers closed around his shaft, stroking him as she took his tip deeper into her mouth. It was too much. Far, far, far too much.

In one swift movement, Ilya pulled her up higher on his body.

"You're killing me," he barely uttered as he lifted her over his engorged shaft and slowly lowered her down.

"You didn't let me finish."

"Oh, we'll finish. I promise."

As her body engulfed him, he closed his eyes and gritted his teeth, calling on every last ounce of restraint. This wasn't about him anymore. It was about both of them. Together.

His hips began to move and Yasmin met him, thrust for thrust. He could just make her out in the low gleam of moonlight from the window. Her slender body was rising and falling—undulating like waves on the sea. His climax was near, but he had to be certain she was going to fall over that edge with him. He fought the urge to give in. Felt her body grow tight around him, felt the rhythmic pull of her orgasm beginning.

He could hold on no longer. She was his absolute undo-ing. He let go, riding the intense swell of pleasure, again and again. And she let go with him, her body tensing and releasing on her own waves of delight, until she collapsed over him.

Ilya wrapped his arms about her, felt the last tiny trem-ors course through her body before she went completely slack in his arms.

"Yeah, wow," he murmured into her hair.

"I can't move," she said languidly. "You're going to have to push me off."

"I kind of like having you right here," he replied, clos-ing his arms a little tighter and relishing the feel of her body against his.

Her breath came in short little puffs of warm air against his chest and he felt her body relax as she sank into sleep in his arms.

He'd never thought it could be like this. The depths of passion, the heights of satisfaction, the closeness of re-maining joined when he finally lost hold on consciousness and drifted into a satiated sleep himself.

It was still dark when Yasmin woke. She remained sprawled over Ilya's chest, her legs splayed on either side of his. Her entire body hummed with a sense of completion she'd never known before. A part of her wondered why the heck she'd waited so long to give in to the attraction that had driven her crazy this past week. The other part told her she was simply being careful.

This changed things. Making love to Ilya had taken their marriage to a new level of permanence for her. Had it been the same for him? She gave a little shiver as she re-membered the things he'd done, the reactions he'd wrought from her. She was no shy violet in the bedroom but he'd brought her to the precipice of something new and exciting. Something she knew would be addictive.

Was she ready to do this? To give herself over to that level of commitment? They'd known each other and been married just a week. It was all kinds of madness to be feeling this way so soon. He was her enemy in business and yet, here in his bed, she knew he was anything but.

Was this the real Ilya Horvath? A man who rescued puppies? A man who saw to her every daily need? A man who reduced her to a puddle of loose limbs and fulfillment after just one sexual encounter?

So where did this leave her? Confused, yes. Wanting more, most definitely.

But did Ilya feel the same way? How did a girl go about asking a man something like that?

"You're thinking too hard," Ilya said sleepily from beneath her.

His voice rumbled in her ear. His hand, which only moments ago had rested limply on the small of her back, now began to drift gently, tracing the knobs of her spine. Up and down and back up again.

"Is that even possible, to think too hard?"

"It is when you should be sleeping or making love."

Desire unfurled in her like petals opening on a full-blown rose.

"And which would you suggest in this instance?" she asked, lifting her head and looking at his face.

His eyes glinted in the dark.

"The latter, of course."

"Is that so? Didn't you have enough the first time around?"

He shook his head. "That was only a starter to whet your appetite. Did I fail?"

She laughed at the mock mortification in his tone.

"No, you didn't fail. But, then again, I don't expect you know what that's like."

His hand stilled on her back. "You think I've never failed?"

"Have you?"

"Enough to know what it feels like," he said grimly. "But I don't want to talk about that right now. Right now, I'd rather do this."

He rolled them over so she was beneath him, and he settled between her thighs. She could feel his arousal, already hard and heavy, probing at her entrance.

He hesitated. "We didn't discuss contraception," he said, his voice blunt.

"I get the birth control shot. And I know we're both clean. It was one of the tests we had to have before the wedding, remember?"

She flexed a little, felt the tip of him enter her. She gasped on a flood of awareness.

"Too soon?" he asked, nuzzling the curve of her neck.

"Not soon enough," she replied, pushing her pelvis forward so she could take him in farther.

He withdrew teasingly. "Oh, I don't know."

She dug her fingernails into his buttocks and felt him flinch.

"Not soon enough," she repeated.

"Then I had best continue as the lady demands," he said, punctuating his sentence with a thrust of his hips.

"That's more like it," Yasmin sighed in approval.

"I aim to please."

"There's nothing whatsoever wrong with your aim," she managed to say before ripples of desire built up inside her and threatened to sweep away any capacity to speak.

This time her climax was deeper, more intense than before, and she knew, through every step, that Ilya was with her all the way. When he came she felt it through her whole body, her pleasure and his mixing and blending and radiating through them until they were both left spent and breathing heavily.

She'd known pleasure and satisfaction before, but nothing—*nothing*—came close to this. Boneless, sated beyond belief, she drifted back into a deep sleep, oblivious to the screen on her mobile phone on the nightstand next to her, lighting up with an incoming email notification.

Nine

He hadn't expected it to be like this, Ilya thought as he and Yasmin walked hand in hand along the beach the next day. They'd driven out to the coast. Feeling the salt air buffet them as the wind whipped down the sandy shoreline and watching the huge breakers roll in, Ilya felt as though the landscape was a fine analogy for the turmoil that churned inside him.

He certainly hadn't expected this depth of connection with another person so quickly. Oh, sure, he knew a lot of how he was feeling was due to their incredible sexual connection. What man wouldn't feel bonded to a woman who made him feel the way Yasmin did when they made love? But it went deeper than that, and that knowledge scared him.

He'd loved a woman before. Believed, with every cell in his body, that she was The One. Yes, they'd been young, but there was no rule saying young people couldn't love each other forever, was there? Although, in their case, forever had only lasted three years. When he'd discovered that the Jennifer he'd fallen in love with had been a fake, that the true woman beneath the smiles, the affection, the plans for the future had, in fact, been a cruel, lying and scheming bitch, the damage to his heart had been total.

Ilya was the kind of man who, once he committed to something or someone, did it totally and utterly. And he'd committed himself to her. Discovering her web of lies had been shattering—not only to his heart but to his very belief system. His trust in himself, his ability to judge others, had been damaged, and in every relationship since, he'd held a part of himself back—unwilling or unable to go that extra distance to commit to another person.

He knew all about heartbreak. The loss of his father and then his mom in his teens had almost brought him to his knees. Nagy had been his foundation through those years. His rock. His stability. And when she'd seen him off to college, she'd encouraged him to find himself and to test his place in the world. When he met Jennifer at a rival college game, he'd honestly thought she was the woman he would grow old with, and discovering her true nature had been as wrenching as a bereavement. It had made him hard—he knew that, accepted it—because being hard meant being invincible. The only trouble was that he could already feel the cracks forming in his carefully constructed walls. And opening yourself to another person meant opening yourself to hurt.

He'd thought full emotional engagement wouldn't be necessary in his unconventional marriage. That loyalty, kindness and devotion would be enough. But the way his feelings were developing for Yasmin was taking him on a roller-coaster ride he wasn't sure he was ready for.

"Shall we go and sit over there, out of the wind?" Yasmin asked, interrupting his thoughts and gesturing to a hollow between a couple of low sand hills.

"Sure." He tucked her hand into the crook of his arm as they ploughed through the loose sand and settled in the spot she'd indicated.

"It's so gorgeous here, so different from the valley. But it looks better from the air," she commented.

"Are you missing flying? We can go to the airfield if you're suffering withdrawal."

"I could take you up in the Ryan if you like," she offered after a short silence.

He felt his pulse kick up a beat. Her Ryan was her pride and joy from what he knew. He admired the amount of time she had to have spent with her grandfather on its restoration. A project like that was a true labor of love. He also knew that she would be in command of the controls and that was something he struggled with. Not because she was a woman, but because ever since his father's death Ilya had rarely relinquished being the pilot in command. Even on commercial airliners he struggled with the concept of someone else being in charge. These days, in most cases, he flew one of the company jets when traveling long haul, even when he went to Europe or to any of the Pacific Islands for a break. He wasn't rated to fly anything like the Ryan, though, so Yasmin would be at the controls, meaning a complete surrender of his instinct to remain in charge.

"You don't have to if you don't want to," she said hastily when he didn't reply. "It's not everyone's cup of tea."

"It's not that."

"You're a control freak, I know. I get it."

Did she? Did she really understand? How could anyone know what it was like to know you faced certain death if you didn't get everything one hundred percent right and that the only person you could trust or rely on was yourself?

"A control freak?" he asked. "Do I come across that way to you?"

"It's possible you're hiding your true nature," she surmised, looking up at him and smiling.

"Humph," he grunted.

"Are you? Hiding your true nature, that is? I know we've been on best behavior with each other since the wedding. It's like we're living in an artificial bubble, really. Don't you think so?"

"That's one way of looking at it, I guess. But, in answer to your question, I'm not hiding my true nature from you. I am what I am. The man you see right here, right now."

She reached up to kiss him. "I'm finding you surprisingly okay for a Horvath. Who knew?"

He laughed. "Yeah, that old family feud thing."

She started to say something but stopped when his cell phone began to chime. He pulled it from his pocket and checked the caller ID.

"It's Danni," he said and thumbed the screen to accept the call.

Yasmin squirmed beside him as he listened to his cousin, keeping his responses to a minimum. When he ended the call he looked at his wife.

"Well?" she demanded.

"We can pick him up later today. If you still want him, that is."

She punched him on his upper arm. "Want him? He's ours. Of course I want him. What are you waiting for?"

She stood up abruptly, leaving him in a shower of sand falling from her jeans. He swiftly followed suit and they laughingly raced each other back along the beach to where they'd parked. As they reached the car, he caught Yasmin's eye across the roof and sent her a smile, realizing, with a small measure of shock, just how much it made him happy to make her happy, as well. Which brought him back to his original turmoil.

No, this connection, this sense of belonging with another person—it wasn't what he'd expected at all.

They were curled up on the large L-shaped couch in the family room, watching the puppy sleep in his crate. The floor was strewn with his toys and puppy pee pads, although Ilya suspected they wouldn't need those as the dog already appeared to have been toilet trained somewhere along the line. Danni suspected he was between three and four months old and a mix of border collie and who knew what else. They had yet to name him.

"He's so cute when he's sleeping, isn't he?" Yasmin commented.

"You said the same when he was awake."

"Well, he's cute. Don't you think so?"

Ilya studied the little guy. They'd been surprised to discover that, once cleaned up, he had quite a bit of white hair interspersed with the patches of brown and black. "Sure, he is."

"I think we should call him Blaze, for the white blaze down his face."

"Yeah, that fits."

"Good. He has a home and a name."

"What are we going to do with him when we go back to work?" Ilya asked.

"I can take him with me."

"And when you're flying?"

"My office manager will look after him...or you could."

"Ah, yes, take-your-dog-to-work day. It has a certain ring to it." He shuddered visibly.

"You're teasing me," she said, struggling to disentangle herself from where she was nestled comfortably against his side.

"Of course I'm teasing you. We'll work something out.

Besides, there's always Hannah or doggy day care. Danni mentioned one not too far from here."

"Well, I guess if she recommended it…" Yasmin's voice trailed off.

It occurred to Ilya that his wife had trust issues similar to his own, especially when it came to what was important to her. He wondered what was behind it, although being dumped by your parents on a cantankerous grandparent probably had something to do with it.

The house phone began to ring and Ilya reluctantly rose from the couch to answer it. His grandmother was the only person who called his landline anymore, and he had no doubt she was calling to check on the state of his marriage.

"I expected you to have rung me by now," she said imperiously the moment he answered the phone. "Why aren't you still up in Port Ludlow?"

"I've been busy getting to know my wife. You know, the one you paired me with? And besides, we wanted to come home. When did you find out?"

Of all the cousins, he was always the one who got away with the most with Nagy. None of the others would dare be as cheeky.

"When and how I found out is neither here nor there. Is all going well?" she asked, blithely ignoring his dig.

He looked over at Yasmin, who was flicking through a sports aviation magazine she'd picked up off the coffee table.

"As well as can be expected."

"Oh, for goodness sake, Ilya! Stop beating around the bush."

"I don't know what you mean," he teased.

"Would you like me to visit, then?"

There was a steeliness to his grandmother's voice that left him in no doubt that she would breach the family's agreement to leave the newlyweds to themselves during the honeymoon period.

"You know you're always welcome, but in this case, I think we should leave it a while. You can be assured that my wife and I—" he paused to smile at Yasmin who'd looked up at that point "—are getting on very well and enjoying learning more about each other. Oh, and we have a puppy."

"A dog? Already?" His grandmother sounded flabbergasted. "Well, that's quick."

"We found him when we were out on a walk in the hills. Danni brought him back to health for us. You'll love him."

"That remains to be seen. You know how I feel about animals."

"Was there anything else, Nagy?"

"No, you go back to your wife. And Ilya?" She paused. "Yes."

"I know you two can make this work."

She hung up without saying goodbye, but he was used to that. She never wasted time on small talk. It was one of the many things he respected about her.

He settled on the couch again and pulled Yasmin back under his arm. He liked the way she fit there. In fact, he liked the way she fit in his life, period. And despite its being what he should have wanted in a relationship, it still made him uneasy because he wasn't ready to fully let her in—to his mind or his heart.

Alice hung up the phone and allowed a small smile to play across her face. It was working—better than she'd hoped, in fact. She hadn't been wrong yet with her pairings, but it was always reassuring to know she hadn't lost her touch.

A puppy? She smiled again, a small chuckle bubbling up from deep inside. Her first-born grandson was actually settling down. She'd begun to fear it would never happen. He'd been so shy of commitment since that awful eye-opening time back in college. Oh, sure. He had a beautiful home in the hills fit for a family. He had money socked away for a rainy day. He had a satisfying career and more family support than a man could ever need. But she knew he'd only been going through the motions these past ten or more years.

When her Ilya gave, he gave everything. Having that love, that trust, abused by a gold-digging, lying piece of… She shut down her thoughts before rage could take over and trigger another of those blasted angina attacks that only she and her doctor knew about. Alice calmed her breathing, cleared her mind and allowed herself to only think about what made her happiest. Family.

Her earnest boy, her knight crusader, was finally learning to give of that most precious part of himself, his heart. She only hoped she'd done the right thing because she knew, without doubt, that if his heart was given and, perish the thought, broken again, nothing would repair it.

Ten

Yasmin walked around the Ryan doing her preflight checks. It felt a bit strange to be at the airport and not go into the office. Her plane was hangared separately from the Carter Air charter planes, but Riya had threatened her with all kinds of harm if she so much as set foot in the office before her official honeymoon period came to an end.

Riya might be small, but she was a force to be reckoned with, and while Yasmin's instinct was just to pop in and check on things, she didn't want to incur her friend's wrath. If there was a serious problem, Riya would let her know. Besides, if Ilya could stay away from his work for two weeks, then she could most definitely do the same.

Excitement bubbled in her veins. She hadn't flown since before the wedding and she was itching to get behind the controls and dance across the sky. And Ilya was coming up with her. He'd surprised her this morning, on their last Friday before they went back to work, saying he'd decided to take her up on her offer of the flight in the old trainer.

Hannah was minding Blaze for them and Yasmin was thrilled at the idea of taking her husband up and showing off a little. But even more important, he was showing her he trusted her, which was pretty incredible, given his own admitted preference to be the pilot in command.

The only shadow on her day was the latest email on her phone. The words had burned themselves into her memory, leaving her wondering who on earth from her past *hisgirl* could be. It obviously had to be someone from her time in college—the photo suggested as much—but she'd ceased to have contact with any of them after that humiliating night.

If you know what's good for you, you'll walk out of his life and never go back.

The inherent threat had made her blood run cold, especially on the heels of the photo *hisgirl* had sent earlier in the week. Was the sender specifically warning her that if she didn't leave Ilya the photo would be used against her somehow?

Perhaps it was someone Ilya had gone out with, but then, how would that person have access to photos taken at the hazing? And what on earth did they hope to gain by threatening Yasmin? If Ilya had been invested in a relationship with anyone else, he wouldn't have put himself in his grandmother's hands for a Match Made in Marriage arrangement. He wasn't that kind of guy.

Her head ached the more she thought about it. The only thing she knew for certain was that there were far more questions than answers. She'd decided to ask Ilya if he'd been seeing anyone prior to marrying her, but the opportunity hadn't arisen. Or maybe she was just too scared to bring it up in case he pressed her for reasons why she was asking.

She trailed a hand along the leading edge of the wing and, putting all her confusion aside, completed her pre-flight inspection.

Ilya was waiting for her beside the plane. "All good?"

"As it should be," she replied with a smile. "You're ready?"

"When it comes to flying, and some other things, come to think of it, I'm definitely ready," he said with a smile that made her stomach flip and her legs turn to jelly.

She growled at herself to pull her act together and focus on the flight plan she'd created for today. "All right then," Yasmin said. "We'd better climb aboard."

The airport was less busy than usual and the tower quickly gave Yasmin clearance to take off. In no time they were taxiing down the runway, engine noise filling the open cockpit. Yasmin keyed her mic.

"You doing okay?"

"I'm not having to sit on my hands to stop myself from touching the controls just yet, so, yeah, I'm fine."

She laughed. She could only imagine how he'd be feeling right now in the front seat of the plane. Visibility wasn't that great while taxiing in the taildragger, but once they were airborne? Well, that would be a different story altogether.

Yasmin felt the tail lift off and experienced the accompanying thrill she always got when she took the Ryan up. A few seconds later they were climbing out. She reached her chosen altitude and keyed the mic again.

"I'm going to take her through a few maneuvers. Hold on to your stomach!"

He gave her a thumbs-up and she pushed the plane into a gentle roll.

"Is that all you got?" he taunted once she'd righted the plane again. "C'mon, I know you have more tricks up your sleeve."

"You asked for it," she said, taking up the challenge.

The aerobatic sequence she did was one she often performed at air shows, and the exhilaration was no less for having an enthusiastic passenger on board. But as she came out of a stall and into a spin she wondered if she was taking things a step too far. After all, Ilya was a self-confessed autocrat when it came to being in a cockpit. It wouldn't feel natural to him to be in the front passenger seat and not take the controls, especially when it felt as though the plane might plummet to the ground any second.

Maneuvers completed, she leveled out and flew out toward the coast. There was something about watching the sea from the air that always calmed her, no matter what kind of day she was having. Her headset crackled to life.

"That. Was. Amazing."

Her lips curved into a grateful smile. "I'm glad you enjoyed it."

"Seriously, you're a brilliant pilot."

Yasmin felt her chest swell with pride. She didn't often hear praise so heartfelt, and having it come from Ilya? Well, that just made it all the more special.

"Do you want to fly her for a bit?" she asked. "Nothing too fancy, but just to have a taste of how she handles."

"Hell, yeah."

Yasmin ran through a few of the basics, underscoring some of the touchier tendencies of the aircraft. "You have control," she said after Ilya relayed the details back to her to indicate he'd understood.

Her heart shuddered a little in her chest. Since rebuilding the Ryan with her grandfather, she was the only person to have ever flown the aircraft. Giving control to Ilya now was the deepest mark of respect and trust she'd ever shown anyone. And doing so felt completely natural to her, which came as another shock. Tomorrow, they'd have been married two weeks. How on earth had she, the quintessential distrustful soul, as Riya called her, come so far in this relationship already that she was prepared to relinquish control of her greatest pride and joy? She rubbed at her chest, at the lump that had settled there. Was this what falling in love was like?

She hadn't counted on this feeling. Didn't quite know how to handle it. Marrying Ilya—well, whoever would have been waiting at the altar for her, to be honest—had merely been a means to an end. A solution to a problem that had grown beyond her ability to manage. Developing feelings like this for him so soon? It was ridiculous, she told herself firmly. People didn't fall in love that quickly.

But they did, her conscience whispered. Hadn't her parents met and fallen and love and married all within the space of a few weeks? Hadn't they always said that they'd known, the moment they'd laid eyes on each other, that it was meant to be and they shouldn't waste another moment beating around the bush and following courtship rituals when they could simply begin their lives together immediately? And even Riya, whose marriage had been arranged by her family back in India, had only met her husband a handful of times before they married. When Yasmin had mentioned how archaic she felt the concept of arranged marriage was, Riya had simply smiled in contentment and told her that *When you know, you just know.*

Did Yasmin know? Not for certain. *So, let's look at this logically*, she told herself. *Despite your reasons for marrying, you're married to a guy who is very likely every straight woman's dream of perfection. He isn't the overbearing jerk you heard he was. In fact, he's nothing like that. In many ways, he's a lot like you. Focused. Businesslike. Ready to start a family. To carry on a legacy.*

Yasmin stared unseeingly at the coastline that zipped along beneath them, not liking the direction of her thoughts.

"I think we should head back now," she said abruptly.

"She's all yours," came Ilya's voice through the headset.

Yasmin took the control column in her hand and turned the plane back to the airport, completing a textbook-perfect landing and taxiing back to the hangar. She'd no sooner completed her routine of putting the Ryan to bed, as she called it, when Ilya wrapped his strong arms around her from behind and spun her around. In the next instant he was kissing her as if his life depended on it. If this was how he reacted when she took him up with her, she'd have to do it more often.

Desire for him flamed hot and fast through her veins and she gave back every bit as good as he was giving her. It was only when she realized that her hands were at his shirtfront, her fingers feverishly plucking at his buttons, that she came to her senses.

"Not here. My apartment. Upstairs."

She grabbed his hand and tugged him out the back door to the external stairs that led to her grandfather's old apartment. She'd made it her own after he died, not seeing the point in paying rent anywhere else. Its proximity to work couldn't be faulted. Right now, though, proximity to a bed was uppermost in her mind as she led Ilya up the stairs. His feet hammered on the steps behind her and her blood was pumping fast when she fitted her key in the lock and pulled the door open.

The second they were inside she turned and pushed Ilya against the door, kissing him with all the hunger she'd bottled up since he'd kissed her in the hangar. They shed their clothing, leaving it in scattered heaps as they made their way to her bedroom. Seconds later, they tumbled onto her mattress in a tangle of limbs. She straddled him and their joining was fast and heated, her climax coming so quickly it shocked the air from her lungs and left her in a state of limbo between pleasure and unconsciousness before she felt Ilya shudder in completion beneath her.

His hands pulled her down to him and he rolled them onto their sides. Now he faced her with a silly grin. His breathing was about as irregular as hers and she put her hand out, flattening her palm against his bare chest, feeling the erratic beat of his heart that matched her own.

"Is this where I say *wow*?" he asked, his voice uneven.

"Yeah, this would be a good time," she answered, as breathless as if she'd just completed a half marathon.

"Wow."

Yasmin laughed, the sound gurgling up from deep inside her and taking her over. Joy filled her from the soles of her feet upward. Ilya joined her, and together they lay there, laughing like a pair of idiots on her bed. Eventually she calmed, lacing her fingers through his.

"Is this what you're always like when you relinquish control?" she laughed, squeezing his hand.

"I could get used to it," he admitted with a rueful expression on his handsome face.

"We should do this more often," she said. "Go flying together, I mean. Although the rest was pretty good, too."

"I couldn't agree more." He rolled flat onto his back. "Thank you."

"For the sex?" she teased.

"For everything. I didn't know how I'd feel not being the pilot in command."

His voice trailed off, and Yasmin heard him sigh deeply.

"It wasn't as bad as I thought," he said on a huff of breath. "In fact, it was pretty damn incredible. *You're* pretty damn incredible—and fearless."

Yasmin felt his praise roll through her and savored it. It had been a long time since anyone had told her she'd done well.

"Thanks. I'm glad it was okay for you. I... I understand

what it can be like facing your fears. But I would never say I'm fearless. I have plenty of fears—in fact, I could barely stand to put my head under water until a few years ago—but flying...no, that isn't one of them."

She traced little circles on his chest with a finger, enjoying the fact that they could lie here together so comfortably with no urgency to leave. She felt the vibrations of his voice when he spoke.

"Tell me about your biggest fear, then. Maybe we can get you over it, since you've apparently cured me of needing to be the boss all the time."

Should she tell him? Could she? Even though they were husband and wife they essentially remained strangers to each other. Yasmin had never told another soul about that night —about her desperation to fit in and belong with the in-crowd at college. Why she'd even let it be so important to her back then still embarrassed her.

"Yasmin?" he prompted.

She drew in a deep breath, made a decision. She had nothing to fear from Ilya, did she?

"My biggest fear is not being able to see. To be blindfolded, to have all vision restricted and be led into a situation so dangerous it almost kills you—" She paused and let go a deep breath. "Yeah, that's my greatest fear."

Ilya stiffened beneath her touch as her words sank in. Coupled with that sense of having seen Yasmin somewhere in his past, somewhere outside of the rare times they'd run across each other at industry affairs, the mention of a blindfold and almost being killed dragged him back to a time he'd chosen to push to the back of his memories.

"Almost kills you?" he asked, seeking confirmation that she was indeed talking about the incident he thought she was.

"I guess I should tell you everything," Yasmin said, withdrawing her hand from his.

She sat up in the bed, pulled her knees up against her chest and wrapped her arms around her legs, making herself seem smaller. Ilya reached up and traced his fingers down her spine, determined to ensure that she didn't feel alone in this.

"Only tell me if you're ready," he coaxed gently.

"I'm ready. It's just that I've never trusted anyone enough to share this before."

"Are you worried I'll use it against you somehow?"

"Oh, heavens, no! I—" She stopped and drew in a breath. "I just wouldn't want you to think of me any differently, y'know? Because of what happened."

"Why don't you let me be the judge of that," he said cautiously.

"Fine," she said with a broken little smile that scored at his heart. "All my life I'd worked so hard to be the best student and athlete I could be. I guess a part of that was the hope that if I proved to my parents that I was a really good kid, they might come back and we'd live as a family again. When I realized it didn't matter what I did, they were never coming back, I constantly sought my grandfather's approval. It took a lot to impress him."

She laughed. It was a bitter sound that lacked any humor, and it made Ilya angry at the old man all over again. Yasmin had deserved better than that.

She continued, lost in her memories. "Because I was so driven, I never made close friends at school. When I wasn't studying, I was training, when I wasn't training, I was competing or helping Granddad out at the airfield. So when it came to fitting in at college I was determined to be just like everyone else. It's ridiculous how hard I worked to be normal," she said, making air quotes as she spoke the last word. "I was prepared to do anything to fit in. Anything."

Ilya felt his skin crawl with damning inevitability as she mentioned where she'd gone to college. The same college as Jennifer. He wanted desperately to reassure her. To tell her that she was normal, that she'd always been. That it had been the others who weren't. But doing so would be admitting to his own involvement, his own shame.

"When I tried to join the most popular sorority, the hazing was intense. The final test was held at a secluded lakeside beach after midnight. The list of challenges was extensive, and involved drinking a lot of alcohol if I did or said anything wrong. I've never been much of a drinker and the vodka shots hit me hard. I ended up doing things I would never have done sober but I was desperate to fit in—to be a part of something other kids my age did as a matter of course. I was already pretty drunk when they blindfolded me and told me I had to swim off the beach to a diving pontoon and then back to the beach again. Any normal day I would have done that without any trouble, but with all that alcohol in my system it didn't end well. I nearly drowned. I failed the challenge and someone, I don't even know who, had to pull me out of the water.

"I ended up in the hospital emergency room getting my stomach pumped and being put on IV fluids to sober me up. It was the most shameful experience of my life. I'll never forget the lecture the ER doctor gave me. Of course I didn't make it into the sorority and I was shunned by the girls I'd so pathetically wanted to be my friends. It was a tough lesson but I took it on the chin. I transferred back home and finished my degree at Cal State and carried on with my life. But it left its scars, you know? I conquered the fear of swimming that it gave me, but I still can't bear to have my eyes covered or lose my eyesight in any way. It totally freaks me out."

He could well believe it.

"And you've never told anyone? You didn't report it to the college administration?"

He already knew the answer, but he didn't understand why she'd chosen not to report the people involved.

"How could I? I chose to participate and I did some pretty disgusting things, again by choice. I could have walked away, given up at any time like a few other girls did when the challenges started getting too bizarre. Some of the kids there took photos that night." Her voice caught on a hitch. "I was warned that if I said anything, those pictures might come out. I couldn't have borne that. It was easier to leave than to be judged for what I'd done."

How on earth could she feel as if she would be judged for what happened that night? She'd been the victim and then blackmailed into the bargain. As if all of that hadn't been bad enough, his then-fiancée had been the bully behind it all.

He couldn't believe that Yasmin was the one he'd pulled from the water that night. Looking at her now, it was difficult to reconcile the slender, blond and competent woman he was getting to know with the broken girl he'd hauled out. She'd been considerably plumper then, her hair long and much darker—more a shade of brown than the blond it was now. She looked completely different now, unrecognizable. He'd never heard her name spoken that night or known who she was. He'd only known she was in trouble and needed rescuing. So he'd saved her.

At the time Jennifer had begged him not to call the authorities. She'd promised that the girl would be looked after and convinced him that what had happened was simply a silly prank that had gotten out of hand—that there was nothing malicious in it.

Saying nothing had gone against everything he'd ever been taught about right and wrong and he'd been furi-

ous with Jen. But she was his fiancée. He'd loved her. He
planned to have a life together with her. He had to believe
her, trust in her, didn't he? And he had, right up until the
moment a few days later when he'd overheard Jen boasting
about the hazing and laughing about how he'd spoiled her
fun. That had been the moment his eyes had opened and
he'd realized that his friends, who'd said early on in their
relationship that she was using him, were right about her.
He could never spend the rest of his life with a woman as
callous and as cruel as that.

He'd been a fool and, at that point, the person he had
lost most faith in was himself.

Looking at Yasmin through new eyes, he realized he
wanted to save her now, too. Save her from the dreadful
guilt she still carried for her part in that night.

He was desperate to reassure Yasmin, but for the first
time in his life words completely failed him. How could
he tell her he had been there that night, though not until
after she'd entered the water? How could he tell her how
he'd been linked to the woman who'd put her through hell?
Whose actions, even now, continued to have an impact on
Yasmin's life?

At the same time, he was in shock himself. His *wife*
was the woman he'd rescued from the water that truly
awful night. Was it some crazy coincidence or had his
grandmother somehow known about the incident? She'd
orchestrated their union. Was this some twisted idea of
hers, pairing him and Yasmin now? It wouldn't surprise
him. She'd always had an uncanny instinct when it came
to others and when he'd returned home to tell her in person
about his broken engagement she hadn't pressed him for
details. She'd only offered her sympathy and told him that
she trusted he would always do the right thing. He itched
to grill her on the subject now, but that would have to be a
discussion for another time. Right now, he had to reassure

Yasmin that she had done nothing wrong. Her fear was a direct result of what others had done to her that night and she herself was not responsible.

If he'd acted then as he should have, and reported the whole sorry situation to the college, it would have been handled appropriately. And Yasmin wouldn't have had to bear the guilt she continued to carry to this very day. It was too late now. He couldn't undo the past. But he could help Yasmin in the future.

He'd told himself he was committed to their marriage—now he had to prove he was committed to her.

Eleven

He owed it to Yasmin, he told himself. If he couldn't or wouldn't take that chance, then he had no business being married to her at all. And right now, her openness, her honesty, deserved a response. He pushed himself upright and gathered her in his arms, pulling her body to his and offering her comfort. Too little too late, he realized, as he chose his words carefully. But he had to start somewhere.

"You're being too hard on yourself. From what you've told me, it's clear you were never to blame. Not for any of it."

She shook her head and he put his hands on either side of her face, tilting it up to look her in the eye.

"Trust me, Yasmin. I know what I'm talking about. You put your faith in the wrong people, that's all. What came next was out of your control."

Tears shone in her eyes and a spear of guilt shafted through him. He hated that this strong, proud woman was still so wounded by that night. Somehow, he had to make it right. Had to restore her to her full strength and heal the pain her experience had left behind.

"You're not to blame," he said emphatically.

Her lower lip trembled and one tear formed a silvery trail down her cheek. He'd never been able to cope with a woman's tears and seeing his proud wife crumble like this was absolutely his undoing. He captured her lips with his and tried to imbue that kiss with all of his admiration for her. For her courage, for her talent as a pilot, for her determination to put the past behind her and to stride forward with the life she'd chosen. When they broke apart he stared straight into her eyes. Her pupils were dilated with the desire that burned like an eternal flame between them.

"You're not to blame," he repeated.

He made love to her then. Slowly, intensely. Taking his time to explore her body, to discover every hidden pleasure point, to learn and imprint her in his mind, to make her understand just how much he admired her, how much he wanted her. He renewed his fascination with the silky texture of her skin, the essential flavor of her. And when he entered her he felt a stronger connection to her than before. A connection that thrilled and terrified him in equal proportions. When they reached the pinnacle of satisfaction, they did so together, tumbling into the abyss of pleasure and satiation with a joy that took his breath away.

She dozed in the aftermath, securely nestled against him. But Ilya couldn't rest. His mind twisted and churned over the facts. Over his involvement. She deserved to know it all. She blamed herself for everything but his judgment had also been lacking—after all, hadn't he believed himself in love with Jen? Believed her when she'd said things had gotten out of control when what happened had been part of her plan for Yasmin all along? He should have known better.

He didn't want secrets between Yasmin and himself,

but how could he tell her without destroying the fragile beauty of their growing closeness? These past two weeks had been an exercise in learning about one another, about developing trust. Would telling her shatter all of that? She'd been so brave telling him about what had happened, he feared disclosing his involvement with her nemesis would crush any chance they had of continuing to build this marriage of theirs.

He pulled her more firmly against him, breathing in her subtle fragrance and relishing the sensation of her bare skin against his. Savoring the trust she'd imbued in him with her words today. He owed it to her to tell her and he would, eventually, but the timing had to be right. He had to be sure that in doing so he wouldn't push her away from him forever. And, in the meantime, he'd do his best to show her every single day how important she had become to him.

Ilya felt an unexpected listlessness as they drove back home to the hills. Today had been a revelation for him in more ways than one. Not only had she opened up to him—which had been a gift in itself, even though it had opened a whole new can of worms—but she'd been the instrument that had made him face his own need to constantly be in charge and, more importantly, to learn when to relinquish control. She'd opened his eyes in a way he hadn't believed possible. There was a freedom in trusting others—a lightness in his chest that had been missing for a very long time. That it was his arranged wife who'd introduced him to the concept was a complete about-face from the self-sufficiency he'd prided himself on for most of his life.

He was glad they'd stopped at her apartment. Not only because of the pleasure they'd found in each other while they were there, but because it gave him another window into Yasmin's life. Her apartment was furnished comfortably but sparsely, with an eye for function rather than beauty. He doubted she ever had spent any more time there than absolutely necessary. In fact, there was so little of *her* in the apartment, aside from the occasional photo of an aircraft on the wall, that if he hadn't known her as well as he was learning to, he would have thought her dull, boring, uninspired.

His body tightened on a memory of exactly how inspired she truly was as he remembered their lovemaking. No, her apartment was not a reflection of her at all. Unless it served as a reminder of her ability to compartmentalize her life. She was a conundrum, this wife of his. More at home in an aircraft than in a car. Happiest throwing said aircraft around the sky than making a house or apartment feel like a home. And there were so many more facets to her still to discover, he told himself as they turned into the driveway.

But opening her up, getting to understand her better, meant opening himself up more to her, too. Putting himself in the line of fire, giving her the power to hurt him. If that was the case, his rational mind argued, didn't he have the power to hurt her also? He rejected the idea. Hurting Yasmin was not an option. But getting to know her better, to understand exactly what made her tick, that most definitely was.

Blaze greeted them exuberantly from inside his crate when they let themselves into the house. Ilya took him outside to do his business in the garden while Yasmin took the clothes she'd brought from her apartment upstairs to their room. She was back downstairs in no time.

"Hungry?" she asked as Ilya walked back to the patio with the puppy bounding along beside him.

"Ravenous. Someone gave me a workout today."

"Aerobatics will do that to a person," she answered flippantly.

"I'm not talking about the aerobatics. At least, not the ones in the air."

Her pupils dilated and a flush lit her cheeks. For a few seconds they were both thrown back into the memory of the passion they'd shared. But then Blaze yipped, breaking the spell. Yasmin bent to give the puppy her attention.

"Hannah told me she'd leave a roasted vegetable salad and steaks for our meal tonight," she said after giving Blaze a good rub that had him rolling onto his back in pleasure. "Do you want to do the meat on the grill?"

"Sure."

It was all so normal, so domesticated, and he liked it. A lot. They walked into the kitchen together, the puppy trotting along beside them. This was the life he'd told himself he always wanted and yet never dared wish for. After his father's death his mother had broken inside. She'd been completely rudderless without Ilya's dad and, once she'd worked through the initial stages of her grief, she'd changed on a level that left Ilya confused and worried for her—both her sanity and her safety. She'd thrown herself into dating just about any man who showed an interest in her, once admitting to doing so because she had to find a way to light the darkness that losing her husband had left inside her.

He'd seen his mom go from a loving wife, a doting mother, to a brittle, insecure woman. Not being able to fill the gaps of what was missing in her had been torture for him. When she and her current boyfriend had been killed in a reckless driving maneuver on the 101, no one had been surprised. Devastated, yes, but not surprised. And for Ilya, it had been a horrible awakening. He hadn't been able to save his father and he hadn't been able to save his mother, either. He was under no illusion that his need to control the world around him stemmed from that year of sheer hell, which made this normality all the sweeter. Or would, if he could think of a way to tell Yasmin about his involvement in her past. That night had been a defining moment in her life—would she ever be able to not think of that experience every time she looked at him once she learned the truth?

As they were cleaning up together after their meal he heard Yasmin's phone buzz on the counter.

"You gonna get that?" he asked, rinsing dishes and loading the dishwasher.

"Later."

"Might be important."

"It's not a number I recognize. If it's important they'll call again."

The phone stopped its vibration, then almost immediately started again.

"I'd better get that, then," Yasmin said with a wry look on her face.

He watched her. She looked a little scared to answer the call. Maybe not scared, exactly, but apprehensive. She walked out onto the patio and after what sounded like some stilted pleasantries, he heard the tone of her voice change and become quite animated. She came back into the kitchen after a few minutes with a cautious smile on her face.

"This is awkward. I have a potential new client who wants to meet my husband and we've been asked out to dinner. I totally understand if you decline, given our agreement not to discuss our businesses in our marriage."

"It was your stipulation," Ilya pointed out carefully.

"Which you didn't argue."

"True. If I had, the wedding wouldn't have gone ahead, right?"

She had the grace to look embarrassed. "Right," she answered tightly. "Look, forget it. I—"

"Yasmin, relax. It's a dinner. I think we can waive our

rules this one time. It's obviously important to you or you wouldn't be asking me. When is it?"

"Tomorrow night?"

"Sure," he said, wiping his hands dry on a towel. "We can do that."

He saw her shoulders sag in relief. "Thanks. Um, you weren't competing for the Hardacre contract, too, were you?"

He shook his head. Horvath Aviation had considered it when the job went out for bids, but he had heard rumors about the guy and he didn't want to put any of his staff on the firing line should Wallace Hardacre make the type of inappropriate advance he was rumored to make. Yasmin obviously had put in a bid for the Hardacre contract, however, and he didn't quite know how that made him feel.

Immediately his protective instincts surged to the fore, and he wanted to warn her about what Hardacre could be like. But then an insidious thought wormed through from the back of his mind. Somewhere he'd heard about a deal Hardacre had made with his long-suffering wife, Esme—that he would never touch a married woman.

Was that why Yasmin had suddenly put her single status in the hands of Match Made in Marriage? Had she married solely to secure a business contract? And if she had, where did that leave him if she won it—or didn't? He was developing feelings for her that he hadn't expected. But was she using him? Had he, through no fault of his own, simply repeated the mistakes he'd made in his early twenties?

Oblivious to the turmoil racing around in his mind, Yasmin made them each a mug of decaf coffee. She looked happy. Genuinely happy and completely relaxed. He hated that he had to question it and wonder whether it was because she was with him or because she was on the cusp of reaching some business goal. Suddenly her insistence that they never discuss business took on a whole new meaning. And he didn't like it one little bit. But if she had her secrets, didn't he also? And until he was able to bare his truth to her, how could he demand the same of her?

Yasmin could barely contain her excitement as she got ready for bed. The dinner with Esme and Wallace Hardacre had gone extremely well and she felt certain that Carter Air was the Hardacres' preferred carrier.

She'd had a moment of discomfiture yesterday when she'd wondered if Horvath had bid for the Hardacre contract, as well, but Ilya's assurance they hadn't lifted her heart and her hopes for Carter Air. Maybe now they'd have the stability they so desperately needed. She wouldn't need to let any of her respected team go and she'd be able to pay her loan back in full. And the icing on the cake was the burgeoning relationship she had with Ilya.

The only fly in the ointment right now was those emails. Another one had come through while they'd been at dinner.

You're not listening to me. Leave him now or everyone will know what you're really like.

She'd seriously thought about blocking *hisgirl* but caution had stayed her hand. So far the emails had been empty threats—more nuisance than anything. Certainly nothing she felt she could take to the police. And did she want the police involved, anyway? One thing was certain: she couldn't possibly comply with the demands. And even if she did what she was being told and left Ilya, what would that achieve for *hisgirl*? Was she standing in the wings, waiting to swoop in and take Yasmin's place in his life? She shook her head at her reflection in the mirror. She had to hope it would all just die a natural death if she continued to ignore the messages.

Ilya was already in bed when she finished in the bathroom. She snuggled up to his back and put one arm around his waist.

"Tired?" she asked, her fingers stroking his bare belly.

"Yeah," he answered.

His fingers closed around hers, halting her slow but inexorable movement down his stomach. She accepted the rejection without taking it to heart. Since that first night they'd made love, sleep had been low on their agenda when they'd gone to bed.

"Tonight went well, don't you think?" she said softly against his back.

He grunted an assent. He really must be exhausted, she thought.

"Ilya?"

"Hmm?"

"Were you…?"

She struggled to find the right words, and when she fell silent Ilya sighed and rolled over to face her.

"Was I what?" he prompted.

"Were you going out with anyone before we got married? Anyone you were serious about?"

"No."

His answer was short and emphatic.

"Oh."

"Why do you ask?"

"No reason. Goodnight."

He rolled back onto his side. "G'night."

She lay in the darkened room and listened to his steady breathing. She was almost sure he wasn't asleep. Something was bugging him, but what? When she thought about it, she realized he'd changed after she mentioned the Hardacres last night. In fact, last night had been the first night they hadn't made love since their first time together. She'd put that down to the fact they'd sated themselves with each other at her apartment but maybe there was something else.

Had he been lying to her when he'd said Horvath Aviation hadn't bid for the contract? No, surely not. It would have come out in the conversation at the dinner table tonight. Instead, Esme had talked about their wedding and the joy of being newlyweds, as if reinforcing to her husband that Yasmin was completely out of bounds. Wallace had been happy to discuss golf and the latest ball game results with Ilya. In fact, the conversation had been completely social—not touching on business at all.

So what had gotten under his skin? She wanted to know. Wanted to make it better for him. After yesterday and opening up to him about her college hazing, he'd been so loving, so gentle. And fierce, too, when he'd told her that none of it was her fault. She'd believed him, not only because she'd wanted to, but because she trusted him.

Trust was a fragile thing. Like spun glass. In the wrong hands it could be shattered into a thousand painful shards. But in the right ones, it could be treasured and loved. Was that what she was learning to feel for her husband? Love? She had nothing to compare the feeling with, but the way both her mind and her body reacted when she was with Ilya seemed to indicate that she was very definitely falling for him. It was more than she'd hoped for. More than she'd ever thought she deserved. And all because of him.

She shifted in the bed, trying to get a bit more comfortable, but it felt strange now to try to fall asleep without her limbs entwined with her husband's.

She found herself thinking about her grandfather. He most definitely would have disapproved of this union, but he wasn't here anymore. He'd been her guide growing up, but at her darkest moment she hadn't been able to turn to him for support. She'd struggled through the worst time of her life on her own and had come through on the other end stronger and more determined to succeed without the help of anyone else. But sometimes, she acknowledged, she couldn't do it all on her own.

She considered Jim Carter's bitterness toward the Horvaths purely because he'd been the jilted lover. Alice had broken his heart and he'd built a lifetime of resentment over the fact, poisoning Yasmin's mind about the other private aviation company and its owners from the day her parents had parked her on his doorstep. But Ilya was nothing like the type of man her granddad had told her he was.

You barely know him and you think you're in love with him? She didn't know if the voice in her mind was her own or an echo of her grandfather's, and as it played in her thoughts she couldn't sleep. Something had shifted between her and Ilya. Something she couldn't put her finger on. Something wasn't right.

Twelve

It felt odd to drive toward work together, especially with this awkward new invisible wall that had appeared between them over the weekend. They'd left Ilya's Lamborghini in the garage, taking his brand-new Tesla, instead.

Ilya dropped Yasmin at the front door of Carter Air. He hadn't rebuffed her attempt to kiss him as she'd gotten out the car, but he hadn't exactly turned it into a fond farewell, either. Maybe it was because of the puppy, she thought, as she snapped a leash on his collar and undid his puppy seat belt harness to get him out of the car. Blaze had shown an unholy interest in the armrest next to him and the leather upholstery now bore a less-than-charming set of tooth marks. Ilya had not looked impressed when he'd seen the damage.

Or maybe Ilya was just worried about something waiting for him at Horvath Aviation and had switched into work mode already. She let the puppy go to the bathroom before taking him into the office building attached to Carter Air's main hangar.

The moment Yasmin set foot inside, Riya shot out of her chair to envelope Yasmin in a massive hug.

"Welcome back!" the petite office manager gushed before stepping back to appraise her boss. "Well, well, well, marriage obviously suits you. Look at that glow!"

Yasmin felt her face suffuse with color. "It's just a tan. I laid around the pool a lot."

"Oh, sure, I believe you," Riya answered with a giggle.

"It's true," Yasmin protested, then couldn't help but join in her friend's laughter. She looked around the office. "So, what's new? What do I need to attend to first?"

The two women went into Yasmin's office. Blaze flopped down in a corner and dozed off. Yasmin had taken him for a long walk earlier this morning, to burn off some of his energy so she'd be able to concentrate on work for a few hours, at least. Hannah had suggested leaving him at the house but she wanted to get the puppy used to a varied routine, which included having him learn how to behave at work with either her or Ilya.

"This courier delivery arrived just before you did," Riya said with a massive grin and handed over a legal envelope to her boss.

Yasmin felt her heartbeat speed up. She recognized the name of the attorneys printed in the corner of the envelope. They acted for the Hardacres. She took a deep breath, opened the flap and shook the contents onto her desk. And there it was, the signed contract in black and white. Joy and relief competed for equal space inside her.

"We did it," she said triumphantly, looking up at Riya with a big grin. "We got the contract."

"That's great news. I never doubted you for a minute. They'd have been crazy to accept anyone else's offer. What a great way to kick off the week. I'll let the team know. When do we start with them?"

"Friday," Yasmin said scanning the letter that accompanied the contract. The *signed* contract, she thought with an inner shimmer of happiness. "They have a family trip to Palm Springs."

"It's a good thing we can fit them in, then, isn't it?" Riya said with a wink as she headed out to the main office.

Bookings had been well down these past few months and the relief Yasmin felt was huge. She took her time to read through the contract again, her eyes lingering on the morality clause. Esme Hardacre had insisted upon it, partly to keep her husband's wandering hands in check but also to act as a warning to anyone who looked at the charismatic motivational coach and speaker as fair game. Yasmin hadn't balked at it when she'd bid for the business and had read the initial contract draft as part of the tender process. But now? Given the weird emails she was getting?

She pushed her concerns about the morality clause aside as something that would not be a concern. She'd met Esme's strict criteria and she would continue to do so. That's all there was to it.

Blaze sat up and barked, his nap quite clearly over.

"Wanna go and meet the team?" she said to the little guy, clipping his leash back on. "C'mon, they're going to love you."

As the days went by, getting back into a routine work-week was both satisfying and a little frustrating. Yasmin found herself missing Ilya at odd moments during the day. Even Riya had caught her wistfully staring out her office window toward Horvath Aviation. All the staff had been thrilled about the new contract, approaching their work with renewed vigor and enthusiasm. Yasmin realized the problem hadn't just been hers to bear alone and it was good to know that they were going to be okay. Now, if only she could get to the bottom of why Ilya had become withdrawn in the past few days.

Yasmin had started to use her own truck to get to and

from work. It was much older than anything in Ilya's fleet and more dog-friendly. He hadn't argued when she'd suggested she transport Blaze in the old Ford, but also hadn't suggested he accompany them in it, either. The last two nights, Ilya had worked late into the night, sliding into bed after she'd finally given in and fallen asleep. The honeymoon was very definitely over.

Ilya arrived at his grandmother's on Thursday morning. As he got out of the Tesla, his eye caught on the damage wrought by Blaze, and he made yet another mental note to book an appointment to get it repaired.

He straightened his suit and walked toward the imposing front door of the house his grandfather had ordered built for his bride when he'd made his first million dollars. Old Eduard's love for Alice showed in every line and curlicue of the building; it represented nothing less than a small Hungarian palace. It should have looked incongruous here in California, but with the landscaping and plantings that had been done, it fit into the surroundings as if it had been there for centuries.

The front doors swung open and Alice stood there waiting for him.

"Nagy," he murmured, leaning down to kiss her crepe-soft cheek.

A whisper of her fragrance swirled around him, the floral, powdery scent one he always associated with her, no matter who he encountered wearing it.

"My boy," she patted his cheek. "What brings you here today?"

"We need to talk."

Her smile faded and a serious look crept into her eyes. "Well, then. You'd better come through to my sitting room. Can I offer you anything to eat or drink?"

"This isn't really a social call."

She sniffed in response and straightened her already ramrod-stiff posture even further before leading the way to her private sitting room. Ilya preferred it to the larger room she used when she entertained the extended family or large groups of friends. This room was more intimate and definitely more her.

"What is it?" she demanded.

Alice was nothing if not direct, and Ilya had inherited that from her. But now that he was here, the words that hovered on the edge of his tongue sounded churlish. He knew his grandmother took her matches very seriously. Questioning her about Yasmin was questioning Alice's integrity at the same time. But his grandmother also had a great respect for honesty so he decided to come straight out and ask her the question that had been plaguing him since the dinner with the Hardacres.

"Did Yasmin marry me to secure her new client?"

His grandmother blinked at him. "I beg your pardon?"

Ilya quickly explained the situation with the Hardacres. To her credit, Alice didn't immediately shoot him down for being an idiot. Instead, she sat back in her armchair and studied him carefully.

"And how does that make you feel? To think she might have used you?"

He gave her a sharp look. "Angry, exploited."

"Have you asked her about it?"

"Of course not."

"You're husband and wife, aren't you? Shouldn't you bring your concerns to each other before you seek outside counsel?"

He snorted. "Nagy, you're hardly outside counsel."

"That's true," she acknowledged with a small smile. "But if your marriage is to work, and your reaction to your suspicions makes me believe that you're already well invested in this coupling, you need to learn to work through issues like this together."

She was right, and it irritated the hell out of him to have to admit it. It didn't stop him asking his next question, though.

"You investigated her, didn't you?"

"As my people investigated you also. You agreed to that, if you remember, and it's a prerequisite for being accepted as a client with Match Made in Marriage. No exceptions."

He waved his hand in acknowledgement but then he froze and looked her directly in the eyes. "Just how far back did your investigation go, Nagy?"

Alice's lips formed a straight line. "As far as was necessary, my boy."

"You know about her hazing, don't you," he said with sudden clarity.

The barest inclination of her head gave him the answer he sought.

"How long?" he demanded through clenched teeth.

"Since you finally saw Jennifer Morton for the person she truly is. You hardly think I wouldn't have made discreet inquiries into what led you to break your engagement, do you? You arrived home a broken man. I had to know why."

She'd seen him at his worst—not once, not twice, but three times as he'd lost the three people in his life he'd thought were most important to him. Those losses, the scars they'd left deep inside him, had held him back. And, as much as he hated the reminder, when it came to Yasmin he was still holding back.

Alice drew in a breath, and he saw her fingers tremble slightly as she began to speak again. "Ilya, the only way for a relationship to thrive is with love and honesty. I believe the two of you are likely on the path to love. You both need to work on honesty. I cannot tell you anything that you can't find out for yourself simply by speaking to your wife. Settle this between you. Don't let your pride, or what happened with Jennifer, ruin what could be the best thing to happen to both you and Yasmin."

"But what about her reasons—?"

Alice put up a hand to stop him. "No buts. You each had your reasons for entering your marriage. What you do with it is now up to you. You didn't expect to find love, and I imagine that Yasmin didn't either, but you belong together, I cannot stress that enough. Work this out, Ilya. *Talk* to your wife."

She rose from her seat and Ilya did also, knowing he was being dismissed.

As Ilya drove back home, his mind was whirling. Nothing Nagy did should surprise him and yet today she'd trumped everything with her revelation. Her conviction that he and Yasmin belonged together was unshakeable. And he had to admit yet again, on the face of things, everything appeared to support that conviction. The time he and Yasmin had spent together so far had underlined their deep compatibility on so many levels. So why did it bother him so much that Yasmin might have used their marriage to leverage her chance to win the Hardacre contract? As his grandmother had so rightly pointed out, he'd entered into their match with his own agenda of companionship and children. He'd never expected love...

He wasn't being entirely fair to Yasmin. Carter Air had to be struggling. It was a tough industry and, up until his death, Jim Carter had been holding on by the threads that bound his overalls. Ilya knew Yasmin was proud and stubborn and determined. They were characteristics he was intimately acquainted with himself. Would he have turned to marriage as a solution if their business circumstances were reversed? If he was totally honest with himself, he knew he'd do whatever it took, which was exactly what Yasmin had done.

All that self-talk about commitment had been a crock. At the first hurdle, he'd fallen. He needed to do better and make it up to her. Nagy had impressed honesty upon him. That meant he had to quit putting off telling Yasmin about his part in her hazing. He had to open up the lines of communication between them and approach her about this like a reasonable and rational human being and, if not entirely rational, then like a husband who had truly begun to care for his wife.

Thirteen

Yasmin looked up from her flight plan for the next day as a message notification pinged on her laptop screen. She opened her email program. One unread message. Her skin crawled when she saw who it was from—*hisgirl*. There'd been nothing since the night of the dinner with the Hardacres and Yasmin had been hoping that the person had given up. Apparently not.

Her eyes scanned the subject header: I warned you.

She clicked on the message but there was no content. Nothing. Just that header. What the heck did that mean? They'd warned her. So what?

The phone on her desk started to ring, dragging her attention away from the computer.

"It's Esme Hardacre for you," her receptionist informed her before switching the call through.

"Esme, how lovely to hear from you. I'm just finalizing the flight plan for tomo—"

"You can forget it. In fact, you can forget everything.

We're canceling our contract with you." The woman's voice was cold and hard, as if every word spoken was carved from ice.

"What? Why?" Yasmin blurted out.

"I thought you were better than that. Was my husband to be the next feather in your cap? Seriously, you need help."

"Esme, please. Can you explain?"

But she was talking to dead air. Yasmin quickly punched in the number for Hardacre Industries, her fingers trembling. What the heck had just happened?

"This is Mrs. Hardacre's assistant," came a disembodied voice in her ear when she identified herself and asked to be put through to Esme.

"I need to speak with Mrs. Hardacre, please."

"Mrs. Hardacre is not taking calls."

"Look, she just called me. I really need to talk to her. I'd like some explanation."

"Explanation?" the tone of the man's voice just about shriveled her ear. "The photos were bad enough but I think the video is all the explanation the Hardacres needed."

"What video?" Yasmin demanded, but she felt an icy finger of inevitability drag through her. Was this what *his-girl* had meant about being warned?

"I just sent you an email," came the assistant's succinct reply before the call was abruptly disconnected.

On cue, her computer pinged again. Yasmin shifted her mouse, the cursor on the screen hovering over the new message. It had been forwarded, and she immediately saw that the original message was from her nemesis. As usual, it was succinct.

Be careful who you trust. Yasmin Carter is not as squeaky clean as she seems.

There were four attachments. Three photo files and one movie file.

Yasmin swallowed against the bile that rose in her throat as she opened the first photo. Her blood ran cold as she recognized it immediately as the one sent to her two weeks ago. She flicked through to the next photo and the next, feeling sicker with each one, but the video was by far the worst. It had been taken just before she had her last vodka shot and entered the water for her final challenge.

While so much of that night remained a blur, parts of it she could recall. They'd blindfolded her and spun her around. She'd dropped to her knees. She could still remember the sensation of the gritty sand embedding in her skin, remembered the vertigo and the nausea that had assailed her. In the video she'd been told to strip down to her underwear, to the shouts and catcalls of the young women surrounding her. She'd tried to stand, she remembered that, and lost her balance, sprawling on her back in the sand. A sex toy had landed on the ground next to her and a disembodied voice could be heard coaxing her to use it or forfeit.

Yasmin closed the window before she saw the rest. Her stomach heaved and she shot to her feet and raced for the bathroom. Riya looked up from her desk as Yasmin ran down the hall.

"Yasmin? Are you okay?"

She couldn't speak. She made it to the bathroom just in time, only just managing to lock the door behind her before her stomach erupted. Even though she couldn't remember all the details of that night, it had been her worst nightmare. It had been something she'd done her best to get over, to forget, to rise above. And now it had been broadcast to her client. Whoever was behind this must hate her very much. Sending those files to the Hardacres was vindictive and cruel. And it had lost her everything.

Her stomach heaved again, but there was nothing left.

How symbolic, she thought bitterly. There really was nothing left.

What on earth was *hisgirl*'s agenda? And how on earth
was she going to hold her company together, let alone repay
her loan? She had to take this to the police now. The damage that had been wrought by *hisgirl* was criminal, surely.
But the thought of showing the files to the police, of reliving it all again and again had her dry retching once more.

"Yasmin?" Riya was at the door, gently knocking.

"I'm okay," Yasmin croaked. "Be out in a minute."

She hauled herself up to her feet and flushed the toilet,
then went to the basin, rinsed her mouth and splashed her
face with cold water. She eyed her reflection in the mirror. A pale face with stricken eyes stared back at her—her
features a far cry from those of the girl in the video. But
they were one and the same person and, it seemed, tarred
with the same brush.

Ilya had said what had happened to her that night hadn't
been her fault but she knew how others would see it because she saw it that way herself. She could have walked
away before it got to the point where she was no longer
able to make decisions for herself. She could have called
a halt to the increasingly degrading activities the queen
bee of the sorority demanded of her.

Yes, she understood that others were also to blame,
that essentially she'd been in their care, but deep down inside she still felt *she* was ultimately the one who'd made
the choice to sacrifice her dignity just to fit in. And with
what she'd chosen to do that night, she'd sacrificed everything her grandfather had worked so hard to build—
everything she herself had worked so hard to hold on to.
She'd failed. Again.

Riya was still on the other side of the door when Yasmin came out of the bathroom.

"Something I ate," she said in explanation as she

brushed off Riya's concern and moved past her friend to head back to her office.

Changing her mind partway there, she went through the door that led to the hangar. She stood in the high-ceilinged building that her grandfather had built from the ground up nearly seventy years ago. The building that had consumed him, that had been his sole source of satisfaction his whole working life. The building she'd put up as security for her wedding loan. She looked at the Beechcraft she'd added to the small fleet, at the mechanics doing the final check for the flight plan that would no longer be executed tomorrow.

That would be the first plane she'd have to let go. She'd opted to buy rather than lease—a business tenet she'd inherited from her grandfather. It had left Carter Air with no financial buffers. She loved flying the twin, but without the demand for it, she'd have to sell it—and hopefully for enough to cover the short-term loan she'd taken out to get married.

She wandered through the hangar, feeling as though her heart was breaking, and let her eyes drift over the smaller craft. There was a chance she might be able to pass them to the flying school that operated out of the airfield and recover something of her losses there if she was lucky. Despair and helplessness threatened to drive her to her knees. Bit by bit her fleet and her team would have to go. She had no avenues left open to her anymore. She drifted into her private hangar next door, to her Ryan. It would have to go, too. Her plane, the hangar, her apartment. She couldn't afford to hold on to any of it if Carter Air crumbled. She was numb with grief and all the while questions kept echoing in her head. Why? Who? What next?

She breathed in the air redolent with fuel. A smell that was as much a part of her as her DNA. Maybe she'd get a job working for someone else, but would her staff? They were her responsibility and she'd let them down.

Yasmin sensed a movement behind her, caught a familiar hint of pine and sandalwood. Ilya. She turned to face him.

"Riya called me. She said you weren't well."

"She didn't need to do that. As you can see, I'm quite fine."

He looked at her. Really looked, and she felt as if he was probing beneath the surface, seeing the rot that lay beneath.

"You don't look fine. Maybe you should let me take you home."

"Really, I'm okay. Besides, I have to pick up Blaze from puppy day care," she hedged.

She couldn't go home yet. Not when she had to explain to her team that things had taken a turn for the worse. That there was no Hardacre contract anymore. Ilya reached out one finger, touched her cheek and then held his finger, moist from the tears she hadn't even realized she was crying, up for her perusal.

"That doesn't say fine to me."

She closed her eyes for a moment, her hands forming tight fists at her sides. Then she forced herself to open her eyes. She had to tell someone about losing the Hardacre business. She might as well start with him.

"The Hardacres changed their minds. They no longer wish to use Carter Air as their carrier."

"What? They can't do that. You have a contract."

She swallowed and looked away for a moment. "Had a contract. There was a morality clause that they insisted on, that I agreed to."

"Okay, but I still don't see why they ditched you."

Yasmin dragged in a breath. "Do you remember what I told you about my hazing?"

He nodded, his face taking on a serious cast that gave her a glimpse into the hard-nosed businessman she'd always understood him to be.

"I don't see what that has to do with anything."

"It seems that conduct unbecoming has no expiry date. Someone sent them photos and video of that night. As a result, they no longer require my services."

Ilya couldn't believe the words that came from Yasmin's mouth. No wonder she looked so haggard. He reached for Yasmin, pulled her to him. She came willingly, her slender form fitting against him, her arms sliding around his waist. The front of his shirt grew damp with her tears and he felt his heart shatter with the knowledge that she was in so much pain.

He'd planned to tell Yasmin everything tonight. To lay his own misjudgment of Jen's character and his involvement with Yasmin's hazing on the table and beg her forgiveness for both not telling her sooner and for not reporting Jen long ago. But with Yasmin as shell-shocked and vulnerable as she was, how could he throw that in her face now?

The way he saw it, there was only one person who could be attacking Yasmin and that was his ex-fiancée. If he'd acted earlier none of this would be happening now. But one thing was for sure. It stopped now. He'd track Jen down and he'd make sure she faced the full consequences of her actions. But first he had to make things right for his wife.

"We'll work something out," he said firmly.

"There's nothing left to work out. I'm going to have to wind up. Not immediately, but over the next couple of months. We're barely making enough to cover fuel and wages as it is."

He'd had no idea that things were so bad.

"We'll find a way, Yasmin, I promise."

"You can't promise something you have no control over!" she retorted, pushing herself away from him.

Ilya reached for her hand, determined to keep a connection with her. To try and infuse in her some level of trust that together they could sort this out.

"Let's go into your office. We can talk better there and you can show me Carter Air's current financials. There must be something we can do."

Several hours later Ilya pushed back from Yasmin's computer and rubbed at the tension in his neck. It was a miracle Yasmin had held onto Carter Air this long. He'd suspected the company had been in a bad position long before she'd taken over and he'd speculated that the only way she'd survived was by shaving costs dramatically to be able to undercut her competition on contract bids, but he'd had no idea by how much.

She'd barely been drawing a salary. Probably only enough to cover her utilities, food and fuel for her truck and the Ryan. But she hadn't stinted on costs where it mattered most: staff and maintenance. And then there was the loan she'd admitted to taking out to go ahead with the wedding. He sighed in frustration. He could see why she'd done it but she'd had no safety net in case things fell through. And they had fallen through.

There was a way forward, but only if she'd put her pride and fierce independence aside. Would she go for it?

For a brief moment, he wondered where she'd be right now if Carter Air had closed before she'd taken it over, if her grandfather had let go of his own inability to admit defeat when the writing had been on the wall for more years than Ilya cared to think about. It seemed so grossly unfair that Jim Carter had pushed the yoke of expectation onto his granddaughter. What would she have wanted to do if this hadn't been the expectation thrust upon her most of her adult life? And what kind of a husband was he, that he hadn't even asked her that simple question?

"It's bad, isn't it?" Yasmin said.

"Yeah, I can't sugarcoat it, Yasmin. You've done a great job keeping things going so far, but as you pinpointed a while back, you need a long-term, steady flow of income to push you over the hump and into a more viable position."

"And I don't have that anymore."

"Are you sure you're not willing to discuss it further with the Hardacres?"

She vehemently shook her head. "I tried. They won't even take my calls. As far as they're concerned I'm in breach of contract and, Ilya, to be honest, I don't want this to blow up any further than it already has."

"And you're not prepared to let me have my legal team look at it?" Maybe if he got his people onto this they might be able to confirm his suspicions about who was responsible for sending the photos and video. But Yasmin was adamant.

"Absolutely not."

"Then there's only one thing left."

"Declare bankruptcy."

"No, not yet, anyway. I have some ideas that might allow you to continue operations and get you on your feet. But you're not going to like them."

Yasmin chewed on her lower lip. "You're not going to offer to buy me out, are you?"

"That is an option. Do you want me to?"

"No. I'd rather close tomorrow than do that."

Ilya took the blow like a punch to the gut. "That makes your feelings pretty clear."

"I'm sorry. I just couldn't. You don't understand. My grandfather—"

"Your grandfather let his pride and bitterness get in the way of far too much. Are you going to do the same?" he demanded, too frustrated with himself to realize he was beginning to lose patience with his beautiful but stubborn bride. "He's dead, Yasmin. And you're not. You're facing some serious financial issues here—it's not just you, it's your whole staff and the clients you currently have who will be affected—and yet you're just as stubborn as the old man was. You need help."

She blinked and looked away. *Oh, hell, no.* Not tears again. His mother's tears had always been his undoing and he'd never felt so helpless in his life as when he faced a crying woman—especially one he had feelings for. He hated that he had to be so blunt, but there was nothing else left to do. He watched Yasmin as she pulled herself together and turned back to face him.

"What's your suggestion?" She enunciated carefully, as if every word had to be pulled from her.

"That Horvath Aviation assign our smaller contract work to you." He held up a hand as she started to interrupt. "No, hear me out. It's not a pity offer. It's purely a business decision we've been batting around in the boardroom for a while already. We considered branching out with another arm of Horvath Aviation that concentrated solely on the kind of work you do. As you know, it's a fiercely competitive niche and after completing our studies, we decided it wasn't viable for us to pursue it with our existing fleet. So this is what I suggest."

Ilya spent the next half hour outlining how he thought they could handle it.

"And, in doing this, I want to make you a personal loan to cover the money you borrowed for the wedding."

"No!" She shot out of her seat.

Ilya looked at her and willed her to understand where he was coming from with his offer. He had to make this right, even if he couldn't explain the full reasons why right here and now. Guilt plucked at him. If only he hadn't allowed Jen to persuade him not to report the hazing for what it really was. If only he could turn back time. Was this what Nagy had expected of him? That he'd finally repair the damage done to Yasmin more than ten years ago? Well, he accepted that challenge. Right here, right now. He put every ounce of persuasion he could into his voice as he continued. "It's a personal loan, Yasmin. Between you and me. No one else needs to know about it. You can make payments to me when you're drawing a regular salary again, which I'd advise you commence as soon as we've ironed out the finer points of the subcontracting deal. Either that, or you're going to have to allow me to invest in Carter Air—either personally or through Horvath Aviation.

"You can see the writing on the wall as well as I can, Yasmin. Without an injection of money somewhere, you have no choice but to close. You won't be able to meet your loan repayments, you won't be able to meet fuel costs, wages, insurance. It's your choice. Are you going to insist on standing on your pride, or will you accept a hand offered in a genuine expression of help?"

Fourteen

None of what he'd said came as a surprise, and yet there was a part of her that still wanted to argue she could do this on her own. Sell a few planes, downsize and then just possibly be able to hang on by her fingernails for just a bit longer. But at the same time, she couldn't let down the staff that relied on her to make the kind of sound decisions that would keep them in stable employment. And what would she be left hanging on to? A skeleton of what Carter Air had been?

She felt sick to her stomach. She knew she had to accept Ilya's offer of assistance—at the very least accept the subcontracting offer. It would be a start, even though it left her beholden to both him and his company's largesse. A month ago she would never have considered this as an option, but right now, it was the only thing standing between her and bankruptcy. Yasmin forced herself to calm down and settle herself back in her seat. She pressed her hands down on the tops of her thighs to try and stop them shaking.

"Okay."

She had to do whatever it took to make it all right. And *hisgirl* needed to be stopped before they did anything else. Maybe if she'd taken the earlier emails to the police this wouldn't have happened. As soon as she'd ironed things out with Ilya, she was going to the police.

"Okay?" Ilya repeated.

"Yes, I agree to Carter Air subcontracting work to Horvath Aviation and I accept your offer of a personal loan to repay the bank for the money I borrowed for the wedding."

Even as she said the words she felt the weight of sole responsibility begin to lift from her shoulders. The sensation was such a release. She'd been so adamant about not involving Ilya in Carter Air in any way, but his insights proved invaluable. And there'd been no blame or recrimination from him, either. Just solid strength and support. Was this what a real marriage felt like? The knowledge that someone always had your back, without judgment or recriminations, no matter what?

Ilya heaved a huge sigh and smiled. "We'll work it out, you'll see. Would you also consider agreeing to my financial people taking a look at the long-term situation for Carter Air?"

Yasmin looked at him in surprise. In the back of her mind she could hear her grandfather's howl of outrage that she could even consider relinquishing so much control to a Horvath. But, from what she'd seen in the past few weeks, Jim Carter had been wrong about Ilya and his family. All they'd done was be helpful. She firmly pushed the embedded suspicions aside.

"Yasmin?"

"Fine, do what you have to, but I insist on being involved every step of the way. No decisions will be made without my okay."

"And what about the information that went to the Hardacres? Will you let me look into that?"

"No. Absolutely not. I will handle it," she said unequivocally.

Ilya reached across the desk and wrapped his fingers around her clenched fist.

"I know this isn't easy for you, Yasmin. I'll make sure my people keep you in the loop. Now," he said, rising from his seat, "shall we go home?"

She looked at the clock on the wall and realized, in horror, that she was supposed to have picked Blaze up from doggy day care by now.

"Oh, no, I'm running late!"

"I asked Hannah to collect Blaze for us when you went to get the files from Riya."

"You think of everything, don't you?"

"Control freak, remember?" he said.

His lips curved into a smile that, even through all the turmoil she was facing, managed to hit her square in the chest and spread warmth through her body. She laughed.

"How could I forget?" she answered drily as she gathered her things. "You're totally in your element."

"Let's ride home together," he suggested. "I can drop you off here in the morning."

She was about to protest but exhaustion pulled at every part of her. "Okay, thanks."

"What? No argument?"

"I'm bowing to your control freakiness, all right?"

He gave her another one of those smiles. "Yeah. And, Yasmin…" He paused reaching for her hand and threading his fingers with hers. "We've got this. Together we'll get you through."

I hope so, Yasmin thought to herself as they exited the building and got into Ilya's car to go home. All the way back to Ojai she remained silent, her mind churning with the day's events, how Ilya had strode in like some knight in shining armor and saved the day. Was that what their marriage was to be like? Her making mistakes, him coming along and solving her problems and making her depend on him more and more? It felt so unbalanced, so unlike her to rely so heavily on another person.

No, whichever way she looked at it she had no other choice than to accept Ilya's offer of help. She made the right decision for her company and her staff. But there was one thing she would do on her own—tomorrow she would contact the police.

Yasmin went to bed early that night but Ilya wasn't far behind. She felt the mattress dip slightly as he got under the covers. They hadn't made love for days and right now she wasn't sure if she even wanted to, but her body craved him. Craved being close to him. Craved that sense that no matter what was wrong, she was safe in his arms. When he reached for her she went willingly, curving her body against his and resting her head on his chest.

Beneath her ear his heart beat was strong, steady and true.

"You okay?" he asked in the dark, the rumble of his voice tickling her ear.

"I'll be fine. It's a lot to get my head around."

"You've made the right choice."

She nodded. She knew that. Sometimes the right choices weren't the easy ones, were they?

Ilya stroked the back of her head. "I've missed you."

"I wasn't the one who pulled away."

"I know. I'm sorry. I had some stuff to work out."

"And you couldn't discuss it with me?"

He huffed out a breath that could have been a laugh. "Seems we both have a lot to learn about being married and sharing, doesn't it?"

He was right, as much as she hated to admit it. He
spoke again.

"Shall we agree that in the future, if you need anything,
any kind of help, you'll come to me. In work and here, at
home. I'm your husband. You need to tell me when something's wrong."

She stiffened, her extreme self-reliance protesting. But,
she reminded herself, without Ilya's help and suggestions
today, Carter Air would be facing a very different future.

"Okay, yes, I agree."

The words came from her reluctantly. Years of being
her grandfather's sounding board and right hand had left
their mark. You didn't just undo a lifetime of condition-
ing in one horrible day.

Ilya's arms squeezed her tight. "Thank you," he murmured against the top of her head. "We can make this
work, if we work together."

Despite his reassurance, Yasmin realized he hadn't
mentioned anything about coming to her if the need for
support was reversed. Did he still expect to be there for
her, while not needing her in return? Or maybe there was
something else holding him back. Something she didn't
know about. Maybe he had some other agenda behind his
offer of help? She told herself to stop being so silly, to
simply take his very generous offer at face value. But she
wasn't Jim Carter's granddaughter for nothing, and even
though Ilya had come through for her today in ways she'd
never have anticipated, something felt off.

Ilya woke to the delicious heaviness of Yasmin still
sprawled across him. He traced one finger down her back.
Her skin instantly broke out in a trail of goose bumps following the path of his touch. She stretched against him
and his body quickened the way it always did when she
was around. His hand continued on its journey, his fingers

tickling the base of her spine where her back curved in just so, then traveled lower to cup the curve of her bottom.

"Good morning to you, too," she murmured against his chest.

He rolled Yasmin onto her back and bent to nuzzle the side of her neck. "It's about to be a very good morning," he whispered in her ear.

His phone rang.

"Ignore it," she whispered in *his* ear.

Her hands moved swiftly to his body, skimming his shoulders, his chest, his belly. The phone continued to ring.

"I'm going to have to take it," he groaned in frustration and dragged himself away from her.

He grabbed his phone from the nightstand and, seeing it was the general manager of his East Coast subsidiary on the line, stabbed the screen with one finger to accept the call. It was hard for him to concentrate on the message being relayed to him as Yasmin sat up on the bed and whipped her nightgown off in one sleek movement. She tossed the garment at him and he caught her scent as he snatched the slip of silk from the air and let it slide through his fingers onto the bed. There was already a flush of arousal on her chest and her nipples were taut. He felt the deep throb of need pull through his body.

But suddenly the words "heart attack" and "hospital" caught his attention and he realized what was being said to him.

"I'll be there as soon as I can," he said, disconnecting the call.

Guilt and regret rippled through him at the thought of leaving Yasmin so soon after the turmoil of yesterday. Plus, as he'd finally drifted to sleep last night, he'd promised himself he would talk to her today about the secret he still withheld. Now he wouldn't have time to do either as his presence was urgently required in New York. He stopped her hands as they skimmed over him and dragged them to his lips, kissing her knuckles.

"I'm sorry. I'm going to have to take a rain check. Emergency at one of our subsidiaries."

Yasmin's demeanor changed in an instant. "Is it really serious?"

She slipped from the bed and pulled on a robe, tying the sash tight at her waist.

"Unfortunately, yes. The general manager of our East Coast office has had a massive heart attack. I need to go and fill in for him for a few days until we know what's happening."

"There's no one else you can send?"

He heard the silent plea in her voice and her vulnerability struck him to his core. If only it had been anyone other than Zachary Penney. He quickly explained to Yasmin. "This guy is a close friend of Nagy's. I owe it to his family, and mine, to be there."

"Of course. What can I do to help?"

She was instantly all business and he was infinitely grateful she was there. In no time she had him pushed in the direction of the bathroom while she packed a suitcase for him. By the time he was dressed and downstairs, she was already in the kitchen with a smoothie at the ready.

"You're going to regret not sharing your recipe with me," she said with a grin as she handed him the glass. "I had to guess."

He took a sip, grimaced, then downed the rest in one gulp. "You're right. It'll be first thing on my agenda when I get back."

"First thing?" Yasmin asked coyly, one fingertip tracing the outline of her nipple through the thin fabric of her robe.

He grinned. "Okay, second."

He leaned forward and gave her a hard kiss. "Thanks for everything. I'll call you tonight. And don't worry. I'll instruct the bank to make that transfer so you can settle your loan later today. Make sure you get the figures. My bank manager will be in touch."

"Don't worry about that now. It's not urgent."

"I'll deal with it."

Outside they could hear the beat of helicopter blades in the air.

"Sounds like your ride to the airport is here," Yasmin said, stepping close and hooking her arms around his neck. She pressed herself against his body and kissed him again. "Take care, huh?"

"You, too," he said.

In no time he was up at the helipad. He stowed his case in the back of the chopper before taking the left-hand seat. When he took off, he circled over the house before heading to the airport. He usually relished tackling a challenge like this. Normally by now he'd be planning ahead as to how he could best ensure that the necessary contingencies were put in place quickly and efficiently. But this time, every cell in his body was attuned to the woman waving at him from below. He didn't just wish they'd been able to complete their morning together; he wished he didn't have to leave her, period.

He wasn't used to wanting someone like this. Sure, he had to make everything right for his family and loved them fiercely. But this was different. It left him daunted. After losing first his father, then his mother, and then being betrayed by his fiancée, he'd always believed that loving someone outside of his immediate family circle was inviting weakness, vulnerability. But he could no longer deny his growing feelings for Yasmin.

This was more than a crush, more than a lust-filled haze of need. Thinking she was using him to win the Hardacres' business had caused a knee-jerk reaction to pull away, as if he'd been looking for a reason for their marriage to fail, he could see that now. He was grateful to his grandmother for her guidance. He fought a smile. The older woman's knack for giving advice had been right on target. He did need to learn to open up, and so did Yasmin. As Nagy had so astutely pointed out, with honesty between them, they could do this.

Which brought him back to the secret he was holding back.

Would telling her destroy the fragile links they'd forged after yesterday? He had to tell her; it was a huge risk not to. The past had a way of coming back to a person and even though he hadn't been an instigator in the torment she'd endured, both back then and more recently, he had to act now to protect her as he ought to have done before.

He landed the helicopter at the airfield. A Gulfstream was waiting for him on the tarmac close by.

He wished he'd told her already. Of course, the right time to have done so would have been after she'd first disclosed to him who she was. But he couldn't turn back time. Nor could he turn around and go back to her right now. It would have to wait until he got home. He'd find a way to tell her everything because he hated having this secret lingering between them like a malignant stain on their relationship. And, despite Yasmin's refusal of his offer, he had every intention of discovering exactly who the Hardacre's informant had been so he would bring them to justice.

It was no longer enough to just be married. He realized now that he wanted it all. Everything that marriage to another human being entailed. Love, honor, respect, togetherness—right down to the very last wrinkle.

Fifteen

It had been four days—and four desperately lonely nights—since Ilya went away. For Yasmin, the days had been filled with walking and playing with the puppy, dealing with the contracts that had come across her desk from Horvath's legal team and flying the occasional client to their requested destination. But her nights were a different story. Sleep had become a fractured thing; she frequently paced the moonlit bedroom floor when wakefulness drove her from the bed.

Ilya had made a point of calling her each evening, and she found herself hanging onto the phone long after they'd said their goodbyes, reluctant to sever that ephemeral contact with him. A glance in the mirror this morning told her that pining for him was taking its toll, leaving dark shadows under her eyes. Ridiculous, when this coming weekend marked four weeks since they'd been married.

And what a roller coaster it had been so far, she thought as she settled Blaze in his crate for the night and wandered through to the office to fire up the computer. She had brought some work home with her and Ilya had told her to use the home computer if she ever needed it. On top of everything else going on, her laptop had died and she'd taken it in to get repaired.

She settled herself in the leather chair at the desk and sat for just a moment, closing her eyes and imagining him sitting here. She'd missed her parents when they'd gone traveling; she'd missed her grandfather when he'd passed away. But this felt different. It was a physical ache. She couldn't wait for Ilya to return home. Quick phone calls simply weren't enough.

How had he come to be such a vital part of her life so quickly? She'd always been the self-sufficient one, the solver of her own problems. The one others could rely on. It had often been a heavy responsibility to bear, but now it was as if Ilya had lifted that weight from her shoulders and bore it on his alone. Somehow they had to find a middle ground. She didn't want to give up every last bastion of control and independence, and she knew he didn't either, but she had growing confidence they could make it work.

He'd been as good as his word, and the money to repay her loan had appeared in her bank account the day he left for New York. Thankfully, there'd been no further fallout from the Hardacre debacle and she'd filed a complaint with the police, but Yasmin still walked around feeling as though there was yet another hammer blow still to drop. She hated feeling like this—as if turning the corner past that situation was just setting her up for another fall.

She spent about an hour checking through the Horvath subcontracting paperwork, making small notations here and there, before scanning the documents and emailing them to her lawyers for a final read through. Provided Ilya agreed to the minor tweaks she wanted, Carter Air had a future. She sat back in her chair for a moment and heaved a massive sigh of relief. She knew that good business generated more business. Working with the Horvaths might have been her grandfather's idea of hell on earth, but right now it was a godsend.

The deal with Horvath Aviation was ironclad. She knew Ilya would stand by his word because he was that kind of guy. This past month had taught her a lot about him. Not everything, obviously, and she looked forward to what she had yet to discover about her husband. Like, his most ticklish spots, she thought with a secretive smile. Or what movies he liked. She was a sucker for the old Bogie and Bacall black and whites herself. Maybe she'd organize a movie night for the two of them when he got back, and cook her special eggplant parmigiana.

She started mentally making a grocery list to give to Hannah as she logged into her mail before shutting down the computer. All thoughts of cooking and movie nights fled, however, when she saw the new message waiting in her inbox. Yasmin swallowed against the sick feeling that threatened to choke her as she opened it.

Your husband knows a lot more than he's telling you.

"What do you mean?" Yasmin all but shouted at the computer screen. "Enough with these stupid cryptic messages." Her fingers flew across the keyboard as she drafted a reply.

She kept it short and sweet.

You've done your worst. Now leave me alone.

She hit Send and went to close the window but a new message popped straight back up in her inbox.

You think that was my worst? He was at your hazing, did you know that?

"You're lying," Yasmin whispered in shock before keying those very words into the computer.

Again she hit Send but this time she waited for a reply. It didn't take long. Seconds later, email after email began to flood her inbox, each one with an attachment. Yasmin hesitated to open the first one but she figured that with Ilya's computer security being top-of-the-line she'd be safe. If the attachment had come with any viruses or malware, his software would block it.

The photo filled the screen and as she identified the people in it, Yasmin's skin crawled in horror. It was a picture of Ilya—younger, certainly more carefree, but just as handsome as ever. But it wasn't Ilya who caused the visceral reaction that crawled through her body like some insidious vile disease. It was Jennifer Morton. The woman who'd strung her along, devised challenge after challenge for her, then almost killed her when Yasmin wouldn't back down. And she was tucked under Ilya's arm and looking up into his eyes, their smiles speaking volumes about their feelings for each other.

One by one, Yasmin trawled through the rest of the pictures. Her head was spinning by the time she got to the last one. It was a picture of a just-woken, sleep-mussed, naked Ilya in a bed. In the foreground was a photo of a woman's hand wearing an engagement ring. The picture was captioned, "I said yes!"

Another message came in. Feeling a sense of the inevitable, Yasmin opened it.

He was there that night. He knows how pathetic you are.

Ilya had been there?

Yasmin stayed frozen in her chair, staring at the screen. Emotions tumbled through her. Shock. Revulsion. Anger. But most of all, betrayal. Ilya knew it all. He'd seen her at her worst. He'd been party to her ultimate degradation. He'd been engaged to Jennifer Morton.

Why had he hidden the truth from her? She'd opened her soul to him that day they'd gone up in the Ryan. Sure, she'd skirted a few of the more sordid details, but she'd bared virtually everything to him about what had happened and how it had affected her. Her eyes glazed over until she could no longer see the screen, but that didn't do anything to assuage the clawing pain that ripped inside her chest.

She'd trusted him with her greatest fear, and yet he'd known it all along. How could he have sat there, after they'd made love, and listened to her pouring her heart out and said nothing at all? Had this been some kind of joke to him? Was he, even now, laughing behind her back about how pitiful she'd been back then? How pitiful now? Was he somehow still in touch with Jennifer and were they laughing together? Or worse, was this all some elaborate scheme to wrest control of her business from her? Ilya had already said his firm had looked into branching out in the smaller client contracts market Carter Air flew, but that it hadn't been viable to establish a new division with that focus. But how much more viable would it be to take over an existing operation?

Yasmin could only be relieved that she'd refused to allow him to buy into Carter Air. Yes, she was still beholden to him for the personal loan, but her business, her life's blood, was still hers. Then there was the Horvath Aviation subcontract. But thinking about it now, it made her feel distinctly uncomfortable. How long had he been planning this? And was Jennifer involved? Were they in this together? Still quietly laughing at her behind her back?

And what about Alice? Was she in on it, too? While every
instinct urged her to email her lawyers immediately and
tell them to instruct Horvath exactly where to shove its
business, she couldn't do it to her staff. But no one said
she had to stay here, or stay married to a man who'd withheld a vital truth from her.

She didn't sleep a wink that night. Instead, she spent
all her time removing every last personal item she owned
from the house and packing it into her truck. By the time
Hannah arrived first thing in the morning, Yasmin was
running on coffee and not a lot else.

"Are you okay, Mrs. Horvath?"

Yasmin barely managed not to roll her eyes. No matter
how often she'd told Hannah to call her Yasmin or, if she
must, Ms. Carter, she insisted on calling her Mrs. Horvath. Yasmin had begun not to notice so much, but this
morning it succeeded in rubbing salt into an already exposed wound.

"Just a little tired is all," she answered, reaching for
the coffee carafe and pulling a face when she realized it
was empty. Again.

"Oh, you leave that to me. I'll make you a fresh pot,"
Hannah said, bustling past her and refilling the machine.
"You must be missing Mr. Horvath, yes?"

Yasmin had been. She'd missed him as if a vital part of
her was suddenly gone. Which, altogether, made her even
more laughable, she realized. She closed her eyes a moment as they began to burn with more unshed tears and
shook her head slightly.

All night she'd tried to understand why he hadn't told
her the truth about him and Jennifer. Would it have been
so very hard? She was exhausted from wondering about
his reasons, wondering what kind of man he really was,
wondering why she'd allowed herself to fall in love with
him. And that, she felt, was the biggest betrayal of all. He'd

presented himself to her as the kind of man she'd only ever dreamed of meeting, but beneath it all, he was a fake.

She watched as Blaze walked outside on the patio, playing with a leaf that fluttered past before getting distracted by a chew toy that had been left under a sun lounger. Ilya had been so compassionate with the puppy. So determined to give him a home. Had that, too, been a lie constructed to somehow win her trust? For what purpose? None of it even made sense. All she knew is she needed to create some distance between them. She couldn't think here in his beautiful home because everything reminded her of him.

Blaze bounded in through the open patio doors and sat on her foot. She bent down and absently scratched his head and gave his chest a rub. What would she do with him? Was he even hers to take? He'd been found on Ilya's property, his care had been provided for by Ilya's cousin and paid for by Ilya himself. As much as it would break her heart, she had to leave Blaze behind.

Overhead, she heard the sound of a helicopter approaching the house. Her stomach tightened in a knot. Ilya had said nothing last night about coming home today. How on earth was she going to face him now, knowing what she did?

Ilya alighted from the chopper and gave Pete a thumbsup after he'd taken his case from the back and walked clear of the helipad. He was exhausted but, as Valentin had wryly pointed out to him over a quick dinner together last night, what was he doing hanging around in New York when he had a beautiful wife waiting for him at home?

It had been a grueling few days away, but he was satisfied that not only was his general manager on the road to recovery, but everything else was in good hands for their operations to continue as normal. And, if old Zachary wasn't well enough in a few months to resume his duties,

there was a succession plan in place so they could cross
that bridge, too.

For now, though, all Ilya wanted was his wife. As busy
as he'd been, he'd found his thoughts straying to her in
unguarded moments and he'd missed her more than he
would have thought possible. He'd kept his early arrival
home a surprise, but given the fact he'd arrived by chopper, he figured she probably knew he was there by now.
He felt strangely nervous, knowing what was coming—
that he was about to reveal his part in her hazing and his
desire to press historical charges—but not knowing how
she would respond. He could only hope that the feelings
they'd developed for one another would see them through.

It kind of surprised him that she hadn't come up to the
helipad to welcome him home. Maybe she was out walking Blaze. If that was the case, he might have time to have
a quick shower to erase the grime of travel before taking
up again where they'd been interrupted before he'd had
to fly East.

As he walked along the path, he heard the sound of
Hannah's car going up the long driveway that led to the
main road. It was strange that the housekeeper was heading out so early in the day when she normally would have
only just arrived at the house. But it was nowhere near as
strange as seeing Yasmin's truck parked in front of the
house loaded with suitcases.

The front doors opened and the chill of foreboding that
had begun to tickle at the back of his mind gave him a
swift hard yank into reality when he saw the look on Yasmin's face.

"I wasn't expecting you," she said bluntly.

No welcome. No smile. No *Honey, I missed you.* Just a
blank wall of…what? He wasn't sure exactly. All he knew
was he needed to go into damage control mode.

"Hey," he answered her with a tentative smile. "I wanted to surprise you. Looks like I succeeded, huh?"

She gave him a bitter look in return. "Surprise. Yes, I guess you could call it that."

He swallowed. This wasn't going how he'd planned at all. When he left, he'd felt like they were on a pathway to a stronger future together. Even last night, when they'd spoken on the phone, hadn't there been affection and longing in her voice as they'd ended the call? What the hell had happened between then and now to change her into this cold effigy of the warm and caring woman he'd left only five mornings ago?

He drew nearer. "Where's Blaze?"

"Hannah took him to day care for me."

"I see."

Ilya didn't see at all. Why was Hannah taking the dog when the day care was on Yasmin's route to work? He looked at his wife's closed expression, trying to figure out what had changed between them since they spoke last night on the phone. He reached out to touch her.

"I missed you," he said, infusing his voice with all the longing that had been building since he left.

She neatly sidestepped his outstretched hand. "Please don't touch me."

Her words were delivered oh, so politely, but they felt like a vicious slap.

"Yasmin, what the he—?"

"You tell me what the hell," she demanded, her gray eyes dark and stormy. "Remember Jennifer Morton?"

If he'd walked straight into a propeller he couldn't have been more shocked. She knew. He'd left it too late.

"I can guess by the look on your face you do remember. How nice. But then again, it might have been nicer if you'd actually told me about it."

"That's not fair, Yasmin. We've barely begun to get

to know each other. Jen, well, that was another time and place."

"Yes, exactly. A time and place that involved me, too, if you'll remember. A time and place I told you about when you asked me what my greatest fear was and yet, even despite my pouring my heart out to you about that night, you didn't think I deserved to know that you, my *husband*—" she spat the word as if it was a bitter, nasty taste in her mouth "—were there, too?"

"I can explain—" he started.

"I think it's gone beyond explanations, don't you? Have you any idea how betrayed I feel? I trusted you. And you were a part of that night all along. You and her!" She made a sound of disgust. "I should have kept on going when I left you at the altar. This whole charade, this fake marriage, was a disaster from the start. I can't help wondering why you even bothered to marry me. If all you wanted was to get your hands on my company then you could have just sat back and watched me go completely bankrupt and you could have picked up the bones of Carter Air for a song. You certainly didn't need to go to the bother of marrying me or having all those threatening emails sent to me.

"Which brings me to Jennifer—nice to know you two are still such great friends that she was prepared to help you. Exactly what is her stake in this? Were you planning to ditch me somewhere along the line, after your contemptible games with me, and renew your engagement with her?"

Her words came at him like machine-gun fire. They penetrated his mind but none of it made sense.

"We're over," she continued. "I will repay your loan as soon as possible. I will continue to subcontract to Horvath Aviation for as long as the offer remains. But I will not stay here as your wife."

She moved toward the driver's door of her truck but he

beat her to it, pushing his weight against it so she couldn't open the door.

"What emails?"

Yasmin laughed. The sound was high-pitched, artificial.

"Out of everything I just said, that's what you focused on? Look, thanks for the memories, Ilya, and the sex. It was great while it lasted but I can't stay married to a man I cannot trust." She tugged her wedding ring off her finger and thrust it at him. "We're over."

Sixteen

Ilya wanted to stop her. Wanted to throw himself in front of her truck, if necessary. But he could see the pain and determination on Yasmin's face and he knew that nothing and no one could change the way she felt right now. She was furiously angry with him, but more than that, she was bleeding inside, he was sure of it. Because he was hurting inside like he'd never hurt before, too.

Ironic, he thought, as he watched Yasmin's truck disappear up the driveway, that he should only come to realize that he loved his wife in the instant that she left him. He'd fought the feeling, fought the truth, and now it was gone. Self-loathing and remorse engulfed him as he turned and went into the house.

She wouldn't listen to him now, and he could accept that. But it didn't mean he had to remain passive and accept her leaving him. They belonged together. He knew it in his bones. He hadn't wanted to need someone the way he needed her. He shook his head. And here he'd thought losing control was his greatest fear. He'd been a complete and utter fool. Love had been his greatest fear all along. With that, sure, came a loss of control, but he'd finally come to accept that the gift of love far outweighed anything else.

He would get Yasmin back, come hell or high water. Her reaction was understandable. He only hoped that when the dust settled, she'd be prepared to listen to him again.

Yasmin threw herself into work over the next few weeks, refusing to discuss anything with anyone, even Riya, unless it pertained to business. By day she either worked in the office or took the flights on her roster. If there were more flights allocated to them than she'd expected from Horvath Aviation, then that was all well and good, too, although she'd expected the reverse to happen after she left Ilya. The fact that he hadn't canceled their contract had given her pause for thought. Maybe he genuinely had been reaching out to help Carter Air. After all, there were easier routes for him to have taken rather than the convoluted scheme that had raged through her head. But that didn't absolve him from having kept his secret from her. Not at all. The cutting sense of betrayal sliced her anew. All those nights they'd spent together, all the times he could have brought it up…

No, she wouldn't allow herself to think about him. And if she woke up at night with her body screaming for release, her heart breaking and her cheeks wet with tears because she'd been dreaming about him again, then that was just too bad. She'd get over it, just like she'd gotten over every other shitty thing that had ever happened in her life.

Each day there was a text, a telephone message or an email from him. Each day she ruthlessly deleted them. Last night he'd even had the gall to show up at her apartment, knocking on the door and asking her to please talk with him. She'd remained frozen in position on her sofa, staring silently at the door and willing him to leave before she did anything stupid like actually let him in.

No, there would be no further communication between them, unless it was through their lawyers. She didn't need any other reminders of how stupid she'd been to think she'd fallen in love with a man who'd not only witnessed her greatest humiliation, but who'd been party to it. She racked her brain, trying to remember if she'd seen him that night with Jennifer, but the hazy images she could recall all involved Jennifer in queen bee mode, surrounded by her sycophantic sorority sisters.

Which meant that Ilya had to have been in the background. Watching. She shuddered. Whatever his part in that awful night, it no longer mattered. Inasmuch as she could engineer it, he was out of her life. So, too, did *hisgirl* appear to be out of her life. The emails had stopped altogether. Yasmin had followed up with the officer handling her complaint but so far there'd been no new developments. She could only hope that *hisgirl* would leave her alone now that she'd achieved her goal. And on the cop's advice, she'd blocked *hisgirl* from her email.

Yasmin sighed and stared at the proposals piled on her desk. Each one was a pitch for new business. She'd methodically created and reviewed them over and over to make them as sharp and as appealing as they could be. She needed new clients so she could ditch the work that was being provided to her by Horvath.

There was a noise down the hall from her office. Strange, that sounded like a bark, she thought, pushing up from her chair and heading out to see what it was.

"Blaze!" she said, dropping to her knees and accepting an effusive welcome from the puppy who'd managed to slip his leash and come barreling toward her.

"I'm sorry, Yasmin," Riya said as she followed on the puppy's heels. "Ilya dropped him off a minute ago and handed him to me. I couldn't get his leash on him and he knew you were down here. I couldn't stop him once he took off."

"It's okay," Yasmin said, burying her face in the puppy's fur and inhaling the scent of him. "Ilya was here?"

"Only briefly," Riya hastened to tell her. "He asked me to give you this."

She handed Yasmin an envelope. Her first instinct was to tell Riya to take it away and burn it; she wanted nothing to do with it or the man who'd written it, but in light of the fact that he'd brought Blaze and left him here, she supposed she'd better do the right thing and read it.

"Oh, and he also dropped off Blaze's bed, his crate, his food and bowls."

"He did?"

Yasmin looked from her friend to the puppy in confusion.

"Well, are you going to open his letter?"

"In a minute," Yasmin answered, getting to her feet and giving Blaze a command to sit.

To her surprise, the puppy did exactly as he was told. She gave him a pat and told him he was a good boy before sliding her finger under the flap of the envelope and tearing it open. Her hand shook a little as she extracted the single folded sheet of paper from inside.

"Jeez, Yasmin, the suspense is killing me," Riya commented drily.

Yasmin glared at her friend before unfolding the letter. It contained only one line.

He's pining for you.

She turned the paper over but there was nothing at all on the back.

"So, what did he say?" Riya prompted.

"Here, read it for yourself."

Yasmin thrust the paper at her friend and wondered

why on earth the simple missive had left her heart pounding and her stomach doing barrel rolls.

"Hmm," Riya said, pursing her lips. "Not big on words, is he?"

"Not big on anything. Look, if he comes here again just ask him to leave. Okay?"

"If you say so, boss. Do you want me to get one of the boys to take Blaze's things up to your apartment?"

"Thanks, I'd appreciate it."

Yasmin snapped her fingers at the puppy and he followed her into her office where he flopped down on her floor with a happy sigh. She reached into the bottom drawer of her desk for a chew toy she hadn't quite been able to bring herself to throw out. Blaze nosed it then ignored it, instead putting his head on his front paws and closing his eyes.

"Yeah, I wouldn't mind doing that, too," Yasmin said softly.

She tried to turn her focus back to the proposals but her eyes kept drifting to the puppy and her thoughts to the man who'd delivered him here. Why had Ilya given her Blaze? She knew he loved the dog as much as she did. Was this another of his attempts at manipulating her? Did he expect some kind of visitation rights?

"Well," she huffed, making the dog open his eyes and lift his brows a little to look up at her. "One thing's for sure. I'll never know what is going on in that man's mind and I'm better off not knowing anyway."

Ilya picked up the phone in his office, tearing his eyes away from the view of the Carter Air hangar a couple of hundred yards away.

"Yes?" he demanded.

His tone was about as short as his temper lately.

"Hello to you, too," answered his grandmother on the

other end of the line. "I see your temperament hasn't improved any since Yasmin left you. I'm beginning to see why she did."

Ilya closed his eyes and swallowed against the retort that sprang to his lips.

"I'm sorry, Nagy," he said in a voice that filtered out all his frustration and tension. "How are you today?"

"I'm tired, my boy."

Ilya sat up a little straighter in his chair. Tired? Nagy never admitted to any physical infirmities, ever.

"Are you all right? Have you been to the doctor?"

She laughed. "Not that sort of tired. I'm tired of how long it's taking you to sort this mess out. I expected more of you, Ilya."

Her censure was a palpable thing through the phone line.

"She's a stubborn woman, Nagy." *Like another woman I know*, he added silently. "I'm working on it."

"Well, work more efficiently. If you really want to prove to her how much she means to you and how much you want her back, you have to understand why she left you in the first place."

"I know why she left me. She thinks I betrayed her trust."

"Then you had better earn it back, hadn't you?"

Before he could answer her, she hung up. He put the phone down on his desk and shook his head. She was a piece of work, his grandmother. But she was right. These past two weeks he'd been attacking the problem of losing Yasmin head-on, trying to win her back through appeals to her emotions. And she'd blocked him every step of the way. He had to approach this from a different angle.

It would help if he could track down Jennifer and see if his instinct about her involvement in all this was correct, but so far, he had nothing to go on. He didn't have access to any of the pictures or videos that the Hardacres had been sent, and wasn't even entirely clear on how Yasmin had found out about his presence at the hazing that night. Why would Jennifer risk bringing the hazing up again after all these years? She could still get in trouble for that in fact he had every intention of pursuing that angle once he tracked her down. But maybe the trouble had come from someone else who had been there that night.

He forced himself to think logically, to recall exactly what Yasmin had said when he first arrived home from New York.

She'd mentioned emails the morning she walked out. If only he could see them for himself. Then he realized something—Yasmin's laptop had been in the shop for repairs at the time. Sure, she usually checked email on her phone, but there was a chance she could have accessed those emails on his home computer. He could only hope so.

He looked at his day planner. There was nothing today that was so urgent it couldn't be postponed, which meant there was nothing stopping him from going home to find out if Yasmin had used his computer. He got up from his desk, shrugged his suit jacket on and headed for the door.

"Deb, please clear my calendar for the rest of the day," he instructed his assistant as he passed through the outer office.

"Sure thing."

He continued out of the office without breaking his stride and was in the Tesla a few minutes later. He really needed to get that armrest seen to, he thought as he peeled out of the driveway of Horvath Aviation and turned toward Ojai Road. He pushed the speed limit the whole way home. When he got there, he stalked into the house, slamming the double doors behind him. The house was quiet, which meant Hannah had already gone home for the day. He was grateful for that. He had the utmost respect for the housekeeper but he wasn't in the mood for idle chatter right now.

Stripping off his jacket and flinging it to one side, he sat down in his office chair and turned on the computer. He opened the web browser and immediately began to search its history. There. That URL had to be Yasmin's email server, he thought, as a sense of relief vied with the exhilaration of finding something concrete to work with. Of course, she had to have remained logged in to her email account when she closed out of the program if he was going to get any of the information he so desperately sought. He clicked on the link and held his breath.

A massive surge of relief rocked him as her inbox appeared on the screen. Yes, he knew it was an invasion of her privacy to be doing this, but in this case he had to do it. He couldn't fight for her unless he knew what he was fighting against. He scanned the mail marked *read* in her inbox, specifically mail from the night before he'd arrived home.

There were more than fifteen messages from one sender, each with an attachment. He checked them, feeling his ire rise with each and every one. By the time he got to the last one—the photo Jennifer had taken the morning after he'd proposed to her—a red haze of fury blurred his vision. She would pay for this and pay dearly, he silently vowed.

He reached for the phone and called the Horvath Corporation's IT department, asking to be put through to his cousin Sofia. She was a complete computer geek and what she couldn't find out wasn't worth knowing. She was also the soul of discretion. He explained what he needed and allowed her remote access to his computer. He hung up and sat back, watching the cursor race around his screen as she worked her magic.

She called him back a few minutes later.

"You were right. She tried to cover her tracks but she's

not as good as she thinks she is. While it took a while to get through the aliases, the activity stems from an account registered to Jennifer Morton."

"Thanks, Sofia. I owe you one."

"I'll add it to the list," she said with a chuckle. "Anything else I can help you with? Tracking Ms. Morton down, perhaps?"

He grimaced at the eagerness in his cousin's voice. No doubt the idea of tracing his ex was far more appealing to her than whatever software issue she was dealing with at Horvath Corporation. "I've got it from here, thanks."

"Okay, then. Well, no doubt I'll see you at the next family wedding."

"Next wedding?"

"Yeah, didn't you hear? Nagy got her claws into Valentin. Seems he was so impressed with the bride she found for you that he said she could find him one, too. He was probably joking but you know Nagy. She isn't going to let it go."

"Strange, he didn't mention anything to me when I saw him the other week," Ilya commented.

But then again, was it so strange? Valentin had always been an intensely private person. Ilya knew he'd been married once before. It was a whirlwind affair that had happened overseas, while he was working on an international medical aid mission. After his return to the States five years ago Valentin had started working with Horvath Pharmaceuticals, mostly out of New York. Ilya wondered if his cousin would be so keen to enter into another marriage if he knew the mess Ilya had made of his own. So far Ilya had kept the news of his separation from his wife between himself and Alice, whom he'd sworn to secrecy, because he refused to believe he couldn't win Yasmin back.

Now, hopefully, with the information Sofia had given him, no one else in the family would ever need to find out, because he planned to find Jennifer Morton and do what he should have done years ago.

"Yeah, well, you know Valentin," Sofia said, interrupting his thoughts. "All I can say is Galen had better keep his wits about him. If he isn't careful, Nagy will be clipping his playboy ways next."

Ilya forced a laugh. "Then you'd be next if we're going in birth order," he warned.

"Let's not go there," Sofia said hastily. "Well, if there's nothing else…?"

He knew that once he turned the conversation to her private life, she'd end their call.

"No, but thanks again."

When Ilya hung up, he made a note to send her a case of her favorite wine. Then he turned his attention to tracking Jen down. With today's social media, how hard could it be, right?

Harder than he thought, he discovered. If she had any social media accounts she kept them very private. Ilya found himself looking up several old acquaintants to track her down. He was on the verge of giving up and calling in a private investigator when one of her sorority sisters replied to his private message, gushing about how excited Jen would be to hear from him again.

Apparently his ex was living in a trailer park outside of Las Vegas. He looked at his watch. It was a two-hour flight to Vegas. Plotting the flight plan in his head he figured he could be there before dark.

In the next instant he was on his feet and heading back out to the car. It was time to put a stop to Jen's cruelty once and for all, and win Yasmin back in the process.

Seventeen

He pulled his rental to a stop outside a single-wide trailer that stood out from its neighbors due to its obvious signs of neglect. The paint was peeling, weeds were growing all over the lot and one of the windows was broken and covered with a piece of cardboard. But he didn't waste a moment getting out the car and going to knock on the door.

"Well, hello there, handsome," Jen said as she opened the door. The sour smell of alcohol wafted off her. It was overpowering and turned his stomach.

He looked at her in shock. The years hadn't been kind, but then, neither had she, so he couldn't be entirely surprised. She still wore her hair the same way, but it was uncombed and looked like it hadn't seen shampoo in several days. Her skin held a dingy tone. And she was unmistakably drunk, or high, or both. But he wasn't here to enquire about her welfare.

"Why did you do it?" he asked straight out.

"I'm fine, thank you. And you?" she answered with a sly smile. "It's been a while."

"Let's not beat around the bush, Jen. Why did you do it? Why hurt Yasmin more than you already did?"

She met his eyes and for a second he thought he saw a flicker of bravado there. But then she averted her gaze, her entire body sagging in surrender.

"You'd better come in," she said sullenly.

He couldn't think of anything he'd rather do less, but if he was to get the answers he needed he'd have to accept her less than gracious invitation.

"Take a seat," she said, gesturing to a sagging couch strewn with tabloid magazines and newspapers. The coffee table was covered in empty wine bottles and dirty glasses.

"No, thank you. I'll stand."

Jen reached for a packet of cigarettes and put one in her mouth, lighting it with shaking hand. She took a long draw and blew out a steady stream of smoke, obviously in no rush to talk. Clearly she needed a reminder as to why he was here.

"I know you're behind the emails. What I don't know is why."

She shrugged and took another drag on her cigarette. "She deserved it."

"I beg your pardon?" His voice was icy cold.

"Why should she have you when I couldn't? Living the high life when all I have is this," she said, vaguely gesturing toward the room. "I saw the write-up about your wedding in one of these magazines. To be honest, when I heard you'd married her I couldn't believe it. Her, of all people. She was the reason you left me. I don't see why she gets to have you in the end. It pissed me off. So I sent her a little message. No crime in that."

He couldn't believe what he was hearing. She was obviously in an altered state, but her hatred had a cold, hard logic to it. "What you did was threatening and a criminal nuisance."

She looked at him again; this time he saw fear in her eyes. "You can't prove anything."

"I can, Jen. It's easy to prove those emails to Yasmin and the Hardacres came from you. It's how I found you."

She'd been a clever woman in college. How on earth had she come to this?

"So, you found me. What are you going to do with me now? I can think of a few things." She ground out her half-smoked cigarette, took a step closer to him and reached out a hand to touch him. "We used to be so good together. We can be again."

Ilya fought down the bile that rose in his throat. He wrapped his fingers around her wrist and very deliberately removed her hand from his body.

"That is never going to happen."

"What a shame," she said with a flippant toss of her head.

"You're going to face charges for this."

"Oh, says who?"

"Me. I've already lodged a complaint with my local police and forwarded them all the emails you sent to my wife." He placed special emphasis on the last two words. "I also contacted the Hardacres. They're cooperating with the investigation, too."

"Always the upstanding citizen, aren't you?" she sneered.

"Look, I let you get away with bullying Yasmin once before. I'm not doing it again. The way I see it, we can do this the hard way or the easy way."

"I always liked it hard," she said with a sleazy smile. He ignored her, wondering what he'd ever seen in her in the first place.

"Look, one way or the other you're going to face charges, but if you want leniency, you'll need to cooperate with me. It's is entirely up to you."

She sniffed and reached for another cigarette. "So what's in it for me? What is it that you expect me to do?"

"For a start, you will send a written apology to my wife for your recent and past actions. You will also explain to Esme Hardacre, in person, why you sabotaged my wife's contract."

"And if I don't?"

"I'll make sure you face the full weight of the law and I'll ask the police to file additional charges against you for the hazing incident while we're at it. Thanks to the photos you sent to Yasmin, I'm fairly sure we can make a pretty good case."

"You stuck-up bastard. You don't leave me any choice, do you? Fine, I'll do it. Although leaving all this behind is going to be such hardship."

He couldn't stand to be in the trailer with her a moment longer and went to wait outside while she gathered a few of her things together. It wasn't until they were in the plane and headed back toward California that he began to hope that maybe, just maybe, he might be able to earn his wife back.

Yasmin had had Blaze back for a whole week and was grateful for the company. He listened—while she raged and while she wept. Without judgment, without censure, without advice. And she was getting there—recovering from the emotional strain of the last few weeks. Not quite out of the woods yet, but stronger every day.

None of it stopped her missing Ilya, though. Her longing for him was a deep physical ache and she continued to throw herself into long hours at work in between exercising Blaze and seeing to it he had sufficient socialization time at a new doggy day care closer to the airport. He was there today and she kept checking the clock, aware his pickup time was looming.

There was a knock at her office door. Yasmin looked up from her desk, grateful for the interruption. It seemed she spent more time at her desk than flying aircraft these days.

"What is it, Riya?" she asked her friend, who hovered in the doorway with a look of uncertainty on her face.

"Esme Hardacre's here to see you. She says it's very important."

Yasmin's heart skipped beat. "She's here to see me?"

"Oh, yes."

Yasmin took a minute to tidy up the papers spread everywhere and quickly checked her appearance in the small mirror she kept behind the door. She rarely wore makeup but she should at least slick a little color onto her lips. She dabbed on some of the tinted gloss she kept in her top drawer and shoved her fingers through her short hair, giving it a touch more lift, then straightened her shoulders.

"Please show her in," Yasmin finally said, taking a deep breath. It was time to see what Esme Hardacre wanted.

Eighteen

By the time Yasmin let herself and Blaze into the apartment later that evening she was exhausted. The meeting with Esme Hardacre had been both awkward and intriguing. Most surprising of all: Esme had come to apologize. Long story short, Jennifer Morton had shown up at Esme's office and admitted to sending Hardacre Incorporated the damning photos and had confessed they were out of context.

According to Esme, Ilya had tracked Jennifer down, taken her to Esme, and when their conversation was finished, turned her over to the police.

Esme was truly sorry that she and her husband had assumed Yasmin was at fault. She'd asked Yasmin if she would consider signing a new contract with them on revised terms. The ball was now in Yasmin's court.

She'd wanted to tell Esme Hardacre exactly what she could do with her offer; that had been her knee-jerk reaction. But reason had prevailed. In the end, Yasmin had asked for a few days to consider things, and that was where they'd left it.

Could she do business with someone who'd seen the evidence of the degradation she'd suffered? Would she see censure, or worse, pity, in their eyes every time she saw them again? Her thoughts tumbled round in her mind, over and over. Fiscally it made excellent sense to agree to renegotiate terms and she had to admit to a certain grudging respect for the woman who'd shown up in person to make her apology. Logically there was no room for emotion in all of this. Maybe it really was time to stop allowing that night to define the rest of her life.

Then, as she was showing Esme out, a courier had arrived with an envelope addressed to her. Inside was a letter with "I'm sorry" for a subject line and a detailed apology. The letter was signed by Jennifer Morton. A raft of emotions assailed Yasmin, but through it all was an immense sense of relief that Jennifer's malicious mischief was over.

While Yasmin reheated the takeout she'd bought the night before, she fed Blaze his evening meal. It was only after she'd eaten, and had taken Blaze out for a toilet stop, that she accepted that she'd allowed herself to be a victim for far too long.

Yes, she'd forged on with her grandfather's company. Yes, she'd fulfilled both his and many of her own dreams along the way. But all along, she'd given Jennifer far more power and sway over her life than she ever should have. She'd allowed what had happened to her to color everything she did from that night on.

Yes, it had been shocking, but by holding on to it, by nurturing the fear, she'd only made it worse. She'd thought she'd worked through it all, but she hadn't. She'd only worked around it, never actually facing what had happened to her head-on. Reading Jennifer's humble apology today—in which she'd mentioned that Ilya had tracked her down and made her come clean—had ripped the blinkers from her eyes. Jennifer wasn't an ogre to fear and resent. She was her own kind of mixed-up and messed-up human being. And now it was time for Yasmin to shed the past and take back control of her life.

But where to begin? With the Hardacre contract? With Ilya?

Just thinking about her husband made every internal muscle in her body seize up with longing so intense it brought tears to her eyes. It was only when she felt the swish of Blaze's feathered puppy tail against the back of her leg that she blinked her eyes clear and forced herself back to the here and now.

"C'mon, boy. Let's get back upstairs."

He'd become surprisingly agile on the stairs, even in the week she'd had him. It amazed her how quickly he'd grown and how much he'd changed since she and Ilya had found him on the trail that day. Was it only six weeks ago? She swallowed against the lump of emotion in her throat. So much had changed in that time.

Could she even begin to hope that she and Ilya could patch things up? Did she dare trust him again? No matter what he'd done since she left him in tracking Jennifer down and forcing her to face her behavior, he had still deliberately withheld the truth of his involvement in that night. Jennifer's letter had said he was not a part of the hazing and that he'd only arrived at the beach at the end. But he had been there. So, how had he been involved?

Blaze trotted through to her bedroom, and she heard him settle on his bed with a contented sigh. She switched on the television and desultorily flicked through the channels, not finding anything that held her attention longer than two minutes. In the end she switched the TV off and stared at the blank screen.

Was it an analogy for her future? she wondered. A blank

canvas waiting to be written? She started at a knock on her apartment door. She flicked a look at the time on her watch. It was late for someone to come calling. She opened the door.

"Alice?"

The older lady swept past her into the open-plan living-dining area of the apartment and looked around.

"It's as though your grandfather still lives here," she commented with a haughty tone.

"Thank you, I like the decor, too."

Alice sniffed, clearly not a fan. "He always was a minimalist—in life as well as in love."

"That's hardly fair. He loved you with his dying breath," Yasmin snapped back. At the stricken look on Alice's face she reined in her temper. "I'm sorry. That was uncalled for. I've had a rather trying day and I took my frustration out on you. I shouldn't have."

Alice rubbed her chest a moment before nodding gently. "No, it was called for. I apologize."

Yasmin sighed internally. Apparently it was a day for apologies and unexpected visitations. "Would you like to sit down?"

Alice moved to the only easy chair in the room while Yasmin resumed her position on the couch. From Yasmin's bedroom, Blaze bounded across the floor and sniffed at the newcomer.

"So this is the puppy?"

"His name is Blaze."

Yasmin wondered why Alice was here. She was a little breathless. Whether it was because of the climb up the stairs that led to the apartment or because she didn't like the dog, Yasmin wasn't sure.

"Are you okay with him here? I can put him back in my room if you'd like."

"No, no. He's fine."

Alice looked around the room again, her eyes alighting on one of the photos of Yasmin's grandfather. The older woman rose gracefully to her feet and walked over to the frame, lifting it up and looking at it more closely.

"Such a handsome man and such a clever engineer," she said in a faraway voice. "And he could dance better than any man I knew."

Yasmin looked at her in surprise. "Granddad? Dance?"

A soft smile curved Alice's lips. "Oh, yes, he was quite the dancer back in the day." She set the photo down and turned to face Yasmin. "I loved him very much, you know."

"But not enough to marry him, apparently." Yasmin found it hard to keep the bitterness from her voice.

"He never asked me."

Yasmin looked at her in shock. "But you knew he loved you."

"*Suspected* it, yes. And I loved him in return. But I also loved Eduard." Her voice broke a little and Alice took in a deep breath. "You have no idea how hard it was, loving two men. Men who had always been friends, whose friendly rivalry turned into a fierce competition over me. Sometimes I think it would have been better if my father had never taken us from Hungary and brought us here to America. But then I would never have had my family, never have built our dynasty."

"How did you choose between Granddad and Eduard?"

"In the end it came down to one thing. Eduard was the man who *told* me he loved me. He was the one who asked me to marry him. I was a bit of a silly young thing then, lost in the romance of being pursued by two handsome men without considering the consequences of what would happen next when I chose one over the other.

"Don't get me wrong. I don't regret my decision, but I'm truly sorry for the unhappiness that I caused Jim. I'm sorry for how it impacted on the relationship he had with

the woman he eventually married and on his relationship
with your father and you."

Yasmin didn't know where to look or what to say. Alice
walked back to her chair and sat down again. Silence
stretched between them until Alice spoke again.

"Do you love my grandson, Yasmin?"

"I beg your pardon?"

"It's quite simple really. Do you love Ilya?"

"No, it's not simple. He betrayed me. I can't trust him
anymore."

"Did you know he was the person who swam out to you
the night of your hazing? He saved your life."

"How did you—?"

"Oh, I have my ways," Alice said with a wave of slender, wrinkled hand. "I'm a firm believer in fate, my dear.
There was a reason he was there that night, and it wasn't
because he was a party to what that evil girl did to you.
He was there for a far higher purpose."

"I didn't know. He didn't tell me."

"Did you give him a chance?"

The question hung on the air like an unwelcome guest
in the room. Yasmin shook her head.

"No, to be brutally honest, I didn't give him a chance."

"Nor would I under similar circumstances," Alice ac-
ceded with a sad smile. "There's a lot my grandson doesn't
share—with me or with anyone else. He is fierce and loyal
but careful, too. He's a good man. An honest one. But he
doesn't give his love easily. Nor do you. My dear, you
need to decide if your love for Ilya is worth putting aside
your past hurts."

"I didn't say I loved him," Yasmin answered with all
the stubbornness she'd inherited from her grandfather. It
was an instinctive reaction, one that came from a place
of self-protection.

Alice simply smiled at her, understanding clear in her

eyes. "You're a lot like Jim, but you have your father's sensitivity, too. I think that if you and Ilya can weather this, and overcome it, you will be an unbreakable force together in the future. But you have to want it—and you have to fight for it if you do want it."

"I don't even know if he loves me. He's never said as much."

"No, he isn't the kind of man who wears his heart on his sleeve. He used to be, but, like you, he was hurt. Are you willing to risk the rest of your life not knowing what the two of you could have had together? Are his past transgressions so bad that you can't forgive him and move on?"

Yasmin let the words sink deeply into her heart. She'd barely let Ilya get a word in that day she'd left him. She'd still been filled with all the shock and hurt and confusion at the news he'd been engaged to Jennifer Morton. And now she knew he'd been the one who actually dragged her from the water and prevented her from drowning. Had she misjudged him so badly?

She thought about what he'd done since she left him. Giving her Blaze, hunting down Jennifer, pressing charges and making the other woman apologize—not only to her but the Hardacres, as well. And then there was what he'd done to help her hold on to Carter Air, sending Horvath Aviation business her way. Giving her the funds to repay her loan. She hadn't asked for any of it, and yet he'd done all those things *for her*.

At the very least, she owed him a hearing.

"Well," Alice said, rising to her feet again. "I have said what I came here to say. I hope to see you again soon, my dear."

"Thank you for coming," Yasmin said automatically as she saw Alice to the door. "I mean it. It's been a difficult time."

"Life's never easy, but it is what you make of it."

Yasmin closed the door behind Alice and leaned against it, letting Ilya's grandmother's words filter through her racing mind. Could she make it? Could they? Did it matter so very much that Ilya hadn't told her the whole truth and if it did, could she forgive him?

There was only one way to find out.

Nineteen

"Come on, Blaze. We're going for a ride."

The puppy bounded toward her, tongue lolling in his mouth and his eyes bright with excitement at the word.

She took her time driving to Ilya's hillside home, wondering all the way whether or not she should have called ahead first, at least to see if he was home. But it didn't matter now; she was committed to seeing this through. Weariness pulled at her whole body. It had been a heck of a day so far and it didn't look like it was letting up any time soon.

Next to her, harnessed in his special seat belt, Blaze got excited as she pulled up outside the gate to the house. She'd left her auto opener behind, believing she'd never need it again. She hesitated, debating whether to turn around and head back to the airfield or to press the buzzer and ask for admittance.

The gates ahead of her slowly rolled aside. That meant one of two things. Either Ilya was on his way out, or he'd seen her on the security camera and opened the gate himself.

She put the truck in gear and started her descent down the driveway. She passed the helipad, noting that one of the choppers from the Horvath fleet was there. Was Ilya planning on heading out somewhere? Or did he have visitors? Her hands were shaking as she pulled up outside the front of the house. Ilya was framed in the doorway.

Her heart all but beat itself out of her chest the moment she saw him there. Tall, strong and so handsome there should be a law against it. And so dear to her fragile heart that she barely knew what to do or say anymore. Beside her, Blaze gave a happy woof of recognition. She unclipped his harness and leaned across the door to open it and let him bound out.

Ilya bent to welcome the puppy, who wriggled and yipped and licked with all the joy and exuberance of a puppy who'd been parted from a loved one for months or years rather than days.

"Are you getting out?" Ilya asked, looking up at her across the bench seat of the truck. "Or were you just dropping him off for a visit?"

A surge of anger filled her. How dare he be flippant at a time like this? She fought the urge to pull the door closed, put the truck in gear and head back up the driveway. Didn't he know how difficult this was for her?

How could he, a voice deep inside her asked, *when you won't even talk to him?*

Yasmin released the breath she was holding and forced herself to get down from the truck. She walked toward Ilya, feeling distinctly lightheaded while at the same time feeling as though the weight of her future, both hers and Ilya's, hung around her shoulders like a leaden cloak.

"Do you want to come in?" Ilya offered, standing up.

"I think that's best," she managed, her voice sounding stiff and unnatural to her own ears.

She walked through to the family room off the kitchen and stood at the sliding doors looking out to the patio. Blaze scratched at the glass, desperate to get outside and hunt out a play toy. She let him through and followed him outside.

"Can I get you anything?" Ilya asked from behind her.

"Some courage perhaps?" she answered wryly.

"Courage? Oh, I don't know. I kind of think you're one of the bravest women I know."

"I don't deserve that."

"What makes you think that?"

"At the first sign of trouble, I run."

"Self-preservation. There's probably many an extinct species that wishes they'd perfected the art of running."

She smiled at his attempt at humor.

"I had a visitor or two today," she said. "And received a letter by special delivery."

"Ah, yes." Ilya nodded and looked across the patio to where Blaze was happily sniffing his way around the edge of the garden. "Shall we sit down and talk about that?"

She took a seat at the large granite outdoor table and rested her arms on the surface. The warmth of the sun still emanated from the smooth rock and she took strength from it.

"Did you always know?" she blurted out.

"Know?" Ilya looked directly at her.

"That it was me you saved from drowning."

"No. Absolutely not. Not until the day we went up in the Ryan. When we talked, after…y'know."

His eyes flared a deeper blue. She felt an answering curl of heat deep inside at the memory.

"Why didn't you say anything?"

"I couldn't. You'd just shared your worst experience with me. Telling you about my part in it right then would have compounded what was already a terrible memory. After that, well, everything unraveled around us so quickly after that. I know it's my fault and I shouldn't make excuses, but I didn't want to risk damaging the tentative relationship we were building."

"Shouldn't relationships be built on trust?"

He nodded and looked away briefly before turning his attention back to her. "They should, and I will always regret that I didn't tell you sooner. That you had to find out the way you did. But I can't undo the past. I'm always going to be linked to the worst thing in your life.

"When I got there, you were just entering the water. I could see you were already in a bad way. I asked Jen what she was thinking, letting you swim in that state, but she said you wanted to. I watched you, saw the moment your arms looked like they were getting too heavy for you, when you started to sink. I went after you and brought you back to the beach."

"Thank you. I never knew who pulled me out, never got the chance to say thanks."

"It was what any decent person would have done. Unfortunately, decent people were thin on the sand that night."

There was an undercurrent of fury in his voice, as if the whole episode still made him incredibly angry. Judging from his fists clenched on the table, it probably did.

"And you got Jennifer to apologize to me?"

"I did."

"I'd begun to suspect her, but when were you sure it was her?"

He scrubbed a hand over his face. "The first couple of weeks you were gone I didn't know what to do—you kept rebuffing me at every turn so I had to find another way. I remembered you saying something about emails."

He explained how he'd checked his home computer, apologizing for invading her private email, and told her how he'd asked his cousin for help in tracking down where the threatening emails had come from.

"So you went all bounty hunter on her? Even the police didn't uncover all that," Yasmin said incredulously.

"They probably didn't see the urgency like I did. I had a lot more riding on it. I had to prove to you that I wasn't who you thought I was. You needed to know who was behind that whole thing and you needed compensation for that."

He explained how he'd turned Jennifer over to the police and the charges she was facing. It was something that the police would be in touch with Yasmin about. But he also mentioned how Jennifer clearly had an addiction problem, and she'd come willingly to apologize to the Hardacres and written the letter to Yasmin essentially admitting her guilt. He hinted that with Yasmin's agreement, Jennifer may be eligible for treatment for her addictions in lieu of serious jailtime. As he spoke Yasmin realized just what a special person he was.

"Well, I'm glad you did all that. It allowed me to close a door on the past. By the way, Esme Hardacre stopped by today."

He looked at her, waiting for her to say more. "And?"

"She wants to renegotiate our contract. I said I'd think about it."

"If you do that, you won't need my help any longer."

Something in his voice made him sound lost. As if he thought that without the work he was putting her way, she wouldn't need him anymore.

"Do you want me to need your help?"

He swallowed. "Not my help. To be totally honest with you, Yasmin, I want you to need me the way I need you. I love you."

Yasmin's eyes widened into giant slate-gray pools. Was it fear, rejection or hope that he saw reflected there? He prayed it was the latter. He'd done everything he could to make this right, everything in his power. Leaving it in her hands now was the hardest thing he'd ever done. Harder than landing a plane knowing that there was nothing that could be done for his father. Harder than standing at his mother's grave and knowing that he hadn't been enough to fill her life and keep her safe. Harder than admitting he'd been a poor judge of character when he'd chosen Jennifer to be his future bride.

But Yasmin was a chance at a future he'd never expected. A future he now wanted with his heart and soul. He'd move heaven and earth if she asked for it. But she wasn't the kind of person to ask for anything. She was self-sufficient. An island. How did a man get across that sea of independence she surrounded herself with? How did he get her to understand how very much she meant to him, especially when he'd only just begun to understand it himself?

Yasmin's voice was hesitant when she spoke. "Needing someone else scares me. It makes me feel less worthy. Certainly, less worthy of love."

Ilya shook his head fiercely. "Never less worthy of love. You are an incredible woman. You've done so much. You never give up."

"I gave up on us."

"Extenuating circumstances." He rushed to absolve her of any guilt.

"No, Ilya, I need to own this, the same way I need to own the fact that I let Jennifer—all the Jennifers of this world—drive my decisions and my idea of my own worth for far too long. The thing is, it wasn't until I married you that I actually started to learn what love really was."

Ilya let her words sink in, felt the burning spark of hope flicker to life in his chest.

She continued. "You weren't what I expected at all. You have to realize, I was conditioned to hate you on sight."

"I got that impression when you ran away from our wedding ceremony."

"Not my finest moment and, again, one driven by fear. I don't want fear to rule my life anymore, Ilya. I want to be in control."

How could she not see that she was already in control? That she'd always been. Didn't she understand that a weaker person could have been completely broken by what happened to her—from her parents abandoning her to a grumpy old man, to constantly trying to win his approval, to being the outsider even when she was at college? Each piece on its own was enough, but she'd dealt with all of that. He told her as much.

"Thank you for the compliments. It's not often I get to see myself through someone else's eyes."

Blaze abandoned his circuit of the garden and came and sat on the patio between them, a contented little sigh coming from him before he put his head down and drifted off to sleep. Ilya looked at the puppy and, for a moment, envied him the simplicity of his life. But then, if Ilya's life were that simple he wouldn't have this beautiful, strong, complicated woman sitting opposite him. A woman who held his heart in her capable hands.

"I meant every one of them, just as I meant it when I said I love you. I know I let you down by not telling you the truth about me and Jen. I regret that more than I can say. Your trust is important to me, Yasmin. It's everything. Without it I feel like I'm only half a person. You are my other half. Will you forgive me my silence? Will you give us, give *me* a second chance?"

"Ilya, I came here tonight not really knowing what I wanted to say. Trust is the biggest thing for me and I did feel betrayed by you. But my perception of that night, of your part in it, was warped—just like my perception of you when I saw you standing at the altar was warped by all the hideous things my grandfather used to say about your family." She took a deep breath and reached across the table to grip his hands. "I don't want to work against you anymore. I want to work with you. To be honest, I don't want to accept the Hardacre contract. I want to work with you, properly, the way our grandfathers started to, the way they should have continued to. If you're willing.

"I'm not going to let what other people say or said, or do or did, stand in the way of my happiness any longer. I'm the one who makes my decisions, my choices, and I choose you. For far too long I strove to find where I fit in this world. I didn't fit with my mom and dad, and I never truly fit with Granddad, either. At school I was that kid who won the prizes but who no one wanted to sit with at lunch. At college, well..." She shrugged and took a deep breath. "I never felt like I fit anywhere, but I know where I want to belong. Here, with you. I love you, Ilya, and I want to tell you that every day for the rest of our lives. They're not words that come easily to me, nor am I used to hearing them. I never thought I needed them, but I do. Can we try again? Can we make our marriage work?"

Ilya was out of his chair and pulling her into his arms before she even finished talking.

"I will tell you every minute of every day for the rest of my life how much you mean to me. I might not always use the exact words, but you will never need to doubt me or my love for you, ever again," he vowed.

She looked up at him, her hands bracketing his face. "I'm going to need help on this one, on understanding what it takes to be a part of a couple, on learning that I don't have to stand on my own two feet on every issue, every single day. I'll need help to learn how to open up to you, to be worthy of your love, too."

"I'm here for you, always. No more secrets."

"No more secrets," she repeated softly.

Ilya kissed her, his lips sealing a promise that transcended words and he knew, in his heart of hearts, that they'd work everything out together. And, as he removed her wedding ring from his pocket, where he put it each day, and replaced it on her finger, he knew they'd get there. Maybe not today, maybe not tomorrow, but they had the future. A long, long future.

Together.

* * * * *